Give Me Tomorrow

A Novel by
CLIFTON LABREE

© 2004 by Fading Shadows Imprint

Published by
Fading Shadows Imprint
New Boston, New Hampshire

Paperback ISBN-13: 978-1-943329-00-7

Cover Design by Vivian LaBree

FORT LEWIS SERIES

Fort Lewis is a fictional Cree Indian village in the vast Canadian boreal forest on the shores of the beautiful Lake Diamante. It has a Hudson Bay Store, a Catholic Church, a Royal Canadian Mounted Police barracks, and a newly-built infirmary. The Crees are in a transition period trying to adapt to modern civilization. The infirmary was established by Bright Cloud, a beautiful Cree nurse who saw the need for a medical facility to care for her people. For centuries they have survived the brutal winters with plunging temperatures and deep snows. They had traditionally followed the reindeer herds which provided them with sustenance and shelter. Survival has been their greatest achievement. It's a tribute to their woodland skills, undaunted courage, and a triumph of the human spirit.

The four books that make up this series portray a Cree family in cataclysmic events during World Wars I and II, the Korean War, and the Vietnam War. The series pays tribute to the brave men and women who served to defend our right to live as a free people. The beauty and tranquility of Fort Lewis helps to heal their troubled souls. The families return every summer for renewal and spiritual growth.

Book 1 – Edge of Tomorrow

Book 2 – Starlight Starbright

Book 3 – Give Me Tomorrow

Book 4 – Beyond the Horizon

Dedicated to my wife Pauline, and my family, with thanks for all their support and encouragement

Chapter One

Captain Scott Taylor listened to the carillon chimes playing in the bell tower overlooking the parade ground at his alma mater, the United States Military Academy at West Point. He wistfully watched the rugged granite hills west of the campus fade from sight. Night enveloped the campus like a giant black curtain as the sun set. The veil of darkness helped to conceal the simmering torment that raged in his heart. His grief was evident in the tears that ran uncontrollably down his face, trickling to his chocolate brown tunic and the rows of medals and ribbons that covered the uniform over his left chest. He could no more stop their flow than he could have prevented the tragedies that created the anguish and pain he bore in his heart. His thoughts were dominated by the searing visions of combat during the past war, questioning his ability to continue with a military career in the Army. The Army was his life, and if he could not live up to its expectations, then he would voluntarily resign his commission, as painful as it was to contemplate.

Tall, muscular, with angular features, Scott looked every inch the soldier that he was. He was not a handsome man by conventional standards, but there was an engaging look about him that inspired respect and trust. He had a reputation of being a gentleman who spoke with conviction and sincerity, but he had a low tolerance for individuals who failed to live up to expectations.

Standing at his favorite promontory overlooking the campus of the Military Academy and the mighty Hudson River on its eastern border, Captain Taylor's thoughts drifted back over the events that had brought him here. The war had already started when his Class of 1942 graduated. He and his classmates

1

were immediately rushed to take over the numerous new platoons being formed with the thousands of draftees the Army was training to fight the war thrust upon the country by the surprise Japanese attack at Pearl Harbor. Like hundreds of other newly commissioned officers, he rose to the Herculean task of turning raw civilians into disciplined soldiers capable of meeting and defeating the armies of two of the most militaristic nations in the world, Japan and Germany.

Kasserine Pass in Tunisia, Africa, was the place that Captain Taylor first experienced combat. The platoon that he led from Fort Dix, New Jersey, to the shores of North Africa was virtually wiped out by German artillery fire during its first day of combat. Incredibly, he received only superficial wounds that soon healed. The ugly memory of his first combat command being turned into grisly heaps of bleeding flesh was forever etched in his soul.

During that same battle, fifteen of his classmates lost their lives while leading their platoons against the deadly accurate German artillery barrage. One of his closest friends, Jim Lucas, a lanky farm boy from Illinois, was blown into oblivion before Taylor's eyes. When the dust cleared, there wasn't anything left of him except small pieces of his body and a couple of buttons from his fatigue jacket!

Taylor recalled how proud he and his classmates had been to finally receive the second lieutenant gold bars on that now dimly-lit parade ground below. Two hundred and fifty-one officers graduated with him that warm summer day. At the reunion conference earlier today, he was stunned to learn that only thirty-eight men from his class survived the war. Other classes suffered similar losses. My God, he thought, what a horrible price to pay for victory!

He fought all the way through the North African Campaign, then across Sicily and up the southern boot of the Italian peninsula. The fighting was dirty, exhausting, and costly to the members of his battalion. He was promoted to Captain during the Italian Campaign, becoming a company commander. Once they invaded Continental Europe by way of the English Channel, Taylor was amazed and horrified to learn that the fighting ahead of them would be even more intense than he had experienced in the earlier battles. The campaign across Europe was going to require the first string of players. The winter months of 1944 were especially ferocious when the Allies were poised for the final strike into German territory. The end was in sight.

It was during this time that no matter how hard Scott Taylor tried to stop reliving certain events, he could not forget two men from the Class of 1944 that served as replacement platoon leaders in his company, Second Lieutenants Arnold Robinson and Daniel Joseph Leroux. They were positioned at a relatively quiet area of the front near the Ardennes Mountains in Belgium.

Robinson had received some mail during a rare lull in the fighting near the German-Belgium border. The mail had been sporadic at best over the past weeks and was a welcome respite when it finally caught up with the soldiers. During this lull, the mess sergeants were able to supply hot meals to the battalion. The men knew that the resistance of the Germans was stiffening by the yard, so they gorged themselves with all the hot chow they could lay their hands on. Too soon the slow spell ended, and Lieutenant Robinson's platoon found themselves out-flanked by a powerful German armored force that seemed to come out of nowhere. Without hesitation, Robinson organized a small patrol to assault a nearby hilltop where he could insert artillery spotters to direct supporting fire, which might eliminate enemy pressure on their right flank.

Scott was in the Battalion Command Post and answered the phone when Lieutenant Robinson volunteered to lead the assault himself. With the limited amount of information at his disposal, Scott was skeptical that the maneuver would be successful, and he suggested that maybe another way could be found that was less risky.

"There's no other way, Captain," responded Robinson impatiently. "If we sit here any longer, we'll be sitting ducks for their armor."

There was a devil-may-care-attitude about him that troubled Taylor. Robinson had been more conservative and deliberate in his judgments than any other platoon leader in his company. Robinson's response was out of character, and it troubled Scott.

Scott had gotten along well with Robinson, so he asked him matter-of-factly, "Do you want to get yourself killed?"

Robinson snapped back. "Captain Taylor, it doesn't matter now. I died a few hours ago at mail call, so this mission won't make any difference..." Robinson hung up. He quickly gathered his men around him, and led them towards the hill at a dead run. The men anxiously followed him. Halfway up the hill, well-camouflaged German machine gun emplacements opened fire, wiping out the entire patrol. Scott was watching part of the assault from the top of a scout car. Lieutenant Robinson made no effort to try to conceal his person from the chattering machine gun above. The guns almost cut him in half as he came into their direct range of fire. Robinson had wanted to die, thought Scott with disbelief.

After years of combat experience, he never could turn an indifferent eye to losses in his command. He took the loss of lives personally and searched his soul for something that he might have done differently with the hope that casualties could be minimized in future altercations. Combat was a deadly game of maneuver and timing. The potential for disaster was constant. It was never a question of whether or not it would take place, the only unknown was the magnitude of its eruption. Robinson's death, and the way it happened, troubled Scott.

While collecting Lieutenant Robinson's personal things, Scott made a grim discovery that helped explain his irrational behavior. He knew that his parents were both dead and that he listed a young lady, Marie Poole, to be notified in the event of his death. He had heard some scuttlebutt that Robinson was a little agitated at mail call. After his company had retrieved the dead bodies of Robinson's platoon, Scott found a letter in the Lieutenant's vest pocket and conceded that the letter would have been difficult to accept, regardless of who it was intended for. Taylor read it quickly and was convinced that the letter was the cause of Robinson's death. Robinson had used the attack on the observation hill as a way of ending the pain.

In the letter, Miss Poole had just shut down the romance and prospects of a happy life together between her and Lieutenant Robinson. She ended the letter with the following words: "…Don't ever try to contact me again, Arnold. Whatever we had in the past is gone forever, and it would not be good for either of us to try to recapture moments past." Captain Taylor cursed the woman who so callously wrote those words to one of his men while they were in combat.

The journey from Africa to Berlin was filled with tragedies and triumphs, sometimes on the same day. Scott was a willing participant, but he had to admit he was a different person today after the war, than when he paraded for the last time in 1942 on the hallowed field below him. He mourned the sacrifice and loss of so many men and searched his soul for some kind of meaning in their deaths. Sleepless nights were filled with questions he could not answer.

Part of Taylor's torment involved a search for his own destiny. Better men than he had perished on the battlefield, and it was impossible for him to escape the haunting question that accompanied many of his sleepless nights. "Why had he been spared?" He was no closer to answering it today than he was on that cold, terrifying night at Kasserine Pass.

The death of Second Lieutenant Daniel-Joseph Leroux was another loss in his command that touched him in more personal ways than some of the others. The death of Robinson and Leroux left open memories filled with anguish that needed closure. In order for that to come about, he talked with his former regimental commander about the possibility of accompanying the exhumed bodies of the two men to their final resting places. His commander thought it was an excellent idea that would also add a more personal touch for the family members.

On the first evening of his West Point Class reunion, Scott received word that the body of Lieutenant Leroux was on its way to Fort Devens, Mass. Taylor could link up with the ceremonial guard at Devens and proceed to Wells, Maine. An accompanying letter from his former Regimental Commander, Colonel Hartwell, explained several things:

Dear Captain Taylor;

I'm sure that you will be surprised to learn that the things we discussed in private are now underway. I hope it comes at an opportune time since you are already at West Point.

I have made arrangements for you to be the accompanying officer in the ceremony for Lieutenant Leroux. A summary of his file is waiting for you at Fort Devens with the body. The base will provide and make travel arrangements. In case you did not know, Leroux's father is a marine combat veteran of both World Wars. He received a Medal of Honor for bravery at New Britain and was badly wounded during the incident.

In regards to Lieutenant Robinson, he has no living family and had a Miss Marie Poole listed as next of kin. She returned Robinson's remaining personal effects to the Army, unopened. The Army has buried Robinson at Arlington National Cemetery. I am forwarding the items to you at Fort Devens and rely on your judgment to dispose of them.

There you are Captain, I hope things work out. The War Department assured me that you will be reimbursed for expenses while attending to these duties.

All of the above and more is covered in formal orders that await you at Devens. Your next duty assignment is something you have wanted, the Command and Staff Course at the Army War College in Carlisle, Pennsylvania. Congratulations, Captain Taylor, your star is beginning to rise.

> Wishing you the best of luck,
> Colonel James Hartwell, USA

Scott was relieved to learn that preparations for returning Lieutenant Leroux's remains to Maine were well underway. Robinson was another matter. Scott sighed, his breath showing in the evening air and wondered what was ahead for him. His affairs at the Point were completed, except for the traditional banquet tonight. He was anxious to head for Fort Devens first thing in the morning. Tonight, he planned to celebrate his selection for the War College course with his friends and classmates.

Next morning Scott was on the road bright and early after a hearty breakfast at the West Point Hotel with a couple of classmates. Last night's festivities brought a smile to his lips. He had shared his thoughts about continuing in the Army with some old friends and learned that most of them felt the same way. His appointment to the War College was the envy of the group. Lieutenant Leroux's death had left him with a great sense of loss, not just for himself but for the Army and for the country. There was something special about the young officer that was difficult to define. The moment Leroux took over the platoon, he was prepared to take responsibility for the men under his command. Scott knew that some officers were just interested in being "in charge." Leroux had a determined way about him, but it was tempered with a calm demeanor and a natural concern for the welfare of his men. Loyalty in a platoon begins with their leader and has a trickle down effect.

Lieutenant Leroux's habit of making eye contact with the person he was talking to was disarming to some, for his penetrating look seemed to be reading the person's unspoken thoughts. There was never any misunderstanding about who was in command! Once the men became aware of his genuine concern and desire to do what was best for the platoon, they responded dutifully to his style.

His Cree heritage was evident. He had the bronze complexion and the unique chiseled facial features of the American woodland native typified by the Algonquins of New England, to which the Crees were related. Those who harbored prejudice were ignored. Lieutenant Leroux was intensely proud of his heritage. Scott knew that Leroux's mother was a full-blooded Cree whose ancestors were chiefs and tribal leaders. It was easy to visualize Leroux as a leader.

Scott clearly remembered the first time he had the opportunity to talk alone with Lieutenant Leroux. They were on board a transport ship in the middle of the English Channel heading for the Normandy invasion beaches. It was evening on the forward deck where the spray from the turbulent English Channel was a welcome contrast to the stuffy crowded quarters below deck. Several men were leaning against the rail, each one lost in his own thoughts. Scott recognized Leroux who was staring across the waters, a troubled look on his face.

"It's quite a sight, isn't it, Leroux?"

"Yes, Sir" acknowledged Lieutenant Leroux, turning toward his superior officer.

"I don't mean to intrude, Lieutenant, but you appear troubled. Is there anything I can help you with?"

"Well, Captain, I just received a letter from my mother. She wrote about how extensive my father's wounds are. My Dad's a colonel in the Marine Corps and was wounded on New Britain. He's being recommended for a Medal of Honor," said Leroux, his voice stronger and full of pride. "My mother wrote that he may never walk again. To be honest, I'm having a hard time accepting it."

"I sympathize with your concern, Lieutenant," commented Taylor. "I grew up without a father in my life; he was killed in France during the First World War. My grandfather tried to make up for his absence, but it wasn't the same. There's one comforting note to dwell on, Leroux, your father won't have to face the enemy's guns again."

"My mother mentioned the same thing in her letter. She's a nurse and is looking forward to having him back home."

"It sounds like you've been blessed with exceptional parents."

"That's for sure, Captain," retorted Leroux proudly. "I only hope that I can live up to their expectations of me. We've been busy, as you know, and I haven't had much of a chance to think about home. I grew up on the coast of Maine, so the water is always a link back to home for me. My father's wounds and the invasion we're a part of made me think about casualties and how I might handle them within my platoon. I've become quite familiar with most of the men, but I'm prepared to do what has to be done."

"I'm confident you'll do just fine, Lieutenant. It's been my experience to not get too close to the men, it can have bothersome consequences when casualties are taken. But how do you define 'too close'? I don't know where the line is even for myself. I guess each officer has to find that level of familiarity on his own. Or maybe it's just an inherent part of leadership, I'm not sure." He gave Leroux a friendly slap on the shoulder. "The evening is still young, and I have a mountain of paperwork to complete. That's one thing that they neglected to tell us about at the Point."

"Goodnight, Captain. Thanks for the sympathetic ear."

"It was my pleasure. Sometime when this war is over, I'd like to meet your parents. Goodnight, Lieutenant."

Recollection of that casual remark so long ago in the middle of the dark Atlantic Ocean sent a shudder through his body. He was going to have that chance to meet Lieutenant Leroux's parents after all, he thought grimly as he was heading toward Massachusetts. Some of the bodies of fallen soldiers remained in cemeteries near where they were killed. Several were brought home to family burial plots and others to military cemeteries all over the country. Scott never investigated why some remained, and others were selected for reburial.

Oblivious to the scenic countryside along the road, Scott was busy making plans for what lay ahead of him. Obviously, he would attend to the burial ceremony for Lieutenant Leroux first. Provided that did not take too much of his time, he was determined to collect the personal effects of Lieutenant Robinson and make a visit to Miss Poole at the small town of Monson, Maine near Moosehead Lake, and leave the package to the designated person Robinson had selected.

Scott was uncertain as to what he would say and how it would sound to the woman, but it was something that he had to do. Robinson's suicide haunted him. Why would a healthy young man choose death rather than life? What circumstances had contributed to the tragic situation? Robinson was commissioned from Officer Candidate School and proved to be a competent commander with his platoon. There never seemed to be anything amiss that Scott could detect. Scott acknowledged that Robinson was more distant than the other officers in his company and often appeared uncomfortable around him, but whatever Robinson lacked in warmth, he made up for in efficiency.

Robinson was a by-the-book platoon leader who sometimes pushed further than Taylor thought necessary. Robinson handled his platoon more like a drill sergeant handled recruits, yet they performed well. They never had the relaxed, confident style that Leroux's platoon displayed, especially when the going got rough. Robinson had slowly developed a more surly attitude towards the men as they continued across France toward Germany. He was frequently ill-tempered. Taylor cautioned him several times to "lighten up," but it continued.

There was no doubt in Taylor's mind that Robinson's feelings for the "girl back home" was responsible for his erratic behavior. He realized that it was none of his business, but he needed to find some logical explanation for Robinson's death that made sense.

The trip to Fort Devens would be his first prolonged trip in his new Ford automobile. He was not allowed to own an automobile while attending the Military Academy. Now, with his latest assignments tied down, he realized that an automobile would be useful and make his life more enjoyable. Scott decided to stick to as many local roads as possible so that he could correctly break in his brand new 1946 Ford Deluxe V/8 sedan at slower speeds. It was his most prized possession and his most extravagant expenditure. He had picked it up from a Ford Dealer at his home town of Dauphin, Pennsylvania. There still was a long waiting list for new automobiles.

The dealer was an old friend of his mother and had promised her one of the first trucks that came to the dealership. The farm operation desperately needed a new truck. However, the first few months after the war when production was gearing up, no trucks were available, but the dealer agreed to reserve an automobile that had just arrived if she wanted it. She was less interested in a car than a truck so she called her son to see if he wanted a new vehicle. She encouraged him to reward himself with something that he would enjoy. He jumped at the chance, and bummed a ride from a friend stationed with him at the Aberdeen Proving Grounds who took him to Pennsylvania to pick up the new silver gray Ford. Scott drove the car across the Hudson River towards Connecticut and Massachusetts. He was making good time. The smooth running V/8 engine ate up the miles effortlessly. He was able to relax and reflect on the past, a favorite diversion since the war. The carefree years before the war were filled with pleasant memories. He had grown up on an active farm in the productive agricultural region north of Harrisburg beside the lazy Susquehanna River. Most of the crop, primarily pumpkins and sweet corn, was sold wholesale to large food processors throughout the country.

His mother managed the farm after his father went to war and never returned from France. His body was placed in a large American Cemetery near Romagne-Sous-Montfaucon. The fact that his father died in battle before he had a chance to see his son, had a major influence in Scott's decision to become a soldier. At the close of hostilities in Europe on April 13, 1945, Scott visited the French cemetery and shrine erected to honor the Americans who had died in the First World War. It was one of several.

It had been a heart-wrenching experience for him to read his father's name on the white cross in the middle of the meticulously manicured cemetery. The recently retreating Germans had taken deliberate steps to honor the sanctity of this field of crosses. There were no signs of combat within the hallowed grounds of the shrine. Even though he never knew his father, his mother kept his memory alive throughout Scott's childhood by telling stories of his gentleness and his kindness. He had a passion for growing things and had worked hard to provide a good living for his family.

Scott's mother continued the farming operations after his father's death. She hired several field hands each year to do the plowing, planting, and harvesting of the squash, potatoes and sweet corn for the markets in Harrisburg. During the dormant winter months, she hired whatever expertise was needed in order to repair or rebuild the machinery necessary to run the farm. His mother did all of the sales and recordkeeping, and other administration work. Sometimes she even operated one of the tractors in the fields.

Scott did his share on the farm while he was growing up. He had worked with agriculture enough to know that there had to be something different for him in the world. The life of a soldier appealed to him early in his high school days. He took the entrance examination to measure his eligibility for admission to West Point and was placed third on the list of his Senator. For reasons still unknown to him, the two names ahead of him were withdrawn, placing him at the top of the list and ultimately to the Military Academy.

From that moment on, his life was filled with the Army and the demands that being an Army officer in the war had placed upon him. After the campaigns in North Africa, Sicily, and southern Italy, Scott was sent back to Fort Devens to help organize new units for the main effort in Europe. The few months that he spent training and equipping units were a relief from the rigors of combat, but he enjoyed commanding troops in the field, and he knew that he was good at it. When his company left Devens in 1944, it was scheduled to be a replacement for any division that needed him. He was pleased to be assigned to one of the regiments of the First Infantry Division, the "Big Red One," possibly the best division in the Army. He wore their shoulder patch with pride and had passed that same pride on to his men.

Driving alone on the road, Scott recalled a remarkable young lady he had met early in the war. Her memory was still strong. He asked himself, "How could anyone ever forget Miss Leslie Kerr?" He remembered their first meeting as if it was yesterday. It was at a small town near Fort Dix, New Jersey, Scott's first duty station after graduation from West Point. One evening he and a few of his friends went to the closest USO Club off base to relax. As soon as he stepped into the Club, the first person he noticed was a young lady wearing a USO blazer seated at the reception desk. She had a cheerful smile and wore her light brown hair loose around her shoulders with a hairpin holding it in place covering her ears. There was a professional air of cordiality about her that was illusive and friendly. Scott was instantly attracted to her.

The USO Club was filled with music and laughter. Scott approached the desk and good-naturedly asked, "Do you have any room for a few more soldiers?"

"Yes, Lieutenant, we'll find room for any number that wish to visit with us," she answered, her dark eyes evading direct contact. "We're here to serve you. No alcohol is allowed on the premises, and you should know that dating of the hostesses is against regulations."

"Everyone has regulations it seems," complained one of the soldiers.

The band was playing a popular love song. "White Cliffs of Dover" echoed through the building. The Club had a reputation of serving home-cooked food and the best cup of coffee in town. Scott noticed the name plate on the receptionist's jacket, Leslie Kerr, Director. There was a mysterious aura about Leslie Kerr that went deeper than the simple smile on her face. He had dated several different girls in high school and at the Point, but there was nobody that was "special." He remembered that the music was inviting. He had danced several times with one of the hostesses.

As the evening wore on, Scott's group of friends decided to leave the USO Club for a lounge at the local hotel. He motioned them to go ahead without him. Scott was not much of a drinker and was looking forward to a leisurely meal in the cafeteria. Later, Scott was sitting in the corner of the cafeteria just finishing off a large roast beef sandwich and a cup of coffee, when Miss Kerr approached his table in an agitated state of mind. The top pocket on her blazer was ripped, holding together by a thread. There was a hint of panic in her eyes.

"Lieutenant, I'm sorry to bother you," she blurted out. "But I've got a problem in the parking lot with some men who've been drinking too much. I refused to admit them and they don't want to accept it. I don't want to be the cause of a riot, so I thought that you, the only officer in the Club, would be able to help me."

"Yes, Ma'am. I'm at your service. Lead me to the troublemakers," responded Scott, pushing his chair away from the table.

"I prefer to handle the situation without calling the police or the MP patrol. Things have a way of getting out of hand when they arrive at a scene."

"I can appreciate your reasoning," said Scott. "Let's see what we've got."

She led him through a side door at the rear of the kitchen area, which opened directly onto the parking lot and a small group of men. As soon as Scott's eyes adapted to the poor light in the parking lot, he recognized that the men were marines, probably from the nearby Naval Yard. Two of them were barely able to stand.

"The lady tells me you men are making a nuisance of yourselves. Why don't you pack it up and..."

"We don't need any goddamn doggie to tell us what to do," shouted a burly marine in front of Scott. One of his buddies in the background emitted the sound of a barking dog. There was a menacing attitude in the air.

"Right now, you men are a disgrace to the uniform you wear. I'm advising you to loosen up and get the hell out of here". Scott deliberately stepped within inches of the big marine's face and looked eyeball to eyeball with him. Moving closer, he saw that the marine was a sergeant. Light from one of the windows of the Club glistened on Scott's lieutenant bars. The moment the sergeant recognized what he was looking at, his whole demeanor changed.

"Sergeant, you know better than to risk those stripes over a drunken misunderstanding. The lady has to enforce the rules, which means that no alcohol or drunkenness is allowed. If you continue to push this thing, you're going to lose, so don't make the situation any worse than you already have. Are you reading me?"

"Yes, Sir, loud and clear," said the marine, saluting Scott. "We really didn't mean to make any trouble, so we'll wait here quietly for the next bus to the Yard."

Scott turned to Leslie Kerr and asked, "Are you all right, Ma'am? What happened to your jacket?"

"Everything will be just fine if they want to wait peacefully for the bus. I don't want any problems."

"It looks to me as if they made the problem themselves. Did they hurt you in any way? Because if they did, then they've got another problem on their hands - me!"

"No, they didn't mean to. I was frightened and tried to push them out the door. One of them tried to push me back, that's all."

"Ok, Ma'am," said Scott, turning his attention back to the young marines. "Let me have your attention, leathernecks. We've got one last thing to settle. You've threatened and frightened this young lady with your boorish behavior. She works hard so that, we servicemen can enjoy ourselves when we're off-duty. I think she's entitled to an apology from all of you."

The sergeant's reaction was instantaneous. "Yes, Sir, I agree. These men are from my platoon, and I can assure you, Ma'am, that I speak for all of them when I say that we're sorry for creating this disturbance. Please accept our apology. We were out of line and regret it."

"I accept your apology, Sergeant." Leslie Kerr was visibly relieved and turned to walk away. Scott stepped into the light ray from the window where Miss Kerr's torn blazer caught his eye.

"Hold it men, we've got one more thing to settle." He pointed to the torn blazer and continued. "Someone has got to pay for this jacket. Does anyone have any objections?"

"I'll pay for the jacket, Lieutenant; then I'll collect from each of the guys later. Is that okay with you?"

"Sounds fine to me, Sergeant. Twenty bucks looks about right. What do you say, Ma'am?"

"They don't have to pay…"

"Oh yes we do, Ma'am," interrupted the sergeant. "It's only fair. We thank you for being so nice about everything."

"Give twenty dollars to the lady, and catch your bus coming around the corner. We all have some days we'd rather forget. So carry on men, Semper Fi." The marines saluted in unison and stumbled off towards the bus stop.

"Mission accomplished," said Scott, escorting Miss Kerr back into the Club.

"You handled that situation admirably, Lieutenant. Thank you for your help."

"In the morning, those marines will be hating themselves, wait and see. I wouldn't be surprised if the next time they get liberty, they show up here at the Club full of contrition," predicted Scott.

About a month later, after the marine incident, Scott went to the Club and was surprised to see an elderly lady at the reception desk. He inquired about Miss Kerr. The receptionist responded saying she was sick and that she could not give out Miss Kerr's phone number or address. Disappointed with her absence, he returned the next evening he had off. Miss Kerr was on duty at the desk.

She recognized him. "I understand you wanted to see me, Lieutenant?"

He was reluctant to tell her that he wanted permission to write to her when he was shipped overseas. The reception room was crowded as usual. "I don't know when my outfit will be leaving for overseas; the scuttlebutt is that it'll be very soon. There's a chance I might not see you again before that happens, so here I am. I wanted to ask your permission to write you. We could keep in touch by mail. It would mean a lot to me. I don't have anyone except my mother... If you're willing," Scott's voice trailed off.

"I'm flattered. It will be nice to exchange letters with you. We hardly know each other, Lieutenant Taylor, and I must say that I'm surprised."

"Thanks for saying yes; you've made my day. I hope to see you at the Club again, but if not, I'll write to let you know my new address," Scott had promised.

"Goodnight, Lieutenant Taylor. If I don't see you again, may God watch over you." She had written her address on a piece of note paper and gave it to him. "I'd appreciate it if you don't share this address with anyone else."

He could still recall her words as he left the club, "If I don't see you again, may God watch over you."

Chapter Two

Lieutenant Daniel Joseph Leroux's mother and father were devastated by the loss of their son. Tomorrow would never be available for DJ; yesterday was his forever. Thankful for the rich memories they treasured, they had painfully adjusted to the fact that he wasn't ever going to be a part of their lives again. The pain returned, more hurtful than ever, when they were notified by Captain Scott Taylor that his body was on its way to Maine. The numbness returned, fresh wounds were opened all over again, and the heartaches started anew.

DJ's mother was a full-blooded Cree Indian known by her tribal name of Bright Cloud. The single most precious part of her life was her marriage to Mark Leroux, a young forester who had come to her village in the northlands of Canada immediately after the First World War as a messenger for the United States Army. He had come north to present the Distinguished Service Cross to her family for the bravery of her brother, Flying Eagle, who was killed in the War. Mark was a young marine officer disillusioned by his war experiences. He and Bright Cloud fell in love the first time they met. Their love created a home filled with serenity and trust.

DJ's father, Colonel Mark Leroux, didn't have much to say when the call came from Captain Taylor. He was, however, thankful that Captain Taylor had offered to spend the evening with them in private before the funeral and burial ceremony. Mark had a lot of questions that he hoped Taylor could answer. It was important for him to be able to retrace every move that was made before DJ's death. The circumstances of his son's death weighed heavily on his mind every hour of every day since the traumatic news. Mark had a feeling that he could start the healing process once he truthfully knew what had happened on the battlefield in Europe. He shared the responsibility for the death of many of his own men in combat, and it was a heavy burden for him. Yet, the finality of death never sunk so deeply into his consciousness until he was forced to accept the death of his only son. It was not his intent to assign blame; he simply wanted to know how he had died.

Scott called ahead to the Leroux family to notify them that he would be available in the evening for as long as they wanted him. The funeral at the local Catholic Church and burial ceremony at the Wells community cemetery was scheduled for the next day. He told the family that they would have an opportunity to spend some private time with their son's casket at the sanctuary of the church. Mark was quick to agree that it was something they would appreciate. Sharing some time with DJ's remains, away from inquiring eyes, might help them get through the ordeal a little easier.

It was mid-afternoon when Scott arrived at the Leroux residence in his private car. The casket was being transported by a regulation Army ambulance with an honor guard of nine men. The Army detachment was assigned to stand a constant vigil over the casket on a rotating basis. They were being housed at a local hotel within easy traveling distance to the church. The detachment included the color guard and the firing squad.

The towering pines around the modest house gently swayed in the soft winds carrying the clean scent of pine needles across the yard. The area that Scott could see behind the house looked like a neatly manicured carpet of brown pine needles on the gently rolling forest floor. It was a scene that radiated solitude and peace. He hoped that the Leroux family would be able to find some sustenance from the tranquil surroundings for the difficult hours ahead of them. Scott was apprehensive about meeting the parents, especially Colonel Leroux. Scott felt responsible for the death of their son, even though there was nothing that he could have done to prevent the tragedy, but they didn't know that.

A moment after Scott rang the bell, a middle-aged woman opened the door with a nervous look on her face. Scott knew who she was before she spoke. Lieutenant Leroux had spoken often about his mother, proclaiming that she was a very beautiful woman.

"You must be Captain Taylor," remarked Bright Cloud warmly extending her hand.

"Yes, I'm Scott Taylor, Mrs. Leroux," answered Scott. There was a gracious air about her that immediately put him at ease. Her beauty had not faded with time. "I want you to know that I'm at your service in any capacity you may desire. I realize that this is a difficult time for you and your family. I share your grief. DJ was one of my men and I was very fond of him."

"We appreciate your kindness, Captain. Please come in. My husband is waiting for us in the living room."

As his wife entered the room with Scott, the first thing that Mark Leroux noticed about the young Army officer was his eyes. He had that look which Mark had seen so often in combat veterans. The eyes looked through you instead of at you, as if the soldier was searching for something that was lost to him forever. Mark already felt a certain kinship to this proud young officer, for they belonged to that select fraternity of brothers who had survived the cauldron of war.

"Mark, this is Captain Taylor. Captain Taylor, my husband, Mark Leroux." Scott thought it was significant that Mrs. Leroux did not say Colonel Leroux, for Mark was wearing his green marine uniform with the Medal of Honor ribbon. He was a slender man with deep set eyes and an easy smile that masked the pain in his heart.

"Welcome to our home, Captain Taylor," greeted Mark, standing in front of his favorite rocking chair with the aid of a cane in his left hand. He grasped Scott's hand firmly. "Please, sit down. We're so glad that you could spend some time with us. There are a number of things that I'd like to discuss with you about our son."

"As I told Mrs. Leroux at the door, I'm at your service, Sir. I'll do my best to answer any questions you may have. I'm available to accompany you to the church tonight, if you wish.

I want you to know, Colonel Leroux, that I consider it a privilege to meet you and your wife. Your son spoke often about you. He was terribly worried about your wounds. The Medal of Honor you wear was a source of great pride to him."

"The Medal would have had more meaning for me if I could've shared the honor with my son."

"DJ's sister and her husband should be arriving anytime now," interrupted Bright Cloud. "We thought it would be better to wait for them before going to the church sanctuary. May I get you some refreshments, Captain? Maybe coffee or something else to drink? My husband is a coffee addict, so I know he will not say no," she chided, gently placing a hand on Mark's shoulder.

"If you're going to make it anyway, I'd enjoy a cup," responded Scott, noticing the wink that passed between his hosts.

"If you two don't mind, you can come into the kitchen and talk while I get it ready," suggested Bright Cloud.

Mark pulled himself out of the chair, deliberately steadying himself with the cane. Scott noticed that his left arm was slightly shorter than the right, and his left hand was twisted outward from his body. Colonel Leroux grasped the cane in his left hand so that the contrast to his right side was not so noticeable. He walked with a limp on his left leg. Mark made no reference to his injuries. It was evident that he was adapting to the limitations and determined to make the best of his condition. Scott admired the man for his courage, and could understand why Lieutenant Leroux was so proud of him. He led the way into a spacious country kitchen with a large table in the middle of the room and motioned Scott to be seated at the well-worn table.

"Captain Taylor, the first and most painful question I want to ask you is, how did our son die?" Mark sat at the head of the table facing Scott with a beseeching look of repressed pain flooding over his face. It was a cry for help and clarification in understanding the death of their only son.

"I knew you would ask that question, Sir," responded Scott quietly. "Before I answer it please allow me to give you a rundown on our situation at the time, so that you can better understand the circumstances facing us." Mark nervously fingered the handle of his cane as Scott continued: "We were in Belgium enjoying a most welcome assignment to a relatively inactive front. Prior to that we had been in continuous combat since landing in Normandy on June sixth. The Germans attacked us in mid-December against the weakest link in the Allied front, which happen to be our sector in Belgium. It was a complete surprise to us and the higher command. The attack erupted with such a fury of concentrated force from the Germans that they succeeded in penetrating our lines in the Ardennes Forest region.

"At the northern limit of the German drive towards the Meuse River and ultimately to Antwerp, they were able to launch their advance. On the road leading from Monschau to Elsenborn and to Bretgenback, the SS Panzer forces came up against the stubborn resistance of the Second and Ninety-Ninth Divisions that were bivouacked in the area. We're proud of the fact that the Germans never succeeded in taking the road connecting the three towns."

"I've read about that portion of the Battle of the Bulge," stated Mark with rapt interest.

"A vicious battle took place at Elsenborn Ridge which was strengthened by elements of the Army's First Division shortly after the battle started. Our battalion was the first unit of the 2nd Division to take defensive positions on the ridge. Your son was a platoon leader in my company. As soon as we set up our perimeter outposts on the ridge, your son was hard at work selecting fields of fire for his heavy mortars and a machine gun section. The battle was tenacious and continued for several days. During the second night of the fighting, Lieutenant Leroux formed a small mobile force to stop a German penetration on his left flank. He successfully pushed them back beyond the perimeter where he established new outposts.

"Daniel Joseph was always at the most exposed outpost in the platoon. The next evening he sent a light patrol to make contact and to verify the German positions. That patrol ran into a German patrol doing the same thing. A sharp exchange of gunfire took place and Daniel Joseph's patrol returned to their lines. Two of the men were left behind in the confusion and darkness. The Germans had peppered the area with mortar fire shortly after the fire fight was over.

"Your son informed the men at the outposts that he was going out alone to look for the missing men, and told them to be alert for their return to our lines before dawn came. Evidently your son found the two men. One was killed, we found his dog tags in your son's pocket. The other man was wounded and was able to walk with assistance from your son. They ran into another German patrol which fired indiscriminately in their direction. Your son and the wounded man were killed in the exchange of gun fire. As soon as daybreak came, I was able to expand our company's perimeter enough so that we could retrieve their bodies. Your son had multiple wounds to his chest and stomach. His empty carbine was still in his hands. We believe that both men died instantly from the gunfire."

The country kitchen was filled with silence when Captain Taylor concluded his interpretation of DJ's death. It was an emotion-packed moment. Bright Cloud had quietly taken a seat next to her husband. Tears flowed down her bronze cheeks. She reached for Mark and sobbed on his chest. Mark gently cradled her convulsive body in his arms stroking her black hair with his disfigured hand. Mark was able to hold back his own tears, but his face betrayed his inner turmoil.

Scott sat quietly while Bright Cloud and Mark vented their grief. He felt helpless and out of place witnessing their personal agony. Maybe he should not have been as graphic about DJ's wounds. Scott had a feeling that Colonel Leroux would want that information, even though it was unpleasant to hear. If Scott had been in his place, he would have wanted to know every detail. After a few minutes, Bright Cloud released herself from Mark's arms and reached for a napkin on the counter beside the table.

"I'm sorry to be the messenger of such unpleasant news. I want you to know that I share your loss with you. He was your son, but he was also one of my own, and I lost him for all of us."

23

"I understand what you're saying, Captain. We appreciate your involvement," said Mark, reaching out to grasp the young soldier's arm.

A soft knock sounded at the kitchen door. DJ's sister, Bright Star, and her husband, Steven Jackson, called from the open door. Bright Star ran to her parents and swept both of them into her arms. It was a sorrowful reunion. Mark's eyes watered as soon as he saw his daughter come through the door.

Scott pushed his chair back from the table and stood silently watching the scene. He noted Bright Star's beauty, which she shared with her mother. She wore the uniform of an Ensign in the Navy Nurse Corps. Her dark hair was swept upward beneath her hat, in contrast to her mother who wore her hair flowing around her shoulders. He thought the women were two of the most beautiful people he had ever seen. An Army Air Corps Captain stood near the door, patiently waiting for the tearful meeting to settle down. Bright Cloud was the first to regain her composure. She reached out for the Air Corps officer and embraced him.

"Forgive me, Captain Taylor. This is DJ's sister, Mrs. Dawn Jackson. We call her Bright Star. This young Air Corps pilot, Steve Jackson, is our new addition to the family," proclaimed Bright Cloud with pride. "Star and Steve, I want you to meet Captain Scott Taylor, DJ's company commander."

"Captain Taylor," acknowledged Bright Star, "we were pleased to learn that you were coming for the ceremony. This is my husband, Steve."

"It's my pleasure to meet both of you. This is not a happy occasion for anybody, but I'm proud to be a part of this chapter of your brother's legacy. I've heard so much about all of you. Now I can put a face to the names."

"Welcome to the circle, Captain Taylor," said Steve, shaking his hand, then turning to Bright Cloud and Mark. "How are you two holding up? My prayers are for these days to pass quickly so that the healing process can begin. You're as lovely as ever, Mother Leroux, and your husband still has that Marine Corps' snap to him." Steve's light-hearted comments brightened the atmosphere in the kitchen.

"It's nice to see you, Steve," said Mark. "We're glad you could make it tonight. We worried that weather in the Fort Lewis area might delay your departure. For your information, Captain Taylor, Fort Lewis is a small outpost of civilization in the forest wilderness of northern Quebec Province."

"Mother and Father, we have one more surprise for you tonight. We brought along an old friend." Bright Star stepped outside for a few seconds, reappearing with an elderly gentleman with white hair who towered over everyone else in the room. Inspector Gerard Clough of the Royal Canadian Mounted Police still projected an air of strength and stability. He searched the room for Mark and Bright Cloud. Scott was instantly impressed with the man.

"Hello, Lass. It's been a long time, hasn't it?" Bright Cloud rushed into the two powerful arms that reached out for her.

"Now the circle is almost complete," she whispered. "I hope the trip was not too hard for you, Inspector. Mark and I are so happy to have you with us at this time."

"Old friend," cried Mark in a wavering voice, reaching out for the Inspector. "I had a feeling you'd come. Thank you for your concern."

"Well, Lad," drawled the Inspector, "it would have taken quite a bit to stop me from making the trip. You're looking good, Yank. It's a pleasure for these tired old eyes to see my favorite family once more."

"Inspector Clough," said Bright Cloud. "You're just in time to meet Captain Taylor, DJ's company commander. Captain, meet Inspector Clough, a very dear friend of many years. He was always there when we needed him. He was stationed at Fort Lewis for years. I have since learned that he refused promotions if it meant being moved to another station. He retired from the Mounted Police a year ago, leaving a legacy of selfless dedication that's legendary in the North Woods. We love him very much."

"I'm glad to meet you, Captain Taylor. I'm old enough to remember a young marine captain who came to the Canadian wilderness after the Great War to pay tribute to a brave soldier.

Perhaps you've heard the story. You remind me of my old friend, the Yank."

"I've heard the story, Inspector. DJ often spoke about a living legend in the wilderness of his ancestors. He held you in high esteem, Sir." Captain Taylor eagerly shook hands with the policeman.

"The feeling was mutual, Captain. I loved that lad as if he was my own flesh and blood. I've had a heavy heart ever since I heard of his death." Inspector Clough shook his head from side to side.

"We're just getting ready for some coffee," exclaimed Bright Cloud, relieving the tensions in the room. "If you would prefer some tea, Inspector, it will only take a minute."

"A spot of tea would go fine, Lass. Thank you."

Early in the evening the family and friends adjourned to the church for private meditation. DJ's flag-draped coffin was positioned in front of the communion rail of the Catholic Church. Two spotlessly dressed soldiers maintained an all-night vigil on either side of the coffin. DJ's family and friends slowly walked down the center aisle of the church, mesmerized by the casket holding their beloved son's last remains. Mark had insisted on walking down the aisle on his own. He was a little unsteady, but determined to stand on his own two feet for his son. Bright Star accompanied Bright Cloud filled with grief. Captain Taylor and Captain Jackson trailed behind them in case they were needed at any time.

With everyone's eyes focused on the casket, they moved to the front row and quietly sat down. During the silent interlude that followed, Captain Taylor walked to the casket and retrieved a package placed on the floor beneath it. He respectfully positioned himself in front of Mark and Bright Cloud and started to speak in a soft voice.

"Colonel and Mrs. Leroux, I thought it would be appropriate to present these awards to you this evening before the public ceremony. Your son had already proven himself to be a respected leader of his men, months before he was killed in action. Since he participated in the brutal campaigns all the way from Normandy to Belgium, he was eligible for the most sought after award in the United States Army, the Combat Infantryman's Badge. It can only be earned by exemplary conduct in a major operation. His courageous concern for the men and his complete disregard for his own safety while trying to retrieve missing men of a patrol from his platoon, were in the finest traditions of the West Point code of Honor, Duty, Country. His actions were above and beyond the call of duty. Other officers of the battalion, along with myself, recommended that he be awarded the Silver Star for his bravery. I take great pride in presenting the medal to you at this time. It's a small token of gratitude for his sacrifice. It's an imperfect way of saying 'well-done', but it's given in a spirit of thanksgiving for such men when our country needed them the most."

Mark accepted the felt covered box containing the Silver Star Medal and the Combat Infantryman's Badge. Bright Cloud was bravely fighting back the tears that sprang from the depths of her sorrow. When Scott released the case to Mark, he saluted the two parents and returned to a seat behind them. Bright Cloud caught his arm as he passed by, whispering in a choked voice, "God bless you, Captain."

Later in the evening, after the family returned to the Leroux home, Scott excused himself from the group. The evening at the church had gone well. The parish priest had joined them for prayers before they left the church. Scott checked in with the sergeant in charge of the detail, then turned in for the evening. His last thoughts before going to sleep were about the young Lieutenant Leroux and the short time they had known each other. Now that Scott had met his family, he appreciated the goodness that was a part of the young man. DJ and his sister, Bright Star, were true products of their parent's value system. They were indeed a remarkable family!

The next day Scott was up early checking on the men and seeing that they were prepared for the ceremony. They ate together in the small dining room of the hotel. Scott intended to accompany the family to the funeral, so he left early and drove over to the house. When he pulled into the yard, he noticed an additional automobile with New York plates parked in the yard. Steve and Bright Star's rental car was still there. They had traveled by plane from Quebec to Portland, Maine, where they rented the vehicle. Bright Star saw Captain Taylor climbing the steps leading to the kitchen entrance. "Good morning, Captain Taylor, please come in."

Scott was surprised to see a marine officer with two stars on his shoulders holding a cup of coffee in his hands. Bright Star immediately introduced Scott to a long-standing friend of the family, Major General Arlo Korsman and his wife Michelle, whom Bright Cloud called Mike. Michelle Korsman's hair was prematurely white. He estimated that she was about the same age as Bright Cloud. Scott was drawn to the energy and directness of Mrs. Korsman. She greeted him with sincerity and thanked him for coming. Her husband, General Korsman, was an impressive looking man with light blond hair and blue eyes that had a penetrating look about them. He was powerfully built and carried his authority with dignity without being overbearing.

Bright Star called the couple her Uncle Arlo and Aunt Michelle. Scott felt comfortable with the new arrivals. He was bolstered by the love and support that permeated the small room. He had a slight twinge of envy for the secure life that Daniel Joseph must have had with this wonderful family and friends.

Scott suggested that they leave early for the church, to beat the anticipated large crowd attending the funeral service. The kindly parish Priest greeted each of them as they took their seats at the front of the church. Within a short time the church was filled to capacity.

The Priest started the introduction to the Mass and introduced Inspector Clough, who walked confidently to the pulpit. He looked at all of the people who had come to pay their last respects, then spoke from his heart: "I never dreamed that in the evening of my life I would be a witness to the burial of the young lad I watched grow to manhood. Our Daniel Joseph was conceived in love. He was born into the brilliance of his own sunrise with a hope and a promise of great things in the future.

"That promise was taken away from all of us when the good Lord called him home. I pray that his uncle, Flying Eagle, will greet him in that special place beyond the sunset and show him how things are done in eternity.

"It's no secret what I thought of this young laddie who made us so proud. I loved him as if he was my own flesh and blood. Good-bye Lad, we shall miss you... Thank you for enriching our lives for the short time you spent with us... such a short time. Farewell, young friend. I carry your memory with a heavy heart.

"I'll think of you when the north winds sweep across the forest and blankets the earth with snow. I'll think of you when the wild geese are threatened and they gracefully wing southward before the snows come, but I will always be closer to you when the earth has kept its promise and springs forth with life renewed for a new beginning. The return of the wild geese is the fulfillment of that promise. Your gifts to those of us who must remain are the memories of hope and sadness that the promise of fulfillment will forever remain...unfulfilled. Good-bye Laddie... you're gone, but not forgotten."

When the Inspector finished, there was not a dry eye in the church. Captain Scott followed the Inspector at the pulpit.

"I'm Captain Scott Taylor. I was Lieutenant Daniel Joseph Leroux's company commander during the Battle of the Bulge in Belgium. I had the unique privilege of watching the young man become a soldier worthy of that title. He embodied the spirit and commitment that he embraced on the windswept plains of the United States Military Academy at West Point.

"However, in a very real sense, those same manifest and noble ideals that made him unique were a part of Lieutenant Leroux's daily life while he grew to manhood. He was a product of his family and of this community which shared in the nurturing of the proud young soldier that I was privileged to call my friend. Those of you that knew him will agree, there was something very special about DJ. His quiet courage was an inspiration to his platoon.

"His final act on the battlefield was an example of his selfless devotion to the men in his command. Without thinking of his own safety, he exposed himself to the enemy in order to search for two men that were missing. He found them. One was dead and the other was wounded and in a state of shock. He directed the disoriented soldier back to friendly lines, and covered their rear. Enemy gunfire killed Lieutenant Leroux while he was in that defensive position. The wounded soldier was also killed.

"I've thought a lot about our losses during the war, and I've asked myself the same question time and time again: 'Where do we get such selfless men who are willing to dedicate their lives and their futures for a noble ideal?' Part of the answer to that question lies here in the homes and hearts of the people in this small community, for you are representative of the rest of the country. This is where the values are cultivated, nurtured, and passed on to each succeeding generation. You are truly the heartbeat of America.

"The flag covering Lieutenant Leroux's coffin has been eloquently described as: All that you hope to be and have the courage to defend. It's a symbol of the heights that man can reach if we have the courage to defend our basic right as a free people who oppose tyranny. Lieutenant Leroux never let that flag down. We cannot pay him for the sacrifice he made for us, but we can make his offering more meaningful by trying to be worthy of his unselfish dedication and courageous sacrifice. May he rest in peace."

Mark sat motionless staring at the simple Army casket when Captain Taylor completed his eulogy. There was a parallel between what was taking place now and the events that sent Mark to the Canadian wilderness so many years ago. For the first time in his life, Mark could understand what Running Deer, Bright Cloud's father, must have been thinking when he presented the Distinguished Service Cross to him in honor of his dead son, Flying Eagle.

At the end of the Mass, the soldiers carried the casket to the waiting ambulance that transported it to the cemetery across from the high school. Scott accompanied Mark and Bright Cloud to a few chairs that had been set up beside the gravesite.

He suggested that they sit and rest until the people gathered around the grave.

Captain Taylor was pleased with the performance of the ceremonial squad. They carried the casket to the gravesite and gently placed it on the ground in front of the chairs where Mark and Bright Cloud sat, their faces filled with pride and sorrow for the loss of a part of their life. The Priest said a few prayers. The firing squad lined up on the opposite side of the grave with sharp precision and came to attention. Off to the right, a lone bugler pointed his instrument into the spring air and played taps. The haunting refrain echoed among the fields of stone and touched the heartstrings of everybody present.

A few seconds later the squad fired a measured twenty-one gun salute. The sergeant of the squad and Captain Taylor folded the flag on DJ's coffin with simple precise movements until it was tightly compacted into the size of a small pillow. Captain Taylor presented it to Bright Cloud, who received it stoically with clenched lips.

"This is presented to you in the name of the President of the United States of America as a token of appreciation from a grateful nation." He slowly and precisely saluted her and took up a position beside her chair.

Several friends gathered around the casket to comfort Mark and Bright Cloud. One of the first was Allyson Perkins, DJ's high school sweetheart. He had given her an engagement ring on his last furlough before going overseas. She was full of tears and reached out to Mark and Bright Cloud for comfort. Allyson had been an important part of their dreams for the future. DJ's death changed everything. Bright Cloud sprinkled sprigs of rosemary, the herb of remembrance, around the grave of her son. It was an ancient tradition of her people.

Suddenly, everybody at the grave site looked up as Bright Cloud pointed at two formations of Canadian geese flying northward. The birds gracefully soared against the clear blue sky. The trailing edges of two large "V" formations slowly contracted and expanded as they passed. A large opening appeared in the second formation of geese on the right hand side of the "V". It remained open until a single bird appeared

31

from behind a small cloud nearby and filled the open space of the flying wedge. As soon as the lineup of the group was complete, they made a complete circle over the gravesite. The formation remained perfectly aligned as the mournful honking sounds grew louder and louder, then dimmer and dimmer as they continued their flight to the north, disappearing into the blue sky. Silence settled over the group, amazed at what they had just witnessed. It was an occurrence that is still talked about in the close-knit community today.

Later, back at the house, the family continued to be busy with friends and neighbors. It was an important part of coping with the grief and loss. Scott and Arlo Korsman stood off to one side. Michelle was with Bright Cloud and Mark.

"Where do you go from here, Captain?" asked Arlo.

"Well, Sir, I'm scheduled to attend the Command and Staff Course at the Army War College in Carlisle, Pennsylvania. However, I've got one more stop in Maine before I report to the school. Since the war I've been busy trying to maintain some resemblance of combat ability in the shrunken forces available to us."

"I attended that same course way back in the twenties," reflected Arlo casually. "I never worked so hard in my life as I did trying to complete its requirements."

"I understand it's a demanding one."

"I made friends with several Army officers, who attended at the same time. We've kept in touch over the years. It always amazed me how often I bumped into them during the course of the war. I'm sure you'll find it the same way."

Mark and Bright Cloud were relieved that the day was behind them. They were emotionally and physically exhausted. There seemed to be no more tears left. It was a turning point in their lives when they no longer looked backward. DJ would have wanted them to get on with their lives. The funeral was a limiting benchmark of their grief. Life must continue. In many ways it is the ultimate expression of love and devotion to those who have passed away.

While Bright Cloud and the other women served refreshments for the family, the men sat quietly in the living room. Local friends and neighbors had filled the kitchen with a large variety of foods. Inspector Clough was uncharacteristically silent. He was touched by the ceremony and remained quiet for hours afterwards. Scott sat next to Mark on the large couch. Steve and Arlo had removed their uniform jackets, for it was warm in the house. It was during this informal gathering that Scott learned that Steve Jackson was actually Michelle's son. According to the conversation in the living room, Michelle gave him up for adoption when he was born and regretted the decision. Bright Star found out about Steve when he was a patient at the Pearl Harbor Hospital during the war and was responsible for getting the two of them together. In the meantime, Bright Star and Steve fell in love and got married a short time ago. Scott enjoyed being a part of the group. He felt comfortable enough to ask Mark about something that had been on his mind since the war.

"Colonel Leroux, did you ever experience any doubts about your military career, such as questioning your ability and fitness to command troops?" asked Scott apprehensively.

Mark looked intently at the young soldier for a moment and admitted, "I questioned it every day, Captain Taylor. Any officer with the experience of leading men in battle who has had to cope with the loss of lives, is a charter member of a unique fraternity. Everyone handles it differently, each according to his own values and experiences. I never subscribed to the familiar 'gung ho' mentality, which seems to be popular today. It implies a reckless irresponsible expenditure of human lives, where the methodology of meeting the enemy becomes glorified and as important as the mission itself.

"In real life it's never that simple, as you must know. The ability of any military formation to excel in combat depends on several things, such as confidence in their ability to do the job, satisfaction with the information that has been supplied to them, a firm belief that every effort beyond their immediate situation is supporting their mission, and, most important of all, the men must have faith and trust in the commander's competence to do the job and trust that he will not spend their lives carelessly. That boils down to character and integrity of the commander. Character is the most important ingredient of successful leadership at any level.

"I fought the Germans in the First World War and the Japanese in the last one. I can tell you in all honesty that the German army was a much more formidable foe than the Japanese. The Japanese may have been more fanatical, but the Germans more intelligently used supporting arms, such as artillery, with a professionalism that the Japanese never came close to matching. The fact that you are able to reflect and ask that question implies a competence to lead men. I don't know if my ramblings answered your question or not, Captain."

"That helped, Sir, thank you for sharing your thoughts with me. Sometimes I've felt that I was the only one troubled by such things," declared Scott, impressed with the range of Mark's knowledge and experience.

"Captain Taylor," volunteered Arlo. "I have some thoughts along that line, too."

"By all means, General Korsman. "I'm still a novice at these things. I place great value on the experiences of veterans from whom I have much to learn," replied Scott.

"The men we serve deserve nothing but our best," commenced Arlo. He had a reputation of being severe on any unit commander when that unit did not come up to expectations. He was a firm believer in the old Napoleon truism that 'there are no bad regiments, just bad regimental commanders'. "We're capable of giving our best only when we have satisfied our own standard of excellence. That search for improvement must be ongoing and relentlessly pursued by any leader. The search for the perfect solution must be a part of our psyche or else we'll become unworthy of the responsibility placed upon us.

"The question of our own unworthiness or competence is not always for us to answer. It's usually answered for us by others who have the experience and wisdom to see who we are, and they either sign our fitness reports or they don't. The ultimate test for your question, Captain, is whether or not the men will follow your leadership. If they continue to do that, then your answer lies in their actions. I have an almost

34

pathological trust in the inherent goodness and acumen of the American fighting man. He judges us more completely and correctly than we do ourselves."

"Now you can understand why my good friend Arlo wears the stars instead of me," smiled Mark.

"I'm indebted to both of you for your insights. Thanks for sharing them with me," said Scott.

Visits to the house from friends and neighbors tapered off after lunch. Scott could see that Mark and Bright Cloud were tired and needed some privacy and rest, so he announced his intentions of leaving in the middle of the afternoon. His job was completed, and he was anxious to continue his journey north in Maine.

"Our home is your home, Captain Taylor," said Bright Cloud embracing him as he moved to depart. "Will you please keep in touch with us?"

"It's a promise, Mrs. Leroux," answered Scott.

He said good-bye to everyone present and left. They wished him well, wherever he was going. Scott honked his horn as soon as he turned on the highway.

"That's a fine young man," declared Arlo. "There's substance to him."

"I couldn't agree more, Arlo," said Mark. "He's a young man in search of his own destiny. The things he saw in the war have shaken his spirit, and we should pray for him. I can empathize with our young soldier. I've traveled that same road."

Chapter Three

Scott estimated that it would take five hours to drive to Monson. After leaving the Leroux's home, he drove as far as Newport, where he stayed overnight at a small resort called Woodside. The cabin he rented overlooked a beautiful pristine lake with large pine trees framing the shoreline.

He was exhausted from the tensions of the past week, and fell asleep against the soft pillow within minutes. In the middle of the night he was awakened by the shrill laughing cries of loons on the lake. It was a new experience for him. He remembered what Daniel-Joseph said about the loons. They were called "moaka", "the mad thing". Partially asleep, Scott listened to the mournful cries answered by other loons in different parts of the lake. There was a primitive echo to the calls which pierced the stillness of the night, making Scott feel alone and insignificant.

The melancholic cries of the loons unleashed a river of memories, mostly about Leslie Kerr. She was a true enigma whose memory lingered. He still had warm feelings whenever he thought about the last time he saw her in October, 1943, when his platoon was scheduled to be shipped out to England. The base at Fort Dix was organized chaos while the troops were trying to draw the materials and supplies they would need in the campaigns ahead of them. He knew the time of their departure was near, so he returned to the USO Club where Miss Kerr worked.

The moment he went through the door, Scott and Leslie spotted each other. It was almost as if she was expecting him to come through the open door when he did. She seemed relieved. Scott looked back upon the incident as if it was yesterday.

"Hello, Captain," Miss Kerr greeted cordially. "I'm glad you could come. The word is all over town that the troops are moving out." She was not the same cheerful person he remembered her to be when he first came to the Club. He attributed it to the bad news about her brother. Under the circumstances, he thought she was holding up remarkably well.

"It's nice to see you again," answered Scott truthfully." As a matter of a fact, this could be my last trip before embarkation. There never seems to be enough time to do things the way we used to do them."

"It's the cruel war, Captain. Nothing can ever be the same again." There was sadness on her face that Scott would have given anything to erase.

"Under normal times, I'm really not as bold as it appears."

A group of sailors checked in at the desk on their way to the ballroom just down the hallway. The sound of loud dance music filled the reception area. Scott was uncomfortable talking with Miss Kerr in the busy hallway. She noticed his discomfort and motioned for one of the hostesses to relieve her at the desk.

"Why don't you and I have a cup of coffee in the office behind you?"

"That sounds like a good idea."

"Some of the noise still filters through the walls, but it's at least a little bit more private," said Leslie, placing a coffee pot on the small table in the room. Scott sat at the table while she took a couple of coffee cups and saucers from a shelf.

"Before I showed up here tonight, I practiced what I would say and how I'd say it. Now that we're here I can't remember a thing," admitted Scott nervously. "I don't know you well enough to make any assumptions. The war and the lack of time to establish a normal relationship, may make me appear to be bolder than I really am, but I can only be honest with myself when I tell you that from the first moment I saw you, I wanted to know you better. Right now, I'm afraid I'll be transferred without ever having known you. That fact bothers me!"

"Captain Taylor, I hope I have not given you any cause or indication for you to feel as you do. These are times for courage and honesty, and I can truthfully answer you that I, also, wish we had more time to get to know each other better. Tomorrow is our most precious gift. Since we cannot guarantee that tomorrow will ever come, why don't we just try to maintain what we have for now? We can be friends, and we can write to each other. Who knows what the future may hold for either of us?"

"You're making it sound easy, Ma'am. I didn't know what to expect tonight. I'll happily settle for friendship," answered Scott, visibly relieved.

"I'd enjoy that too, Captain. I don't mean to be disrespectful of your feelings, because you've given me a wonderful compliment by coming to me with your honesty. I'm proud to be the recipient of your attention. I apologize too for our lack of time, but that's what the war has brought to everyone's lives, not just our own."

"Yes, I understand. You have duties that need to be carried out. I'll say good-bye for now. I have to get back to my men. Until we meet again, Miss Kerr."

"Not good-bye, Captain. So long sounds better. Take care of yourself." She placed her coffee cup on the table. Then deliberately leaned down and kissed him gently on the lips. Before Scott could say anything she left the room.

He could still feel the softness of her lips. It lasted for a fraction of a second, yet the simple act touched his heart for months. She wrote once or twice every week, as promised. Once, in Italy, he received six letters all at the same time. They had been in heavy combat and the mail was erratic, at best. Mail call was a welcome break from the all-consuming-task of beating back the tenacious Germans. The letters were filled with folksy news of the Club and the home front. She related light-hearted events from her life. The marines who had been unruly in the parking lot were now helping to keep the peace for her. She also wrote quite a bit about her father's problems on the farm during the war. Help was almost impossible to locate.

Scott's memories of Leslie Kerr were agonizing and bittersweet. As soon as his outfit crossed the Straits of Messina into the Italian mainland from Sicily, Leslie Kerr's letters stopped without explanation. He continued to write whenever he had a chance, but after a while, his letters were returned with "Address Unknown Returned to Sender". Something had happened!! Once they had become established in Italy, his battalion was pulled from the line and he was granted a two week furlough back to the States. He returned to Fort Dix, New Jersey. The minute he arrived, he took a cab to the USO Club where Miss Kerr worked. He was desperate - no one present at the Club knew her or anything about her. One of the cooks thought that she might have been the one who left town, but could not be sure.

Scott spent several days checking the local newspapers in the library for anything unusual. He checked with the police station and the sheriff's department asking if there had been any accidents involving a young woman of her description. He came up empty handed. At first, the mystery was hurtful to him, but as the days continued without success, it made him more and more angry and frustrated. Finally, he went home to see his mother in Pennsylvania before reporting to Fort Devens where he would be charged with putting his own infantry company together. A night never passed that he did not think about Leslie Kerr, wondering what had happened to her.

Scott rose early the next morning, as was his natural routine. He was anxious to meet Lieutenant Robinson's ex-girl friend. Casualties, whenever they occurred, were difficult to cope with. Scott was still harboring a lot of anger about the way Arnold died. A deliberate suicide was something he could not accept, no matter how hard he tried. He placed some of the blame on the girl who wrote the letter, and was curious to find out why a loved one at home would do such a disastrous thing to a soldier in combat.

The local gas station in Monson was able to direct him to the Poole residence. The attendant looked him over thoroughly before giving him directions to the home. Scott expected that his presence in the small town would be common knowledge before nightfall. Evidently, Marie Poole still lived with her parents. It was a modest bungalow-style home overlooking Lake Hebron. The village of Monson was located on the eastern tip of the lake. The Poole residence was about one mile from the center of town at the southern shore of the lake on a small hill with well-kept fields mowed down to the water's edge. He saw a wharf jutting out from the shore at the edge of the sloping field. It was a peaceful setting. He was surprised. For some reason Scott expected it to be different.

As soon as Scott pulled the Ford into the driveway he had some misgivings about what he was doing. A middle-aged lady working on her hands and knees in the garden beside the driveway saw the car and started to rise. When she saw the uniform she rushed to meet Scott.

"Good morning, is this the Poole residence?" asked Scott.

"Yes, I'm Mrs. Poole. What can I do for you?"

"I'm Captain Scott Taylor, I'm looking for a Miss Marie Poole. Does she live here?" Scott had a distinct feeling that his presence was not welcome. He didn't want to get into the reason for his visit until he was speaking with Marie Poole.

"Yes, she lives here. Right now she's down by the water. You can come around the house by the garden and follow the path down to the wharf. She spends a lot of time down there when the weather is favorable. School is not in session this week so you're lucky to find her at home during the day."

"She's a school teacher then," responded Scott with interest.

"She teaches school in Dover," answered Mrs. Poole. "I don't mean to pry, Captain Taylor, your business is between you and Marie, but I must warn you that her father and I do not wish to see her upset about things of the past."

"I appreciate your concern, Mrs. Poole. I'll do my best to honor your wishes."

"That's all we ask for."

"Thank you," said Scott, heading down the well-worn pathway to the bottom of the hill. Marie Poole was sitting in a chair at the water's edge beside the dock. There were several thick books on the ground around her, with a rather large typewriter sitting on a table beside her chair. She had heard the car door slam when he got out of the automobile, so she was not surprised when he approached her. He announced himself just before reaching her chair.

"Hello, Miss Poole. I'm Captain Scott Taylor. I don't know whether Lieutenant Arnold Robinson ever mentioned me or not. I was his company commander when he was killed."

"How do you do, Captain Taylor," answered Marie Poole, reaching for a cane to help her stand.

Scott did not know what to expect from Marie Poole. He had prepared a mental image of Robinson's ex-girl friend, and the young lady before him did not fit that profile at all. Marie was average height and size with dark brown hair that fell to her shoulders. There was a quiet winsome quality about her. She was proud and confident standing before him with a trace of defiance on her face. She wore dark green sunglasses, so he was not able to look into her eyes. Scott wished that he had found the less than respectable girl he envisioned in his thoughts instead of the lady before him now, it would have made it easier for him to speak freely.

"I hope I haven't caught you at a bad time. Your mother directed me down here." He was increasingly unsure of his position. Marie Poole did not offer her hand. Indeed, she braced herself on the cane.

"Please, be seated, Miss Poole. I was the officer responsible for gathering Arnold's things after he was killed. That's how I know your name. I have the last letter that you wrote to him."

Marie sat down heavily and stared motionless across the water. "What can I do for you, Captain?" Her question was cold, distant and demanding.

"Well, I should start at the beginning, if you don't mind. Maybe then you can better understand why I'm here."

"I don't mind. Please continue."

Scott went over the situation on the battlefield that Robinson's platoon was facing when he was killed. Scott did not spare her anything regarding the way Arnold died or the apparent reason behind his death-wish. Scott watched Marie Poole carefully for some reaction to what he was telling her. The large sunglasses still kept him from seeing her eyes which might have helped him.

"After we retrieved his body," Scott continued. "I found your letter in his jacket pocket. He was a brave soldier. I didn't know much about him. He and I rarely talked together the way I did with some of the other officers in the company. There wasn't much time for friendship. I must confess that the letter from you made me angry. I believed that letter was the catalyst which made him do what he did. I didn't come to judge you." Scott stopped unsure of what else to say.

"Then why did you come, Captain?" Marie demanded sharply.

"That's a fair request, and deserves an answer," continued Scott haltingly. "To be honest, his death saddened me, and I was determined to find out what kind of person could so callously write such a letter when you must have known that we were in a continuous combat situation."

"Oh, no, you didn't come to judge me, did you?" cried Marie Poole mockingly. "If all you see in me is a person who was responsible for Arnold's death, then I feel sorry for you. Furthermore, I don't believe it's any of your business. It was between Arnold and me. You're seeking revenge and placing blame against me when you're not in possession of all the facts, and I'm not so sure that I wish to enlighten you, Captain." She was furious and large tears rolled down her cheeks from under the glasses.

The very condition Mrs. Poole had warned him about had developed and Scott was alarmed that he had incited something that he could not control.

"I'm sorry, Miss Poole. I've made a mess out of this thing, and I apologize for my insensitivity. I regret that I've upset you. Before I leave, I want you to know that I'm authorized to release the uncashed checks which you've returned to the government. Arnold listed you as his sole beneficiary and you have a right to the proceeds of the policy. I also have with me the last letter he wrote to you before his death, if you are interested. I'm going to stay a day or two at the Indian Hotel in Greenville on Moosehead Lake. You can get in touch with me there. I'm sorry for having spoiled your day, Miss Poole. I really didn't intend to do that."

"How could it have been any other way, Captain? Good-bye." Marie quietly sobbed, staring across the water.

Scott slowly walked up the hill toward the house feeling guilty about the confrontation. He looked back and found her still sitting in the chair. He was not very proud of what he had done. She was right. It was really none of his business. He had stepped out of line when he tried to implicate her in Arnold's death.

"I'm afraid I did upset your daughter, Mrs. Poole," exclaimed Scott. "I regret that I came."

"My daughter is a much more fragile person since her break-up with Arnold. His death was a shock to everybody. He was not right for her, and I believe I should leave it at that."

"I told her where I could be reached for the next day or two in case she changes her mind. Good-bye, Mrs. Poole. Please accept my apology for reopening hurtful wounds." Mrs. Poole continued to work in the garden without answering him.

The sanctuary of the automobile was a welcome relief to Scott. He was ashamed of his performance, but he was not displeased with the reasons he went there. He rationalized his mission to talk with Miss Poole, but it still left him uneasy. She was right about him not having all of the facts. His condemnation of her was one-sided and unfair, but she refused to tell him her side of the story.

Moosehead Lake was an attraction Scott had been looking forward to for a long time. He had read a lot about its colorful history in the early days of the lumber and paper-making industry. The view from Indian Hill on the road from Monson to Greenville was picture-perfect. The lake spread out into the horizon with small dots of green islands nestled amongst the blue water. It was the largest lake in New England, and it lived up to its billing as a beautiful body of water not yet spoiled by the hand of man. Even with the warm spring sun, the strong breeze across the lake was cool if one did not have a jacket on.

The Indian Hotel was located on the waterfront. Scott was anxious to get settled into his room. There were a number of things he needed to think about and he was searching for ways to make amends to Miss Poole. A few hours later he inquired about a good place to eat lunch, and was told that the best place in town was just a short walk down the street from the hotel. He had not eaten all day, so he decided to check it out.

A booth overlooking the lake was available so Scott took it and ordered a sandwich and coffee. By the time he had finished his sandwich, a tall broad shouldered man entered the restaurant and walked deliberately towards his booth.

"Excuse me, Captain, may I sit for a spell?" The large man wore the State of Maine Game Warden uniform.

"Sure, have a seat," answered Scott. "The coffee is good. I was just going to have another cup."

"My name is Jonathan Poole, I'm a cousin to Marie. Our fathers are brothers. I stopped by Marie's place for a visit right after you left. She was still crying when I got there. She continues to carry a lot of resentment towards Arnold, yet, deep inside of her, I think she feels responsible for his death."

"I'm afraid I don't understand what's going on," exclaimed Scott. "I feel terrible that I got her so upset."

"The reason I looked you up, Captain, is she asked me to speak to you. I believe she wants to read that last letter from Arnold. If you don't mind, I'll join you in a piece of pie and a cup of coffee." There was a good-natured naturalness about the husky conservation officer that Scott liked.

"Maybe you can fill me in about Arnold," Scott requested, glad to have a chance to find out more about the situation between Marie and Arnold.

"Make no mistake about it, Captain, Arnold was two different people in the same body. Most of the time we saw a caring, courteous side of him that was cultivated and encouraged by his parents, who were decent, hard-working people. Arnold's father had served in the Army during World War One. When Pearl Harbor took place, Arnold had already been at the state college for two years. He quit school and joined the Army. You know more about him after that than anybody else. As for me, I wouldn't be surprised if he was a pretty good officer. Maybe tougher than he needed to be, but always willing to get the job done."

"You could say that about him," Scott agreed.

"All of us carry some kind of a burden, and what I'm about to tell you should stay between us, Captain."

"You have my word on that."

"I knew Arnold as well as anyone in town, and I refuse to speak badly of the dead or violate any confidences that he may have entrusted in me. Having said that, Arnold did have a mean-spirited side of him that did not surface often. When it did, he was a little scary, because he seemed to lose control of himself. It never lasted very long, but when he was in that mood, it was most intense. Could he be violent? I never saw it myself. However, it didn't take much of an imagination to see that the right kind of incentive could possibly trigger a violent response.

"I can also tell you that Arnold worshipped the ground that Marie walked on. I think he was a little jealous of her, too. I was away in the Army when they were dating. Marie and her family are good people. I can't imagine that she would break up from Arnold without good cause. Half the young men around here were in love with her at one time or another, including me, and I'm her cousin.

"Marie and her family don't talk much about her disabilities. When the accident took place I understand that her father used a shotgun and ordered Arnold off the property. My uncle still claims that he would've shot Arnold if he had not left immediately. Marie doesn't get around much like she used to. It's hard to know exactly what happened. She refuses to talk about it. The townspeople talk a lot. You know how small towns can be for loose talk?"

"My home state of Pennsylvania is the same," commented Scott. "Small towns can become mean-spirited to those members of the community who choose to keep their problems and affairs to themselves. Every town has its own little 'click' of individuals who try to impose their opinions and wishes upon the rest of the citizenry. I can imagine that the Pooles' desire to keep their affairs to themselves has spun off a whole lot of local conjecture."

"Precisely, Captain."

"What you're saying then, Jonathan, may I call you by your first name?"

"Since we're about the same age, that sounds right to me. I was just a lowly sergeant in the Army, so I'd like the opportunity to call a Captain by his first name." Jonathan grinned from ear to ear. He had an infectious easy-going smile.

"I'd like that just fine, Jonathan, please call me Scott. What you're saying is that the last time Arnold and Marie were together, there was an accident of some kind."

"Yes. She uses a cane to get around with," stated Jonathan.

"I noticed that when I met her. What happened?"

"I don't know exactly because the family refuses to talk about it. I do know that Marie was taken to the hospital, just down the road from this restaurant, with a broken leg and assorted bruises. I think that she and Arnold were on the second floor of the house in the open porch that looks out on the field and pond, when an argument erupted between them. She must have fallen from the top of the railing which is about fifteen feet from the ground. That was when her father ordered Arnold from the property. Poor Marie - she's been quite withdrawn ever since it happened. When I was discharged after the war, I hardly recognized her. I can't tell you anything else because I really don't know for sure about the actual specifics."

"I appreciate your candid thoughts, Jonathan, and your willingness to share the situation with me. I'll be glad to turn over the letter and anything else to your cousin. I hope that she'll reconsider about the money. It's legally hers. If it can help her or her family in any way, she should take it."

"She doesn't receive any compensation from the special school where she teaches. They provide transportation and equipment, but no salary," commented Jonathan, finishing his piece of pie.

"Marie doesn't drive then," remarked Scott casually.

"Didn't you know, Scott? Marie Poole has been blind ever since the accident!"

Chapter Four

Scott was stunned to learn that Marie had lost her sight in the accident with Arnold. That helped explain her unwillingness to look at him when they met at the wharf. Scott had attributed it to the bright sun reflecting off the water, and to the dark sunglasses she wore. As far as Scott was concerned, her blindness presented a whole new dimension to the situation. He had acted on insufficient information, and he felt like a chump for his accusatory manner during his visit.

That evening, Scott telephoned the Poole residence to find out what time would be convenient for him to visit them. Mrs. Poole suggested that he come first thing in the morning. It would be Saturday, and Marie would not have to go to school until Monday.

The next morning, Scott felt sure of himself turning into the driveway than he did on his previous visit. Thanks to Jonathan, he was much more informed about the situation, but he still felt guilty about leaving Marie in such a sorrowful condition. If he did nothing else today, Scott wanted to make amends for his attitude of yesterday.

"You're just in time, Captain Taylor. Marie and I are enjoying a leisurely cup of coffee on a lazy Saturday morning. Won't you join us?" asked Mrs. Poole, guiding him through the house onto a small open balcony facing the lake in the foreground and a large range of mountains on the horizon.

Marie still wore the dark sun-glasses, but her color was better than yesterday. She greeted him without a trace of anger.

"My cousin, Jonathan, stopped by yesterday to see if we needed anything," said Marie matter-of-factly. "He and I have always been the best of friends. He mentioned his talk with you at the restaurant. I'm glad you came back."

"We had a good chat. He told me about your accident and the circumstances of the fall. I'm sorry, I wasn't aware of your blindness yesterday. Do you object to talking about it?" asked Scott.

"No, it's a fact of life, and we have learned to accept the reality of it. We don't try to skirt around it here at home. That would make it even more uncomfortable to live with. It would be easy to pretend that it's not there, but honesty helps me to face it straight on. That doesn't mean I'm not bitter about what happened, because I am. I went through a long period of self-pity before I could accept the limitations of blindness." Scott saw a different person in Marie Poole this morning. She was a fighter with spirit, who did not give up easily.

"Here's a fresh pot of coffee," announced Mrs. Poole. "My favorite bran muffins are hot out of the oven, too."

She placed the pot in front of Marie, who felt for the handle and proceeded to pour coffee for the three of them. She held each cup under the pouring spout and filled them until the liquid touched the index finger she had looped over the rim of the cup. Scott watched with fascination. There was a proud air of accomplishment about her when she placed the cups in front of each of them.

"Your muffins live up to your description, Mrs. Poole."

"They're Marie's favorite too, Captain," answered Mrs. Poole. "Thank you."

"I was pleased to learn from Jonathan that you reconsidered about the letter from Arnold. It may help to put the whole tragic episode behind you. I have the letter with me." Scott pulled the letter from a large manila envelope and placed it in Marie's hands.

"Would you please read it, Captain?" asked Marie.

"I have not read the letter and I prefer not to, Miss Poole. I suggest that your mother read it. I'll excuse myself from the table. It's a private communication meant for you, and I'd like to respect his last thoughts by not intruding."

"I think Captain Taylor is right, Marie."

48

"Under normal circumstances, I'm sure he's correct, too," said Marie, passing the letter on to her mother. "Captain Taylor has been loyal to one of his men who died in combat. I can respect his compassion and concern. Therefore, I think he has a right to know exactly what happened to us, because it has a bearing on Arnold's performance under Captain Taylor's command."

"I appreciate you taking me into your confidence. It's true, I would like to know what happened. I've been laboring under some false assumptions. The truth would be helpful."

"Perhaps it would be better to bring the Captain up-to-date, Marie. Afterwards, I'll read the letter if you want me to."

"Before the war, Arnold and I grew up together in this small town," stated Marie matter-of-factly. "We were good friends through our school years. We occasionally dated in high school but we didn't go steady until we both attended the University of Maine at Orono. Two years later, when the war started, Arnold joined the Army and went to Officer Candidate School. We were serious with each other then and planned to marry. Arnold could be a wonderful caring person most of the time. There were other times when he could become possessive and jealous. It wasn't often, but during those periods, he was not the same man I had fallen in love with. The manipulative episodes became more and more frequent, and I became afraid of him.

"The most explosive time we ever had was during his last furlough home. We were sitting at this same table when I received a telephone call from a young man who was a classmate of ours at Orono. It was a call about one of our assignments in child psychology, and I remember vividly of telling him that I'd give him my notes when I returned to school. Arnold literally exploded over the innocent exchange.

"To make a long story short, Arnold frightened me and backed me up against the corner railing behind you. I was afraid he was going to hit me, so I leaned out over the rail where I lost my balance and fell to the ground. I was unconscious and badly bruised. I remember hearing my father threatening

Arnold while my mother was getting the car ready to take me to the hospital in Greenville.

"I was in a state of shock. The fear I had of falling, along with the broken leg was nothing compared to the terror of what had happened between Arnold and myself. I knew that he was going overseas, and I had a premonition that something horrible was going to happen to him.

"When I recovered from the anesthesia at the hospital, my left leg was already in a large cast, and I was unable to see. The doctor said my eyes appeared to be perfectly normal. Something must have injured the optic nerve because it affected both of my eyes.

"Arnold and I communicated back and forth several months afterwards. It was never the same again. I wanted to break it off but was reluctant to do so because he was at the front most of the time. I never told him I was blind, but it had reached a point where we had to be truthful and stop living a lie. That's when I sent him that final letter. I've agonized over it for a long time. When you arrived yesterday, I didn't blame you for wanting to know what happened. I've condemned myself much more often and more severely than you could ever do, Captain."

"I apologize for bringing up the subject again," said Scott, relieved to know the truth.

"To the contrary, Captain," said Mrs. Poole. "Maybe we can get on with our lives and look to the future."

"That is my sincere wish, Mrs. Poole."

"Why don't you read the letter, Mom."

"Okay."

My Dearest Marie;

I just received your letter telling me that what we had together is finished. I understand how you might feel that way, but it has cut me like a knife. The only thing that has sustained me during the long days and nights of battle is my love for you. I admit that I was wrong and that I was responsible for your accident. Can you ever forgive me?

I'm not sure what it is that makes me do those crazy things I end up doing every once in a while. My mother and father were always concerned about my mood swings. They called it a repressed tantrum syndrome. Whatever it is, I can't use it as an excuse. It's my cross to bear and I hope I can make amends to you for your hardships.

No matter what happens to me, Marie, I don't blame you for wanting to be free of me. Don't blame yourself. I, alone, must carry that burden. You should remember that I have treasured your love and loyalty to me ever since our high school days. Our love has been the one thing I could count on. Without it, the future looks bleak.

I carry my memories of you in my heart. If something should happen to me over here, then that love will accompany me into eternity.

Remember me as we were in happier times, when we were able to laugh together. There were quite a few good times. I'd like for you to remember me that way. I will always love you.

Arnold

Scott and Marie listened with rapt attention. When Mrs. Poole finished, large tears swelled into her eyes. Marie just stared into her blackness.

Scott broke the silence first. "It's a tragedy for all concerned. There are no winners, only those who have lost. I recall reading somewhere that a love that is lost can be the sweetest one of all. It probably applies to all of us at one time or another in our lives."

Marie tried to maintain her composure, but the need for release was too great for her to hold it back. She cried for a long time. She cried for herself. She cried for Arnold, and she cried for the destruction of the future they had planned together. And in the end, she wept for her own limitations, mourning for what might have been. When the last lament pierced her lips, it was almost like a cleansing of her soul. She cried until there were no more tears to shed, and a peaceful silence settled over the room.

Marie broke the spell by sharing something she had carried in her heart for a long time. "It seems I've been shackled to a memory of what might have been in a dream world that could never become a reality. I always knew that, but it's much clearer to me now. I carry no remorse towards Arnold, I loved the person he used to be. I will pray for his salvation so that he can find the peace of mind that eluded him on earth. I'll also pray for his forgiveness. There was a lot of goodness in his heart, and I'll always treasure those kind memories."

Scott felt privileged to be included in their circle of intimate confidences. Marie's catharsis filled the room with a soft calmness. Scott was moved by the emotions he had witnessed around the table.

"As soon as Marie came home from the hospital, she had already made up her mind that she needed to study Braille," remarked Mrs. Poole proudly.

"Bravo, Miss Poole," exclaimed Scott. "I admire your courage. My trip to the State of Maine has certainly broadened my horizons a great deal. The soldier on the battlefield is not the only human being who acts courageously. The definition of courage that I've always understood, taking positive steps in the face of fear, has been amply manifested on this trip. I saw it at a funeral ceremony in Wells a few days ago, and I have witnessed it here in this household with you, Miss Poole.

"When I met you yesterday down by the lake I noticed your typewriter. I thought it was the biggest portable typewriter I'd ever seen. I realize now that it's a Braille typewriter."

"Are you stationed nearby?" asked Mrs. Poole.

"No, Ma'am, I'm going back to school at the Army War College in Pennsylvania. I think the course will take about fifteen months, then I'll be assigned to troops again. I grew up in a small town in central Pennsylvania. My mother still manages the family farm in Dauphin. I intend to head back to Pennsylvania tomorrow morning."

"So this is your first time in Maine?" asked Mrs. Poole.

"Yes. Northern Maine is especially beautiful. Moosehead Lake is all that I expected it to be. I made reservations at the Indian Hotel."

"We're experiencing an early spring. Today is as warm as a day in June; yet, it's only May." Mrs. Poole was musing over something or other. Marie quickly picked up on it and calmly protested.

"Mother, I think I know where you're going with those comments," scolded Marie. "Please don't continue with that line of thinking!"

"Nonsense, Marie, I was simply thinking that Captain Taylor might like to know about Mount Kineo and some of the other features of Moosehead Lake. If he's interested in any of the history of the area, you could point them out to him. After all, you're an authority on the region's history. Maybe Captain Taylor has other plans, it was just a thought," Mrs. Poole quickly added.

"Mother, how could you?"

"In answer to your mother's question, I was planning to take a closer look at the lake by driving along the southern shore towards Moose River, the Pittston Farm and on to the Golden Road. A tour guide would be welcome."

"But I can't, Mother, please. Captain Taylor is just being kind. Sometimes you can be terribly bold when you want to be." Marie didn't try to hide her displeasure with her mother.

"It sounds like a wonderful idea, if you'd be willing, Miss Poole. Your mother is right. It's a beautiful day, and I'll enjoy your company."

"But I can't see, Captain," exclaimed Marie with a beseeching look on her face. The statement had a tone of impossibility to it.

"So what," exclaimed Scott. "I'm an expert on reading maps. When we get to where we want to go, you can tell me what to look for and tell me what's significant about what I'm looking at."

"Oh, Marie, it would do you good to get out from the house." It was almost a plea from her mother.

"It sounds like a good idea to me," repeated Scott, pleased at the turn of events. "How about it, Miss Poole? It would be swell spending the rest of the day touring the area."

"Since you put it that way, I'll get my purse and jacket."

As soon as Marie left the room, her mother turned to Scott with a triumphant look on her face.

"It will be good for her, Captain. She spends too much time alone. Your visit has turned out different from what I expected. Thank God the war is over. There is so much healing that needs to take place in the country."

"I'm lucky. I survived relatively unscathed. For a lot of men, the war will never be over. No matter what he did to Marie, which was monstrous and uncalled for, Arnold was a brave soldier. His last act was not cowardly. I've felt so helpless about his death. I confess that I blamed your daughter for what happened. That's why I insisted on coming here. Now that I know what actually took place, I can accept it as a tragedy that was inevitable. Marie is as much a casualty of the war as Arnold. I'm so glad that Jonathan asked me to come back here. I feel as if a giant hand has reached out and removed a load from my conscience. I thank you and your daughter for that."

"It's time to put the past to rest," said Mrs. Poole, reaching across the table clasping her hands over his. "I'm so glad it was you who came, Captain Taylor. Your visit will be a milestone for us. Marie hasn't been doing very well, and we've been worried about her."

"Well, I guess I've got what I need," announced Marie, sporting a bright red and yellow sun bonnet.

"You two run along and enjoy the day."

"I promise to drive carefully, Mrs. Poole."

Scott escorted Marie out to his new Ford, opening the door for her. The minute they turned down the road towards the village, Marie leaned back in the seat and relaxed.

"Here we go," Scott announced light-heartedly. "The freedom and independence to go wherever we want is one of the miracles of the modern automobile."

"I'd almost forgotten how pleasant it can be," Marie softly announced, as if she was talking to herself.

They drove north to Greenville, then along the southern shore of the lake toward Rockwood. Marie talked freely about the area. She mentioned that the view of Mount Kineo from the Rockwood landing was especially beautiful. "The steep cliffs rise from the water almost perpendicular." She told Scott about the famous Mt. Kineo Hotel that was built at the top of the Mountain. It burned at the turn of the century. She became enthusiastic about the steam-powered elevators, the first of their type in the world, which operated at the face of the cliffs for years.

Once they arrived at Rockwood, Scott could appreciate what Marie had been telling him. The sheer cliffs looked as if some giant ax had shaped them. There was a sightseeing boat loading a few passengers at the landing. The trip took about three hours.

"Would you be up to taking the trip on the boat? The water seems to be quite smooth today."

"Yes, that would be fun. I haven't been on a boat since the accident," answered Marie. "Before we go on the boat, Captain, I'd like to explain something to you that makes people feel awkward around me. Let's face it honestly. I'm blind and I do have limitations. There are things a person with sight can do that I can't. I have to accept that fact honestly, for my own safety. I'm a very independent person by nature, so you can imagine that I don't like being treated like a baby. I've lived with blindness long enough to realize that false pride can get me into trouble. When we're walking, I still feel more comfortable and secure if I can take your arm. I prefer your left arm so that I can use the cane with my left hand, if necessary."

"It's great that you're able to speak so candidly. I like that attitude. I promise you that I'll do everything I can to keep you safe and comfortable while we're together."

"If I did not believe that, I wouldn't be here with you. If I'm uncomfortable in any situation, I'll tell you. There are a lot of things I miss not being able to do, of course. One of them is driving an automobile. I don't dwell on my condition as much as I did. I want to live as normal a life as my condition allows. I hope that my days of self-pity are over."

"I admire your courage, Miss Poole. Incidentally, you and I are about the same age so what do you think about calling each other by our first names? It's kind of formal to keep calling each other Miss Poole and Captain. My first name is Scott. When I was young, my friends called me Scottie. Whenever my mother called me Scott, I knew I was in some kind of trouble."

Marie smiled at him. "I've been thinking the same thing. Everyone calls me Marie. I'll call you Scott. I like that better than Scottie."

They boarded the boat together. Scott carefully guided her to the gang plank and to the step up to the boat's deck. When there were steps he warned her ahead of time. He located a couple of comfortable seats at the fantail of the boat where they would not be subjected to a direct breeze. The boat had just pulled away from the landing when Marie lifted her head to feel the wind on her face.

"Mt. Kineo is really beautiful from the west. When we came aboard the ship I could feel the sun in the west. So we must be going in a westerly direction. Am I correct?"

"Yes, you are, Marie. Kineo is pretty from this perspective. I like the small islands that dot the lake, also. I can almost smell the forest."

"It's true, Scott. I can smell the spruce and fir trees, too. Mother Earth is coming back to life after a long dormant winter. I believe that people spring back to life at this time of year, too."

"I agree."

Scott and Marie talked a lot about their lives. School experiences were a favorite subject. He was anxious to tell her how, as a young boy, he dreamed of being a soldier while he labored in the fields of his mother's farm. When he graduated from West Point he applied for the infantry branch instead of the more technical branches such as artillery, engineering or logistics. The infantry demanded more leadership skills and he believed he excelled at leading troops. Evidently others thought so too, or he would never have been selected for the choice billet at the Army War College. Scott shared some of his doubts about continuing in the Army with Marie. He told her of his conversations at the Leroux's home place after the funeral, and how they helped convince him that he was well-suited for his chosen career.

Marie also talked about her school days at Orono. She always wanted to be a teacher, so she majored in Education. She was able to laugh about some comical incidents in a public speaking class and an English class. Laughter came easily to her and that pleased Scott. It was an indication that she felt secure in his company. He watched her closely while she talked. She used her hands a lot to make a point or to emphasize something. She was intensely thorough and precise in the things she talked about. After being with her for a while, Scott came to the conclusion that she probably was a perfectionist by nature.

By the time the cruise boat returned to the landing at Rockwood, Scott had learned a lot about Marie. Just the way she adapted to her blindness was a reflection of a very self-reliant person. Scott admired her independence and positive attitude, questioning if he could handle such a tragic accident half as well as she was doing.

"This is your territory, Marie. Have you got any suggestions as to where we can get a good meal and a hot cup of coffee?" asked Scott, helping her into the passenger seat.

"Let me think for a second. Believe it or not, I haven't been up this way for a few years. Most of the places don't open until Memorial Day. I think that the Squaw Mountain Inn is still open year round. It's just up the road to the west a mile or so. If you want we could try that. A cup of hot soup would be nice after the boat ride."

"Squaw Mountain Inn coming right up," said Scott. "This has turned into a great day. I'm glad you could come. It was nice of your mother to suggest it."

"It has been a pleasant day, Scott. I guess I was a bit harsh on her when she brought the matter up. She's a very independent woman. She has a lot of friends. My father is much more reserved, but they have a wonderful relationship. After all of these years, they still love and support each other. I'm lucky to have grown up in such a household."

"You certainly are," answered Scott, turning into the driveway of the Inn. It was open for business, as Marie expected it would be. "I never knew my father. He was killed in World War I. I was a furlough baby. I never had any brothers or sisters. My mother is an exceptional woman and I love her very much. She has worked hard all her life."

A long set of stairs led to the entrance of the Inn and dining room. Scott assisted Marie to the first stair tread. She paused for a moment to feel it with her cane. With a look of determination she then climbed the stairs without stopping again.

"Twelve steps up and nine steps from the top of the stairs to the entrance door," Marie reported to Scott. "I find that I'm constantly creating maps and mental images of the places I've been. Knowing the approximate distances helps me when I return to them in reverse. Counting steps is one way blind people measure distance for themselves."

"I never thought of that, but it makes sense."

The dining room was not too crowded, so they took a booth near the fireplace in the center of the room where a small fire crackled. The decor was rustic and relaxing, adding a warm glow to the atmosphere.

As soon as they settled into the booth, Marie leaned over to Scott and spoke to him in a whisper. "I'm a little embarrassed to ask, but would you help me to the women's restroom? If you walk me to the door, I can find my way back without any help."

"Of course," answered Scott gently. "Give me your arm."

The restrooms were on the opposite side of the fireplace. Scott paced the way with Marie and placed her hand on the door.

"Thank you, I can handle it from here," Marie whispered in his ear.

Scott returned to the booth and looked at the menu. He was starved. A few minutes later Marie returned to the booth. Scott watched her pace off the distance from the restroom door to the booth with amazing accuracy. There was a triumphant look on her face when she announced: "This must be our table, Scott."

"It is, Marie," he answered, thinking how difficult it must be to live in a world of total blackness.

Scott ordered soup and a steak dinner. Marie ordered soup and a ham sandwich.

"When I'm at home, I usually eat from a dish with sides like a soup bowl. That way I can eat it with a spoon and not make too much of a mess. A sandwich is easier to eat in public than a steak dinner like you're having. I can eat soup just like everybody else, once I've felt it. It isn't nice in public, but a blind person has got to determine how full their dishes are. The only way to do that is to carefully touch it with your finger hooked over the rim. I would not dare to eat a steak in public until I've practiced more. Sandwiches are always a safe bet, and I really like them."

When their meals were served, Scott quietly watched Marie cover the distance from the end of the table next to her body with her hands until she located the soup and sandwich plates. She repositioned them to suit her. After she checked the soup level with her left index finger, she proceeded to eat as if she could see everything in front of her. If somebody at a distant table watched her eat her meal, they would never have guessed that she was blind.

"I feel a little guilty with such a large steak. My, it does smell good. I haven't touched it yet, so why don't I cut off bite-size pieces and put them in your minestrone soup, so that we can share it."

She giggled like a young girl at the suggestion. "Okay, Scott, if you can do it without being too obvious. I don't like to be the subject of curious people."

"I'll be very careful, Marie. Never mind what other people think. You're doing great. I admire your spirit."

"Thank you for the encouragement. You're a kind person, Scott Taylor. I didn't think so yesterday, but I do now."

It was late when they drove back to Monson. "I hope your parents aren't worried about you." said Scott, turning the car radio to some soft music.

"No, they won't worry. As a matter of fact, I think they were going to my cousin Jonathan's house for the evening. The music is nice. When I hear it now, I'm surprised at my ability to hear the different components and instruments in any particular song. My hearing has intensified a lot since I lost my sight."

"Well, here we are back where we started. The house is dark, so your parents must be out. I'll see you to the door. This trip to Maine has certainly turned out differently than I expected. I apologize again for my conduct and attitude at our first meeting. I'm glad we could spend some time together."

"I accept your apology, Scott. I know it's sincerely offered. It's been a fun day for me, and I appreciate your helpfulness. When you return to school, maybe we can write to each other, if you want."

"I was going to suggest the same thing. I'll write to you first to let you know what my address will be. The Army has its own way of doing things. Here we are at the front door. The lights are all off, but I'd like to see you safe and sound inside. Where I came from, that's what a gentleman is expected to do."

"If you insist. The doors are never locked. I don't even know where the key is to the old door." She flicked a light switch on. "I do it by habit. I don't need it to get around."

"Good night, Marie. Thanks for a pleasant day. It was fun for me, too. I'll be leaving in the morning. As soon as I reach Carlisle, I'll be in touch."

"Good night, Scott. Thank you for sharing the day with me. I wish you well in the new course at the Army College, and will be looking forward to hearing from you. I can type a letter back to you as soon as you give me your address. I'm so thankful that I learned to type without looking at the keys. It's paying dividends now."

Scott started to leave, then changed his mind. He reached out to take Marie into his arms and gently kissed her on the lips. She accepted his embrace. They said good-bye one more time. Scott left her standing in the doorway waving to him.

Chapter Five

Later that evening, Scott awoke from a recurring dream that continued to hold him in bondage. The dream always included faces of the men killed in action. The men were standing all together with their arms extended, reaching out toward him, as if they were trying to say something, but he could not hear any of the words. Scott woke from the dream awash in sweat. One of the faces from the dream was that of Lieutenant Robinson. Scott spent sleepless hours trying to figure out the significance of the dream. It was very real to him. He could feel the glare of the dead men's eyes and hear their soft cries, but he could never discern what they were trying to tell him. The look of disbelief and horror was not easy to forget.

Unwilling and unable to sleep, Scott got out of bed and opened the window overlooking Moosehead Lake. The cool air flowing over the glistening waters was refreshing. On the distant shore majestic spruce trees shown in silhouette against the blue-black void filled with an infinite number of blinking stars. There was a restlessness in him tonight that he could not explain. Marie Poole's face looked down from the heavens with that beseeching smile she sometimes wore. He could not help wondering what the future held for Marie. Perhaps the parting kiss was out of line, but, at the time, it seemed the appropriate and natural thing for him to do.

Marie was in Scott's mind for the rest of the night. He was reluctant to read any more into their time together than the fact that it was pleasant being with her and he could not help admiring her perseverance and discipline. Perhaps he harbored a certain amount of pity for the blind lady. He wasn't sure, but, one thing he was certain about, she did not deserve the tragic consequences of blindness.

The following morning Scott began his long journey back to Pennsylvania. Normally he would have broken it up into two days, but his restlessness forced him to continue on into the evening until he reached his mother's home in Dauphin, Pennsylvania. He called her from a roadside diner in New York State so that she would not worry about him when he pulled into the yard late at night.

The trip to Maine had put to rest many of the misgivings he entertained about Arnold's death. Now, he could accept it without placing any blame on himself or Marie Poole. That in itself was a source of relief. Scott's discussion with DJ's father and General Korsman helped to alleviate some of the nagging reservations he entertained about the way he handled his company in combat. Colonel Leroux admitted that he had also questioned his own decisions every day of his life. It was reassuring to hear that comment coming from a Medal of Honor recipient.

The lazy Susquehanna River was like an old friend to Scott. He drove through the empty streets of Harrisburg and turned north along the east bank of the river. He had spent his childhood days swimming in it, boating on it, and playing near it. The river was as much a part of homecoming as the fertile fields of his mother's farm in the picturesque valley beside the river.

Scott could remember the time when he and two friends built a rather unstable raft out of flotsam and old boards near the edge of the river. When it was completed, they decided to have a launching and a christening ceremony for their creation. The construction process had consumed their collective energies for several days. Charlie der Blatz and his younger brother, Matt, were able to "borrow" an unopened fifth of whiskey from his father's meager stockpile in their cellar. Before they broke the bottle against the large tree trunk which formed the keel and main frame of the raft, the boys decided to drink a toast to the fruit of their endeavors.

The three friends each took a large swallow from the bottle. It nearly choked them to death. Scott and little Matt were given the scare of their lives when poor Charlie laid on the shore and rolled his eyes back so far that only the white portion was visible. After several anxious minutes, Charlie came to, a little embarrassed because the other two boys kidded him that he could not hold his liquor! Then Charlie broke the bottle against the log while Scott and Matt pushed the heavy raft further out into the main stream of the river. The raft quickly turned sideways in the swift current and ceremoniously disappeared down the river out of sight. The spectacle of the three enterprising young boys still touched Scott's heart. The two brothers were killed in action when their cruiser was lost in the battle of the Philippines.

Scott's mother's family were immigrants from the Netherlands in the early part of the 19th century. He proudly proclaimed himself as a Pennsylvania Dutchman even though his name was English. He turned into the long driveway leading to the house. The musty aroma of freshly plowed earth was like a tonic to him. The porch lights were a welcome sight. When the headlights from the Ford flashed across the yard, he could see his mother heading for the door on the porch.

"Land sakes alive, Scottie, I'm happy to have you home." Mrs. Taylor leaped into his arms and buried her head against his chest. She was a small slender lady who could not make it to Scott's shoulders even in her high heel shoes. Scott thought that her hair had grown a little whiter than the last time he saw her. She was an uncomplicated woman who did not readily show her feelings. She was a hardworking country woman who spoke her mind freely, without emotion. She appreciated it when others did the same, and she never took offense with differing opinions. She had a well-earned reputation in the agrarian community of being dependable and reliable. Even though she was not well-educated, she was an undisputed authority on truck farming in the area. She passionately read everything she could lay her hands on about soils, crops, and the constantly changing markets. Her son was the shining joy of her life.

"How long are you home for, Son?"

"Just for tonight Mom. I'm not sure whether I'll be able to stay here or not while I'm attending the War College Course. I should be able to find out when I report in tomorrow."

"Well, come in," she said impatiently with her arm around his waist.

"I know it's kind of late, Mom, but I could still use a cup of coffee. It'll help settle me down after the long drive. The Ford ran like a charm. The trip was a good way to break it in."

"I'll put the coffee percolator on. I may be able to find a piece of fresh apple pie. That was always your favorite." She was in good health after all of the years of hard work on the farm. There was still a spring to her steps. She seemed to bend forward slightly so that she could move faster. Scott had to hustle to keep up with her. Though life had been difficult for her, she kept her own counsel and never complained about the heavy load. To the contrary, she embraced life with such enthusiasm that Scott drew strength and satisfaction from her boundless reservoir of energy. She encouraged him to run with his dreams, and that no matter where they took him, she would rejoice in his accomplishments. Scott had absorbed her integrity and her love of life by sheer osmosis.

"I was just thinking about the time when Charlie and Matt der Blatz and I built our raft," reminisced Scott. "It's probably a blessing that it floated away from us or else we could have all been drowned out in mid-stream."

"I understand that Mr. der Blatz never mentioned a thing about his missing bottle. Evidently, Mrs. der Blatz didn't realize he had it in the first place," his mother told him, placing a piece of pie before him. "The death of those two boys on that ship has just ripped the heart out of their mother and father. They haven't recovered from the loss yet. I saw Mrs. der Blatz at the grocery store the other day. She asked about you and then started to break down. They're good people and I pray that God can bring some comfort to their lives."

Scott was silent. It was hard for him to imagine that two such energetic young men were gone forever. He couldn't help feeling the pain of the family. "I should stop by to see them. We were such close friends in school."

"They would like that. You boys were inseparable. My, it seems like only yesterday. I wish your father could see you in that uniform with the Captain bars on your shoulders, Scottie. He would be as proud of you as I am." She stood behind his chair and ran her fingers through his close-cropped hair.

"Maybe he does see me, Mom. I hope he's proud of me, but he should be especially proud of you. He must have been someone special to have a girl like you as his wife. I hope I'm as lucky as him when I make that choice."

"Just follow your heart, Scottie, and it will never lead you astray."

Mother and son talked quietly together well into the evening before they went to bed. Scott warned her that he would not disturb her when he left early in the morning for Carlisle and that he would let her know for sure about his boarding status. Scott fell asleep instantly in his own familiar bed.

The Command and Staff Course at the Army War College was designed to prepare career officers for command of full regiments and divisions in combat situations from equatorial jungles to arctic operations. The officers attending the courses were from all of the branches of the Army, including infantry, artillery and engineers. In the same class with Scott there were two marine officers, two Dutch Army officers and one Canadian Army officer. Most of the officers had experience as company commanders. The main goal of the college was to elevate the outlook of the junior officers so that they could handle the command of increasingly larger formations of fighting men, and be able to coordinate attached supporting arms and service units into a dynamic force capable of performing any missions assigned to it.

Scott immersed himself in the demanding schedule of the school. It was several days before he had a chance to write a letter to Marie Poole. Classroom instruction and field exercises took up all of the student's time and energy, so Scott would not be able to commute from his mother's place. The students did have weekends free of organized study, but even then, they had to dig into the assigned work just to stay abreast. General Korsman called the course the most difficult in his career. Scott was inclined to agree.

One of the field exercises took place at the Indiantown Gap Army Base outside of Harrisburg. On that occasion, Scott and his classmates were studying close ground support techniques from aircraft. At the briefing conference Scott thought that an Air Force officer looked familiar to him. He could not immediately place the man until the air officer reviewed the demonstration to be performed that afternoon. It was the fighter pilot Scott met at DJ's funeral. Later in the evening, Scott spent some time with Captain Steve Jackson at the temporary officer's quarters at the airfield.

"I thought you were discharged from the Army," remarked Scott.

"Well, I was discharged," said Steve pleased to see a familiar face. "I recovered from my injuries better than expected, so I was able to transfer to the Reserves in the New York National Guard. My eyesight has returned as good as ever and my legs are rarely a problem anymore. It's great to be back flying again."

Scott liked the gregarious pilot. There was something solid and dependable about Steve. He had confidence in his abilities but he was free of the swagger and cockiness that was a trademark of many fighter pilots. Steve never mentioned the burn scar on the left side of his face. He shaved closely every day to hide the fact that his upper lip failed to grow facial hair after it healed. He was still self-conscious about the injury.

The next day Steve led his New York pilots in another demonstration of air support for ground troops. Everyone at the school was impressed with the accuracy and skill Steve and his squadron displayed with their P-51 Mustangs. The planes dropped bombs filled with napalm, a gelatin-like form of gasoline that ignited on contact. It was a horrifying weapon that proved effective during the war against any type of enemy stronghold.

In general, the Army Air Corps did not view air support of ground troops as a fitting role for their aircraft. A few innovative pilots however, had successfully cooperated with the infantry by using their fighter planes as mobile artillery platforms when the ground troops were unable to utilize their own artillery support systems. A squadron of P-51 Mustangs in Alaska commanded by an aggressive commander was the first to use airpower as an integral part of an attacking force. The commander of the New York Air National Guard had been a part of the squadron in Alaska and was convinced that support of ground troops would help insure the establishment of an autonomous national air arm. The New York Air National Guard enthusiastically embraced the concept and trained endlessly to perfect its execution.

Steve confided to Scott that the demonstrations the day before were the first time he had flown the Mustang. He had just a few hours to familiarize himself with the aircraft before the demonstration. Up to that time, he had flown the P-38 Lightning. It was still his favorite fighter even though the Mustang was slightly faster.

"Are you going to return to your New York base for the coming weekend?" asked Scott.

"No, our planes and radio equipment for the ground forward controllers will stay here for a while," answered Steve, checking a calendar hanging on the wall beside their table. "Evidently they're going to have us run more demos for several different groups. I'm on my annual three-week tour and have been put up at quarters here on the base for that period."

"I was just wondering if you'd be interested in going up to my mother's place for part of the weekend? I'd be glad to give you a lift unless you planned to return home," suggested Scott casually.

"I appreciate your offer, Scott, but I'm not returning to New York. My wife is at a small outpost in northern Canada working as a nurse at an infirmary her mother established years ago. It's a small tribal village in the wilderness of the Province of Quebec. It's called Fort Lewis. I flew from the lake adjacent to

Fort Lewis, to Lake George, New York just before I started these flying demonstrations."

"I remember DJ talking about Fort Lewis. It was his ancestral homeland, right?"

"His mother, Bright Cloud, was born and raised there. Bright Cloud's father, Running Deer, was a well-respected leader of the tribal council at Fort Lewis for several years. My wife's Indian name is Bright Star. Her biological mother died giving her birth, her father was Bright Cloud's brother, Flying Eagle. He served as an Army officer under Colonel Leroux during World War I. I suppose that all sounds confusing to you, but it becomes more logical when you're familiar with the family."

"DJ looked a lot like his mother and your wife. When I met them I was struck with the similarities," admitted Scott. "You're a lucky man to have such a family."

"There are strong ties between General Korsman and my biological mother, Michelle Korsman, and the Leroux family. Inspector Clough is also very close to all of them. He's an interesting character, isn't he?" asked Steve.

"I met him briefly at the funeral, but I can remember DJ talking often about the strong arm of the law as represented by Inspector Clough in the North Woods," answered Scott. "I wouldn't want him on my trail."

Steve smiled, "I guess the Inspector was a force to be reckoned with. He's become a living legend in an area full of legendary strong men. My wife and her mother have him eating out of their hands and they all like it that way. I've become very fond of him."

"How does it feel having a marine general in the family?"

"I still can't get out of the habit of calling him general, even though he's repeatedly asked me to call him Arlo and sincerely means it. We've never gotten into the familiar Army/Marine rivalries that are so common. Both he and Colonel Leroux, who was a superb combat commander, agree that no single service has a monopoly on courage and competence. We both use the same tactical manual, and share other things in common, so the differences are more or less academic. Arlo is a powerful individual, but he's as gentle as a lamb. He and my mother are very happy together. Well, I've been talking like a babbling idiot. That must mean that I miss Star and it shows."

"Don't apologize, Steve," Scott glanced at his watch. "My life has been pretty uneventful so far. I went from West Point to Africa and the European Campaign during the war. I haven't found the right girl yet. I've been so wrapped up in Army affairs that time has just passed me by. I don't know if it's a sign of ambition or if it's an escape mechanism for my independence. Maybe I'm just a die-hard bachelor!"

"At one time or another, we're all in that category," said Steve approvingly.

"Tomorrow is Friday and it looks as if we're getting off by 3:00 PM. Why don't we go up to my mother's for supper and stay there overnight?" asked Scott. "She'll enjoy our company."

Steve stood up. "Sure, that would be great. The squadron commander is planning to stay at the base for the weekend, so I'll be free. I'm the squadron executive officer. Which reminds me, I should check on the maintenance crew before I turn in. I'll see you tomorrow afternoon then."

"I'll pick you up at your quarters," suggested Scott. "Good luck with your demonstration tomorrow morning."

"Thanks," answered Steve with a wave of his arm.

The next day turned out to be a rainy one, which canceled the flying demonstration. Steve substituted with an impromptu lecture on the subject for the balance of the day. Scott drove to Steve's quarters that afternoon and the two men left the base in civilian clothes which were easier to relax in.

The weekend proved to be restful and uneventful for both of the men and they were able to relax under Mrs. Taylor's watchful eye. Steve told Scott about the float plane that he had stored for the time being at Lake George. They discussed the possibility of making a trip to Fort Lewis during the Fourth of July break. They could fly directly from Lake George to Fort Lewis with one fuel stop at Lac St. Jean, Quebec. The trip would be about seven hundred miles, one way. Steve estimated that they could make it in four hours. Scott was enthused about the idea. It would give him the opportunity to see first-hand the countryside that he had heard so much about.

When Scott returned to Carlisle Barracks late Sunday evening, a letter from Marie Poole was waiting for him. He anxiously flipped on the desk light and read the neatly typed letter:

July 22, 1946

Dear Scott,

A few lines tonight to thank you again for the fun day we had last week.

I've been thinking a lot about the initial reason for your visit. If I had been in your shoes I probably would have had the same kind of thoughts that you had about me. It was logical. I want you to understand that if I had it to do all over again, even with the benefit of hindsight, I would do the same thing, even though I still feel responsible for Arnold's death. Every hour of the day I think of the way he died, and I believe that God has punished me with blindness for enabling the tragedy to take place.

Don't feel sorry for me. I've gone through enough self-pity these past months. I can't stand any more of it. Your visit has been a turning point in my life. I'm starting to look forward to the future with a more positive outlook. More than anything else, I want to thank you for helping all of us bring this episode in our lives to a close in a manner that helps to resolve many of the guilty feelings. Time will help the healing, but it is reassuring to know that the process has begun.

In regards to the day we spent together, I'm having contradictory impressions. When we were together, I had the feeling that you enjoyed yourself. Now, days later, I'm troubled with doubts and fears that I can never know for sure, because I could not look into your eyes and know the truth. I can understand and accept the fact that there is not and never will be anything more between us. At the same time I must tell you with desperate honesty, that I would be crushed if your behavior was motivated by pity or professional courtesy towards me personally.

I wish you well in your school work, and look forward to hearing from you.

Sincerely,
Marie Poole

P.S. Please excuse any typing errors that I may have made.

Scott was concerned that Marie was uncertain about his motives. He thought often about her. The picture of her confronting him with that proud determination the first time they met, was still a very strong image to him. He could not rule out the fact that he had strong thoughts about the unjustness of her tragedy, but he didn't think he acted out of pity.

The day Scott spent with Marie was a refreshing interlude. He would have protected her with his life, if necessary. She made him feel needed and that was comforting to him. Yet, it could easily be construed as a form of pity. Scott unpacked his overnight bag and sat back at his desk to compose a letter to Marie. He had trouble finding the right words to describe his thoughts, so he reached for the phone to call Marie in spite of the late hour.

"Hello, Mrs. Poole? This is Captain Taylor and I apologize for calling at such a late hour. I started a letter to Marie but I know that I can explain over the phone better than I can in writing."

"I understand, Captain Taylor. Just a moment. I'll call Marie; she's in her room," said Mrs. Poole.

"Thank you, Mrs. Poole."

"Hello, Scott. This is Marie," she answered hesitantly.

"I apologize for calling at this late hour. I just received your letter and I wanted you to know that I felt the same as you about our Sunday together. I want to dispel any lingering doubts you may have. I don't pity you, Marie. My Lord, you've accepted your blindness with more courage and perseverance than anyone I know. Instead of pity, young lady, you've won my respect and if you could look into my eyes, you'd know that it's true."

Marie thought about it a few seconds before she answered with a serious tone: "Thank you for the nice words. You've made the evening special. How's school going?"

"Well, they're running us ragged if you want the truth, but I'm getting a lot out of the course. Everything we're studying and practicing is related to the command decisions that we'll have to make in combat. The responsibility of men's lives in combat is something that I take seriously, so I study hard in the hopes that it will make me a better commander."

"I know that you're very dedicated to your work and I admire your devotion to duty. I wish you well. I'll continue to write, and you can write to me. My mother will read your letters to me, but that should not prevent you from telling me precisely what is on your mind."

"I wanted to ask you about that. I promise to write. Thanks for your letter, Marie. By the way, there were no mistakes in your typing. I'm not guaranteeing that mine will match that level of perfection, but I'll try," said Scott wryly. "I use the two finger method! I feel better now that we've talked. Until next time, Marie, goodnight."

"Goodnight Scott, take good care of yourself."

The next day Scott was intensely involved in his studies. He was selected to lead one of the school's demonstration infantry battalions against a mountainous stronghold with a strict time table that had to be adhered to. It was intended to be a simulation of an advance across a broad front of several battalions. He was allowed to use the supporting arms of the field artillery batteries or close support of ground troops by fighter aircraft overhead. How and when he used the support systems was up to Scott.

The attack got underway at 5:00 AM with Scott at the front of his formation in a half-track vehicle that served as his mobile command post. He had radio communication down to every company and platoon in his battalion. He liked to be at the front where he could determine what was going on. He placed his command post close to the forward air controller's radio jeep and next to the field artillery forward spotter's radio jeep. He could use the two supporting arms within seconds of their need on the battlefield. That kind of backup gave Scott a more comfortable feeling of being able to control the battlefield to his advantage.

After two hours of fairly rapid advance, his battalion was stopped by heavy concentrations of large caliber artillery located within the forested hills in front of them. Scott requested an air strike against two prominent lookout points on the mountains. Flashes of the enemy gunfire had been seen and spotted by members of his staff. He requested the air controller to call in a two-plane-strike on each stronghold.

Whereas this was only a training exercise, the bombs to be dropped were only partially filled with napalm, a jelly-like gasoline substance that ignites on impact. Referees were scattered all over the battlefield to rate the performance of the participants. It had been firmly established by mutual understanding between the air groups and the infantry, that an air strike would be made in front of the attackers and at right angle to their line of attack. The forward controller attached to Scott's battalion, requested an attack straight against the enemy strongholds in line with the battalion's advance. By the time Scott realized that the planes were coming in over their heads, instead of in front of the battalion, it was too late for him to do anything about it. He was trying to call off the order when the impossible happened.

The air controller made the decision on his own to have the planes come in over their heads, because he believed, logically, that the mountain peaks in front of them were more readily avoided by a head on approach than flying parallel to them. Changing direction of an air strike was not the worst thing to happen. The pilots were given coordinates too close to the battalions front line for any reasonable margin of safety to the friendly troops. Scott's mobile command post was hit with a napalm bomb injuring several members of his staff. Scott was badly burned on his back and shoulders.

Scott would have been rapidly consumed by the fiery gelatin mass sticking to his body if it had not been for the quick action of the half-track driver who grabbed a fire extinguisher in the cab of the vehicle, throwing Scott to the ground, and turning the extinguisher upon him.

Chapter Six

Steve was listening on the radio link between the airplanes and ground control when the short drop took place. A sickening nauseous feeling came over him when he heard the desperate warning from the controller, "Abort, abort, abort, casualties taken, abort!"

Everyone involved had worked tirelessly to establish routines that eliminated the potential for disaster. There would always be some risk, if flexibility of command was necessary, but if the main procedural guidelines were noted and used by all concerned, then the potential for error was reduced. Now this, their worst nightmare. When the planes landed, Steve was at the field waiting for them. The Squadron commander and Steve took the pilots into a private debriefing room where the facts could be collected and reviewed. The input from the air controllers with the lead battalion had to be included in the information gathering session. It would take some time to ascertain exactly what happened.

In the meantime, a staff officer from the Army War College administration gave the officers at the debriefing center a review of the facts. The forward controllers for the mission had misread the coordinates on the maps that had been issued to them. Distance and contour intervals on the maps being used were a different scale than the maps being used by the air force and the attacking battalion under Scott's command. How that could possibly have happened was under investigation. The whole thing boiled down to the age old Army truism: "There's always someone who failed to get the word." Someone at Supply had pulled the wrong maps from the storage shelves.

As soon as Steve was satisfied that the debriefing routine was being conducted by a competent panel of experts, he raced to the field hospital to check on the injured men. Army Base officials reported that thirteen men had been injured, with no fatalities reported. Captain Scott Taylor was on the list of injured men. The hospital was able to handle most of the cases which were first and second degree burns. Captain Taylor's case was the most serious. He had sustained third degree burns on a large portion of his back and shoulders. The nurse on duty at the information desk told Steve that third degree burns would have to be treated at another facility with specialized equipment and physicians.

Unable to obtain any more information on Scott's condition, Steve returned to the airport command center where he placed a call to Scott's mother, before she heard about the incident over the radio. The demonstration was observed by a large number of the press and foreign dignitaries. He wanted to reassure her that Scott was alive and being treated at the hospital, so she would not worry needlessly.

Mrs. Taylor received the news with apprehension, and asked Steve to call her back as soon as he had more information on Scott's condition. "Be brave, Mrs. Taylor. I'll be in touch with you as soon as I learn more," promised Steve. He could imagine the independent and resourceful lady standing alone at the kitchen phone, full of dread and feeling helpless that her flesh and blood was hurt and she could not do anything about it.

Scott was still unconscious. Thankfully, his helmet had saved his head and face from being badly burned. The extreme heat had burned his eyebrows and eyelashes. Within four minutes after the accident, Scott was on his way to the base hospital. The medics and doctors were not as concerned about Scott being unconscious as they were about the extensive third degree burns on his back and shoulders. He was fortunate that he had received the life-saving benefit of the fire extinguisher. As soon as the fire was out, several men came to his aid trying to remove the smoldering pieces of his jacket and any remaining pieces of hot gelatin clinging to his body. His flesh was exposed to the air showing dark red blotches of dried blood already clotting where the skin had been burned away or had been peeled off with the clothes. The sickening sweet-sour smell of burned human flesh permeated the ambulance transporting him to the base hospital. The attendants feared a tetanus infection might set in with such a large open wound.

Intravenous glucose solutions were immediately administered to Scott to prevent dehydration as soon as he arrived at the base medical facility. His unconscious body was immersed in a lukewarm bicarbonate of soda and water solution to keep the burned flesh moist and to dilute any remaining residues of the gasoline mixture. At one point Scott's body began to jerk and shake uncontrollably so that the attendants stopped the bath until the convulsions were under control. They injected him with heavy doses of pain killer.

Scott's reaction to the soda bath made the doctors more cognizant of the fact that he could be helped or made worse by the immersion. The warm liquid bath should have counteracted some of the effects of blood loss and reduced oxygen deprivation to the rest of his body. At this critical juncture of his treatment, Scott's life was threatened. The doctors silently concluded that he had a fifty-fifty chance of survival.

Another factor that could not be determined until he was conscious, was the amount of damage that may have been done to his lungs. During the few seconds he was on fire may have been enough for him to breath in lung-damaging fumes and heat. All that could be done was to wait. The rest was up to Scott and the God he prayed to!

While Scott struggled for his life, Army investigators were busy trying to determine what had gone wrong. It was a miracle that nobody was killed. At the debriefing with all of his squadron officers, Steve learned that errors were made by the clerical staff at the supply stockroom where the maps were stored. A revised storage system was underway, and different maps were inadvertently issued instead of the ones that had been requested by the War College instructors. No one picked up on the error until after the accident.

A committee of officers representing the different commands involved was appointed to write a report on the accident and submit it to the Department of the Army. Steve was selected to represent the New York fighter squadron.

After the debriefing session, Steve went to Scott's quarters to collect shaving gear and clothing for him to use at the hospital. Steve saw the unfinished letter to a Marie Poole on the desk. Scott had never mentioned her name to him. The addressed envelope told Steve that the person was from Monson, Maine. She must be the person Scott went to see after DJ's funeral. Gathering up a small overnight bag, Steve hurried out the door.

The Base hospital was not much more than a well equipped dispensary, adequate for the relatively small number of people based at the training center. Several other men were waiting to hear about Scott's condition. The base commander, Brigadier General Reardon, a heavy set giant of a man with dark piercing eyes, walked into the waiting room with a flurry, and addressed the men.

"Gentlemen, we're trying to make Captain Taylor as comfortable as possible, but we're not equipped to care for his burns on a day-to-day basis. Therefore, we're evacuating him to Plattsburgh Army Base at Plattsburgh, New York, which has an excellent burn center. We are going to airlift him out within the hour. Are there any questions?"

"Yes, Sir," exclaimed Steve. "May I have permission to accompany him to Plattsburgh and return when the accident committee convenes?"

"Why do you want to accompany the patient, Captain?" The Base Commander eyed him intently.

"Well, Sir, I'm a friend of his, and I have first-hand experience on how painful burns can be especially for the first few days."

Noticing the burn scars on Steve's face, the general granted permission and added: "Use my name to obtain a ride from Plattsburgh when your accident committee needs you, and keep me informed on the captain's condition. Good luck, son."

"Thank you, Sir."

Scott and two other injured soldiers were quickly rolled to a waiting World War II vintage DC-3 specially equipped to transport wounded men and administer to their needs while in flight. Steve leaped on board at the last minute after retrieving a small bag of essentials from his quarters, and notifying his Reserve Commander that he was going with Scott.

Plattsburgh was an old established army training center on the western shore of Lake Champlain. Steve checked in at the hospitality center, while Scott was rushed to the hospital in an old brick building overlooking the calm blue waters of the lake. The doctors warned Steve that it could be twenty-four hours before the pain killers and sedatives wore off enough for Scott to be able to talk.

Steve took it upon himself to telephone Marie Poole and notify her of Scott's accident and change of address. It was early in the evening and Mrs. Poole answered the phone.

"Hello, is this Marie Poole?" asked Steve reluctantly.

"Who's calling please?"

"I'm Captain Steven Jackson, a friend of Captain Scott Taylor, and I have a message for Miss Poole."

"I'm Marie's mother. Is Captain Taylor all right?"

"He's had a serious accident, but is holding his own. Scott doesn't know that I'm calling and I'm not sure if he would approve or not," said Steve, wondering what he was doing interfering with something he knew nothing about.

"Just a moment, Marie is in the next room."

"Thank you, Mrs. Poole."

"Hello, this is Marie Poole.

"How do you do, Miss Poole. I'm Captain Steve Jackson, a friend of Scott Taylor. I'm calling to tell you that he had an accident during a training session."

"How badly is he hurt?" interrupted Marie.

"I cannot tell you how it happen but I can tell you that he has third degree burns on his back and shoulders."

"Oh, my." Her voice was low and pensive.

"I'm sorry to bring this kind of news to you. After the accident took place he was moved to a different base. I went to his quarters to get a few things for him when I noticed your address and a partially completed letter to you on his desk. Maybe I've made a mistake by assuming too much, and I apologize if I've overreacted. He's in the Army hospital at Plattsburgh, New York and he's going to need all of the support he can get."

"I'm glad you called, Captain Jackson. I'll be in touch with him soon. He and I just recently met, and I'm not sure he would want me to visit him. We're really strangers to each other. Thank you for your thoughtfulness though."

"Well, this call was a spur of the moment thing. I'll tell Scott that I called you and he can take it from there. It's been nice talking with you, Miss Poole."

"Tell Captain Taylor that I'll pray for his recovery and will be thinking of him."

"It'll be my pleasure."

Watching Marie slowly hang up the phone, her mother asked, " Is anything wrong, Marie?"

"It's Scott Taylor. He had an accident and is in the Army hospital in Plattsburgh, New York."

"What a coincidence. Your father went there for Army training during the First War."

"I'll wait until tomorrow to call and find out how he's doing. That way they'll have a chance to evaluate his injuries. I can't explain how I feel about what's happened. We hardly know each other."

Mrs. Poole placed her arm around Marie's shoulders to reassure her. Marie was more upset by the news than she wanted to tell, but her mother knew what was in her thoughts. "Things will work out, Marie. Give it some time."

Marie's parents agonized for her at times like this, for the trauma of blindness was a terrible burden to carry. Marie went to her room where she sat motionless in a chair, staring into her blackness.

Back at Plattsburg, Steve Jackson was patiently calling his mother's home at Diamond Point on Lake George just south of Lake Champlain. For the fifth time the line was busy. He kept trying at ten minute intervals and smiled to himself. She must have been talking with her husband Arlo. Arlo and his mother had purchased her family homestead at Diamond Point and used it as their permanent residence and weekend retreat when they could break away from Arlo's current duty at the Defense Department in Washington, D.C. Michelle Korsman preferred the old house to their apartment on the Potomac River in the middle of Washington.

Steve missed being away from Bright Star, his wife, for almost a year. He would have called to talk with her, but it was very difficult getting a clear line to Fort Lewis. Star was continuing to work as a nurse at the infirmary established years ago by her mother, Bright Cloud. Sometimes his mother Michelle went to Fort Lewis to help out, for she was a nurse also, and very much loved by the people at the tribal village.

Steve was thankful that fate had played a role in bringing him and his biological mother, Michelle Korsman, together. His biological father was a soldier in World War I and was killed in France. Michelle gave birth to Steve after she was notified of his father's death. At the time of his birth, Michelle was coerced by family and friends into giving up the child for adoption. Regretting the decision, she began a diligent search for his whereabouts but always ran into a dead end. Then she met Arlo Korsman at Fort Lewis, where Michelle was helping Bright Cloud build the infirmary into the respected institution it is today. After a few more attempts to locate her son, she was persuaded to give up the search for good.

She followed Arlo from one post to another before the war and was in China when the Japanese and Chinese war erupted. She and other dependents were sent to the Philippines, where she was stranded on Leyte when the Japanese bombed Pearl Harbor. The war came quickly to the Philippines where Michelle retreated into the mountains with a group of partisans. One day the leader of the partisans carried a badly wounded American fighter pilot to their hideaway in desperate need of her care. He was shot down off the coast and rescued by the partisans before the Japanese could get to him. He was severely burned and injured in the crash. His legs were broken and he was blinded by the fire in the cockpit of the plane before it crashed into the water. He was in such desperate condition that the guerrilla leader took a chance to call out on their hidden radio for a submarine to pick him up as soon as possible. The wounded Airman was Steve Jackson.

Steve was taken directly to Pearl Harbor, where he was treated for his serious injuries. Bright Star was a Navy nurse working on the same floor where Steve was assigned. They fell in love during his internment. In time, Steve regained the full use of his legs and his sight was miraculously returned after the burns on his face healed. The burn scars around his eyes and the right side of his face barely hinted at the ordeal he had suffered.

It was during this time that Bright Star, who knew about Michelle's adopted son, perceptively put the pieces together. Shortly after Steven was born, he was awarded to a couple that died in a car accident. The baby survived the accident and was awarded by the state to a couple by the name of Jackson. The former couple's name had been Stevenson, so the new couple called the infant boy Steven Jackson in honor of the first adopting parents. Michelle had traced her son to a family by the name of Stevenson, and found that the child had been awarded to a family in central New York State. At that point, her search stopped. Steve was a lucky child for the new parents showered him with love and he was raised in a stable, caring environment. He went to a good college where he earned a degree in education and became a teacher.

When Michelle was rescued by Army rangers during the liberation of the Philippines, she was taken to Pearl Harbor where Arlo was waiting for her. Bright Star confided her suspicions to Arlo, who found her story incredible and believable. When Arlo met Steve at the hospital, there was no doubt in Arlo's mind that Steve was Michelle's long lost son. It was a miracle!

Steven tried one more time to get an open line to his mother at Diamond Point and his patience was rewarded, "Hello," came the long awaited voice

"Hi, Mother."

"Oh Steven, what a nice surprise. Are you all right?"

"I'm fine, Mother. I just wanted to tell you that I'm in Plattsburgh at the army hospital with Captain Taylor. You remember, he was the officer at DJ's funeral."

"Of course, I remember him. Is he injured?"

"He got hit by one of the napalm bombs from my squadron. He's burned on his back. The hospital isn't giving out any information yet."

"That poor young man. I never think of burns, that I don't remember how painful your burns were when I had to set both of your broken legs there in the mountains of Leyte without any medication. It was one of the most difficult things I've ever had to do in my life. Even in that godforsaken place there was something about you that touched my heart. We have much to be thankful for," she mused.

"I wanted to let you know that I may not be home as planned because I've been assigned to help write the accident situation back at Indiantown Gap. However, I'll stay here as long as I can so that Scott will have a friendly face around."

"I just spoke to Arlo and he won't be home for several days. He's in Berlin right now. If you're going to be at Plattsburgh, I could drive up tomorrow and visit with you for a while."

"That would be great, Mother. I'll either be at the base hospitality center or the hospital."

"I'll find you, young man. I think I could find you anywhere, after what we've gone through. Take care and give my best to Captain Taylor. Until tomorrow, son. I love you.

"I love you too, Mom."

Steve smiled at the irrepressible spirit of his birth mother.

The next day, Mrs. Taylor anxiously drove up from Dauphin to see about her son. Steve had notified her of the change in hospitals. By the time she arrived at the hospital reception desk she was almost in a state of shock. The nurse on duty could not give her any information about Scott, but she did call a doctor to speak to her. Mrs. Taylor's face was flushed from the stress of driving non-stop for the past six hours. She had hoped to be able to walk right into her son's room and see with her own eyes how well he was doing. Now that she had to wait for the doctor first, all kinds of thoughts ran through her worried mind, and her heart started hammering even more. She was on the verge of tears when the nurse gently directed her to a comfortable chair in the sitting room around the corner.

Steve Jackson was sitting in the far corner of the sitting room when he recognized Scott's mother.

"Mrs. Taylor, it's nice to see you again," Steve exclaimed, taking a seat next to her.

"Captain Jackson," exclaimed Mrs. Taylor, relieved to see a familiar face.

"May I get you something to drink, Mrs. Taylor?" asked the nurse, still worried that the lady may be on the verge of fainting. "How about something warm like tea or coffee? It would help you relax."

"Coffee would be fine, nurse," answered Mrs. Taylor, breathing heavily.

"Scott is going to be fine, Mrs. Taylor. I don't have any more information than you do. The doctor should be out to see us shortly. He's with Scott now. Is there anything I can do to help you?" asked Steve with a worried look on his face.

"I'll be fine as soon as I see my son. All the way up here, I could think of nothing but the worst. I've been worried sick about him." She reached in her purse for tissues to wipe the tears from her eyes.

Steve grasped both of her hands in his and tried to comfort her. "Go ahead, Mrs. Taylor. Let it all out, you'll feel better afterwards. I'm here to show support for him, too."

"Here's a hot cup of coffee, Mrs. Taylor," interrupted the nurse cheerfully. "I found a corn muffin fresh from the kitchen oven. You look as if you could use a little something to eat." The nurse placed them on the table beside her.

"Thank you, I appreciate it," said Mrs. Taylor, visibly calmer.

Moments later, an Army major presented himself to the group in the waiting room. The nurse introduced him as Dr. Horace Conklin, a tall, thin middle-aged man with a small mustache.

"Doctor, this is Captain Taylor's mother and a friend, Captain Steve Jackson," said the nurse before she returned to her station.

"How's my son doing, Dr. Conklin?" asked Mrs. Taylor, her voice charged with emotion.

"Your son has a nasty burn on the upper portion of his torso, Mrs. Taylor. All things considered, he's doing remarkably well. He's got some difficult days ahead of him but don't be alarmed, Mrs. Taylor, your son has the strength to fully recover. Take heart in that fact. I think he'll do just fine, but it would not be prudent to minimize the severity of his condition.

"His lungs have survived in good shape. The first and second degree burns around his face and hands will clear up within a month. His eyebrows and eyelashes should start to grow back shortly. Our main concern is the large burned area on his back and shoulders where all of his skin was burned with such intense heat that it's a miracle his lungs and muscles survived the ordeal. The accident was a serious and potentially lethal incident. He's lucky to be alive."

Mrs. Taylor gasped at the graphic description of Scott's wounds and started weeping. Dr. Conklin kneeled down before her and tucked a clean handkerchief into her hand. The air of professionalism that Dr. Conklin projected could give one the impression that he was a disinterested scientist without feelings for his patients. Nothing could be further from the truth. He was articulate, decisive, and always in control, and had a reputation of demanding the best his subordinates could deliver for his patients. He was a burn specialist with a lot of experience in treating badly-burned casualties during the war. Doctor Conklin was the main reason the War College sent Scott to Plattsburgh.

"She's been going on nerves ever since this happened, Doctor," said Steve.

"I really came out here to tell you that Scott is awake now, and I think it would be good for him to see you. The good Lord was with him on that command car yesterday. Now that he's here in our care you can be certain that no effort will be spared to return your son to good health. I give you my word."

"Thank you, Dr. Conklin. I appreciate your honesty and consideration," she replied.

Chapter Seven

Scott regained consciousness for a short period of time on the flight to Plattsburgh. His body felt confined and pain gripped him so intensely that he cried out for relief. The slightest movement of the plane was like a sharp instrument being driven between his shoulder blades. As soon as the flight nurse heard Scott's plea for help, she administered another shot of morphine to ease his pain.

He woke up from his medicated limbo next when Dr. Conklin was working on him under intense lights. They felt warm to his naked body. He didn't feel any pain, and he couldn't move any parts of his body.

"Good morning, Captain Taylor. I'm Dr. Conklin at the Army hospital in Plattsburgh, NY. We're treating your burns. You had an accident during your latest field exercise and were badly burned."

"Yes... I remember," said Scott warily. "I feel as if I'm burning up, Doc; then I'm chilled right to my bones. It might sound like a contradiction, but..."

"To the contrary," interrupted Dr. Conklin. "It's an apt description of what's happening to you. As soon as I'm finished cleaning up and sterilizing the burned area on your backside, you'll feel more comfortable. Your skin was burned from your belt line to your neck. You're a lucky man to be alive, Captain.

"You also have a few scattered burns on your arms and legs that will heal fairly fast as long as we keep them free from infection. Avoiding infection is our main concern for the next few days. Your back is going to need extensive skin grafts. With your approval, we'll take the healthy skin from parts of your buttocks and thighs. We can start tomorrow if there are no infections."

Doctor Conklin explained that they needed to keep his back moist at all times with a mist of soda water and sterilizing agents. He would be confined to a swivel bed that allowed reasonable comfort. It would be a lot like leaning over a barrel. The misting apparatus would keep the open wounds moist and enhance healing. He stressed that pain medication would be administered as needed, but the less medication used, the better the body would heal itself. It all depended on Scott's threshold of pain tolerance.

"Has my mother been contacted?" asked Scott groggily.

"I don't know. Your friend, Captain Steve Jackson, is just down the corridor waiting to see you. He accompanied you from Pennsylvania. I'll let him know how you're doing, and as soon as the nurses are finished setting up the mist tent you can see him. One last thing, be sure to drink as much liquids as you can. Dehydration is a very real threat to your recovery."

The nurses completed their chores, and Mrs. Taylor rushed to his side reluctant to touch him for fear of hurting him. Scott reached out for her and she buried her face in his hands. Steve quietly looked on.

"I really got fouled up this time, Mom," said Scott, slurring his words, and trying to be nonchalant. The nurse had warned Scott that he may have trouble talking because of the medication he was receiving through the glucose liquid. "Thanks for coming, Steve. How many men were hit by the fragments?"

"I understand that twelve others got hit. You're the most seriously injured," answered Steve.

It was not easy to carry on a conversation with Scott. He kept falling asleep in the middle of a sentence, so Steve and Scott's mother decided that he needed the healing power of rest more than he needed to talk.

Steve took Mrs. Taylor to lunch at the Officer's Club where she could relax in comfortable surroundings. Halfway through their lunch, Steve's mother, Michelle Korsman, entered the Club and walked toward their table.

"I didn't think you'd make it as quick as this, Mother," said Steve, greeting her with open arms.

"Giving my son a hug is still one of the great joys of my life," exclaimed Michelle. "And you must be Captain Taylor's mother. I'm so sorry to hear about his unfortunate accident." Michelle went to Mrs. Taylor and placed a comforting arm of support around her shoulders. The two women were about the same age. Michelle's white hair contrasted with Mrs. Taylor's gray-streaked black hair. They were two active, independent women and took an instant liking to each other.

Michelle joined them for lunch and was able to talk Mrs. Taylor into coming back to Diamond Point with her for the night. Michelle promised to bring her back to the hospital any time she desired. Mrs. Taylor told Michelle and Steve that she planned to return to Dauphin late tomorrow, unless Scott took a turn for the worse. She was in the middle of the planting season, and even though she hired out most of the work, she liked to keep a close eye on the operation. Steve decided to return to Pennsylvania with Mrs. Taylor; Indiantown Gap was right on her way. Scott was in good hands! Steve could assist Mrs. Taylor by driving the car back home with her.

The aroma of Scott's burned flesh still permeated the hospital room. He was resigned to the painful daily routine of having the dead material cut off his back. The misting process continued, even though he jokingly complained about being turned into a shriveled prune. Dr. Conklin was able to start the slow process of grafting skin in half inch strips on the burned portion of Scott's back. The strips were placed about a quarter to a half-inch apart. Within a couple of weeks, the new skin grafts would begin to grow into the untouched area between the strips. In time, the affected area would be covered with a new layer of skin.

The biggest worry that Scott had after the accident was the status of his attendance at the War College Course. He was able to deal with the pain and discomfort of the burn better than he was able to handle the anxiety of his future in the Army. He was told by school officials that he could pick up with the course as soon as he got out of the hospital. Visitors came at frequent intervals, his mother, Michelle Korsman and Army friends that happened to be in the area. Before Steve Jackson left for Pennsylvania, he told Scott about his conversation with Marie Poole. Scott received a phone call from her the next day.

"Hello," said Scott, his speech returning back to normal.

"Hello, Captain Scott Taylor?" asked Marie hesitantly.

"Is that you, Marie?"

"Yes, I was reluctant to call because I wasn't sure you would be able to use the phone. How are you doing? A friend of yours, Captain Jackson, called to tell me about your accident."

"Steve just told me this morning. I'm glad he called. It's nice to hear from you. I'm not doing too badly; everyone thought it would be worse than it is. The healing process will have to take its course. I'm already getting impatient and the process is only beginning."

"You must listen to the doctors. Frequently they're out of touch with how their patients feel and sometimes they lack compassion, but most of them are competent. I promise not to give you any platitudes about being a good patient and so forth, because I hated to hear the well-intended advice myself," chided Marie.

"So far the staff seems to be top-notch. I have faith in my doctor," said Scott, tilting his bed so that he could hold the phone easier. "I'm strapped into a moisture cocoon on a swivel bed. Actually it's more comfortable than it sounds."

"Is there anything I can send you that would help you pass the time of day? I have quite a collection of paperback novels."

"Thanks for the offer, Marie, but I'll spend all the time I can studying for the course. That way, when I get out of the hospital, I'll be more prepared for it."

"You sound better than I expected. Before we hang up I want to tell you that, ever since your visit, I've been able to put some of my doubts and fears about Arnold's death in a more positive light. I'm not blaming myself like I did. For that I'm thankful to you, Scott. I'm not ready to take on the world yet, but I'm making progress. My mother sends her best wishes and, of course, I hope your stay in the hospital is a short one. Let's stay in touch… Good-bye, Scott."

"Thanks for calling, Marie. My visit with you was important to me also. I've changed my thoughts about the whole episode. I believe it's best for all concerned that we put it behind us the way you have been trying to do. I think often about our day at Moosehead Lake. Good-bye, Marie."

Steve talked with Scott several times over the next two weeks while the board of inquiry was collecting information and documenting the incident. It was pretty much an open-and-shut case with no winners and no losers. It was a tragic chain of events that demanded more safeguards. Steve told Scott that the report was almost completed, and he would soon be leaving New York for Fort Lewis, Quebec.

Steve was excited and his enthusiasm obvious as he described what was taking place at Fort Lewis. Bright Star had called Steve to let him know that the Province of Quebec had not refused their proposal for a school based at Fort Lewis that would serve the larger geographic area. Trying to get the necessary permits and approvals was a time-consuming job. Thankfully, the Catholic Church was a staunch supporter of the endeavor and their influence was important in presenting a solid case for the proposed institution. The French-speaking Province had opposed it solely on the grounds that the proposed school would conduct its instruction in English; yet, Bright Star happily reported that Provincial permission was imminent, according to the Church officials.

"What's so special about this place called Fort Lewis?" asked Scott. "I remember Lieutenant Leroux frequently talked about it. It seemed to take on mythical dimensions whenever he spoke its name."

"It's hard to understand unless you've been there, Scott. It's a wilderness settlement with no other vestige of civilization for hundreds of miles in every direction. Fort Lewis sits on the western shore of Lac Diamante, a relatively small body of water about ten square miles in size, shaped like an exquisite diamond when viewed from the air. The water is crystal-clear. From the air you can see rocks on the bottom of the lake. I've pulled some of the most beautiful whitefish and trout from its waters that you've ever seen. There's a beauty and an awe about the place that defies description. The lake is surrounded by tall conical white spruce and balsam fir trees that reach for the sky in perfect symmetrical splendor. I fell in love with the area on my first visit. The winters are a very real challenge to those who must endure its severity, but preparation for the reality of winter makes it easier to handle. I had never been in the wilderness before I married Bright Star. Once you've experienced its isolation and solitude, you gain a respect for its deadly beauty, and if you're lucky, you may find a reservoir of strength within yourself that you never knew existed."

"You sound as if you've already been hooked," commented Scott with an easy grin.

"I guess I am," answered Steve. "By the way, have you heard anything from the young lady I called in Maine?"

"Sure. She called when I first started treatment. I've talked to her a couple of times since then. She's a special person."

"Is it serious?"

"I don't know," answered Scott. "We met under strange circumstances. I'm not sure about how I feel. I do know that I respect her independence and her guts for handling her blindness the way she does."

"I didn't realize she was blind."

"The subject never came up before. One of my platoon leaders was killed in action after getting a 'dear john' letter from Marie. I blamed her for his death and confronted her with the accusation. Then I saw how badly she was used by Lieutenant Robinson. An argument between them turned ugly and she fell from a balcony during the scuffle. She ended up with a broken leg and blindness. We spent a pleasant day around Moosehead Lake, and I enjoyed her company a great deal. She's not as bitter about her situation as I might be if I was in her shoes. Since my accident, I've thought a lot more about her and about the limitations that blindness places on a person."

Steve watched one of the grounds keepers mow the large lawn outside the hospital. Hearing Scott talk about Marie's blindness brought back his own bittersweet memories. He talked to Scott about his accident in the P-38 on Leyte and how he, too, was badly burned on a large part of his upper body. It was easy for him to appreciate what Scott was going through. However, the injury that had cultivated panic was the blindness that accompanied the other injuries. He would never forget how the loss of sight had shrunk his world and had introduced him to abject fear of the world of blackness, fostering doubts about his ability to handle it.

"I didn't know you had been in such bad shape, Steve," said Scott, looking at his soft-spoken friend with new admiration. "If I ever complain again in your presence, give me a punch. Not too hard though. I've got a feeling that you've been thinking of something other than what we've been talking about."

"I plead guilty. Listen! An idea just came to me. Maybe I can be of some help to you and Marie before I leave for Canada. This weekend, if weather permits, I could crank up our float plane at Lake George, then fly to Monson to bring Marie back here to Plattsburgh. I could land on the lake near her house and land up here on Lake Champlain. When I return to Canada in a few days, I could drop her off on the way to Quebec. It would not be out of my way at all. My squadron has already returned to base in New York. When the report is printed, that will finish my commitment for the reserves for the summer. What do you think about it, Scott?"

"It would be fine with me, but I'm not so sure Marie would approve," said Scott hesitantly.

"Well, you can ask her," said Steve decisively.

Later that evening, Steve checked on living accommodations for Marie. The base commander was obliging enough to reserve a ground floor room at the hospitality center with easy access from the main entrance lobby. The commander also offered the services of his own aide-de-camp while she was on base, if she wanted an escort. When Steve told Scott about the arrangements available for her visit, Scott realized he was enthusiastically looking forward to seeing her.

Scott called Marie that evening to determine if she was agreeable to making the trip. She did not object to the idea of a visit, but there was a certain amount of reluctance to the airplane ride. Scott was able to build Steve into such a super pilot, that she finally agreed to make the trip.

Every detail of Steve's flight plan left nothing to chance. He realized that a round trip without refueling was impossible, so he planned to land at Moosehead Lake for gasoline before stopping at Lake Hebron to pick up Marie. From the air, Steve could easily make out Marie's dock on the southern side of the lake. Steve carefully landed in the center of the lake, then slowly idled the plane to the wharf. He was greeted by a strapping young man in a Game Warden uniform who caught the line Steve threw him and secured the aircraft to the wharf.

"Hello, there. I'm Steve Jackson."

"Hi, Steve. I'm Marie's cousin Jonathan Poole. Your landing on the lake this morning is going to be the main topic of conversation in this little town for a spell. How about a cup of coffee while Marie gets ready?"

"Sounds great, Jonathan."

"Marie is a little apprehensive about the trip, but she'll come around. She's a pretty spunky lady. I think it'll be good for her."

"I'm glad to hear that," commented Steve as he rushed to keep up with Jonathan. "Scott told me what a remarkable lady she is. I think her visit will be good for him, also."

Mr. and Mrs. Poole met Steve at the head of the balcony steps. They were excited and nervous over Marie's airplane ride to New York State.

"It isn't every day that an airplane ties up at our dock, young man. I'm Harold Poole, Marie's father, and this is my wife, Avis." Harold Poole was a tall, thin man with curly black hair. His sharp facial features and deep set eyes gave him a rather gaunt and somber look. The smile that crossed his face when he met Steve was genuine and sincere.

"It's nice to meet both of you," responded Steve.

"This is going to be quite an adventure for me," interrupted Marie, walking into the room. "It's generous of you to offer your airplane, Captain Jackson. I'm Marie Poole."

"It's my pleasure, Miss Poole."

"Of course I must tell you at the very beginning that I'm scared to death. I've never been in a plane before," exclaimed Marie excitedly.

"I promise to make it a pleasant experience for you. I've flown a lot of hours in and out of the service. My wife and I are partial owners of the plane along with my mother and her husband, so you can be assured that everything on the aircraft has been meticulously maintained. Otherwise, I would not be here."

Mrs. Poole suggested that they all have coffee together before Marie and Steve commence their journey. A fresh pot was perking on the stove. Marie nervously excused herself when she had finished her coffee and muffin. She had to finish packing her suitcases. After a few minutes she called to Jonathan to grab her two cases and take them to the plane.

"I intend to return within a week, depending on the weather, Mr. and Mrs. Poole. I'll drop your daughter off on my way to Canada," Steve informed them, offering his arm to Marie. "I'm at your service, Miss Poole."

"Thank you for your arm, Captain, but I'm all right going down these stairs by myself. I'd appreciate your arm to the wharf and plane, though."

"The plane is straight ahead of us at the end of the dock. It's a four-seater aircraft of Canadian manufacture called the Norseman. I want you to sit in the seat to my right. Your cousin has got the door open for us, just step up about ten inches. You can feel the seat in front of you. Take your time and climb up into the seat. It's the one I'll use to fly the plane."

"I hate being so helpless," admitted Marie under her breath. Her fears of the unknown were making her shake. She could not control feeling the way she did. Steve squeezed her hand gently. "Take your time, Miss Poole. Sit back in the seat and try to relax. I realize how you must feel. Take some time to reach out in front of you. There's a wheel, not unlike an automobile steering wheel, directly in front of you. Beyond the wheel, you can feel an instrument panel filled with a lot of gauges, just like a car, also. Above the instrument panel is the windshield. As soon as you're comfortable with the cockpit area, move over into the seat to your right. The seats are quite close together, but there's plenty of room for the two of us. Your purse and cane can be tucked under the seat."

"So far, so good," said Marie with a small nervous laugh. "Good-bye, Jonathan, tell Mom and Dad I'm doing fine."

"I will, Marie. Have a good trip and enjoy your visit. Happy landings, Captain, I'll release the mooring line and give you a shove out from the dock."

"Thanks, Jonathan. Don't worry about your cousin. No harm will come to her."

"If I thought she was in any danger, I wouldn't have let her come aboard. Bon Voyage."

"Well, Miss Poole," said Steve, closing the door. "Before I start the engine, I want you to feel both sides of the seat for the seat belts. Bring them around you and fasten them so that you're comfortable. That's fine. Now I'm going to start the engine."

The rumble of the powerful engine sent nervous spasms through her body. She was so tense she was starting to sweat. Steve lifted her left hand above her head to grasp a radio headset and helped place it properly on her head. Then he adjusted the microphone about two inches from her mouth doing the same with his own radio.

"Now we can talk in normal tones without shouting to overcome the engine noise. Is the headset comfortable for you?"

"Yes, it's just right."

"I'm going to increase engine speed and pull out into the center of the lake. I'll take off in a westerly direction away from the town."

"I'm still scared, Captain, but there's something terribly exciting about what we're doing, too."

"The lake is free of boats and swimmers, so here we go. The engine will be loud and the plane will feel rough. That's normal, so don't be alarmed."

The powerful Dehaviland Norseman did not need a very long stretch of water for takeoff. Short takeoff capabilities and its rugged dependability were two of the reasons why it was the aircraft of choice for most wilderness bush pilots. A few seconds later the aircraft left the water and the engine leveled off to a pleasant sounding hum. Marie had the exhilarating sensation of being lifted from Mother Earth for the first time.

"We're airborne and heading westerly towards Lake Champlain. We'll fly at about three thousand feet at a cruising speed of 150 mile per hour. Now, all we have to do is sit back and enjoy the ride."

"It must be wonderful to see the ponds and forests from the air. It's times like this that I feel cheated."

"You wouldn't be normal if you didn't feel that way. I don't think anyone can ever know what another person actually feels under certain circumstances, but I can tell you that I have some experience with blindness, also. I was blind for six months during the war, and I wasn't sure I'd ever see again. I owe my recovery to a great doctor team at the Pearl Harbor Naval Hospital and to my wife, whom I met while she was a nurse at the hospital."

"Thank you for telling me that. Sometimes I think I'm the only one so afflicted, and it's easy to get carried away with self-pity. I'm still angry over what happened, and I pray every day that my sight may be returned to me," Marie confessed.

"Incidentally, why don't we use first names? It will be easier for us both."

"You took the words out of my mouth," smiled Marie. "How serious are Scott's wounds, Steve?"

"The burn injuries had the potential of being fatal, but Scott was lucky and will come through the ordeal without any deformities. It will take a long time for him to heal, but complete recovery is expected. We're going to land right outside his window on the lake."

The steady drone of the engine increased her sense of security and reinforced the trust she had placed in Steve from the beginning. He continued to speak to her in a calm manner that made her feel at ease flying among the clouds, even if she couldn't see them!

They filled the time with conversation about their lives and hopes for the future and were pleased to learn that each of them had earned degrees in education at college just before the war.

Steve was teaching at a high school in New York when the war started. Marie was into her second year of teaching at her home town of Monson when the accident took place and terminated her hopes and dreams. Her passion for literature pushed her into learning to read Braille soon after the accident. It wasn't the same as reading with her own eyes, but it allowed her to continue to enjoy literature.

Steve told Marie about the school project that he and his wife were trying to organize at Fort Lewis. They visualized a community elementary school for the surrounding area's children five to thirteen years old, with first through eighth grade levels of instruction. They anticipated that approximately one hundred students would enroll the first year. The next closest school was two hundred miles away. Plans and building materials were already available for construction of a dormitory to house students who lived in the more remote areas around Fort Lewis.

A large number of supporters had collected monetary help and pledges of assistance from a diversified collection of people and organizations. Steve eagerly explained to Marie that Bright Cloud and Mark Leroux had generously donated the life insurance money they received from the death of their son, DJ, for construction of the school's buildings and their maintenance. It was imperative to obtain approval for the school's charter as soon as possible, because Quebec Province would have to approve the proposed construction plans at the same time. One of Steve's friends in the New York National Guard was an architect, and he agreed to design the structures free of charge and make any changes that might be mandated by the Provincial officials. The staff for the school could be hired from the inhabitants of the village. The teaching staff could be recruited from several schools in the Province, and a list of volunteer part-time teachers had already been collected.

"My, it sounds like a wonderful project," said Marie. "It's obvious that you have a great deal of passion for it."

"I've never had anything in my life that excited me as much as the proposed school. I've got a lot of things in my life to be thankful for, and the thought of being able to bring the gift of knowledge to those children who live beyond the influence of civilization is at the top of the list. It's one way I can make a contribution. The people in the village and surrounding areas have been most supportive of our efforts. They're the ones who've really made the difference. Actually, we'll probably end up teaching a number of adults, too, who never had a chance to learn to write or read."

"I envy you and your wife, Bright Star, for the challenge ahead of you," answered Marie, wistfully. "I had such wonderful teachers throughout my school days, that I never wanted to be anything else. Now, I teach Braille to a group of blind people, mostly adults. A lot of the new blind, such as myself, are desperate to learn Braille. It helps remove some of the limiting barriers. I often wondered what it would be like to teach at a missionary school. Being able to make a difference is a dream of most teachers."

Marie remained relatively silent for the rest of the trip. Steve observed that her hands were nervously playing with the buckle on the seat belt. Her head was turned as if she was looking out the window. Steve would have given anything to know what she was thinking.

"I can feel the sun on my face," stated Marie, breaking the awkward silence.

"We're not far from Burlington, Vermont," said Steve. "I'm going to call Plattsburgh air control tower. Maybe they can call Scott's room and alert him of our arrival." Steve changed the frequency on the radio and called the tower.

"Private float plane 'Norseman' to tower."

"We have you on radar, Norseman."

"This is Captain Steven Jackson, USAF. If you have access to an outside line, could you call a Captain Scott Taylor at the base hospital and tell him that he'll soon have a visitor."

"We've been expecting you, Norseman. Consider it done. You're free to land at will on the lake."

"Roger tower. Thank you."

"The first step of your adventure is almost over, Marie. For a first-time passenger, I give you an A-plus," chuckled Steve.

"I'm going to turn slightly to the right and start our descent, so don't be alarmed when the plane dips sideways. Here we go."

Steve pulled the nose up slightly while he completed the turn northward then leveled the plane off before starting his gradual descent to the water.

"Hang on, Marie. The water on Lake Champlain is a little rougher than it was on Lake Hebron at takeoff. We're going to touch down right...now."

The sudden roughness of the water made Marie a little more tense during the landing but her fears quickly dissipated.

"That wasn't so bad, was it?" Steve asked as soon as the plane came to a gradual stop.

"It was exciting. I'm glad you invited me to make the trip. I've never had such a thrilling ride in my life."

By the time Steve tied up at the dock near the hospital, the base commander had been notified, and true to his word, provided a car and driver for Steve and Marie. Steve asked the driver to take them to the hospitality center, where he familiarized Marie with the entrance features and the layout of the room assigned to her. Then, Steve took her to the hospital to visit Scott.

Chapter Eight

The first thing Marie noticed when she walked into Scott's room was the pungent smell of strong disinfectants. It was almost overwhelming. She was nervous, like a young teenager on her first date, hoping it wasn't obvious to Scott.

"It's nice to see you again, Marie. I saw you and Steve land in the water," exclaimed Scott. "I apologize for being in such wretched condition to receive you. I'm glad you decided to trust my good friend's flying ability."

"The trip was a wonderful experience for me. How are you doing, Scott?"

"If you two can get along without me," interrupted Steve. "I'm going to shove off and take the plane back to Lake George. I'll be in touch about the return trip, Marie. You're looking better every day, Scott. If this lovely lady doesn't perk you up, then there's no hope for you. See you two later." Steve's remarks brought a flush to Marie's face.

"He's a great guy, isn't he?" asked Scott. "He's right about your presence though. You look lovely, Marie."

"Thank you." Marie reached towards him. He took her hands in his. For a moment, she thought what in the world am I doing here? She was miles away from home in the company of a man she hardly knew. Yet, the excitement of him holding her hands quickly erased any doubts she may have entertained.

"Right now, it's just as well that you can't see what I look like. I lost my eyelashes and eyebrows in the flames. It doesn't hurt and thankfully I don't have any wounds on my face."

Marie touched his face for the first time and gently traced the outline of his features. She could now visualize how he looked, he had a sharp distinct jaw line and prominent cheek bones. "You must feel strange without eyelashes or eyebrows. I don't mean to make light of it, but it sounds amusing to me for some reason." She laughed softly.

Scott took her hands from his face and kissed them. He was aware that he had strong feelings for her the moment she walked through the door with Steve. She walked proud and erect without the cane, with her light brown hair pulled up towards the top of her head, making her appear a little taller than he remembered. There was an air of confidence and a wholesome quality about her that filled the room with her vitality. She wore very little makeup, a light touch of lipstick gave her mouth a sensual allure.

Marie was comfortable and at ease with Scott. She was also aware of something taking place between the two of them. It made her feel warm inside and thankful that she could still experience such feelings. She had not felt the same way about Arnold. She had learned to love him and had successfully closed her heart to his jealousy and possessiveness. She knew now that she had loved his potential, what he could have been, not what he was. It had taken her a long time to understand that she had not been truthful to herself.

Scott and Marie spent two days talking about each other's past experiences. He told her about his infatuation with Leslie Kerr. Neither of them had dated much in high school or college. There was no pledge of commitment by either of them, but there was a refreshing exchange of stories and ideas about hopes and disappointments that helped them to understand one another better.

Marie awoke in the middle of the night on her second day at Plattsburgh, in a state of anxiety. She was certain that Scott shared similar feelings towards her. Things were going almost too quick and too smoothly with Scott. A tiny voice inside of her kept whispering, "Beware, you are a stranger to this man, and he a stranger to you, no matter what feelings you may harbor." Sitting upright in bed, Marie tried to curb the negative thoughts. The joy she felt with Scott after so much bitterness in her life gave her hope.

Feelings of inadequacy overwhelmed her that evening, and cast a shadow of sadness over her newfound joy. If she looked at herself as others must see her, she had little to offer someone like Scott, except a lifetime of dependency. She had a sickening feeling that it could become a troublesome burden as time went by. She believed that her ability to make substantial contributions to a relationship would only decrease with time. Marie's active imagination continued to paint a bleak picture of her future. Surely, she thought, Scott has not been able to think ahead very much, or he, too, would have similar impressions!

The next day, tired and restless, Marie confronted Scott with her fears and conclusions. He listened earnestly with respect and compassion. She liked that about him. Scott was beginning to think that Marie was having second thoughts about their relationship, and he spent a number of hours trying to convince her that such thoughts were natural. He suggested that it probably was her subconscious mind bringing up objections to anything new and different in her life. Maybe it was a way of testing her resolve to take the correct road, and once taken, not to have regrets about the decision already made.

On the third day of Marie's visit, Scott's mother showed up at the hospital. Steve had completed his work in Pennsylvania. He drove with Scott's mother from Dauphin to Plattsburgh. They met Marie and went to a local restaurant for lunch while they waited for visiting hours to begin. Mrs. Taylor was looking forward to meeting Marie. When Scott mentioned Marie's visit to her over the phone, she heard a sparkle in her son's voice that had not been there for a long time. She wanted to meet the person responsible for raising his spirits.

"I must say, Marie, if I may call you by your first name, you've done wonders with my son. Ever since the war ended he's been burdened with guilt. I've been worried and frightened to death about what they would ultimately do to him. When I last talked to him on the phone, I was thankful to hear him talking the way he used to before the war. As his mother, I want to say thank you for giving him back to me."

"I've done nothing, Mrs. Taylor," said Marie. "I only came to Plattsburgh to visit with Scott. We've talked about a lot of things in our lives. If you think it's I who has made a difference, I'm flattered, but you're most likely misinterpreting our relationship. We've only known each other for a few weeks. So don't give me too much credit for your son's improvement."

"I have to agree with Mrs. Taylor," said Steve, sitting at the restaurant table between the two women. "Scott's attitude and his spirits have risen measurably since Marie came on the scene. If I remember correctly, my old class in philosophy called it 'post hoc' reasoning (after this, therefore because of this). Nevertheless, he's improving and holding up extremely well under a very painful procedure."

"I sense a conspiracy around me," laughed Marie.

"My dear girl, whatever it is that has given my son new hope, I certainly support. What a nice trip this has turned out to be for me. Steven offered to drive me up here to meet you and see Scott. It has warmed my heart and eased my mind to see Scott so happy."

As they turned to the food the waiter placed in front of them Steve announced his plans to return to Canada day after tomorrow. "We should leave Lake Champlain by eight AM at the latest. Are you prepared to leave, Marie?"

"Yes, I'll be ready by that time. Before I leave I want to be honest with you, Mrs. Taylor. This has been a very meaningful visit for me. Your son is a wonderful person who deserves the best that life has to offer. I'm not sure where he and I go from here and I don't want you to read too much into what he and I share, because it's still too early to know anything for certain, but my blindness could be an obstacle to the future," stated Marie bravely.

Mrs. Taylor listened carefully to what Marie had said. "My dear girl, I appreciate the way you talk from the heart. All that matters in this life is our capacity to love and be loved. There are no limitations to the human spirit. Your blindness is a problem only if you make it one. All I ever wanted out of life was to be proud of my son and to see him happy. If you can do that, Marie, you'll warm my heart."

"Thank you for your support, Mrs. Taylor," said Marie with relief.

Scott was awake early in the morning with pain so intense he could barely tolerate it without screaming. The duty nurse gave him another unit of pain medication and asked him to drink as much water as his bladder could hold. It was impossible for him to sleep even after the medication started to ease the pain. He thought of Marie and how their relationship had progressed since that first meeting in Maine. His feelings for her had grown these past few days. He knew of her feelings, doubts and misgivings about how her blindness would impact him.

During the early morning rounds of Dr. Conklin, Scott asked him a favor. "Doc, you must have noticed the blind lady that's been to see me for the past few days. Could I ask you or someone else on your staff to examine her and evaluate her situation?"

"I'd be glad to take a look. Much of my work with burn cases has also involved problems of the eyes. I'm not allowed to prescribe anything to her, but I can check to validate her physician's diagnosis."

"Thanks, I appreciate it."

Marie, Steve, and Mrs. Taylor were the first visitors of the day at the hospital when visiting hours started mid-day. Scott had just completed another skin graft session and was still drowsy from the medication. Steve told him that he was heading for Maine first thing in the morning. Steve estimated that it would put him at Fort Lewis by mid-afternoon. If Dr. Conklin was to look at Marie, it would have to be done today. He was hoping to have a little more time to discuss the matter with her, but their departure in the morning did not give him much time.

"I have a request to make of you, Marie," said Scott, hoping she would not think he was out of line. "I asked Dr. Conklin to check your eyes. He can't do anything else for you, but he can give you another opinion that may reinforce what you already know. I had planned to talk with you beforehand, but your departure in the morning makes it awkward. What do you think, Marie? It's up to you."

"I don't mind having another doctor look at me. I would never have asked for it on my own, but since you'd like to be reassured, I'll do it. I just hope that your request is not a manifestation of second thoughts or doubts on your part, Scott. Feelings of being incomplete and inadequate are a daily battle of mine since the accident, and I must tell you that they've been stronger than ever since I've known you. If Dr. Conklin confirms what others have told me, will it make a difference in your feelings towards me?"

"No, of course it would not make any difference to me. You have my word on that, Marie. I feel terrible putting you on the spot like this. I was only thinking of you, not myself. If I had the power, I'd return your eyesight in a heartbeat. Please, don't doubt my intentions... I was afraid of being misunderstood."

"I believe you, Scott," she answered softly.

Later that same afternoon Dr. Conklin escorted Marie into his office and thoroughly examined her eyes questioning her about the accident and what her physicians had done. He arrived at the same conclusions. Her blindness, having taken place at the time of the fall from the balcony, was complete. She was unable to distinguish any degree of lightness. Her eyes were healthy with good blood circulation and color. Marie's problem stemmed from the fact that the signals from her eyes were not being transported to the brain and vice versa. Dr. Conklin had a theory pertaining to her condition. When she fell from the balcony, she probably hit her head hard enough that some of the liquid in her skull collected in a pocket or sac, so that the liquid itself was prohibiting the flow of impulses through the optic nerve to either of her eyes. Exploratory surgery could be used to try and locate the liquid, but he emphasized that it was a theory and he could be wrong.

"I hope I haven't disappointed you, Miss Poole," said Dr. Conklin. "There are so many things we don't understand about the human body, especially the brain."

"Is there any possibility that my sight could be restored," asked Marie hesitantly.

"I would not want to give you any false hope young lady, but nothing is impossible if we have faith." Dr. Conklin handed

Marie back her glasses and watched her put them on. "May I make a suggestion?"

"Yes."

"Why don't you put those glasses in your pocket. The only practical function they serve is to alert other people to the fact that you're blind. You have lovely brown eyes that are still healthy, you just can't see through them, so why wear the glasses?"

"I… don't know. I thought that light would be bad for me."

"Nonsense, young lady. The cause of your blindness is in the nerve system behind the eyeballs, not in the eyes themselves. I understand that glasses can be a good screen to hide behind, but a pretty lady such as yourself doesn't need to hide behind anything. Hold your head up high and show the world that you're only blind, not crippled."

"Thank you, Dr. Conklin," cried Marie. "You've been very kind and helpful."

"Captain Taylor is a lucky man. I wish you the best of luck, Miss Poole."

Dr. Conklin escorted Marie back to Scott's room. Scott instantly noticed that Marie wasn't wearing her glasses. She was a vision of loveliness. Dr. Conklin excused himself after wishing Marie a safe trip back home.

"You look better without your glasses, Marie," said Scott. I can see your brown eyes now."

"I wish they could see you. Dr. Conklin only confirmed what I already knew."

"At least it's another confirmation and opinion, my dear," offered Mrs. Taylor. "Scott's right. You do look better without the glasses."

Mrs. Taylor and Steve left Marie and Scott alone for the evening so that they could have some time together before she left for Maine. Scott was anxious for her to understand how much he appreciated her visit. He was proud of her and he wanted her to know that he understood how much courage and determination it took to travel this far to visit a virtual stranger in a strange place.

107

"A hospital isn't a very good place to get to know people, but it's been swell having you here, Marie."

"I'm glad I came, too. It has been wonderful getting to know each other better. I can return home now with a lot of nice memories. I'm sorry that you continue to endure such painful treatments, but it could have been worse. You could have perished in the accident," said Marie with a shudder.

"I think often about that. It'll be a lonely vigil here after you leave. Is there any future for us, Marie?" Scott asked, watching Marie closely for a reaction. "What I mean is… is this a beginning, or is this an ending for the two of us?" Marie looked directly at him as if she could see his pleading eyes.

"This moment of discovery is a time for honesty and plain talk, Scott. My heart tells me that I want to know you better. If this parting turns out to be the end of us as a pair, then I would accept it, but it would hurt and it would not be easy."

"That's what I wanted to hear…"

"I can tell what's in your heart, Scott. I share those same feelings. It's a relief to be able to freely express our thoughts, but there's something else that we must face honestly. No matter what you say to the contrary, Scott, I cannot ignore the fact that I will be blind for the rest of my life. I don't consider myself a cripple, but I do have a very real disability that could put a strain on any relationship."

"How many times do I have to tell you that I do not care about that? Your eyes may be sightless, but your spirit is more alive and more active than anyone I've ever known. The Marie that tackles problems head on is the person I've come to care a lot for. Let me be your eyes, Marie; you can see the world through mine."

"If you don't stop I'm going to cry, and I don't want to do that before I leave you. This has been the most joyful trip of my life. I know that something serious and meaningful is taking place between us and I pray to be worthy of your attention. My joy is eclipsed by doubt. I'd give anything to be able to see, like normal people."

"Then I have a suggestion, Marie. Why don't we just give it more time? Time will answer all of the questions you may have. I'll miss you when you're gone. I know everything seems to be so sudden, but I'm not going to fight it. Instead, I'm going to rejoice that it has happened to us." Scott grasped her hands and gently kissed each one.

"You'll never know how complete you've made me feel these past few days. Thank you for that."

Scott's bed was rolled so that he was at a forty-five degree angle with the floor, so Marie kneeled down on the floor and kissed Scott on the lips and said: "Until next time, Scott. I'll be thinking of you and praying for your recovery."

"You've just made me the happiest man in the world," he cried. "Until next time, Marie. Thanks for coming."

Steve landed the Norseman on the lake in front of the hospital where he picked up Marie. After lift off, Steve banked the plane in a complete circle above the hospital before setting a course due East for Maine and Canada.

Chapter Nine

Late in the afternoon Steve caught a glimpse of Lac Diamante on the horizon. As the plane drew closer to the lake, the setting sun cast dancing shadows on the rippling blue waters, giving the impression that the lake was moving with the wind. The stark simple beauty of the lake and its surrounding cover of greenery touched him. He felt a strong sense of belonging to the community. It was as much an emotion as an oasis of civilization in a sea of green forest. His heart beat a little faster when he thought of his wife, Bright Star, and what her reaction would be when she heard the drone of the airplane engine.

Steve circled above the western shore of the lake so that he could approach the main dock straight in. The sturdy Norseman turned so sharply it seemed to pivot on an invisible hinge. Steve gently touched down and coasted to the dock against the rubber bumpers. He saw Bright Star running down the path from the infirmary toward the dock, her coal black hair trailing behind her. She caught the mooring line and fastened it to the dock, before she opened her arms to welcome him home.

"It's so nice to have you home again," cried Bright Star. She was dressed in a starched white nurse's smock with her hair full and loose around her shoulders. Usually she wore it pulled toward the top of her head where she held it in place with two colorful combs. The small nurse cap above her forehead was held in place with a hair pin. Her dark brown eyes shined like beacons from her happy face.

"I've missed you, Sweetheart. It's been a long month away from you," Steve exclaimed, holding her at arms length. "You look lovelier than I remembered. How have things gone since I left?"

"We've got good news from Montreal, Steve. That last appeal you wrote must have caught the attention of someone with common sense. The school project has been accepted by the Province. Thanks to your persistence."

"At last we can start the school project," Steve cried, picking up Bright Star and twirling her around the dock. He stopped abruptly when he saw a worried look on her face. "What's wrong, honey?"

"Inspector Clough is not doing very well. To be honest, Steve, we're concerned for him."

"You know, when I left I had a feeling he wasn't doing as good as he let on. It seemed to me that he lost some of the fight he always had after Daniel-Joseph's funeral in Maine. I'm sorry to hear that."

"Mother and Father came up last week just to be with him. The three of them had planned to take a trip to Europe this summer. Father and the Inspector wanted to visit some of the old battlefields and try to piece together what it was like for DJ when he was killed in Belgium. Father also wanted to show my mother where my biological father, "Flying Eagle" was killed. The trip could give all of them some closure to the deaths. All three of them need that."

"Is the Inspector so bad that he won't be able to make the trip?" asked Steve, taking Bright Star around the waist and headed towards the infirmary.

"I'm afraid so, Steve," she soberly answered with a shake of her head. She clung tightly to Steve.

Steve had come to love the elderly policeman, who had decided to stay on at Fort Lewis after his retirement from the Mounted Police. Bright Cloud and Mark insisted that he share their cabin with them, and, if he wished, they would be happy to take him back to Maine where he could live more comfortably for the winter months. The Inspector didn't object to the suggestion, for he enjoyed the seacoast area also. Over the years a strong bond of friendship had developed between the three.

Inspector Clough projected a formal and stiff demeanor to the outside world, but those who knew him understood that he was a caring and compassionate man with a heart equal to the breadth of his shoulders. He was loved by all who knew him. To those criminals which he pursued with a singular purpose, he was feared and respected, because he was uncompromising with his commitment to the law. In the northern forests, where he had spent most of his career, he was a living legend who championed the hard working forest people with a persistent diligence and fairness that was unique in the "Force" he served for so long.

Steve and Bright Star lived in the same cabin that was used by Michelle Korsman when she replaced Bright Cloud as head nurse of the infirmary over twenty years ago. They dropped off Steve's luggage at the cabin and went directly to Mark and Bright Cloud's cabin finding them sitting at the large table in the center of the great room. A small fire crackled in the stone fireplace. An air of sadness filled the room. Bright Cloud's face changed the minute she saw Steve.

"Now that you've returned, things can get back to normal. Our daughter has been like a lovesick teenager ever since you left. Welcome home, Steve," said Bright Cloud, kissing him on the cheek.

"You look a little drawn, Steve," observed Mark. "How's Captain Taylor doing?"

"Well, I think Scott will be coming out of this in good shape. It'll take a while for him to recover, but it should be complete. Star just told me about Inspector Clough."

"It's true, he's not doing very well, Steve," answered Bright Cloud in a faint voice, pointing to the closed door beside them. "He's sleeping now. We're worried about his condition. He has a deep, rattling cough that frightens us. He refuses to be evacuated to a major medical facility. His lungs are slowly filling with fluids even though I've administered penicillin and another new antibiotic that's supposed to work well on pneumonia and lung infections."

Silence filled the room as each person reflected on the situation they were confronted with. Bright Cloud was especially distraught and nervous at being unable to help her friend in his greatest hour of need. "I fed him some soup this afternoon," she said in a shaking voice. "The Inspector looked at me in a strange way I've never seen before. He told me: 'when my time comes... I hope it's going to be quick'. I've never seen him so sick as he is now..."

Suddenly, a familiar voice could be heard from behind the closed door. Bright Cloud and Bright Star rushed to see what the Inspector wanted and were pleasantly surprised to find him propped up on one elbow, prepared to swing his feet over the bed to the floor.

"Am I imagining things or did I hear Steve's voice," asked the Inspector in a weak voice.

"Why don't you stay in bed and rest for a little while longer," pleaded Bright Cloud, buttoning his pajama top. A wracking cough forced him to sit upright so that he could clear his throat. Steve and Mark came into the room when they heard the labored cough.

"Welcome back, Lad," whispered the Inspector, reaching out for Steve's hand between coughing spasms.

It was difficult for the group around the policeman's bed to see him lying helpless on the white sheets. Steve was shocked to see how much weight the Inspector had lost. His eyes lacked that special gleam that was a trademark of the man. His face was drawn. The bushy eyebrows and the sunken eyes gave him a gaunt, drained appearance. He seemed to be having trouble focusing his eyes.

"I'm glad all of you are here." Inspector Clough spoke haltingly. There was a sense of urgency in his weak voice. "I've some things to tell you that have weighed heavily on my heart for a long... long time..."

"Do you think this is the right time, Inspector?" pleaded Bright Cloud, trying to ease him back down on the pillow. It was a tense moment. Everyone in the room could see that Inspector Clough was struggling to say something that was important for him to tell.

"I see your sad faces around me and I'm touched to be the object of your concern," the Inspector continued. "I was never blessed with a family of my own. The flu took my dear wife when I was at the front in France years ago. I thought my world had stopped turning. I gave up and lost my direction for a while, but I was able to start life anew, thanks to my old friend, Running Deer and his family, who took me into their home and extended their friendship. I gratefully accepted it as a drowning man grasps for a life line...

"Not long afterwards, a young American, fresh from the trenches of France, came into our lives and into our hearts. It was a proud day, Yank, when you presented Flying Eagle's medal to Running Deer and Bright Cloud. You've been a true friend to this old man and I have valued your friendship more than you will ever know..."

"I knew, Inspector," answered Mark, choked with emotion. "I always knew."

"I owe you and Bright Cloud an apology that is long overdue. I'm old enough to be Bright Cloud's father, yet I've loved her ever since she was a young girl. I knew then that it was wrong, but I was not able to control my feelings, and I kept that knowledge to myself all these years. I was unable and unwilling to express my feelings to Bright Cloud. I made a promise to myself and to my God that I would protect you whenever it was possible, Bright Cloud."

"Dear Inspector, the things you've said don't come as any surprise to me. I believe I've known what was in your heart and went unspoken," admitted Bright Cloud, turning away from the stare of the sick policeman.

"Do you remember the time you fell and hurt yourself beside the river when you first started the forestry work for the Tribal Council, Yank?" Inspector Clough seemed to gain strength with each word. He reached out to take Mark by the arm and continued. "When I found you, Yank, and carried you back to the infirmary, I became privileged to learn just how much you meant to Bright Cloud. You had won her heart, and my secret fantasy would never become a reality. A part of me resented your presence at Fort Lewis at that time. I'm so ashamed to admit it to all of you. I've felt guilty all these years for harboring such unkind thoughts over something I should have had the courage to overcome. Of course those thoughts were short-lived and I ask your forgiveness, Yank. You and Bright Cloud have given me the only home I've ever known. Our lovely Bright Star has warmed this old policeman's heart ever since she was a baby. I've been so proud to watch you become the lady that you've become, Lass. And I was also filled with pride for our dear young Laddie, Daniel-Joseph. May God rest his soul. I hope to be seeing him soon. Don't mourn for me. I have no regrets in my life now that I've confessed to you, Bright Cloud and Mark. I'm sorry for my failings..."

"Don't be hard on yourself, Inspector," interrupted Mark. "There's nothing to excuse you from. You had natural feelings that any human being would have had, and as far as I'm concerned, no apologies are necessary. Your friendship has been one of my most precious possessions. My life with Bright Cloud has been enriched by your generosity and thoughtfulness. It is I who am indebted to you."

Bright Cloud and Bright Star helped the weakened Inspector to lie down flat on the bed. They supported his head with a pillow and tucked a blanket around him.

"Thank you... I do feel a chill... I'm sorry to be such a burden..."

"Hush, Inspector," said Bright Cloud, touching his parched lips with her finger. "You rest for a while before supper time." She wiped several strands of white hair from his bushy eyebrows and felt his forehead. He was still running a fever!

Later that night, Inspector Gerard Clough watched the moon rise over Lac Diamante. Just before the moon passed from his sight, he closed his eyes and stopped breathing. His legacy to the forest people of the Canadian north woods was already a part of the folklore of the primitive wilderness he served so faithfully. His legacy would continue to live in the hearts of those who knew him.

The inhabitants of Fort Lewis prepared for Inspector Clough's funeral with heavy hearts. Most of the villagers remembered him as a permanent fixture in their midst. One of their most influential benefactors now belonged to the world beyond the sunset. News of his death spread rapidly. Many of the forest people responded to the news by heading to the scene of his passing, Fort Lewis. There was a somberness in the air at the outpost. The tiny hamlet slowly filled with people who came to pay their respect to a man who spent his life defending their way of life.

Steve and Bright Star sent a radio message out to Arlo and Michelle. Within an hour the RCMP station received a message they would be coming in for the funeral, for they were a part of the Inspector's intimate family, too. Shortly after Mark and Bright Cloud married, Arlo came to Fort Lewis with Mark for a fishing vacation. Arlo and Inspector Clough hit it off the first time they met. Their friendship grew steadily through the years. Arlo was exceptional, for he was the only person that the Inspector confided the location of his best "fish holes" on Lac Diamante. Even Mark did not have that distinction. Arlo was pledged to secrecy and never betrayed the trust. Whenever he returned to Fort Lewis, he was anxious to go fishing, his one passion. He visited the special "fish holes" only when he was alone on the water. On those occasions, he consistently returned to shore with a bountiful catch.

Arlo and Michelle shared fond memories with the Inspector about their courtship. The two fell in love on Arlo's first visit to the village. Arlo and Inspector Clough were serious cribbage players, and they played at every opportune moment when Arlo was at the village. They maintained a point list that covered all of the years of their relationship. At the end of each calendar year, the one with the most points was rewarded with a bottle of the most expensive champagne money could buy. Over the last twenty-five years, Arlo recollected that he had presented the gloating Inspector with twenty-one bottles of fine champagne. That was bad enough, but the Inspector never once offered to share a glass with Arlo!! Arlo selected his friends with care, and he treasured his friendship with the Inspector, who was an important link to the happiest years of his life.

Steve and Bright Star anxiously waited at the landing dock to meet Arlo and Michelle's plane. Steve was concerned because the weather was turning bad. They were relieved to hear the engine of a circling aircraft overhead. A few seconds later the plane came into view and lightly touched down on the water.

Arlo stepped out of the plane first and reached out to help Michelle. He was wearing his forest green uniform with two gold stars on the shoulder straps. He looked as if he had been poured into it. The gray streaks in his hair were the only clue to his actual age.

At a distance, Michelle looked older than Arlo because of her pearl-white hair. The hair color was deceiving, for she was five years younger than Arlo. She had an energetic bounce to her walk and a sparkle in her eyes that belied the whiteness of her hair. She wore her hair short, preferring to have it cut just below the ears. She wore a black dress with a snug-fitting black blazer. The years had been kind to her - she was still a very young-looking woman. The fact that Arlo and Michelle survived the war years and were successfully reunited at its end had tested their love, which had never wavered for either of them.

Bright Star sadly greeted them with an embrace. "It's so nice to see you two again. Isn't it sad that it takes a death to bring us together?"

"These are difficult trips," said Michelle, reaching out for Bright Star and Steve. "Seeing you two together makes my heart pound. Family and friends are so important at times like this."

"I missed you, General, when I left Lake George at the end of my summer camp," said Steve.

"Your mother told me about your bad luck at camp. I hope Captain Taylor is doing well," remarked Arlo. There was a grave look in his eyes as he looked out over the waters of the lake. "I just can't believe my old friend has passed away. He seemed so indestructible and so permanent. I hadn't noticed much change in him over the years, but of course we all have that date with destiny that cannot be denied."

Steve grabbed the two bags of luggage and followed the new arrivals up the path to the village. "Mother and Father will be relieved to know that you've arrived safely." Bright Star linked her arms with two of her favorite people, Aunt Michelle and Uncle Arlo.

The funeral for Inspector Clough consisted of a simple Mass at the Catholic Church in Fort Lewis. The day started out with dark overcast clouds and a wet, cold drizzle. The small Church was filled to overflowing. Mark, Bright Cloud, Steve, Bright Star, Arlo and Michelle sat at the front of the congregation. After the Mass, the mourners went to a site selected by Mark and Bright Cloud for the Inspector's final resting place. The procession followed the worn path to an open spot directly beneath the "lookout rock" located on the ridge to the west of the village where it had an unobstructed view of the village and Lac Diamante. The location was selected so that the spirit of the dead policeman would still be able to watch over the village that had captured his heart.

The casket was carried by six uniformed men. Arlo and Steve carried the two front corners of the modest pine coffin, while four Royal Canadian Mounted Policemen were positioned at the center and rear of the casket. It was a demanding climb, yet the six strong men never faltered in their solemn trek. Once they arrived at the gravesite, the casket was lowered into the freshly dug grave. A detachment of RCMP riflemen lined up a short distance from the grave.

Bright Cloud, Bright Star, and Michelle accompanied Mark at the end of the procession. His determination to make the climb unaided, even though it was a heavy strain on his legs, was successful. The three women were prepared to assist him if necessary. The fact that he was walking at all was a miracle. It was typical of the man who never once complained about his wounds from the war. By the time Mark reached the gravesite he was perspiring heavily. Before he took his place at the edge of the grave, he wiped his brow and straightened the Medal of Honor sash he wore around his neck.

The village priest led them in prayer for the committal, then nodded to Mark at his side. The rain had stopped and the wind increased in intensity at the top of the ledge outcrop. A silence fell over the scene and the mourners could see that Mark was having difficulty saying good-bye to an old friend. He took his time to place a rose and a sprig of rosemary, the herb of remembrance, on the casket. The wind filtered through the tall pine trees nearby filling the air with gentle rustling sounds of the pine needles being caressed by the wind.

"Good-bye, old friend. May the path you travel through eternity be paved with soft moss and princess pine. We will miss you more than it's possible to express, but you already know that. Our paths first crossed a long time ago in that horrible place of death and destruction near Soissons, France. You were an observer from the Canadian Army, and I was a marine captain in charge of an Army company. Little did I know then how much of an influence you would have on my life.

"For two generations you've been the glue that held the small outpost of Fort Lewis together. Your legacy will always be with us. I want to thank you for your support in all that I tried to do. Your friendship has been treasured by me and my family much like a precious jewel is enjoyed through the ages. Your memory lives in our hearts.

"Tell Flying Eagle and Daniel-Joseph how often we think of them. I know you'll look after them the same way you did for us. May the stars light your path to eternity, and may you find the peace and love that eluded you here on earth. Good-bye, dear friend."

Bright Cloud stepped beside her husband and grasped his hand in hers, while the Priest read a final prayer. The committal service ended with a stirring rendition of an old Irish folk song - *Danny Boy*, a favorite of Inspector Clough. The young Mounted Policeman bugler stood straight and formal as he played. The sad refrain echoed from the top of the ridge into the wilderness beyond. The song of love, devotion and loyalty touched the heartstrings of those who attended. The bugler ended the ceremony with a Canadian rendition of a British service tribute to a fallen soldier – *Last Post*. That was immediately followed by a salute from the riflemen standing tall and straight in their scarlet tunics and wide-brimmed hats. Three volleys of fire filled the air to announce that an old warrior was coming home to his final resting place.

Mark took his time descending the trail. He was not anxious to leave the place. Death, it seems, had become a central theme to his life. It started during the First World War with Flying Eagle's annihilation from an artillery blast which almost unbalanced Mark. He was able to overcome the trauma with the help of Bright Cloud's love, which was severely tested when the two of them faced a tragic situation involving Flying Eagle's twin brother, Red Fox. He had kidnapped Michelle from the infirmary during a raging snow storm. Bright Cloud and Mark took up pursuit and confronted the depraved brother, and Bright Cloud was forced into a situation where she had to decide which of the two persons, Mark or her own flesh and blood Red Fox, lived or died. Red Fox was posed above Mark with an ax aimed at Mark's head. She was faced with a horrific decision. Before the swing of the ax was completed, Bright Cloud fired three shots from her .35 Remington Automatic Rifle into the body of her brother, slamming him against the wall of the cabin. The ax fell harmlessly at Mark's feet.

World War Two added another chapter of death and mutilation of young men's bodies around him. It was for their welfare that he charged a Japanese pillbox with a satchel charge of explosives. He was instantly cut down by a machine gun and would have died if not for a miracle intercession on the part of his departed friend Flying Eagle. In the midst of recovery from his wounds, Mark and Bright Cloud received word that their son DJ was killed in action during the Battle of the Bulge. Death always seemed to accompany Mark. He did not brood over it, but he reflected on the fragile nature of man.

The oil lamps burned late into the evening at Bright Cloud's and Mark's cabin. Arlo and Michelle stayed with them. Steve and Bright Star joined the group later in the evening after they had stopped at the infirmary. It was not a jovial gathering, but it was reassuring for all present to be in the company of true friends. The fact that they were all together was reason enough to be thankful for the moment, and to draw strength from their fellowship. It wasn't long before the main topic of conversation was the proposed school for Fort Lewis.

Approval for the school was in hand. The school was a logical addition to the growing community at Fort Lewis, which served the forest inhabitants for a radius of two hundred miles.

Most of them were members of the Cree Tribal Council at Fort Lewis. The Tribal Council administered a large tract of forest land which Mark had helped secure for the tribe with his development of a forest management plan. The plan was an important step in insuring the stability and pride of the local Tribal Council.

Annual harvests from the forestland were conducted on a scale well below the annual growth of the forest. Therefore, the forest as a productive entity was more valuable now than it was back in 1921 when Mark completed the first plan. It helped the tribe sustain their pride of self-determination. The addition of a school would fulfill a basic need and desire for education. The physical building complex for the school was addressed by the Council with the introduction of a sawmill on the forest tract which could saw the lumber needed to build the structure. As a matter of fact, the logging crews had already produced enough lumber to build the complex in accordance with the plans Steve had proposed to the officials in Montreal.

Steve's proposal for the school included three classrooms, a small library for school and community use, a separate barrack-style room for boys and girls and a kitchen-dining area. The school would be able to share the ample water system previously installed for the infirmary. Whereas supplies had to be flown or carried into the isolated village over long distances, it was determined that the Tribal Council would make available enough seasoned firewood from the forest tract to heat the structure and cook the food. It would have been ludicrous to have even contemplated oil or gas heat when a renewable resource was so close at hand. Preparation of the firewood became a community effort and a source of pride. Utilizing the low grade trees from the tribal forest for firewood increased the productive capacity and quality of the residual forest stand.

Just as the group was ready to retire, Michelle asked; "What name are you going to give to the school?"

"We haven't decided on anything, yet," answered Steve, looking from Bright Star to Bright Cloud for suggestions. "Wait a minute, I just thought of one. We could call it 'Eagle Nest' in honor of Star's paternal father, Flying Eagle. What do you all think?"

"I think it's perfect," said Mark. "If nobody objects, I'd like to carve the school's nameplate while we're at Fort Lewis this summer. I can't help much with the actual construction, but I can at least do that."

"That would be great," approved Bright Cloud. She knew that it was moments like this that Mark's wounds limited his participation. She saw a resigned look come across his face. She smiled at him but his smile in return was hollow and unconvincing.

In the early hours of the morning a weather front blew through the small hamlet sweeping away all of the rain clouds. In its wake cool clear air rolled out of the north over the ridge where Inspector Clough's fresh grave shone in the moonlight. The skies were filled with a myriad of dancing stars as if to celebrate his homecoming. The northern lights hummed and crackled lighting up the skies with a display of color and fireworks stretching to the horizon.

Late in the fading hours of the night, a large eagle silently circled the grave several times coming lower and lower with each flyover. When the powerful talons of the eagle touched the damp soil of the grave, an intense light shone from directly above for several seconds. As soon as it disappeared the lone eagle catapulted into the air where it was met by another eagle. Together they circled the grave three times before heading easterly into the first rays of the rising sun.

Chapter Ten

Steve landed the Norseman on Lake Champlain in front of the hospital. Scott heard the unique sound of the aircraft's engine and was sitting up in bed when Steve came through the door.

"What brings you to these parts?" asked Scott.

"I offered to bring Arlo and my mother to Lake George. They chartered a plane to come to Fort Lewis for Inspector Clough's funeral. So, I figured I could bring them back and check on your progress at the same time."

"I'm sorry to hear about the Inspector. I'm finding that the hardest part of my recovery is filling up the hours of the day. It's great of you to stop by. I'm bored stiff. How is everybody?" asked Scott, slipping his legs over the side of the bed.

"Arlo has been assigned to command the Marine Corps Schools at Quantico. The rest of the gang is doing as well as expected in the aftermath of the Inspector's death. Bright Star is taking it pretty hard."

"I liked the General when I met him at the funeral," mentioned Scott. "He'll probably be a positive influence on the schools. The Marine Corps Schools are pretty thorough in their coverage of amphibious operations and small unit operations, but they're not as broad or inclusive as the Army Schools. The Army schools of Artillery at Fort Sill and the Infantry Schools at Fort Benning continue to be the best in the world. They always have several marine officers attending them."

"Do I detect a slight rivalry on the part of an Academy man?"

"Maybe some," laughed Scott. "I really don't mean to put down the Marine Corps, for I'm an admirer of some of their accomplishments. However, one has to admit that they've got the best public relations, or propaganda programs in existence. They saturate the papers and magazines with pronouncements of their activities regardless of whether it was a squad action or a full division. They paint a picture for the public that is not always reflective of the facts. They have the highest rate of desertion and suicide than any of the other services, yet they never mention that fact. While I'm on the subject, criticism of the Marine Corps is tantamount to dismissal if it comes from another marine. I like marines, but I have some reservations about the accuracy of many of the claims of the Marine Corps as an institution. There, now that I've got that off my chest, I feel better."

"Well, I guess you do have some feelings on the subject. Seriously, I think the other services have the same opinions. Listen Scott, I can't stay too long. I want to reach Fort Lewis by night-fall. Darkness comes earlier up there than it does here and as soon as the sun goes down, it descends at an even faster rate," said Steve checking Scott out closely. "Is there anything I can get you?"

"You can make time go by a little faster if it's in your power. Marie has been swell. She's sent me a radio and a lot of reading material. Her letters help, too. She frequently mentions her trip in the airplane," said Scott. "I appreciate your bringing her. It was nice to see her again. I'm glad she's become a part of my life."

"She's a very special woman, Scott. The two of you deserve each other," said Steve. Suddenly, Steve unexpectedly excused himself and left the room in search of Dr. Conklin, who was at the nurse station on Steve's floor.

"How is Captain Taylor coming along, Dr. Conklin?"

"He's doing better than expected," answered Dr. Conklin. "We've completed the grafting procedures. All he has ahead of him now is the wait for the grafts to heal and grow together. He seems to heal rapidly, a gift of youth and a healthy body."

"Would it be possible for him to be moved?"

"What do you mean? Moved to another facility?" asked Dr. Conklin guardedly.

"No, no, Dr. Conklin. I mean could I take him on a trip for a visit of a few days? He would be staying with me and my wife, who is a Naval nurse. She helps run a regional infirmary, just a few feet from our cabin in Canada," related Steve with excitement.

"It's highly irregular, Captain, but as long as his dressings are changed as needed, and there is an experienced eye to check for infection, I don't see any reason to not let him go with you. He should avoid excessive movement; however, moderate exercise will promote healing." Dr. Conklin paused for a few seconds to examine Scott's charts, and continued. "If you want to assume the responsibility for his care, I'll approve the trip. He's getting restless and it'll probably do him good."

"That settles it then. Can you get him ready for transport as soon as possible? I have a deadline with darkness that can't be postponed."

"You don't ask for much do you, Captain?" grinned Dr. Conklin. "We can have him ready and instructions prepared for your nurse wife within fifteen minutes. Does that meet with your approval?"

"Sounds great. Thanks, Doc," said Steve, rushing down the corridor to Scott's room.

"What's going on, Steve?" asked Scott.

"Well, Scott, I just got official approval from Dr. Conklin to take you back with me to Fort Lewis for a few days if you feel up to it. What do you say?"

"No kidding? What about my dressings?"

"You'll be in the care of the two best nurses in the country, my wife, Bright Star, and my mother-in-law, Bright Cloud."

"That sounds great to me, Steve. This place is beginning to drive me nuts."

"We'll head off into the wild blue yonder very shortly. Fort Lewis, here we come."

Four hours later Steve and Scott arrived over Lac Diamante as the sun dropped behind the western ridge. Steve pointed out some of the places described to Scott, such as the center cabin, the Cenotaph to Flying Eagle and the grave of Inspector Clough before positioning the plane for a straight-in approach to the docking area. Bright Star was waiting for them at the dock.

"Welcome to our village, Captain Taylor. It's nice to see you again. How was the trip?" asked Bright Star, ready to lend a hand in case it was needed.

"Steve made the trip as smooth as silk, Mrs. Jackson. I can't twist sideways yet, but I'm improving."

"Can you walk a short distance?" inquired Bright Star watching him gingerly climb out of the plane.

"Oh yes. I've walked almost everyday since I was taken off the rocking bed a week ago. That was a relief. Steve let me take the controls of the plane for a while. I guess I didn't do very well."

"Now I know why he's a ground pounder," laughed Steve.

"To each his own, I always say," answered Scott. "This is a lovely spot. I've forgotten how much I missed getting away from things for a while. That fresh air filled with the scent of cedar and balsam is a tonic to the senses."

"That's our Canadian wilderness for you. I've lived here most of my life and I still appreciate its mystical charm."

"This reminds me of the area around Moosehead Lake in Maine," said Scott, thinking of Marie. "Marie would feel right at home here."

"Steve told me about your friend, Marie," admitted Bright Star, pointing out the way they had to walk. "The infirmary is down this path. We don't have streets here, only paths. If you don't mind, I'd like to check your injuries, Captain, so that we can take care of you properly."

"Lead the way and I'll follow. A little slow, but I'll make it. Incidentally, this Captain stuff is way too formal for me. I'd like you to call me Scott."

"You took the words out of my mouth," answered Bright Star. "I prefer to be called by my Cree name of Bright Star rather than my Christian name of Dawn."

"Then it will be my pleasure to call you Bright Star."

Steve grabbed the two suitcases and followed behind Scott to the infirmary, where he helped Bright Star remove Scott's outer clothing. Dr. Conklin insisted that Scott continue to wear the metal frame around his back so that clothing did not irritate the healing of the wounds. It was awkward for Scott but it enabled him to move more freely. He was positioned on his stomach when they removed the lightweight cage.

Steve didn't admit it, but he was experiencing a lot of pain. It started the moment they became airborne at Plattsburg. Cradling his head in his arms, Scott could feel Bright Star gently remove the heavy bandages Dr. Conklin had prescribed for the trip. Scott could not see the look on Bright Star's face when she exposed his grafted back, but Steve saw it and instantly knew that something was not right.

"Steve, honey, could you ask my mother to come over? I want her to see Scott's backside so that we're both familiar with his condition." Bright Star's voice gave no hint of the anxiety reflected in her eyes.

"I'll be right back."

A small part of the dressing caught on an area of newly grafted skin causing Scott to wince.

"I'm sorry, Scott. I'll be more careful. Are you uncomfortable or in any pain?"

"Yes, but it's been worse than this. I'm tired. I think I might have overdone a little today."

"Of course you're tired. That's only natural after what you've gone through."

Steve and Bright Cloud entered the room with a flourish.

"How's our new guest?" asked Bright Cloud, slightly out of breath. She placed her hand on his forehead. Scott was running a fever.

"I hope I'm not a burden to you."

"My dear young man, we're pleased to have you visit with us. Now, take this thermometer and place it under your tongue. I want to see just how high your temperature is. You just relax and let us pamper you for a while."

Bright Cloud was correct. Scott had a fever of 103 degrees, enough to be concerned. Both Bright Cloud and Bright Star were perplexed at the fact that Scott's back was newly infected in several places over the grafted area. It was possible that the medication applied in New York was not strong enough. They conferred together at the end of the hall, where Bright Cloud read the instructions from Dr. Conklin. After she read the sheets in front of her, Bright Cloud checked the secured medication closet to determine if they had the required medication, then she spoke to Bright Star in a calm measured tone.

"If the infections are not arrested, you realize that we've got a major problem on our hands. We'll have to send him back to Lac St. Jean or Quebec City."

"I know, that's why I asked Steve to get you, Mother. What do you think? I doubt the medication on hand is strong enough to do the job all by itself."

"I've got a suggestion. It's going to be uncomfortable for Captain Taylor, but it could slow down the spread of infection so that the prescription would have a better chance to take effect. I'd like to immerse his backside in a salt bath for an hour or so, then apply the medication full strength. We'll also supplement the ointment with penicillin antibiotic."

"That could be painful for him, but it should do the trick, Mother."

"What's wrong with Scott?" asked Steve, interrupting their secluded conference.

"Shhh Steve," said Bright Cloud, grasping his arm and walking with him further from the door to Scott's room. "For some reason, the infections have spread to some of the new growth between the grafts of skin. If we can't control it tonight, Captain Taylor will have to be flown to a hospital tomorrow. We're going to give him a warm salt water bath."

"Listen, Honey," requested Bright Star calmly. "Mother and I will take care of Scott. You must be exhausted after your long flight. Run along home to rest, and I'll see you in the morning."

"Okay, but you better call if you need me."

Bright Cloud informed Scott of his condition and what they proposed to do about it. He already knew that something was wrong. He knew that one of the most effective treatments given to him was a salt water bath. He agreed with Bright Cloud and Bright Star.

"Go ahead with the brine bath. I had a lot of them earlier at Plattsburg," said Scott.

"It could be painful."

"I can handle it. The alternative would be harder to take. I apologize for being such a bother."

"Hush, now, young man," said Bright Cloud. "No more talk like that. We'll do our best for you. Besides, it's not as if you were a total stranger. It's an opportunity to say 'thank you' for your kindness and concern for DJ."

Bright Star poured liberal amounts of hydrogen peroxide over Scott's back. Suddenly, the infected areas began to boil and bubble until his entire backside was covered with a foaming mass of bubbles. It helped take away some of the sting that made Scott uncomfortable. A tub, large enough for his upper body, was filled with warm water mixed with sodium chloride. His arms and legs hung out over the rim of the tub, while his back remained fully immersed in the healing solution. It hurt more than expected. Scott's whole back felt as if it was on fire when the salt started to react with the raw open wounds. They gave him a medium strength sedative to help dull the pain and penicillin to help control the infection. They agreed that he was better off remaining alert and mobile rather than being medicated to a lethargic state, but sleep finally came, and Scott surrendered to the weariness.

By the next morning, Bright Cloud and Bright Star were exhausted and relieved by two native Cree nurses. They would know within twenty-four hours if the crisis had been averted. Throughout the night and following day Scott was subjected to an hour of soaking in the brine solution, then given a heavy coating of antiseptic cream which felt cool and soothing on his infected skin. The routine was exhausting on Scott, and he readily fell asleep even though he was in pain.

Steve quietly watched his wife and mother-in-law work over his friend. He questioned his judgment of putting Scott at risk by bringing him to Fort Lewis. A lot of things required Steve's attention including the structure for the new school complex which was under way. It wasn't easy to concentrate, but the two nurses in his life seemed to have Scott's situation under control. He was able to apply his modest experience in carpentry and construction to the benefit of the local volunteers doing the work. Steve had worked on several construction projects during summer months and between college semester breaks, therefore, he became the general supervisor for the job. He thought the target dates of completion could be met with a little luck.

Besides the physical building, other issues occupied Steve's mind. Books and supplies for the school had to be ordered, transported and stored in a dry condition after they arrived. The accumulation of foodstuff, furnishings, and living supplies were as important as the educational material. Feeding and housing the students that had to live at the school would require as much effort and work as instructing them in the classrooms.

Local families volunteered to help administer the large amount of supplies and equipment that would soon be arriving. Steve was a stickler in regards to the prompt payment of goods for the school. He stressed that the most valuable lesson the school could teach was accountability, and it began at its infancy with the way it conducted business with its vendors who supplied their needs.

The accelerated tempo of activity was proceeding according to plans, with one exception: another teacher was needed. The school curriculum required three full time teachers. Steve shouldered the responsibility of being director or principal for the school and would handle one of the full-time teaching jobs. A young female Cree from Fort Lewis had just finished college in Ottawa and was anxious to become one of the teachers. The third position was accepted by a college graduate from Quebec, who agreed to come for at least one year. After Steve returned to Fort Lewis with Scott, he learned that the third teacher had canceled his agreement, leaving a very short time to make arrangements for another by the time school opened. Steve recognized the valuable asset of the nurses at the infirmary, who could serve as substitute teachers in the event of a temporary absence or illness, but it was out of the question to think of using any of them on a full-time basis.

He immediately sent an urgent request back to Quebec for another suitable teacher.

Late in the afternoon of the second day of Scott's visit, Steve dropped by to chat with him at the infirmary, and have a cup of tea with Bright Star. Scott was sitting at a small table drinking coffee and eating a sandwich.

"Well, old man. Seeing you like this makes me feel better. I hope I was not wrong in bringing you up here."

"Hi, Steve," answered Scott with a grin. "I feel much better than I did last night. Your wife said that the salt water bath and ointment licked the infection. The infected areas are much improved she says. My back feels better, too."

"That's good news, Scott. You had us all worried for a while there."

"I have to tell you that your wife and mother-in-law are swell people. I've been treated like royalty since we got here. Colonel Leroux stopped by to visit for a while this morning. I like him. DJ talked a lot about his father. He's really a grand person."

"Colonel Leroux is my father-in-law as well as a dear friend. You aren't the only one to feel the way you do about him."

"By the way, Steve, how's your school project coming along? Something must be happening. I can hear the hammers pounding all through the day."

"We're on schedule with the building so far. Our supply situation is tenuous this far from civilization, but the Canadian Air Force Reserves have volunteered to deliver our bulky equipment with some of their large float planes such as the Martin Mariner or the Catalina PBY. The lake is large enough to handle them. I've been flying with one of their squadron commanders who flies periodic forest fire patrols in the area. He's committed them to making delivery 'on demand'. When they fly the missions, they promised to bring an amphibious truck capable of handling the equipment from the water to the school site, which will certainly help the situation."

"It doesn't matter if it's civilian or military, supply problems have a way of dictating what, when, where, and how things are done. My education really started after I graduated from the Academy. In the real world of military operations, logistics require eighty percent of your time and effort; whereas, tactics take less than twenty percent."

"Sounds like you've been studying up on your service and supply manuals," remarked Steve.

"I've been trying to cover as much as possible while I'm out of commission. I'll be glad to return to the War College course again. I want to be prepared. It's an important opportunity for an infantry Captain."

"How much longer will it be before you're able to return?"

"Dr. Conklin estimated that I'd be ready by mid-August. He thought I could draw limited duty by that time and by Labor Day I could carry a full schedule of courses. It's beginning to be a long summer."

"I wish I could say the same thing. If I get everything done by Labor Day I'll be lucky. But then, if our school opening is delayed a short time, no real harm is done," Steve told him, shrugging his shoulders.

Scott stayed at the infirmary one more night and moved into the spare room in Steve and Bright Star's cabin the next morning. He spent part of every day getting better acquainted with Mark. They shared hours on the lake fishing. Mark used a flat bottom rowboat instead of a canoe because it was more stable for both of them. On rainy or inclement days he played cribbage and checkers with Mark in front of the fireplace. Warmth and fellowship contributed to Scott's feeling of contentment. It seemed as if he was constantly eating. The crisp clean air made him hungry. He indulged himself probably more than he should have. The ample supply of fish were exciting to catch and delicious to eat. He and Mark kept the two homes and the infirmary supplied with fish from the lake.

Early in the evening of the fourth day of Scott's visit to Fort Lewis, Bright Star casually asked him if he would like to take a walk down the path to the police station. It seemed a little unusual to him, but he needed the exercise, so he gladly fell in beside her. Scott's back was protected from his large outer shirt by the brace that created a pocket so that his skin could "breathe". It was uncomfortable to wear because it held him at an exaggerated position of attention with his shoulders held back and his head tilted slightly upward.

Steve was at the school site when they walked by. Seeing Scott walk made him chuckle. "You look like one of the King's guards at Buckingham Palace!"

"Steve, that's not fair," scolded Bright Star.

"That's okay, Star," replied Scott with a laugh. "I've seen myself in the mirror and it does look funny. But, what can one do?"

The RCMP Station was directly across from the school. It had changed very little from the time Mark first came to Fort Lewis in 1920. It was a rambling log cabin with rooms added so that they formed a hollow square in the center, which was used as washrooms and toilets. It looked like what it was, a frontier blockhouse capable of being defended by its inhabitants. The Canadian flag snapped in the wind above the main entrance door. There was a clean efficient look about the structure which reflected the professionalism of the policemen who were carrying on in the same tradition set forth by Inspector Clough.

"We have a surprise for you at the police station, Scott," said Steve with a gleam in his eyes. "I think you'll approve. The nearest phone line is located at Lac St. Jean, about two hundred miles away. The Canadian government has developed a wireless phone connection to remote places such as Fort Lewis. They've been working on it for a long time. At strategic points, the Army has built generating stations to pick up and relay messages to Lac St. Jean, where it's tied into the existing telephone system. Since you're an honored guest, we thought it would be fitting that you make the maiden call out. I knew the system would be completed today, and I took the liberty of sending a telegram to Marie preparing her for your call from Fort Lewis."

"I've been thinking a lot about her lately," exclaimed Scott truthfully. "Thanks for the thoughtfulness."

Steve held the door of the police station open for Bright Star and Scott. The station held a lot of memories of Inspector Clough for her. She still found it difficult to accept the fact that

133

he was gone. Steve introduced Scott to the resident officer, Constable Snow.

"Welcome to Fort Lewis, Captain Taylor. I've been looking forward to this moment for a long time. Now, the advances in electronic communications have given us a direct link to the rest of Canada."

"Thank you, Constable Snow, the pleasure is all mine."

"We're going to leave you in the good Constable's care while you make your call in private. We'll be at the school," said Bright Star as she disappeared out the door.

"Steve gave me the number for Monson, Maine, in case you don't remember it. You can sit here at this table, Captain, where you'll have more privacy. Place the headset on and talk into the microphone in front of you on the table. I'll clear the lines to Lac St. Jean. When they answer, just give them the number and location just like you would over any phone. Feel free to talk as long as you want, Sir."

"I'm amazed."

"The line is now open for your call," said Constable Snow, quietly stepping into an adjacent room.

Scott gave the operator the number and listened to the rings on the line. Marie answered with an excited, "Hello."

"Marie, this is Scott. I'm calling from Fort Lewis. I'm up here with Steve."

"It's nice to hear your voice, Scott. I've been worried sick over your taking such a long trip in your condition. How are you feeling?" She was thrilled to be speaking to him once again.

"I'm doing great, Marie. They've taken good care of me up here at the infirmary."

"Steve sent me a telegram to expect a call by mid-week. I didn't know what to think. So you're at that place Steve talked so much about?"

"It lives up to its description."

"Has he started the school yet?"

"Yes, he's pretty busy orchestrating everything in preparation for opening day this Fall. He just told me he's still looking for a teacher, but other than that, he's optimistic about meeting his deadline."

"You sound wonderful, Scott. Are you able to get around much?"

"You won't believe it, but I've been fishing just about every day. That's more fishing than I've ever done in my life. To be real honest, Marie, I'm ready and anxious to get back to the War College course. With all the idle time on my hands, I've been studying a lot for it. I think often of you and appreciate your letters."

"Ever since my return from Plattsburg I've been thinking a lot about the future, and everything else," admitted Marie. "Sometimes I'm so frightened of what I feel... I can only bring dependence to a relationship."

"Marie, stop beating yourself up! I wish I could be with you right now. I don't like to hear you talk that way. I've changed since you came into my life. I can't tell you how many times I've regretted the thoughts I harbored toward you and Arnold. I was so wrong to accuse you without knowing the facts. I know you forgive me, but I find it hard to excuse myself."

"Of course I've forgiven you, Scott. You've been nothing but kind and thoughtful towards me since then, and I thank you for that. I only wish that things could be different with my condition."

"Please don't prejudge my feelings for you, Marie. And please don't place obstacles in our path that aren't meaningful. Do you understand what I'm trying to say?"

"Yes."

"Before we hang up, Marie, I want you to know that my injuries are improving daily. I'm stronger than when you last saw me. Don't worry about me. When I get back to New York State, I'll call you. This call was arranged by Steve and his wife, Bright Star."

"Thank both of them for being so considerate. Hearing your voice again has brought light into my world. So...until next time, Scott."

"You must realize that I've fallen in love with you, Marie. Until next time!"

"I love you too," answered Marie, hanging up the phone. Tears of joy filled her sightless eyes.

Chapter Eleven

Marie placed the phone back on the receiver with trembling hands. She sat back against the chair and thought about the conversation with Scott, her heart bursting with happiness. "He does love me," she shouted to herself. When she was with him, the world around them seemed to be in order. She felt a level of understanding and trust with Scott that she had never obtained with Arnold, even though they had known each other since childhood.

She prayed that Scott, and all that he represented in her dreams and hopes, would not think less of her because she was blind. He berated her about such thoughts, but her affliction was real to her and it could not be ignored. She had no doubts that Scott and she could be happy with each other. It just felt "right".

Later that evening, when sleep was impossible for Marie, a plan of action developed in her mind. She went downstairs, fixed a cup of coffee for herself, and sat down at the typewriter with a determined look on her face. She started composing a letter to Steve Jackson.

Dear Steven,

It was nice hearing Scott's voice last night. Thank you for making it possible. He brought me up to date on your school project and I must say it sounds exciting.

After we hung up, I couldn't stop thinking about your search for a teacher. I've decided to ask you to consider me as one of the teachers, if you haven't already hired one.

I realize that my blindness limits me in many ways, and I'm not positive that I can do the job. I know that some blind people have been able to teach effectively. If I could not successfully handle the job to everyone's satisfaction, I'd be the first to step down and leave the area. The fact that you and I have met should be helpful in arriving at a decision.

My qualifications as a teacher are supported by a Bachelor of Science degree in English and a minor in Education from the University of Maine. I taught fifth grade in Monson for five years and have a very flattering letter of recommendation from the school board.

I'm not asking for a permanent job. I'm only asking for a chance to prove to you and myself that I can successfully teach in the classroom again.

I'll anxiously wait for your reply. If you agree with my request, I'll need to equip myself with a certain number of specialized Braille teaching aids, which may take some time to procure.

As you already know, my passion is literature, but I can handle everything included in the curriculum for first through eighth grades. I've enjoyed teaching Braille to adults in a remedial reading class, and I would not object to teaching adults in a similar remedial class at Fort Lewis if there was a demand for it. I fervently believe that the inability to read or write is the most cruel handicap to those unfortunates who must bear the burden. Reading and comprehending what one reads places the full experiences of mankind at our finger tips.

I'm sending this letter to you by way of the address you gave me. I hope you receive it shortly, for I will be sitting on pins and needles until I hear from you. I want to stress that if you honestly feel my blindness will prevent me from doing the job, then you owe me the courtesy and honesty to tell me so. I expect nothing less from you.

Good luck with your project, Steve. Even if I cannot be a part of it, I share your enthusiasm for the endeavor.

Sincerely yours,
Marie Poole

Scott's condition continued to improve at Fort Lewis; however, Dr. Conklin was anxious to have him return to Plattsburg where he could monitor Scott's progress. After all, he was responsible for his patient and took that responsibility seriously. Several days after Scott spoke to Marie, he was shaking hands with his new friends, thanking them for their warm hospitality. Good-byes were something he had learned to hate, for they had resulted in last farewells at an alarming frequency during the war.

Steve lifted off the clear waters of Lac Diamante and headed for the ridge to the west of the village where he pulled a hard right turn before pointing the nose of the Norseman due south. Scott watched the tiny settlement beside the lake become swallowed up by the endless green forest below. As far as the eye could see was nothing except bodies of water and the endless miles of spruce-fir trees. Scott's eye for terrain and its logical defense or assault potential were a natural part of his thought process, and he shook his head at how difficult either mission would be to carry out in such a vast remoteness.

An hour later, Lac St. Jean was visible in the distance. Steve landed for fuel at the waterfront RCMP station. A young constable recognized him.

"Captain Jackson, we have some mail here waiting for delivery to Fort Lewis. Do you want to take it now?"

"Yes, Constable, if you've got it handy."

"No problem, Sir."

Steve and Scott climbed back into the cockpit of the plane. Steve curiously opened the mail pouch to quickly check the contents. The letter from Marie was on top.

"It's a letter from Marie Poole," Steve announced, reading it carefully. "Of course, why didn't I think of her? She would be perfect."

"What does she say?" asked Scott.

"We've just found our new teacher! Here, you read it for yourself."

Scott read the letter, smiling at her enthusiasm. "She's one spunky woman, that's for sure. I have no doubt that she will find a way to be effective in the classroom. Her blindness is not as much of a handicap to her as some people would expect it to be."

"I could see that the first time I met her. We'll call her from New York."

Once they landed at Lake Champlain, the Army hospital staff expertly rushed Scott into the examining room. Dr. Conklin was anxious to check Scott's injuries, watching his patient with interest while he made his examination.

"You've been in good hands, Captain Taylor. We could not have done any better by you than the nurses in your wilderness infirmary. The trip seemed to have agreed with you. Your color and disposition are much improved."

"It was great to get away from the hospital, Doc, no offense intended. I ate my fill of fresh fish. Wow, you should have seen the size of some of them! I also rested a lot as you suggested, but now, I'm ready to return to duty as fast as I can, even if it's limited activity."

"Wait a minute, Captain, your back was seriously injured and you're not going to gain anything by rushing it too much. You do heal quickly. I'd guess that you could be posted to the College on a limited field duty basis within a couple of weeks."

"I'd appreciate it if you could put me in for that, Doc," said Scott. "I'm going to call Marie and tell her the good news."

"Give my best to the young lady, Captain," remarked Dr. Conklin on his way out the door. "I'll send in your Air Force friend."

"Thanks, Doc."

"Well, Steve," said Scott as Steve entered the room. "I've got good news to share with you. Looks like I can return to school within a couple of weeks. What do you say we call Marie and share it with her?"

"That's good news, Scott. I'd like to speak to her for a minute, then I'll get on my way and give you two some privacy."

The phone rang several times at the Poole residence. Just as Scott was ready to hang up, he heard the familiar voice of Marie answer, slightly out of breath. "Hello."

"Hello, Marie. I'm back in Plattsburg. Steve is here in the room with me and he wants to talk with you. Don't hang up afterwards, for I have some good news to share with you."

"Ok, Scott. You sound in good spirits. I was out on the lawn when the phone rang and had to run for it."

"Here's Steve."

"Hi, Marie. I just read your letter, and I can't tell you how happy we would be to have you come with us as a teacher. I don't have time to go over specifics, everything seems to be happening so fast."

"I didn't expect an answer this quick. I'm glad to hear that you accept my proposal, Steve."

"I'm going to spend the night with my mother at Lake George. I hope to start back to Fort Lewis first thing in the morning. Wait a minute! I just happened to think of something. Is it too short a notice for me to stop at Monson on my way back to Canada and pick you up? That way you could get a feel for the situation at the village and gain a better idea of what's ahead of you. We'll be glad to bring you back to Monson whenever you wish. What do you think?"

"I don't have much to do right now; my Braille classes in Dover are suspended for the summer... Yes, I'd like to fly to Fort Lewis with you. Thanks for asking."

"I'll stop about 9:00 AM tomorrow, weather permitting. If it's bad weather, I'll call to let you know. Here's Scott again." Steve handed the phone back to Scott and motioned to him that he was leaving. Steve disappeared down the hall with a happy smile on his face.

"Steve's a good friend," stated Scott, watching him leave the hospital.

"He certainly is," answered Marie. "I'm so glad you called. I wanted to speak to you about the impetuous letter I sent to Steve. What do you think about the teaching job at Fort Lewis?"

"I think that the school and children are going to be lucky to have a schoolmarm like you," answered Scott truthfully.

"I hope my condition is not a factor."

"If you're going to tell me that your blindness will limit you, then I won't listen, Marie. Sure, it's going to be a factor, and it won't be easy. They'll love you at Fort Lewis, Marie. Mark my words, they'll take you into their hearts and make you feel at home. I'm very proud of you."

"Thank you for saying that. I guess I needed to hear it from you, Scott. Now, what's the news you have for me?"

"Dr. Conklin just gave me a thorough checkup, and he's pleased with my progress so far. Within a couple of weeks he's willing to recommend to the War College that I be placed back on limited duty. I'm getting restless just filling up the days. I feel myself getting stronger and stronger with each passing day."

"That's wonderful, Scott. I've been so worried about you. If I end up teaching at Fort Lewis, that means we're going to be so far apart. I want to do the job, but I don't like the idea of being so far away."

"I know. I promise to get up to see you as often as I can. I'm not sure what to expect for a duty assignment after I finish the course. A soldier's life is difficult on families and relationships. But don't worry, we'll cross that bridge when we come to it. In the meantime, this teaching job is a challenge that will do you good, Marie."

"You make it all seem so easy," commented Marie lightheartedly.

"When I was in Europe during the war," answered Scott in a serious tone, "a day never passed when I wasn't afraid of dying. Once you've experienced moments like that, everything else becomes easier by comparison. Nothing is impossible when two people want the same thing. I'm assuming you feel the same way, Marie. Something very special is happening between us."

"Yes, I've felt that same way. I haven't been the same person since you came into my life. It's easy to tell you that I love you, Scott."

"I love you, too, Marie. You take that trip to Fort Lewis with Steve. Check the place and people out and then decide if it's something you want to do. Whatever decision you make, I'll support you."

"Thank you for being so special. Until next time, Scott. I pray for you all the time."

"Good luck on your trip, Marie. With all my love, until next time."

The next day, Steve picked up Marie as planned, and headed towards the great North Woods. Marie's new adventure was about to begin. Steve followed his normal route to Lac St. Jean where they filled up with gas and refreshed themselves before commencing the last leg of their journey to Fort Lewis. Two hours later, the faithful aircraft settled onto Lac Diamante and coasted to a stop at the dockside, where Constable Snow was waiting to secure the plane.

"Welcome back, Steve."

"It's good to be back, Constable."

"You're not going to believe some of the changes since you left yesterday morning. The Army engineers moved in with two plane loads of material and transported it to the school building site with an amphibious truck. They've set up tents and a mess for a platoon of men."

"Well, I'll be darned," exclaimed Steve, momentarily forgetting that he had an important visitor on board the plane. "Constable Snow, I want you to meet Miss Marie Poole. We hope that she'll be one of our school teachers this fall."

"Welcome to Fort Lewis, Miss Poole." Constable Snow watched Marie carefully step from the plane to the dock with help from Steve. She was dressed in a dark green pant suit with a white blouse, her sand colored hair falling loose around her shoulders. She carried herself straight and proud as she clung to Steve's supporting arm. There was a confident air about her that the young policeman admired.

"Thank you, Mr. Snow. My legs are a little wobbly after the long plane ride. I'm glad to meet you," said Marie, reaching out towards his voice with her right hand.

"I think you'll like it here, Miss Poole," answered Constable Snow, shaking her hand.

"I cannot see it because I'm blind, in case you've been wondering, Constable. However, I can smell the fragrance of the forest and feel the crispness of the air which makes you feel good to be alive. I like it already."

"It doesn't take much salesmanship to sell Fort Lewis to newcomers," said Steve proudly.

"May I get your luggage, Steve?"

"Thanks, Constable. Marie has a suitcase on the floor in the rear seat. She's going to stay with Bright Star and me."

"I'll bring it to your cabin. Enjoy your visit Miss Poole and call on me if I can help with anything."

Marie could "feel" the vastness of the forest around her. The only sound she could hear was the sound of the wind brushing through the needles of the trees around the village. The silence was as vast as the forest itself. She imagined that Fort Lewis would be similar to the forests north of Moosehead Lake. She wasn't disappointed, but there was an added element of remoteness that increased her perception of the things around her.

Marie's blindness had taken away her ability to distinguish light, color, and the distinctions of shapes and tones; while, at the same time her other senses of hearing, smelling, touching, and tasting became more acutely utilized to compensate for her loss of sight.

"I hear construction sounds off to our left. That must be the school."

"You're right; the school site is behind us nestled between the Hudson Bay Factor's house and the Cree Tribal Council building. The Army engineers have not been idle while I was away. We'll check on their work later." Steve continued to guide her along the path. "On our right is the RCMP station, which has a barracks and mess facilities for several men. Our radio link to the outside world is located there. The path we're taking is about three hundred yards inland from the lake and runs parallel to it. All of the individual homes in the village are made from cedar logs. On our right, behind the police station is the Catholic Church and rectory. Immediately adjacent to the Church is the infirmary complex where my wife works as a nurse. Her mother, Bright Cloud, is also a nurse. As a matter of fact, she founded the infirmary back in 1919."

"It sounds like quite a family."

"I admit, I'm biased. You'll soon be able to judge them for yourself."

"I love the feeling of solitude and freedom that fills the air. You can actually hear your own heart beat in the stillness. What a place to get to know oneself."

"This far from civilization isn't for everybody, but for those of us who are comfortable with it, there's a feeling of self-discovery and fulfillment."

"That's the word, self-discovery," Marie thought out loud.

"Oh, yes. I want to get you settled in our cabin."

"That sounds fine to me."

"My wife and I stay at a cabin next to the infirmary. She works such crazy hours, the convenience of being so close makes her job easier. We have a spare bedroom and you're welcome to use it as long as you want," said Steve, checking to see if he could see Bright Star through the windows. The cabin seemed empty. Steve called out for Bright Star. Suddenly, a voice from the infirmary to their right called out to them.

"I heard you land. I would have been at the dock to meet you, but I couldn't leave," called Bright Star from the infirmary door. She didn't recognize the woman walking beside Steve.

"Bright Star, I want you to meet our newest teacher for the school, Miss Marie Poole. Marie, this is my wife, Bright Star."

"So you're the woman Steve flew to New York," remarked Bright Star, recognizing the name. "I'm so happy you could come, Marie. My Christian name is Dawn but I prefer to be called by my native Cree name of Bright Star."

"The pleasure is mine, Bright Star," answered Marie, reaching for Bright Star's hand.

"Is it really true that you're our third teacher?"

"When I got to Lac St. Jean with Scott, a letter was waiting for us from Miss Poole. She's a highly qualified teacher looking for a challenge," explained Steve.

"It sounds wonderful. Listen, Steve, why don't you take Marie to the cabin. I've got a couple of things I must complete before I'm off for a while. I took the liberty of having one of our village friends come in to do some cooking for us. We've been so busy at the infirmary."

"I don't want to be any extra trouble," stated Marie quickly.

"You're no trouble, Marie," said Bright Star reassuringly. "You must be tired and hungry after the trip. By the time you get settled, I'll be home and we can get better acquainted over supper."

"Thank you, Bright Star."

Later that evening, everyone enjoyed fresh baked bread and venison steaks prepared by a neighbor. Bright Star was exhausted, too. The infirmary was packed with sick people who needed attention, and the staff was pushed to their limit. Bright Star told Steve and Marie that her mother, Bright Cloud, insisted on working the evening shift so that the three of them could share some time together over a good meal.

Marie was anxious to hear all she could about this place called Fort Lewis. Steve told her that Bright Cloud and Colonel Mark Leroux returned to the village every summer. When he related the story of their meeting at the close of the First World War, Marie was captivated by the story.

"They sound like interesting people. Scott has told me about them and about your brother, Daniel-Joseph. Scott still holds himself somewhat responsible," said Marie softly.

"All of our family and friends are thankful that DJ had a commander like Scott. His visit with us at DJ's internment has been a milestone in our ability to pick up the pieces of our lives after his sudden death. Scott's a very special man. It's nice that you two have become such good friends."

Marie blushed at the comment from Bright Star. "We met under unusual circumstances and it has turned out wonderful so far."

"We had a chance to get to know Scott better when he visited us here at Fort Lewis. He's very proud of you and it showed whenever he mentioned your name. Wait a minute, I'm becoming very personal to a new friend, and I apologize for my boldness, Marie."

"It's I who must thank you for taking such good care of him when he needed it."

The three adults sat around the large tavern table in the great room and became better acquainted. The subject of the proposed school was the center of conversation. Marie was surprised at the size of the school complex and the number of children who would be attending. She had not realized that so many of the students would be cared for at the barrack-like dormitory rooms, or that two small rooms were being constructed for chaperons to live with the students.

Marie jumped at the chance to be with the students in a capacity other than that of a teacher. Steve seemed pleased at her response, because they needed another proctor or house-mother. The enthusiasm of Steve and Bright Star for the school was contagious, and Marie found herself sharing their passion for the chance to bring knowledge to young minds who would not otherwise have the opportunity. She understood the zeal that missionaries had in their pursuit of serving those in need.

It was late when they retired, and Marie had trouble sleeping. Her head was full of thoughts and plans for the future. The village noises of people talking and doors closing eventually faded away and the night was taken over by the voices of the wilderness that penetrated the walls of her room. She could hear the ripple of the water against the lake shore beside the cabin. In the distance a loon could be heard thrashing and clawing its webbed feet against the water as it prepared to take off. Other loons at different points in the lake sounded their melancholic call to one another in a symphony of sounds. One close to shore near her open window answered its mates across the water. The chattering cry of foxes also added to the cacophony of the night. As the evening wore on, Marie could also hear the sound of great horned owls hooting intermittently into the crisp cool night air.

The night may have been still to the ear of the average person, but Marie's enhanced sensitivity to sounds admitted her to an exclusive club capable of picking up the restless energy of the nocturnal creatures of the wilderness. The silence of the night was a relative thing, for in reality, a large portion of the forest inhabitants roamed the forest trails in search of food, creating a disjointed symphony of sounds. In many ways it was not that different from the sounds she heard through her bedroom window in Maine. The main difference was the feeling of detachment from society that surrounded her as soon as she stepped from Steve's plane to the dock at Fort Lewis.

Marie felt a special relationship to the creatures of the night, for she was a part of their world of darkness. Bitterness and sadness filled her heart, and the burden of her misfortune seemed more difficult to bear at this time of each day. She never let herself slip into self-pity, but fear of the unknown was a constant companion. It was at these moments that she questioned her resolve to be able to function in the world.

Thoughts of Scott readily changed her mind to the more pleasant aspects of her life. She loved Scott; after all, "How could anyone not love him?" she cried out loud. She loved him most for the feeling of wholeness that settled over her when she was with him. She drew strength and courage from him. She rarely thought about Arnold since Scott had entered her life. Arnold needed her more than she needed him. She realized that now, but the steady demands and promises placed upon her by Arnold kept her in a continuous state of anxiety. She grew up with Arnold; yet, she never felt the same depth of feelings for him that she now had for Scott. Arnold had generated dependency. Scott generated strength and independence.

In the distance above the village to the west a long disconsolate cry of a wolf echoed across the land as if to signal to the humans below that the night was his. Marie closed her eyes and surrendered to sleep. Her mental image of Scott accompanied her to the world of dreams.

Chapter Twelve

Time passed quickly for Marie. After a short adjustment period and evaluation of what was expected of a teacher at such a primitive facility, she eagerly accepted the teaching job at the Eagle Nest. She did not deceive herself about the hardships ahead of her. This was a new untamed land in a foreign country with a social culture that she was still uncertain about. In spite of all of the potential problems, she was confident of her ability to perform at the village of Fort Lewis. Marie stayed at the village for two weeks, then returned to Monson, Maine to make preparation for her first year of teaching. Whenever she was ready, Steve promised to come for her.

The Canadian Army transported more construction workers so that the school complex was completed and equipped by the first week of September. Steve remained busy supervising everything that took place. He reviewed and ordered textbooks, teaching materials, and supplies when he was not at the place where he was needed the most on the construction site. His energy and good-natured enthusiasm was contagious to the engineers and the volunteer Cree workers.

The school was organized into three separate classrooms with three distinct age groups; grades 1 through 3 (ages 5-9); grades 4 through 6 (ages 9-11); and grades 7 and 8 (ages 12-14). Steve volunteered to teach grades 1 through 3. A new teacher, Tom Hardy, arrived early in September from Ontario to teach grades 4 through 6. Marie took the older students in grades 7 and 8.

Tom Hardy was a tall, thin, easy-going young college student with long legs and a protruding Adam's apple and a gaunt appearance. He had a peculiar walk that amused the children. The rigid standards that he set were not an instant success with the children, but they soon adapted to his ways and felt special under his regimented tutelage. He was more formal than either Marie or Steve. One day Tom summed up his philosophy to Marie: "We're in this world to do something; we can't just go along for the ride and watch what happens." Steve and Marie categorized Tom Hardy as a lovable eccentric and they worked well together.

Everything the new teachers did established the foundation for a tradition that would probably stand for years to come. It was a historical moment for Eagle Nest, and the significance of the events was not lost on the staff who filled its ranks. Marie caught the spirit that pervaded the walls of the school when she wrote a popular cliché on the chalkboard for her first day of class: "The longest trip starts with the first step."

Marie volunteered to be the housemother to the girl's dormitory. The student's ages ranged from 6 to 13 years old. The added duty did not create any more work for her. The local villagers took care of the cleaning, laundry and cooking chores, leaving Marie with little more to do than to be present for the nights. She monitored the children's activities, and organized the older girls so that they were paired with some of the younger members and held them responsible for each other. The buddy system worked surprisingly well. In time, the relationships turned into caring friendships.

Most of the older students had already attended small mission schools scattered all over the North Country. A few had attended provincial schools in Ontario and Quebec. Marie acknowledged her blindness and her limitations as a result of the blindness, to the students on the very first day. She laid a foundation of mutual cooperation and understanding that she built upon every day she remained at the school. It was her intention to create a partnership whereby they shared each other's tasks and were responsible for one another's welfare. She tried to impress upon them that she was there for them, and that she expected them to reciprocate by helping her when her blindness created a barrier to the pursuit of any goal. She stressed the essentials of teamwork. What one could not do becomes possible for a larger group. She quickly found that the concept of teamwork was deeply ingrained in the native peoples of Canada.

The students responded to Marie's direct way of doing things. They never misunderstood what was expected of them, and as time passed, they learned that Marie always kept her word and followed through on her promises. Their respect for her soon turned into real affection, and they competed with each other to help her when she needed it. They looked after her as completely as she did for them. It was a remarkable experience for teacher and her students.

It didn't take long for some of the adults in the village who never had the opportunity to learn how to read or write, to inquire about the possibility of Marie teaching those basic skills to them. Marie was not surprised at the request. Indeed, she was thankful for the opportunity because she realized that she was accepted by the villagers. The Crees took her into their hearts as if she was one of their own. Several nights a week she held classes for adults for two or three hours. The classes usually ended with a request for her to read to the group.

At first, Marie selected articles and stories featured in the textbooks so that each member of the class could follow along with her recitations. The adults listened with rapt attention, for they had a natural love of story-telling. Marie sat at her small desk and used her Braille versions of the story selections. Eventually, she was able to expand her reading sessions to some of the classics. A favorite of her adult class was *Last of the Mohicans*, by James Fenimore Cooper. The last chapter of the book, which dealt with the death and burial of Uncas, the last of his proud race, had a special meaning for the forest people, and they asked her to re-read that portion several times. It was a sad ending that moved the adults in the classroom. Marie could not see the sadness on their faces or the tears that trickled across their bronze cheeks, but she shared the same emotions as she read the descriptive passages.

Marie's blindness did not diminish her ability to reach out to the people of the forest. As a matter of fact, her blindness and her courage to not let her affliction limit her, made it possible for them to grant to her a status of respect and affection given to very few. Inspector Clough had won that enviable position, and Mark Leroux had also won them over. She felt a communion of spirits with them, and she matured into a resourceful and even stronger person as she worked to overcome the challenges of teaching at Eagle Nest.

* * *

Scott was able to keep abreast of her activities through her daily letters. The Army War College seemed a long way from Fort Lewis, but Scott and Marie bridged the gap with letters. By mid-September Scott's back had healed sufficiently so that he could accept full-duty status. He was lucky enough, at that time, to tie in with a class that was at the same point he had been when the accident happened.

The conclusion of the six month course ended with a simple graduation ceremony in October when Scott and his classmates were given orders for their next duty station. Scott was ordered to China as a battalion Executive Officer. The posting was accompanied with a promotion to major. It was a bittersweet set of orders. He was pleased to move up to the position of second-in-command of a battalion, but the idea of shipping out to China so soon after graduation had little appeal to him. He was hoping to have more time to spend with Marie. However, he was a good soldier, and he would go wherever he was ordered without complaint.

Scott calculated that he could spend a couple of days with Marie at Fort Lewis before he had to start his journey to the far east. He spent a day with his mother in Pennsylvania, then chartered a float plane to take him to Fort Lewis. He had not told Marie about his plans, so his presence at Fort Lewis would be a surprise. He had already forwarded his gear and personal belongings to the Presidio in San Francisco, which was a staging area and point of embarkation for men and material slated for the battalion. He could reach San Francisco from Quebec as soon as he left Fort Lewis.

The charter plane dropped him off at dockside on Lac Diamante. One of the young Mounted Policeman met Scott at the dock.

"You can leave your suitcase with me, Captain," greeted the policeman. "I'll be glad to take it to Bright Star and Steve's cabin. You look better than the last time I saw you."

"I feel better, too, Constable. Thanks for offering to take care of the bag. Nobody knew I was coming, so my visit will be a shock to Marie."

"Miss Poole's classroom is the door on the right as you approach the school. I'm sure she'll be surprised."

The school looked a lot different than the last time Scott saw it under construction. Each of the three classrooms had their own entrance located on the front of the building facing the lake. The dormitories and other rooms were located in the rear where they had the benefit of sunshine in the rooms most of the day. Scott noticed the neatly carved sign, *Eagle Nest,* fastened to the front of the building. He said to himself with a grin, "Colonel Leroux has kept his promise."

Scott's heart was pounding as he carefully opened the door and quietly stepped inside. Marie was leaning against her desk at the front of the room reading to the class from a book in Braille. The class was taking in every word. They had not noticed his presence yet, so he sat in an empty seat at the rear of the classroom. None of the children detected his presence, but Marie lifted her head in his direction and continued to read while her hands floated over the Braille markings in the book.

"Excuse me," said Marie unexpectedly. "Is there someone at the back of the room?"

The children all turned to stare at the soldier sitting at one of the desks. He bolted from the seat without saying a word. The whole class seemed to catch its breath in unison! "Wow..."

"I apologize, Miss Poole. I just stopped by to see you in the classroom," explained Scott as calmly as he could. Marie recognized Scott after the first word, and she ran the full length of the room into his waiting arms. There was a collective "ooh" from the students who then started to talk all at once.

"The class will be out of control if you don't settle them down," Scott exclaimed, releasing Marie from his embrace.

"Now children," shouted Marie. They stopped talking immediately. "We have a wonderful surprise today. This is the person I've mentioned to you on several occasions. Those of you from the village may remember him when he visited Fort Lewis last summer. He had been injured and was recovering from his wounds at that time. Class, this is Captain Scott Taylor of the United States Army. Captain Taylor, meet the seventh and eighth grades."

"Hello. I apologize for my interruption of your studies, but I was so anxious to see your teacher that I couldn't wait. I just completed several months of school myself. You're lucky students to have a teacher like Miss Poole. Isn't she very special?"

The class gave a resounding "yeh" to his question, and they began clapping. Marie blushed all over and shook her head in dismay. Scott's unannounced visit was a little unsettling for her and for the class. The students always saw her in complete control of herself, and for a moment, when she lost that control, she was embarrassed. The feeling passed quickly, for she was so happy to show him off to the children. Marie regained her grip on the children by announcing a short recess. The room emptied in a few seconds!

"You've succeeded in surprising me completely, Scott."

"You look lovely," Scott whispered in her ear. She turned her head towards him while he swept her into his arms and kissed her. "I apologize for disrupting the class the way I did. It seems like a long time since I've been with you, Marie."

"How long do you have off?"

"I can stay for a couple of days," answered Scott. "I'm not sure where I'm going to stay. I failed to call ahead to notify Steve and Bright Star."

"I'm sure they'll be pleased to have you as a guest. I stay here at the school. Oh, Scott, it's so nice having you here. There are so many things I want to share with you. My life has changed so much from the last time we met. I'm still working hard to make my work relevant to the students. They've been wonderful to me. I really like it here."

Steve entered the classroom and was shocked to find Scott. "Well, Scott. You made it back to Fort Lewis. Welcome! It's great to see you again. How's your back?"

"I had my last checkup with Dr. Conklin this month. I'm as good as new. I had reduced duty status for a while, but that changed soon after I started the course again. I'm impressed with your new school, Steve. I appreciate how much work went into it. I'm afraid I embarrassed Marie in front of the class."

"I was just unprepared for your visit," stammered Marie self-consciously.

"I heard the plane come in and assumed it was for the Hudson Bay Company. Bright Star will be delighted that you're staying for a while."

"I hope I'm not assuming too much."

"Scott," answered Steve seriously, "you'll always be welcome in our home, and I know I speak for Bright Star, too. As you can imagine, Marie has been a blessing to us and to the children. They've responded splendidly to her way of doing things. She's been able to pass on her love of literature and learning to the students in her class. She is, without question, the most respected person associated with the school."

"Now, now, Steve," interrupted Marie. "Let's not get carried away. Would you take over the class for the rest of the afternoon?"

"I'll be glad to take care of the kids. You two have a lot to catch up on. When you go out, send the class in. Enjoy the rest of the day. I'll see you at our cabin this evening for a celebration of your return."

"Thanks, Steve," said Scott, linking his arm with Marie's. On her way out, she picked up a jacket, for the air was damp and cool. The students watched Marie and Scott with curious interest, but they singled out Scott for the most intense scrutiny. He was a well built man with broad shoulders and an easy walk that projected an image of strength and confidence. His uniform fitted his physique and contributed to an air of invincibility. The young men watched with awe while the young girls shyly watched with envious eyes and adolescent coquettishness.

"Right now, you're probably being checked out as thoroughly as you've ever been in your life," laughed Marie softly. "Come, let's walk along the lake. The villagers made a walkway between the lake and the buildings of the village, so that I could walk and exercise with confidence. As you can see they placed stakes and threaded a rope along the path."

"It's amazing," remarked Scott when he saw the evenly spaced stakes holding a sturdy rope railing along the length of the pathway which extended for a mile or more. She guided him unerringly to the beginning of the walkway. "Are you warm enough? It's getting cool up here already."

"Yes, I'm fine, Scott. All of the weeks that we've been apart, I've stored up things I wanted to say to you when we were together again. Now that you're here, my mind has gone blank, but it's so wonderful being with you. I was afraid of the possibility that you might change your mind."

"That will never be, Marie," said Scott, placing a finger against her lips. "I have something for you, Marie. It comes with a message from my heart, and it should answer any doubts you may have about us."

Scott reached into his pocket while he raised her left hand, kissed it and carefully placed a ring on her ring finger. "This engagement ring is a symbol of my love for you. It was given to my mother by my father. She saw how much you meant to me, and she insisted that I take the ring. She believes the ring has the power to protect our love, and I want you to know that it represents my commitment to you and to the future, together."

Marie's heart soared with joy. She caressed the ring on her finger and buried herself in Scott's arms, softly crying, unable to describe the love that filled her heart. It was a time when words were not enough, so they let their hearts speak to one another with a silence filled with expectations and promises for tomorrow.

The cool breeze blowing across the lake carried the promise of winter, but Scott and Marie shut out the rest of the world and made their vows to each other. By facing tomorrow together, they were confident that there would be a future where their dreams would become a reality. Love had propelled them into a new world of unlimited possibilities. It was a magic moment that both of them would cherish forever.

Later, Scott and Marie enjoyed a pleasant evening with Bright Star and Steve. Bright Cloud and Mark had recently returned to their home in Maine. Scott was hoping that he'd have a chance to see them. Bright Star said that her mother and father were anticipating a trip to Europe. For years, Mark nurtured a strong desire to return to the location where Flying Eagle was killed. Bright Star and her mother questioned the wisdom of such a trip because they were afraid it might have a harmful effect on Mark. He argued that it would give him a chance to put that painful episode in his life to rest.

"I've been wondering what you thought about revisiting old sites filled with strong memories, Scott?" asked Bright Star. "If my father went to Europe, I know that we would not be able to stop him from visiting the area where Daniel-Joseph was killed."

Scott thought about the proposal for several seconds, for he had wondered if such a visit would be beneficial for his own peace of mind. "That's a question I can't answer, Bright Star. I know that some people have found meaningful understanding by such visits, and I know of cases where it brought old ghosts and unanswered questions back to their consciousness, making a resolution of the situation that much more painful and still in doubt."

"I'm not sure if I would want to see the place where DJ was killed," said Bright Star with a sad reflective look in her eyes.

"Colonel Leroux talked a lot about the proposed trip. The last few days they were here, it was very much on his mind. I had the feeling it was a trip that he had to make, maybe as much for things left unspoken as anything else," mentioned Steve. "He still carries a burden of guilt about Flying Eagle's death. I personally think that he should go. Bright Cloud will support him and bring a level of stability to the experience. He mentioned a desire to make the trip this fall before heavy winter weather sets in."

"If they did go to the area where DJ was killed, they will find that a lot of things have changed," said Scott. "I wish that I could be with them to explain the conditions that existed at that time and place. I remember it, for a lot of reasons, as if it was yesterday."

Marie detected a hesitation and a sadness in Scott's voice that she had not heard before. She was sure he was also thinking about Arnold's death. She reached for his hand beneath the table to reassure him and offer him a silent expression of support. It was cold and moist. Marie could understood what was going through his mind and said: "I'm not sure that revisiting old ghosts are in any person's best interests, but if it allows that person to reach an accommodation or an understanding at which they can live with the memories, then I think it's something that should be done as soon as possible."

"I think you're right, Marie," exclaimed Scott, anxious to change the subject. "Now, on a more cheerful note, I have an announcement to make. When I graduated from the War College, I was promoted to the rank of Major. My classmates gave me these gold leaves and I've waited until now so that Marie could pin them on me."

"I'm so proud of you, Scott," exclaimed Marie, her voice filled with admiration. She accepted the two gold insignias from Scott and quickly secured them to his epaulettes in place of the Captain bars she removed.

It was a happy occasion for everybody. Bright Star and Steve proposed a toast from a bottle of fine wine they had been saving for a suitable occasion. Bright Star filled fresh glasses with the red wine and looked towards Steve to make the toast. He pushed his chair away from the table and raised the glass in his right hand.

"I propose a toast to Major Scott Taylor, a fine friend who has made us all proud; and to his new fiancee, Marie Poole, who has also made us proud and thankful for her friendship; and, finally, I propose a toast for the future of these two extraordinary people together. They've graced our lives with their presence. For that, may our benevolent God look down on them and grant them peace and contentment and long life together."

The evening passed quickly for the celebrants. It was a milestone day for Marie and Scott. He did not want anything to dampen the festive mood and camaraderie that filled the cabin, but there were some conditions that went with the promotion that had to be faced. A new promotion meant a new set of responsibilities and a new tour of duty. Scott announced the news just before they broke up the gathering.

"My new promotion means I've been assigned to a battalion as an executive officer," announced Scott, watching Marie for her reaction. "The position as second in command of a battalion is like a dream come true. The only drawback to the assignment is that it's in China, where the battalion is part of a regiment that is helping to keep the peace in Formosa."

Marie heard the words Scott spoke and an exquisite sadness displaced the joy from her heart. "Does that mean that you'll be away for a long time?" she questioned, unable to hide her disappointment with the news.

Steve and Bright Star looked inquiringly at Scott, for they understood how Marie must feel about the separation. Steve, more so than Bright Star, understood the multitude of implications that accompanied such a relocation. He had seen how difficult it was on military families, and was aware of the stress that prolonged absence placed on relationships. It was a sacrifice that all soldiers and their families made in the defense of their nation's freedom.

"I understand what's going through your thoughts, Marie," Scott tried to explain. "I'm not happy about being so far away from you either, but I'm a soldier and I took an oath to do my duty. I realize it's not going to be easy. It won't be forever. I really had no choice in selecting my next duty station."

"Oh, my dear Scott, please don't think you have to apologize for doing your duty," cried Marie firmly grasping his arm. She could not read the expression on his face, but she could read what was in his heart. She spoke passionately from her own heart. "I'm so proud of who you are and what you are. Whatever comes along we'll handle it and adapt to it. My first reaction to your duty in China was a selfish one. I only thought of myself, and I apologize for that. I treasure the words you spoke to me when I was thinking of coming here to Fort Lewis. Do you remember?"

"I think so..."

"You said 'Whatever you decide to do, I'll support your decision'. Those words gave me the courage to reach out and grab the challenge offered to me. I want you to know that I support whatever or wherever your duty takes you. My heart and my love will be at your side."

"I've never been prouder of you than I am right now, Marie," said Scott, putting an arm around her shoulders and kissing her on her temple.

Memories of this night helped Scott and Marie maintain their lonely vigil of the months ahead, when they were separated by thousands of miles. Scott left Fort Lewis three days later. It was a sad parting. They had declared their love for each other and planned a future together; yet, the idea of being separated for any amount of time was painful to both of them. Marie was fortified by the demands placed upon her by the teaching position at Eagle Nest and by the love she shared with Scott. She attacked the challenge with her usual determination. Whenever she had any doubts about tomorrow, the ring on her finger warmed her soul and strengthened her resolve to persevere.

Soon after Scott's departure, the Canadian winter swept down and engulfed the tiny hamlet of Fort Lewis in its cold grip. The wind blew and screamed incessantly across the landscape. The placid waters of Lac Diamante were turned into a frenzy of white caps in random rills across its full length. Within a day the water was frozen in permanent furrows. There was something in the air that struck a melancholic chord in Marie's heart. The first announcement of winter's coming was emotional as much as it was physical, and she warmed her heart with more frequent thoughts of Scott. The colors of fall were rapidly wiped out by the howling fury of the north wind. Before long, the area was locked in a thick blanket of white snow and pervading cold.

Chapter Thirteen

When Scott heard that DJ's parents were going ahead with their proposed trip to Europe, a feeling of uneasiness came over him that he could not get rid of. He knew it would not be an easy journey for them, and he felt guilty and responsible for their having to make the trip in the first place.

A small charter plane carried Scott from Lac St. Jean to Quebec City airport where he would be able to get a commercial flight to anywhere in the world. By the time he arrived at Quebec a plan was beginning to form in the back of his mind. It had a lot of conditions attached to it; but nevertheless, it was starting to come together. First he had to determine the itinerary of the Leroux family, so he immediately headed for a phone booth to call them.

"Hello," answered Bright Cloud.

"Mrs. Leroux, this is Scott Taylor. I just returned from Fort Lewis. I'm on my way to California where my battalion is at a staging area preparing for duty in China. I wanted to check with you and Colonel Leroux before you left for Europe."

"How pleasant it is to hear from you again, Captain Taylor. Mark and I were just talking about you, and here you are on the phone. We plan to leave in a day or two for Paris."

"I understand, Mrs. Leroux. We don't have much time, so I'm going to be direct. I'm only speculating at this time, but it may be possible for me to obtain permission from my superior officer to postpone my orders to the battalion if I explain my reason for the delay. If I can get permission, I'm prepared to accompany you to Europe if you think my presence will help."

"Oh, Captain Taylor," exclaimed Bright Cloud. "We were just thinking that the trip would be much easier if someone else was with us. We'd always planned to make it with Inspector Clough, and possibly with Bright Star and Steve. If it's possible for you to rearrange your orders, we would both be relieved and pleased to have you come along."

"It's my pleasure, Mrs. Leroux. What airport are you scheduled to fly from?"

"We're booked on a TWA flight from Boston to Paris. They gave us a choice of either tomorrow or the day after. We can make it on either of the days, so you select the one which better connects with your plans. I hope your battalion commander approves your request."

"Let me get back to you as soon as I have something definite to report. Be patient, I may have trouble getting through to the battalion command center," requested Scott.

"I'll tell Mark. He'll be glad to hear the news. Thank you, Captain Taylor."

Getting a line to California from Quebec was not easy. Eventually, Scott was connected to the communication center at the Presidio, where he was routed to the temporary command post of his battalion. Scott explained to the Battalion Commander, Lieutenant Colonel Friedricks, the reason for his call. Without hesitation Colonel Friedricks gave his permission for the change in Scott's orders, reminding him that the battalion was scheduled to ship out in a month. That would give him enough time to report to California before they moved out.

"Incidentally, Major Taylor," added Colonel Friedricks. "I have a close friend, a Captain Meyers, the Public Information Officer for Army units in the European theater of operations. He's stationed at Paris. Contact him when you get there and tell him your situation. He owes me a few favors, so you can let him know that helping you out would go a long ways in paying me back. I'll send your revised orders to you via Paris command center, they should be there by the time you touch down in Paris. Good luck, Major, give my best to the Leroux family."

"Thanks, Colonel," answered Scott with a smile. He had a feeling he was going to like his new Commander. "I'll report to you within a month, Sir."

Scott then called Wells again. This time Mark answered the phone. "Colonel Leroux, this is Scott Taylor."

"Scott, I can't tell you how much we appreciate what you're doing."

"I have a favor to ask of you, Sir," mentioned Scott reluctantly.

"We're at your service, Scott."

"I bring good news, Sir. My orders have been altered so that I can accompany you and Mrs. Leroux to Europe. I'm embarrassed to ask this; but, I did not bring enough money with me for a trip to Europe. So could I depend on you to purchase a ticket for me? I'll pay you back as soon as I get to my next duty station."

"Of course we can do that. I understand your predicament completely. I've been there myself many times, and don't you dare think of paying us back," answered Mark with a firm tone.

"I have one other request to make of you, Sir. Could you and your wife be at the airport tomorrow morning? I'll be waiting there."

"We'll be there, Scott. The closer we got to the time of departure for our trip, the more I was dreading it. Now that you're going with us, I feel better. We thank you."

"I'll see you tomorrow in Boston."

"We'll be there."

Twenty-four hours later Mark, Bright Cloud, and Scott were sitting in the Captain Meyer's PIO office in Paris. A car and driver were made available for as long as they required. He offered to reserve lodgings along the routes, but Scott preferred that they make their own selections. Mark and Bright Cloud were unprepared for the preferential treatment provided them, but they were quick to acknowledge that it helped them focus on the main purpose of their trip.

Their first night in Paris was uneventful. Mark and Bright Cloud cultivated their own private thoughts about the reasons for making the trip, and the significance that they attached to the actual area where their son was killed in action.

The French countryside was ravaged twice within three decades by invasions. Both of the wars saw massive destruction and loss of lives. The French people were filled with hatred for the savage outrages perpetrated against them. This was accompanied by an uncompromising affection for the American soldier, who was instrumental in evicting the oppressive Germans from French soil in both of the World Wars. The admiration for Americans continued to grow, when the French people realized that the sacrifice of American blood on their behalf was freely given without asking for anything in return. The French people took them into their hearts with a warm "Merci".

When Mark fought with the Second Division in 1918, the battlefields were filled with deep foul-smelling trenches where men could find some shelter from the continuous rain of bursting shells in the no-man's land between the opposing trenches. The terrain was generally pockmarked by artillery explosions that destroyed everything attached to the land. Buildings, bridges and people were pulverized in a cataclysmic plowing of the areas over and over again until there was nothing left except dust and a glue-like mud that stuck to everything, especially after a rain. After the Armistice, the land began to heal itself.

Bright Cloud and Mark were quieter than usual as they left Paris the next morning. Mark wore warm casual clothes for the trip, with the Medal of Honor ribbon on his chest. He thought of wearing his uniform, but decided against it because he did not like to draw attention to his wounds. Bright Cloud wore a black dress with a white lace collar. Her black hair, laced with strands of white, fell loose about her shoulders. She wore a red ribbon in her hair with one of DJ's lieutenant bars pinned on it. She was a beautiful woman who carried herself proudly, radiating an air of warmth and confidence.

They traveled northeast of Paris towards the location where the Germans made their last attempt to capture Paris during the First World War. Verdun, St. Mihiel, and Belleau are names of places forever linked to the bitter exchange between the Germans and the newly arrived American doughboys, who had the audacity to stand before the German onslaught and ultimately reverse the attack.

The picturesque towns of northern France that were lucky enough to escape damage from the war stood in stark contrast to the ones that were bombed or the scene of a battle. The clean whitewashed structures with their red tile roofs were neat and orderly, presenting a warm, inviting picture to the travelers. Villages that had been fought over were still in a sorry state of repair, stark reminders of the destructive nature of wars.

Mark had a feeling of de-ja vu as he watched the landscape pass by. His thoughts spanned backward thirty years to a time when he saw combat for the first time. He remembered the sharp crackle of small arms fire and the ear-splitting thunder of artillery which never stopped. The sounds of the battlefield were accompanied with the stench of the rat-infested trenches that ran for miles like giant mole trails running haphazardly over the landscape.

Bright Cloud knew what Mark was thinking. He always had that determined set to his jaw when he was upset by things he had no way of controlling. She knew, perhaps more than Mark himself, just how much he had suffered these past thirty years. If it had been in her power, she would have taken him into her arms, years ago, and erased all the horror that tormented him. Of course it was impossible, so she settled for second best, making sure she was at his side when he needed her the most. This trip was necessary for him, and she prayed that her gentle Mark would be able to derive some comfort from it.

Scott also appreciated what Mark was going through. No one talked much after they left Paris. Somehow small talk seemed out of place between them. He could feel the intensity of the emotions that filled the car. Scott glanced in the rear view mirror and saw Bright Cloud holding Mark's arm. He quickly turned his eyes away, not wanting to violate a private time for the two of them, and prayed that he and Marie could have the same kind of love for each other. As the driver turned left onto a road marked by a signpost for Bouresches and Vaux, Mark straightened up in his seat and asked the driver to pull over. On their right was a large rambling set of buildings on a small hill overlooking the valley between the road and the structure.

They were traveling on the Metz-Paris highway towards the small town of Bouresches.

"Those buildings," cried Mark with excitement. "Those buildings are the monastery where I was first hospitalized. I stayed there for several weeks at the end of the war."

The driveway leading across the valley had not been used for a long time, so the driver slowly followed the old wheel tracks meandering around several of the out buildings, ending at a cul-de-sac near the center of the main structure. A large entrance pavilion occupied the center with a wide terrace extended all the way around the ruins. It had been abandoned for a long time. Parts of the roof were sagging and the terrace had several years accumulation of leaves scattered around its floor.

Mark knew where he was. "I remember sitting in the chairs that used to line the full length of the terrace. It was crowded with wounded soldiers then. It seems deserted now."

Scott stepped out of the car and walked out on the terrace. He noticed that the building had been hit with a bomb or artillery fire. The damage was not visible from the road or driveway. He held back from Mark and Bright Cloud.

They slowly walked out to the center of the terrace and stood in silence looking across the valley as if they were in search of the young man he used to be. Mark was transported to a time in his life when the world, as he knew it then, came crashing down on him. He released Bright Cloud's hand and walked toward the rear of the terrace. Bright Cloud, sensing his need to be alone, joined Scott at the other end of the terrace.

"The greatest burden that my gentle Mark has had to carry is his experience with 'shell shock'. Today it's called battle fatigue. He's been ashamed of the incident all these years, even though he doesn't talk much about it. I've tried to explain to him that his performance on New Britain should cancel out his self-inflicted condemnation of his performance in the First War. He's proud of the Medal of Honor, but he feels that it was his responsibility to save his men from certain destruction on the beachhead. Any good commander would have done the same thing, he claims."

"But the fact remains that Colonel Leroux saw what was happening and acted, without any thought of himself," said Scott firmly.

"I'm certainly not an expert on the subject of battle-fatigue," Bright Cloud continued: "but I believe that early in his manhood he saw too much death and destruction and it reached the point where some mechanism in the brain simply pulled the plug to wipe out the pain. This is the place where he was taken immediately after he collapsed. They helped him here so that he could eventually return to duty, but the stigma followed him and was instrumental in his resignation from the Marine Corps. Later, he was able to find a workable balance between military service and civilian life by joining the Reserves until the war came along. You've heard what happened after that. You know, Scott, I've seen, on occasion, the same look in your eyes that I used to see in Mark's. When I think of the unspeakable horrors that all of our young men in uniform have been subjected to in the defense of our country, my heart cries out to never let it happen again."

"Wearing the uniform has its rewards, Mrs. Leroux. Your husband and your son understood that, too. I believe it's a noble profession, and is worthy of the people's respect and admiration," commented Scott, accepting Bright Cloud's firm grip on his arm and looked out across the agrarian countryside hoping to see what Mark was looking for. Mark stood silent and erect as a statue for a long time.

"I've always known that Mark would have to revisit this part of his past," she said in a soft voice.

"I understand the significance of that journey, Mrs. Leroux. Your husband is not alone. Every combat leader carries a burden that never leaves them. I continue to question my own ability to command troops," confessed Scott, surprised at his candor.

Bright Cloud clung to Scott's arm looking up at his face. He reminded her of Daniel-Joseph. She was thankful that her son had the good fortune to serve under such a compassionate commander. He has the same qualities that made her Mark so special — he carried all of his men's pain as well as his own. At some point, Bright Cloud thought to herself, there was a distinct possibility that the load may become too heavy for him.

Mark continued to stare at the hills across the valley towards Bouresches. Being here on the terrace where he had to struggle for his sanity, was a strange experience for him. Looking back at the person he was at the war's end was like looking at a stranger. Had he really changed or was he just an older version of the young soldier who had contemplated throwing himself off this same terrace?

He remembered that when he first arrived at the monastery hospital, the sound of guns was a constant companion of the long days and nights. The Germans had made the Americans pay dearly for their success in keeping them from reaching Paris. Now, the countryside was peaceful and quiet. A small pond on the grounds of the monastery was covered with the fallen leaves of autumn. The barren trees now stood naked to the world patiently waiting for their rebirth in the spring. Mark had felt the same way as the trees. His confidence and sense of purpose had been taken away from him, and he resented showing his incomplete and inadequate self to the world.

After the Armistice was signed, his determination to find himself again became more evident. He clearly remembered the simple incident that was a turning point in his recovery. A small flock of sparrows had lit on the stone floor of the terrace to eat the bread crumbs placed there by the patients. The distant guns were silent. It was a strange feeling for Mark and the other patients to be able to hear themselves breathe and to actually hear the singing of birds. The chirping of the sparrows ignited a memory in Mark's head. It was the first time since he was introduced to combat, that he could recall the peaceful setting of his home in Maine.

Towering pine trees were a part of his upbringing. He could almost smell the sweet odor of pine pitch and hear the soft whisper of the wind filtering through the pine needles, but the sounds he had almost forgotten were the soothing sounds of sparrows, robins, juncos, and cardinals. It had been a long time since he had heard their songs. They were a part of his happy childhood, and for the first time since he was carried to the monastery, small gentle sparrows allowed him to reach back and recall a happier time at his beloved home on the Maine coast. After thirty long years, he could still hear the singing of the sparrows on the floor of the terrace.

Scott and Bright Cloud watched Mark for any sign that they might be needed. Bright Cloud held her breath when she saw him turn around looking for her. She saw a look of fulfillment and peace that had eluded him for a long, long time. He held out his right hand to her. She rushed to him.

"This place restored my sanity," Mark cried softly in Bright Cloud's ear. "Even though we could still hear the guns, this place was far away from the trenches to the north. I didn't know how desperately I needed to make this trip until I stood on the terrace and looked backward to see how far we've come. I love you, Bright Cloud."

The three of them walked around the crumbling ruins of the monastery. Mark described how it was when he was there. He admitted to Bright Cloud that he had been infatuated by one of the nurses who worked there. Every man in the place was in love with her. He could not remember her name, but at the time, it was an important step in his recovery.

Mark looked back at the ruins one last time as the driver turned out of the driveway and headed north toward Bouresches. The heavily forested area known as Belleau Woods was on their left. It was the place where the Marine Brigade, attached to the Army's Second Division, drove the Germans out of the forest and occupied the area. The Germans never regained the initiative after that battle.

The road north of Bouresches looked unfamiliar to Mark until they came to a series of rolling hills northeast of the road leading to the town of Belleau. A small pond created by the construction of an earth dam built between two of the hills, caught Mark's eye and he asked the driver to slow down. It was an agricultural pond of ten to fifteen acres in size. He recognized it as the one near where Flying Eagle was killed. The driver stopped at the edge of the road while Mark studied the area.

He could remember the day that Flying Eagle was killed with a clarity reserved for few events in his lifetime. It was a day similar to today, cool and sunny with white puffs of cirrus clouds dotting the sky, and a light breeze blowing from the northeast. The three hills to the east were in German territory. Mark had organized a patrol, led by himself, to scout the enemy lines. They needed intelligence, and he warned his men not to provoke a fight, but they ran into a German patrol in the dark and a fight erupted. At the very beginning of the exchange, Mark was stunned by a bullet striking his helmet, leaving him unconscious in the middle of a battlefield. The next thing he remembered was being surrounded by German soldiers looking for him. He emptied his automatic at the dark figures. Suddenly out of the darkness Flying Eagle attacked the German's with a rifle, a bayonet and his bare hands until they fled. Mark was still disoriented in the darkness, but Flying Eagle guided him to safety.

By the time Mark had finished a warm cup of coffee, the sun introduced a new day. The welcome sun was accompanied by the terrifying warning of a gas attack. A green cloud hung above the trenches. The quickness of the soldiers to pull on their gas masks determined the difference between life or death. Mark was successful in fastening his, but Flying Eagle had lingered a fraction of a second longer.

The memory of Flying Eagle coughing and staggering from the deadly mist swirling around him was still fresh in Mark's memory. He screamed for him to hurry up, but his efforts were in vain. Before Mark could take a step to help Flying Eagle, a German mortar shell made a direct hit on him. He disintegrated in front of Mark. The grotesque image of Flying Eagle being torn to pieces was his last conscious recollection of the war. A blackness overwhelmed him and he dropped into the putrid mud at the bottom of the trench.

Mark walked ahead of Scott and Bright Cloud along the road with his eyes sweeping a steep hill to the north and the areas between the hill and the pond. Satisfied with his orientation, he made his way through some thickets towards the pond. The old trench line was positioned so that it terminated on the western edge of the pond. That way the pond helped to protect their right flank. The wet areas around the pond had reverted back to trees while the drier sections had recently been used for hay and silage. Mark's eyes scoured the terrain for any sign of the trench that was filled in years ago. He was elated when he noticed a slight depression along a contour that ended at the pond.

"Bright Cloud, this is the spot where Flying Eagle was hit." Mark pointed to a small trough in the field.

She always wondered what it would be like for her when she saw this place, and now she was profoundly surprised to experience a feeling of peace instead of sadness and grief. It was as if Flying Eagle's spirit was trying to tell them to mourn no longer for his death. Mark felt the same, free of the burden he had harbored for so many years. It was a comforting discovery.

Mark and Bright Cloud kneeled on the soft ground of the hayfield and prayed for Flying Eagle and for themselves.

Bright Cloud voiced what was in her heart with a sad smile of longing framed by tears flowing down her bronze cheeks. "My dearest Flying Eagle, time has not diminished my memories of you and I as we grew into adulthood on the banks of Lac Diamante. Your daughter, Bright Star, has been a blessing for Mark and me. You would be proud of her. Wherever you are, dear brother, may you rest in peace and be assured that your memory and the legacy of your love for your people continues to be one of our most treasured possessions."

As soon as Bright Cloud finished the prayer, a bright ray of sunlight shone through the clouds with a warm glow of light, until the clouds slowly eclipsed the sun. Scott knew that something had taken place, and he felt the presence of a dynamic force, leaving all of them transfixed.

The driver who had stayed with the car, picked up a thermos of coffee and walked toward the others. The day was not cold, but when the sun was not shining, the breeze was cool. The hot coffee was welcome. They stood quietly in the field reflecting on the sign and the moment. Mark and Bright Cloud were able to say good-bye with a long final glance at the clover field.

By mid-day they had traveled almost one hundred miles to the north in the Ardennes region of Belgium and Luxembourg. They stopped for lunch at the town of Bastogne, made famous by the 101st Division and their gallant refusal to surrender. The town was an important transportation center for the outlying regions in the Ardennes, and the doughty paratroopers were not inclined to let the Germans have it.

The Belgium people still remembered the sacrifices of the young American soldiers who stopped the last gigantic effort of the German Army to push through the Ardennes towards Antwerp, which contained a rich stockpile of supplies. The Germans hoped that they could drive to the coast and cut the Allied armies in two. It was a valid plan that might have worked, except the German Staff failed to take into account the ability of the American soldier to adapt himself to changing situations, and they arrogantly underrated the courage and skill of the American infantryman.

The owners of the small café where they ate lunch made every effort to make their meal a pleasant one. Scott and the driver were in uniform so they were recipients of gifts of wine and cigars and cream-filled sweet rolls, which they good-naturedly accepted. The owner of the café would not allow the party to pay for their lunch. As they were leaving, the owner said, "You have paid enough and we thank you for coming."

Back on the road Scott tried to describe the Battle of the Bulge, which took place in the area they were traveling. The Battle was a series of disconnected actions, some large, some small. Those units that were prepared for the onslaught fared relatively well, while others caught by surprise and without adequate supplies were overwhelmed.

Scott told the story of his Second Division with pride. The battalions of the Division were in the midst of an assault phase towards the German border when the German offensive ran into them. The Second frantically tried to rush men and equipment to the east so that the battalions in the vanguard could be reinforced to hold their ground. Scott's company had actually penetrated the German border when they were struck with massive concentrations of armor and artillery. Allied intelligence had failed to alert them to the surprise German offensive. A vicious battle for survival prevailed for the next several days.

The front was a road known as "Skyline Drive" running north-south along the scenic mountain heights. When they left Bastogne an hour earlier, they took the scenic route northward towards a small landmark called Elsenborn Ridge, which dominates the valley to the north and to the south. It was there that one of the most violent battles of the war took place, involving Scott's battalion and elements of the Ninety Ninth Division. Elsenborn was half way along the Skyline drive between Monschau and Malmedy. Several German Panzer Divisions were assigned the task of securing the road net connecting the two towns. They soon found out how tenacious the American soldier could be!

Scott asked the driver to turn onto a secondary road leading to the now famous ridge. The view was breathtaking and panoramic. Scott pointed out where his company command post was located.

"I've already told you how DJ was killed. If you'll follow me I'll try to reconstruct what took place on the ground. We'd been advancing ever since Normandy. I believe we were the first troops to set foot on German soil. When the Germans attacked, we pulled back to this ridge. If we could hold the northern shoulder, then we could deny the Germans the use of the road network that radiated from Malmedy and Monschau. I had already assigned a mortar section to DJ's platoon because he was extremely resourceful in positioning them where they could be most effective. He had a good eye for terrain and distance."

Mark and Bright Cloud listened closely so that they would not miss a word Scott was saying. Mark nodded in agreement about the positioning of mortar fire. It was what he would have expected from his son.

"DJ's platoon was responsible for this section of the ridge. Over the edge here towards the east, he sent out a small patrol to verify German positions so that he could establish his outposts to the best advantage for the night. The patrol got caught up in a fight that lasted for ten minutes or so. When they returned to the ridge, two men were unaccounted for and DJ went out to find them. He found one man dead, because he had the soldier's dog tag in his pocket. Evidently the other man had been wounded. They headed back up the slope when they were spotted by an enemy patrol. DJ and the wounded man were both killed in that exchange. By daybreak, I decided to expand our perimeter enough to retrieve their bodies.

"We found all three bodies where they fell. DJ had several wounds to the chest and stomach. We concluded that he died fighting. His carbine was empty and still in his hands when we found him. He was a courageous soldier and he was mourned by all of us who knew him. He was your son, but he was one of my responsibilities and I grieve his loss, too."

Mark took in every word and studied the landscape with a trained eye for detail as if he could see what DJ had been up against, wanting to learn everything he could about the circumstances surrounding his son's death. One thing that Mark was concerned about was the possibility that his son's death had been in vain. After looking over the terrain and hearing Scott's words, he was proud of the achievements of his son's unit. Their steadfastness had made a big difference by upsetting the timetable of the German's advance. It must have been one vicious battle, Mark thought to himself.

Bright Cloud and Mark had reconciled themselves to Daniel-Joseph's death. Standing on the scenic ridge where he was killed was difficult; but at the same time, a release of the nagging uncertainties made it easier to accept. Both of them reached out to comfort Scott. Mark's heart went out to the young major, for he knew how tormenting the visions of war could be to those who survived it and were destined to relive the nightmares.

Later, back in Paris, where they enjoyed a view of the Seine from their hotel room, Scott said his good-byes. They had concluded an eventful visit to the past that miraculously left each of them in a reflective mood. Scott was anxious to return to his battalion and get it ready for duty in Asia.

173

Mark and Bright Cloud decided to extend their visit so that they could enjoy Paris. It could be a celebration of his liberation from the ghosts of the past. For years Mark had the feeling that his experiences in France during the war had in some way affected his marriage to Bright Cloud. He could never define just how, but he was always conscious of it. He kept the thoughts to himself, for he knew that when a person insists on dwelling on the past or lives within the shadow of the past, they are in danger of losing the present. The thought of losing any part of his life with Bright Cloud made him vow to accept the past and never look backward again, for their joy was to share as many tomorrows as their destiny allowed.

Chapter Fourteen

Marie wrote to Scott every day. The mail pouch left the village on the average of twice a week in the dead of winter when heavy snows and low temperatures gripped the region. She eagerly listened to the daily wireless radio broadcasts of news from around the world. She knew that Scott was stationed in Formosa and that the war on the China mainland was not going well for the Chinese Nationalists. All of Asia seemed to be building for some unforeseen eruption of violence that Marie feared could involve Scott's battalion.

Scott continued to write her as often as his busy schedule allowed. The gaps in his letters reinforced her worst fears that something was going wrong. He tried to reassure her that he was never in danger, but it failed to quiet her active imagination. She was not certain that he was still on Formosa, which was absorbing all of the retreating troops of the Chinese Nationalist's Army, making the island their last bulwark of defense against the Communist forces.

Marie had lived all her life in northern Maine where the winters were often severe, so she was confident that she could handle the winters at Fort Lewis, but she was unprepared for the severity of the winter storms that raged in the Canadian North Country. The life threatening dangers of temperatures that dropped to thirty degrees below zero for days and weeks at a time were unthinkable to her. By the time warmer weather arrived in the spring, she was ready to take a break from her teaching chores.

After the first year at Eagle Nest, Marie returned to Monson. She was exhausted and felt the need to relax. Her parents saw a weary, but highly motivated Marie return to them. The challenges of the wilderness school were demanding, but it had fulfilled her dreams of being able to teach, even though she was blind. The prospect of a future with Scott was never far from her thoughts, but until that time came, she was thankful for the work at Fort Lewis. The months slowly passed by and turned into another year. Marie and Scott maintained their correspondence with each other, but the long separation left an empty longing that grew as the absence endured.

A welcome event took place during the long cold winter of 1948-1949. Scott was able to get a short leave from the battalion when he was ordered to Washington for a debriefing by Army historical researchers about his experiences in World War II. His battalion commander gave him a few extra days to make a trip to Fort Lewis for a visit with Marie. His first unscheduled visit in winter time broke up the monotony of the routine at the Eagle Nest.

They spent the time alone with each other, and the weather cooperated so that they could take long snowshoe walks around the lake.

On one of the trips, Scott collected dry wood and built a fire to warm them and to toast the sandwiches Bright Star had made. Scott watched Marie as she sat on a log listening to the hiss and snap of the bristling fire at their feet. She was radiantly beautiful and at peace with herself. The brisk temperatures of the north brought a flush to her cheeks. He pulled her closer to him and kissed her softly on the mouth. She wrapped her arms around his head and reassured herself that he was really beside her by carefully running her fingers over his face.

"I have a surprise for you, Marie," he whispered in her ear.

"Having you here beside me is enough surprise for me. I missed you, Scott, and I worried about your safety," she admitted seriously, then smiled holding him at arms length. "Now, what's the surprise?"

"I've just been promoted to Lieutenant Colonel, and given command of the old battalion," proclaimed Scott proudly.

"Oh, I'm so proud of you. I knew it was only a question of time before the Army recognized my fiancee's abilities."

"I have a pair of silver leaves here for you to pin on my shoulders as soon as we get back to the cabin and take off this heavy parka," said Scott, throwing another piece of wood on the hot bed of coals. Marie was pleased about the promotion, certain that he deserved it, but there was something about the announcement that left her uneasy. She quickly spoke what was on her mind.

"Does this promotion mean any changes in your duty status or.."

"Not really," interrupted Scott anticipating her reaction to the news. "The battalion is being transferred from Formosa to Japan where it'll join up with two other battalions to complete the formation of the regiment. Don't worry dear, we're going to be posted to easy occupation duty in Japan for a while. As soon as I return, I'll look into the possibilities of finding quarters for us in Japan. Will you marry me then?"

Marie searched for an appropriate answer. She cried out and buried her face against Scott's chest. "You know I will. I love you, Scott, and I'll never be complete until we're together. Yes, yes, yes… I'll work hard to be a good wife. I'd have to know in advance so that I could help Steve find a suitable replacement for me."

"Are you willing to give it up, Marie?" asked Scott guardedly. He had given the situation a lot of thought, realizing that he was asking her to give up something very important to her. He was somewhat uneasy with the fact that he was giving up nothing, while she was being asked to make the sacrifice.

"Yes," answered Marie quickly. "My life will be centered around you, Scott. Wherever you go, I'll go also. I'll miss Eagle Nest and the people and the students that I've come to love and admire, but to everything in life, there comes a time when change is necessary. I can make that adjustment because my heart is with you."

"The short time we've spent together since you started to teach here at Fort Lewis has been special and important to me. I've worried about you way out in this isolated village, but you've handled it like a trooper. You've made me very proud. I'm a lucky man. I love you for your generosity and your willingness to accept changes so that we can be together. I'll work hard at being worthy of your love," he vowed.

"I'm the lucky one," cried Marie, holding him close.

Early the next day, Steve's ski-equipped plane circled the lake after take-off and set a course due south. Scott watched Marie wave towards the sound of the plane's engine. She cast a dark shadow against a vast sea of white snow. She looked so alone and vulnerable. Scott saw another person walking rapidly towards Marie. It was Bright Star. The last impression he had of them before they disappeared from view was Bright Star comforting Marie in her arms.

"I can understand that this parting is difficult," said Bright Star, gently guiding Marie back to the school. "But you now have the promise of a future with Scott, and you can dream all you want about that wonderful time. We're all so happy for the two of you."

"Thanks, Bright Star," answered Marie, wiping her eyes. "I know that I'm over-reacting, but I do love him more than anything else in the world. I hope God keeps him safe." The two women walked arm in arm towards the schoolhouse, kicking up a dust of light snow that had fallen the night before.

Four days later, Scott reported to the battalion command post. It was stationed on the northernmost island of Hokkaido in the small town of Sapporo near the Sea of Japan. The Far East Army Command under General Douglas MacArthur was located in Tokyo about seven hundred miles to the south. As soon as Scott got settled into his new quarters on the Army base, he wrote a letter to Marie.

Sapporo, Japan
January 5, 1949

My darling Marie,

A few lines to let you know that I'm here with the battalion. The return trip went off without a hitch. I thought of you and the future all the way here. It will be like a dream come true to soon have you with me.

The battalion made the move from Formosa while I was away. The men are looking forward to an easy life doing occupation duty. I plan to disabuse them of their notions when I announce my revised training schedule. I probably won't be very popular with the men, because I'm going to work their butts off so that they don't lose any of their skills. After a while, they'll be anxious to do anything except more training drills and exercises. They'll actually look forward to combat as a substitute for the training routines. If that time ever comes, I'm one commander who is not going to have his men be unprepared for the rigors of combat. We all hope it never becomes a reality, but regardless of the recruiting sales pitches to the contrary, defending Americans and America's ideals is what a soldier does, and the only way that can be accomplished is by being ready to the best of our ability.

The parts of Japan that I traveled through are in bad shape. Many of the cities have been completely destroyed by the bombing raids. Some rebuilding has started already, but it's woefully inadequate compared to what needs to be done. The Japanese are an industrious people and are very courteous and kind to us. General MacArthur has done wonders for the country. He's given the Japanese people a chance to build a new nation. They don't act like a defeated country. Instead, they seem more like partners in the monumental task of rebuilding it. I have no animosity for the people. They suffered horribly in the war and are working hard to rebuild their country. One of the jobs of my battalion is to insure the safety and well-being of the community assigned to us. The regiment should be here at least two more years.

It was swell being with you again, Marie. Our time together was too short. Each time I have to say good-bye to you, it becomes more and more difficult to let you go. I know how much your teaching job means to you, and I appreciate the fact that you're willing to give that up and become the wife of a soldier. It may be possible for you to continue teaching wherever we're stationed. We'll talk more about that when we're together.

I look forward to the time when I can call you my wife. The other officers and their wives will just love you and I'll be so proud to introduce you to them. Give my best regards to Steve and Bright Star. Take good care of yourself, sweetheart.

Until next time---I love you,

Scott

The battalion Commanding Officer job was no more demanding of Scott's time and energy than his previous position as Executive Officer. He was comfortably settling into the routines of the battalion in its role as an occupation force with his usual organizational zeal. The men soon found that their new commander ran a tight unit with little tolerance for slackers who let others do their work. Scott confronted every issue that needed a decision on the basis of how it would affect the well-being of the men and what it would contribute to their mission capabilities. He never tried to be one of the boys, but his respect for the soldiers under his command was well-known throughout the ranks. He always made himself available to the men to discuss any topic of their choosing. This generated loyalty from the top downward, which Scott knew from experience was one of the most important ingredients of unit coherence and morale.

Scott also put the battalion and company cooks on the spot by demanding the best they were capable of at all times. He ate the same rations as the enlisted men. It didn't take many interviews with the men to find out that the rations provided were not up to standards. He immediately raided the base supply depot for additional clothing and bedding which was badly needed by his men in the colder climate of Hokkaido Province, and the Regimental commissary for fresh rations, especially meat. The men reacted to the improved messfare with characteristic griping, but it was tangible evidence that their new commander was a force to be reckoned with. His reputation as a commander who "got things done" made the men proud to be a part of the organization. His attention to the basics of leadership was beginning to pay dividends.

Regimental Headquarters was located next to Scott's battalion command post, so it was natural for the officers to work closely together. Scott liked and respected Colonel Friedricks. They were both West Point graduates with a passion for the Army and all it stood for. One evening, shortly after Scott took over as battalion commander, he and Colonel Friedricks headed for the new Officer's Club that had recently opened on the base. The Club was crowded, but they were able to find a vacant table against the wall opposite the bar.

They ordered wine and settled back to relax. They sipped their wine and casually scanned the other tables for familiar faces. Two tables away, an attractive woman watched Scott with a look of disbelief on her face. It was so unexpected he almost choked from the wine. The woman dressed in a light blue evening dress recognized Scott the instant their eyes met. Scott, too, was shocked. It was Leslie Kerr!

"My God," exclaimed Colonel Friedricks. "You look like you've just seen a ghost, Scott. An old acquaintance?"

"Yes, Sir. A ghost from my past."

"She certainly is a beauty," Colonel Friedricks said, observing Leslie Kerr hesitantly approach their table.

The woman standing at the table was without a doubt the same Leslie Kerr he remembered in the early days of the past war. She was dressed in a revealing satin dress that showed off her voluptuous figure.

"I watched you come through the door, Colonel. It was quite a surprise," she said, shaking his hand.

"It's a small world, Miss Kerr," added Scott. "This is Colonel Friedricks, my regimental commander. Colonel Friedricks, meet Leslie Kerr. The last time I saw her was 1943 in New Jersey."

"It's my pleasure, Miss Kerr," greeted Colonel Friedricks, feeling the tension between the two younger people. "If you'll pardon me, I'll let you two visit in private while I let my Executive Officer at the bar buy me a drink."

"It's been a long time. I thought you were dead. I tried to look you up when I returned from overseas, but it was almost as if you had never existed. Even the Club could not help me," said Scott. He was beginning to be uncomfortable with the situation.

"I can't stay but a few seconds," she said nervously, looking back at the captain sitting at the table she had just left. "He's had a few too many drinks," she muttered softly.

It was an awkward moment. They really had never known each other except for a few moments at the USO Club. "I remember you from the USO Club as if it was yesterday. I wore out those few letters you wrote by reading and rereading them. I think you helped me keep my sanity during the war, Miss Kerr. I couldn't imagine what happened when your letters stopped without any explanation."

"It was not my choice," responded Leslie, sitting on the edge of her chair. A look of desperation came over her. Her fingers were shaking as she gripped the edge of the table. Scott speculated that she was not only unhappy but scared about something.

Suddenly, without Scott or Leslie noticing, the intoxicated captain towered over them in a foul mood. He laid a heavy hand on Leslie's shoulder for support while he introduced himself. "In case she hasn't told you, I'm her husband, Jeff Landers…"

"Jeff, you've had too much to drink. Be careful," she warned briskly, removing his hand from her shoulder and getting up from the table.

"I'm glad to meet you, Captain," greeted Scott, standing so that he met Landers at eye level. The two men took an instant dislike to each other. Scott accepted the extended handshake, but his look of disgust left little doubt in Leslie and Jeff's mind that it was time to say good-bye. Captain Landers lowered his eyes when he saw the silver leaves on Scott's collar.

Scott didn't say another word. He remained standing several seconds after he watched Leslie and her husband exit the front door. He was not bothered by the awkward scene with the husband, but Leslie Kerr's miraculous reappearance in his life was devastating to his peace of mind. When he finally sat down, his whole body was shaking. Colonel Friedricks watched him closely from the bar and returned to their table.

"If you care to talk, I'll listen. If you want to be alone, I'll get lost. I don't want to get involved in anyone's personal affairs; that's their business," said Colonel Friedricks quickly.

"Sit down, Colonel. I don't know what I need right now," muttered Scott with beads of perspiration forming on his forehead. "When I first saw the lady she was a USO manager in New Jersey. I think I fell in love with her, like every other soldier who saw her. To make a long story short, we wrote to each other when I was shipped to Africa in 1943. When I was cycled home for a month before the Normandy invasion, I tried to locate her. It was weird; she had simple vanished without a trace.

"I even told Marie about Leslie Kerr. Now, she crops up on the other side of the world five years later, and gives me a real shocker."

"Are you in an eating mood?" asked Colonel Friedricks without comment.

"Yes, I was hungry before we got here. I'll join you in something to eat, Sir."

They ordered steaks from the menu and an awkward silence settled over the table. The Colonel offered nothing about his reactions to the situation. He was by nature a cautious man who kept his own counsel. Even his closest friends claimed that they did not completely understand him, because he very rarely commented on people or events if it did not relate to the welfare of his command. He learned early in his career not to meddle in those areas where he could not make a difference. Scott knew about his commander's reticence, and appreciated his willingness to be a friend.

"Colonel, do you know anything about Captain Landers? I noticed he's in the Second Division."

"Yes, I know who Captain Landers is," answered Colonel Friedricks, slowly lighting a cigarette. His response was carefully measured. "You'll want to step carefully, Scott."

"What do you mean?"

"Landers is an attorney who works in the Division's Civil Affairs battalion. He's a troublemaker and a heavy drinker. If he was in my command I'd sack him in a heartbeat. His father is a powerful senator who holds an important seat on the Armed Forces Committee. The word is out that Landers is to be given every courtesy possible, so as to not make any waves that could find their way back to those hallowed halls of the Senate. Some of the political aspects of military life are repugnant to me, but there isn't much I can do about it. I've heard that Landers is a brilliant lawyer. This is the first time I've seen his wife. It's a small world."

"What a turn of events!" commented Scott with a sigh.

"Are you going to be all right, Scott? You look as if you've just been kicked in the stomach."

"I'll be fine, Sir. I really haven't thought about her for years. To have her show up at this time and place, I admit, has unnerved me a bit."

Later that evening, Scott had trouble getting to sleep. In the early hours of the morning he was still stretched out on a couch at his bachelor's quarters staring at the ceiling. He was angry at himself and at the response Leslie's presence had triggered. The feelings had been repressed for so long that they were running rampant through his mind as if it was 1943 all over again. The feelings were not something he could pass over and forget, they were too strong for such a simple remedy.

He was frantically searching for something to solve the dilemma. Thoughts of Marie continued to fill his conscience at the same time. Around one o'clock in the morning, a muffled knock sounded at his door. When he opened it, Leslie Kerr was standing on the threshold with her hair and clothing in disarray.

"I know it's late and I know it's irregular, but could I please come in, Scott?" pleaded Leslie with puffy tear-stained eyes.

"Of course," answered Scott, closing the door behind her. "Would you like something, some coffee?" She was distraught and on the verge of collapse when she sat down heavily at a small kitchen chair near the door. Scott had a chilling premonition that something terrible had happened to her.

"I must be out of my mind," she cursed to herself, searching her purse for a handkerchief. Scott placed a box of tissues on the table in front of her.

"What's happened, Leslie?"

"If you don't mind, I could use some strong coffee. I hate to bother you like this, but I just had to get away. We had a terrible fight tonight, again, and I was afraid. I shouldn't be here, but I had no one else that I could turn to."

"I'll put on a fresh pot," said Scott, relieved to do something. He watched her closely while he prepared the coffee. She sat with her head placed on her arms on the table. She had stopped crying. He had a strong desire to help her, although entertaining another officer's wife in the middle of the night at bachelor's quarters was a serious matter.

Neither of them spoke until Scott sat down beside her with two cups of steaming black coffee. He thought she was sleeping but she lifted her head as soon as he sat down.

"This makes the second time I've turned to you for help."

"I remember. It seems a long time ago," said Scott, making conversation.

"It was another world then," she whispered hoarsely, lifting her head to look at Scott. He was struck by the fear he saw in the gray depths of her eyes. She continued haltingly with trembling lips. "I made some choices back then that have proved to be bad ones. I think I realized it then, but chose to ignore it. Over the years I've often wondered how different my life might have been if I had chosen differently."

"The saddest words are 'what if' and 'if only'. Drink some coffee; it'll help you relax," insisted Scott.

"Thank you. You're kind and caring, Scott Taylor. I saw those qualities in you the first time you came to the Club." Her hands shook while she warmed her fingers against the coffee cup and slowly lifted it to her lips.

The light in the small kitchen was not very bright, so Scott had not noticed that the right side of her face was red and swollen until she lifted her head to drink the coffee.

"My God, Leslie, what happened to you? Did Landers do this to you?" demanded Scott.

"Yes, he was at his worst tonight. I owe you an explanation, Scott."

"You don't owe me anything," he exclaimed. "If I made some assumptions that turned out to be wrong, then I must bear the responsibility. You promised nothing."

"You never said a word, but I knew what was in your heart. If only I had listened to my own instincts, I would have encouraged you more, Scott, but, who knows about such things? As it turned out, I listened to a slick talker who painted a rosy picture for the future. I met Jeff at about the same time you were shipping out for Africa. He took me to Washington where I became intoxicated with the feeling of power and importance. Just being where historical decisions were made that influenced all our lives was heady stuff to me at the time. I didn't realize what a sham much of it was until it was too late. Eventually my life with Jeff reached a point of emptiness and total collapse.

"I sold my father's farm so that Jeff would not have to work so hard. I always knew that he drank too much and gambled excessively. Yet, I made excuses for his behavior and ultimately enabled him to continue the destructive habits. Lately, he's been under a lot of pressure because General MacArthur has reduced the numbers of Civil Affairs groups that work directly with the Japanese government. He'll soon be out of a job and his influence, which is directly related to his father's position in the Senate is slowly waning. I'm not telling you this to excuse his actions or to rationalize my own contribution. I've reached a point where I can't take it any more. Tonight, I had the courage to honestly look at myself and see how much my marriage had failed both of us. You may not believe it, Scott Taylor, but it was because of you that I was able to walk out forever. When I saw you last night, it made me ashamed of my life compared to the life I might have had with someone such as yourself."

"I'm sorry."

"Please, let me finish, Scott. I knew that I could find a sympathetic shoulder to lean on and I appreciate your patience and concern. Even though we never had anything more, your friendship has always been a comfort to me. Tonight, I feel liberated, for the first time in years…"

A loud knock at the door interrupted her. "Scott, this is Colonel Friedricks. Open up!"

Scott unsnapped the inside lock. Two military policemen and Colonel Friedricks quickly entered the room.

"What's going on, Sir?" asked Scott.

"The whole base has been turned upside down by the MP's looking for Mrs. Landers. She just killed her husband with a bayonet through his stomach."

Chapter Fifteen

Two stern-looking MPs handcuffed Leslie and started to leave. Before she left the room, she turned toward Scott: "I was going to tell you about the terrible fight tonight and what I did to that monster. Really, I was, Scott." She started to cry and continued hysterically. "I'm sorry that I killed him. I just couldn't defend myself anymore. I was afraid he was going to kill me, so I stopped him."

Scott was speechless. As soon as the door closed he turned to his commander, his face white as a sheet. Colonel Friedricks patiently waited for Scott to collect his composure before he spoke.

"I'm sorry to barge in on you like this. The MPs combed the camp looking for her. When they came to Regiment HQ. I had a hunch she might have come to you."

"I thought she was just looking for a safe place until tomorrow. Believe me, Sir, I was planning to call you and Mrs. Friedricks to see if she could stay at your quarters until she got passage out of Japan and back to the States. She hadn't gotten to the worst part of her story, but I'm convinced she intended to tell me."

"I believe you, Scott. To be honest, I feel sorry for the lady. She deserved better than she got. Landers was a weakling parasite who improved his own situation by feeding on the work of others. Off the record, I don't blame this lady for doing what she did. For once, the little weasel bastard got what he deserved, and I intend to include that in my statement to the Provost Marshall."

The balance of the night passed quickly. Scott was consumed by self-analysis. Beyond everything else, he fostered a powerful condemnation of his actions and feelings toward Leslie. He felt in every cell in his body that he had wantonly betrayed the trust that Marie placed in him. The very mention of Marie in association with the sordid affair that took place, he thought, was a failure on his part to be worthy of what she was offering to him.

* * *

While Scott was preoccupied with the events surrounding Captain Lander's death, the small village of Fort Lewis was experiencing an unprecedented series of storms that continued to produce large amounts of snow while the temperatures plunged to thirty degrees below zero. All activity out-of-doors ceased until the storms abated. It was the worst stretch of weather Marie had ever experienced. In places the wind piled snow over the doors and windows of the sturdy log cabins.

The children who stayed at the school thought it was all great fun, and Marie and Steve did nothing to discourage their optimistic outlook. Small footpaths were maintained between the school, church and infirmary by continuous packing of the snow by the children when they were allowed out as a group to vent their excess energy. The hardy villagers resorted to the traditional snowshoe for winter traveling when they found it necessary to leave the warmth of their cabins.

Marie took advantage of the forced captivity to read and discuss some of the literature the children and some of their parents also enjoyed. Marie's readings had already become a favorite activity for young and old alike. At first, mothers attended more often than the fathers, but there was widespread approval for her efforts to open up the minds of the forest people to distant worlds and experiences. Eventually, she won over as many men as women to her reading sessions. One reason was her selection of the Leather Stocking Tales by James Fenimore Cooper, with *The Last of the Mohicans* being the favorite. They could easily relate to the story of frontier life as portrayed by Cooper.

Marie continued to write daily to Scott. The mail pouch at the Mounted Police Station was bulging with letters that had not been picked up because of the severe weather. Early every evening after the children finished eating, Marie took out her faithful typewriter to compose a letter to Scott and to commune with his spirit on the other side of the world. The children were accustomed to the ritual of the clattering typewriter, and they made a conscious effort to be on their best behavior so that their teacher could "talk" with her future husband far away. Steve's occasional visits to the school over the years had introduced an element of intrigue and adventure into their normally sedate school routine. Marie shared with the children some of the events Scott described to her in his letters. The idea that the young handsome soldier they had played with was in Japan was exciting for them to think about.

A week after the stormy period, the mail and courier plane delivered a single letter to Marie. She was disappointed that she did not get more than one letter after such a long time.

Bright Star stopped by shortly after the mail plane arrived in order to read the letter to Marie, who in turn, transcribed it on her Braille machine so that she could "read" it privately without assistance from another person. From the beginning, Bright Star gave Marie a solemn promise to never divulge the contents of any correspondence to anybody, not even to her husband. Marie was comfortable including Bright Star into the intimate details of her private life. Marie anxiously waited at her Braille typewriter which enabled her to devour every word over and over at her leisure. Bright Star slowly read the letter:

Sapporo, Japan
January 20, 1950

My Dearest Marie,

I'm writing tonight with a heavy heart and a loathing disgust at myself. [Bright Star paused a second and watched the blood drain from Marie's face.] I have a terrible feeling that I've betrayed the love and trust we've shared. I'll try to explain it the best I can and leave the judgment to you.

I've told you about a woman I met early in the war, Leslie Kerr, and that I had strong feelings for her.

I was no different than thousands of young men who yearned to have someone to remember them when they were away in combat. It helped us get through the ordeal.

I can tell you without having to apologize for feelings that existed at that point in my life. It was an infatuation of something peaceful, serene and, yes, even beautiful, that sustained many soldiers in the trauma of combat when all they saw on the battlefield was death, broken bodies of friend and foe, and chaos as a constant companion. So the fantasies and memories took on an importance, at that time and place, that under different circumstances, would not have been nurtured with the same amount of fervor.

I don't know if I'm making much sense, Marie. If it sounds as if I was excusing myself, I'm not. I cannot apologize for having honest and honorable feelings from the heart towards another woman before I met you, and I'm sure you're not asking that of me. However, my feelings for Leslie Kerr never soared to the heights they have for you, Marie. That is true, I swear.

I met Leslie Kerr at the Officer's Club at Sapporo. We recognized each other and spoke briefly. Later that night, she showed up at my quarters bruised and distraught over a fight with her husband. Evidently he was an alcoholic with a pattern and history of violence towards her. That night she tried to defend herself and ended up killing him with a bayonet. She's now in custody of the Provost Marshal's office.

The night has been long, and I'm still filled with remorse and shame for letting old feelings suddenly disrupt the beautiful future we have planned together. My love for you is as strong as ever - you must believe that, because it's true. My feelings towards Leslie Kerr have not been completely sorted out, but I must tell you that if she needs any help from me at her trial, I will be compelled to offer whatever assistance I am able to give. Do you think that statement violates the trust we share, Marie?

Forgive me for hurting you in this long letter. I continue to pray for you every day, and tonight I'm including a special prayer for guidance and peace of mind.

Until next time my precious Marie.

Love,
Scott

Bright Star carefully folded the letter and placed it in Marie's shaking hands. A cry of anguish and sadness burst from her lips.

"I can't tell you what to think, Marie, but it sounds to me as if Scott has bared his soul to you. Of course it's only natural to be hurt when you learn that possibly Scott is in love with the two of you at the same time," exclaimed Bright Star, trying to put herself in Scott's position.

"It can't be true, Bright Star... what does that say about the uniqueness of the things we had together?" cried Marie, searching for answers. "I can understand his feelings for the woman at the time he first met her during the war. I thought I loved Arnold, too. It was only after I fell in love with Scott that I realized how different it was."

"In several ways, the letter is a tribute to your love," Bright Star added thoughtfully. "The fact that your love was strong enough to evoke such a strong reaction from Scott's conscience indicates that he's at least honest and fair enough to confess his dilemma. It's what I would expect him to do."

Marie sat motionless for a few seconds thinking what Bright Star had just said. "He does sound confused and tormented, doesn't he?"

Bright Star looked at her watch and said; "I've got to get back to the infirmary, Marie. We can continue this conversation after I'm off tonight, if you want. Are you going to be all right?"

"Yes, thank you, Star. You're a dear friend. I appreciate your concern, but I can handle it. Scott is worth any effort on my part to insure our future together. It's times like this that my blindness keeps me from understanding things clearly."

"I understand what you mean, Marie. Don't let it pull you apart."

"I'm going to write a letter to Scott tonight. He needs some answers, and I need to sort out a few things. Thanks again, Star."

Well into the evening, while a howling, shrieking wind pounded at her window, Marie sat down to her faithful Royal typewriter and poured out her love and support to Scott.

My Darling Scott,

Your letter about Leslie Kerr has been received with mixed emotions. I can tell that you were distraught when you wrote it, and my immediate impulse was to reach out and enfold you with my love.

I cannot judge what your feelings are for Leslie. I would guess that you just never had a chance to deal with the feelings because the love, if that is what it really was, was never tested or even acknowledged by you until this last meeting with her. I want you to know that I don't feel any betrayal of our dreams or hopes for the future. If our plans cannot weather a revival of old relationships that were never put to any test for soundness, then we never had as strong a union as we hoped.

Just how strong and significant your feelings are towards me and Leslie can only be measured by you. I hope and pray that it's in my favor, but if it's not, then I deserve a direct answer from you as soon as your heart has sorted it out.

We cannot build our life together if our foundation is weakened by the memories of another person, or by dreams that are put into words by the most hateful phrase in the English language: "What if things had been different????" I'm strengthened and comforted by your sense of honor and integrity.

Your letter brought me to an emotional crossroads, where I've put my dreams and expectations on hold until I have sufficient reason to think otherwise. I hope I'm not a selfish person, and I have to fight the tendency to labor in self-pity, but I must tell you straight out that if you and I cannot pick up the pieces of our future where this episode ruptured it, then I think it's for the best to say good-bye and go our separate ways. My God, what a terrible sentence to have to write!

I won't view Leslie Kerr as a threat to our future unless you tell me differently. In a way my heart goes out to her for having made such a bad choice for a husband. You're correct to offer any help you possibly can. That's what friends are for. Help her, Scott, and use the time to evaluate where you want to go from here.

I'm sounding generous and magnanimous, but my heart is torn with the prospect of losing what I believed to be mine alone. It's a sad thought that something which had such a potential yesterday, might be out of reach tomorrow. Right now I don't care about the past. It's always available for us to visit whenever we desire to. It can be an inspiration and a source of strength, but it's still history and cannot be changed.

I had pinned my dreams on the promise of tomorrow. If you can give me tomorrow, I vow to be yours forever. If you take away our tomorrows, then we've reached the end of our journey together.

I pray for you, Scott, and I pray for Leslie Kerr who must be going through her own self-imposed purgatory. Good night, my love. Until next time.

Love,
Marie

Chapter Sixteen

Time dragged for Marie. Her work at Eagle Nest helped to keep her from dwelling on her relationship with Scott. The long difficult winter that interrupted the mails in the northland added to her anxiety and feelings of helplessness. A few letters had arrived from Scott since the Leslie Kerr incident. He still proclaimed his love for Marie and asked for forgiveness. She forgave him because it was not a planned deception or an intentional violation of their love, though she felt the incident had put their future in jeopardy. Scott could have said nothing about the incident and she would never have known. She clung to that alternative because it proved that deception was not a normal part of his makeup.

One day late in February, Constable Snow came to the school to tell her she had a telephone call from Scott. Marie's first thoughts were that something had happened to him, for she recently read about the potential for civil war between North and South Korea. She nervously threw on a hat and coat and let Constable Snow guide her to the RCMP barracks.

"Hello, Marie?" shouted Scott breathlessly.

"My, it's nice to hear your voice again, Scott. You sound so far away!"

"Well, I'm in Japan across the world from you. My CO pulled a few strings for me to use this Signal Corps line to call you. Your letters have been encouraging, but I wanted to speak to you in person, Marie, and we don't have a lot of time on the phone."

"I'm glad you felt that way..."

"What I really wanted to say to you, Marie, is I love you. I know that more than ever now, and I'd like for us to continue planning our wedding day."

"I never gave up any of our plans, Scott. My life began with you, and I can't imagine a future without you. My thoughts and plans never stopped. It was you who introduced an element of uncertainty."

"I accept the blame, Marie. It was foolhardy of me to compare my love for you to the infatuation I had years ago for Leslie Kerr. I've been able to thoroughly think that situation through, and I'm sorry for what I've done to us. Will you still marry me in June?"

Scott heard muffled sighs over the phone line. Neither spoke for a second or two. He listened with every nerve of his body, alert for the slightest sound. Marie searched in her heavy parka coat pocket for a handkerchief to dry her tears of joy. "Yes," she answered softly. "I'll be proud to be your wife, Scott Taylor. Just promise me you'll always love me, and if that should ever change, also promise you'll tell me without any delay. Can you promise me that?"

"Oh, Marie, yes, yes, yes. I'm a lucky man, and I thank God for the gift of your love and understanding," said Scott, fighting to hold back his own tears as the reality of her acceptance sunk in.

"We can plan a June wedding if you like," suggested Marie, thinking ahead. "I'll be finished at the school by early June and will return to Monson shortly afterwards. Can you get leave at that time?"

"My Commander has been really helpful. He guaranteed my furlough in June unless a national emergency demanded that I stay at my post. Marie, I've got to clear this line. I love you."

"I'm so glad you called. I love you, too."

The promise of the coming spring filled the air as Marie and Scott waited for its arrival. Leslie Kerr's murder trial was conducted in Japan by the Army, because the occupation forces still controlled the country by martial law. She was acquitted of the crime; the court recognized that it was an act of self-defense. Colonel Friedricks appeared at the trial as a witness to past abuses by her husband.

Scott came to the conclusion that Leslie was a very socially conscious person who enjoyed and sought the finer things in life that Captain Lander's family was able to provide. She tolerated his brutal treatment so that she would not lose the status she had as his wife. It was beyond reason to ever think that Scott and Leslie could have been compatible. Scott derived a sense of relief and comfort in being able to close that chapter of his life.

The winter temperatures in the Canadian north gave way to the warming rays of the sun that shone brighter and longer as each day passed. Marie counted the days with joy. Soon she would begin a fresh new life with Scott, much like the way nature responded to the warming rays of spring sunshine, and tree buds burst with anticipation of a new beginning.

The Eagle Nest was completing its third year of operation, and Marie celebrated that achievement with Steve and the other teachers who worked tirelessly for the children. Though her heart was filled with happiness, Marie was saddened to think of leaving Fort Lewis. She had come to the wilderness community as a stranger with a desire to again prove herself as a teacher. She succeeded beyond all expectations. The forest people accepted and took her into their hearts. They rejoiced over her plans to wed Scott, but saying good-bye was difficult. Her readings and story telling had opened up a whole new world of wonder and excitement to the people she was leaving behind. Practically every person in the village crowded around the dock where Steve was prepared to fly her back to Maine. Bright Star held her arm as they stepped up onto the wooden dock. "I can feel the people watching," said Marie, reluctant to leave.

"Yes, there are more people on the shore than I've ever seen at any one time at Fort Lewis," answered Bright Star. "There are a lot of folks who want to say thank you for all you've given them. Here comes Constable Snow."

"The villagers have selected me to act as their spokesperson, Miss Poole," said the young policeman soberly. "When you leave this place, you leave a void in the people's hearts that cannot be replaced. We wish you and Scott the very best of everything, of course, but our joy is dimmed by a sense of loss. You've enriched our lives with your example of courage and generosity, and given of yourself with an open heart. May your days be filled with happiness. From all the people in our small outpost village, thank you for the memories you leave behind. May God be with you, Marie."

Marie reached out and embraced the young policeman with a sob on her lips. "Thank you for those gracious sentiments, Constable Snow. I leave here a better person thanks to the wonderful people who have made my stay so memorable, and I thank you, Constable, for the countless acts of kindness you've personally extended to me. There was never a day that I did not feel secure and safe with you stationed at the village. Thank you."

"It's been a privilege to serve you, Miss Poole. Colonel Taylor is a fortunate man," added Constable Snow wistfully.

Marie turned to the crowd of people and waved her hand. "My dear friends, I'll miss you all. You've taught me the true meaning of humility and sharing, and I want all of you to know that your kindness has touched my heart. I'll carry your memories with me wherever I go. Do you remember how we read about the river of life in one of our books? Well, that river is flowing through our experiences even now here on the shore of Lac Diamante. The river never stops. When we are gone, others take our place on the journey to destiny. We can control who we are and what we become, but we cannot stop the relentless flow of the river towards tomorrow. Thank you for opening your hearts to me. I'll remember you always, good-bye..." Bright Star and Constable Snow helped Marie to board the plane.

"I'll see you at the wedding, Marie," hollered Bright Star above the noise of the plane's engine. The village people watched the plane make a loop around the lake before heading south. They stood transfixed until the throb of the engine could no longer be heard and the plane became a tiny speck on the blue horizon.

The wedding plans came together as soon as Scott called Marie at Monson to confirm his furlough for the month of June.

They intended to have a simple church ceremony with a reception at the Hebron Hotel near the center of town. They limited their invitations to the immediate family and friends. Steve volunteered to be Scott's best man while Bright Star agreed to be Marie's bridesmaid. The happy day was set for June 5, 1950.

Scott left Japan on a military transport stopping at Pearl Harbor and Anchorage, Alaska, before landing in San Francisco. He then hopped a commercial flight to Harrisburg, Pennsylvania, where he stayed overnight with his mother. The next morning the two of them started for Monson in Scott's Ford.

The day before the wedding, the small town of Monson opened its doors to more strangers than the town had ever seen at any one time. Steve and Bright Star landed their plane on the lake and tied up at the Poole's wharf. Mark and Bright Cloud drove in with Arlo, Michelle and young Maria. All of them stayed at the Hebron Hotel in bright, sunny rooms overlooking the lake.

Marie insisted that Scott's mother stay at her parent's home so they could have a chance to get better acquainted. Scott was a house guest at Marie's cousin Jonathan and his wife Rena.

The marriage ceremony took place at the small Methodist Church where Marie and her family were regular parishioners. Marie planned to wear her mother's white wedding dress for good luck. The church was filling up with people, leaving the front row empty for the wedding party. Jonathan Poole, dressed in his old khaki Army uniform, acted as an usher, escorting the people to their seats. Mark and Bright Cloud followed Arlo, Michelle and their adopted sixteen-year-old daughter, Maria, to their seats. Arlo and Mark wore their dress blue uniforms for the occasion. Mark wore his Medal of Honor in a sash around his neck. Staff sergeant Jonathan Poole proudly saluted both men, respectfully noting the Medal of Honor.

Young Maria sat between Arlo and Michelle. She was blossoming into an attractive young lady, with an air of confidence about her. Her affection for Arlo and Michelle was obvious to anyone who saw them together. She was the center

199

of their family life. Their love for her created a secure environment in which she developed independence and a sense of who she was. She always had an energetic smile on her face and a flash of fire in her dark eyes.

Jonathan took Scott's mother and Marie's mother, one under each arm, and escorted them to their seats. They were followed by several cousins and friends. The two mothers sat near the center of the church. The Pooles made a sincere effort to bring Scott's mother into their expanded circle of friends and family. She appreciated the grace and warmth of Marie's family and felt comfortable and relaxed as their guest.

Michelle and Bright Cloud sat next to each other, both dressed in light blue dresses which complimented their husbands' blue uniforms. They sat in silence listening to the organist play. Bright Cloud appreciated the skill and technique of the organist, and was soon wrapped up in the music.

Scott and Steve entered the church and stood nervously off to one side at the rear waiting for the appearance of the bride. Scott was dressed in his Army brown tunic with tan pants. Steve wore the new blue uniform of the Air Force. Scott was slightly restless, but when the church door opened to admit Marie and her father, his heart pounded. Marie was beautiful, standing straight and proud in her mother's white dress with the several layers of lace flowing around her. Her shoulders and neck were shrouded with light lace. A veil of the same material covered her head and face flowing out over her shoulders. As soon as she entered the church her lips were parted as if she was going to speak.

"Is everyone here?" Marie whispered to Bright Star.

"The church is full," answered Star reassuringly. "I can see the groom. My, what a stunning couple you two are going to make."

The organist surveyed the wedding party at the rear of the church and started to play the wedding march. Marie nervously started down the aisle with Star on her left and her father on her right. Mr. Poole, tall, reserved and full of pride, guided his daughter to the altar where Scott was waiting. Scott was oblivious to anyone else in the church except Marie. He took her hand in his and gently squeezed it. Marie did the same to him.

The ceremony for the sacrament of marriage went very quickly. After it was over, Scott had difficulty recalling that it had actually taken place. As soon as the minister pronounced them man and wife, he said quietly to Scott, "You may now kiss your new bride, Colonel Taylor."

Marie carefully folded the veil on top of her head and turned to him with eyes full of love and joy even though she could not see her husband. "Were you as nervous as I was," whispered Marie in his ear.

"It was like a dream, Mrs. Taylor."

Immediately after the ceremony, the reception took place at the hotel ballroom. As the happy couple arrived at the ballroom a four piece band started to play and the dance floor was soon crowded with celebrants. It was an occasion that the people in the small Maine town would fondly remember. The softness of a warm June day contributed to the memory.

Steve rapped a fork against his glass and stood up to make a speech: "New friends and old friends, I join you in celebrating the marriage of Scott and Marie. For the past three years I've had the privilege of watching Marie work under conditions that would tax anyone's ingenuity and determination. Yet, this charming lady has been able to turn adversity into an opportunity, by endearing herself and her passion for knowledge to a whole community of people who will always remember her with warm hearts and happy faces. Her courage and willingness to give of herself have been an inspiration to all of us.

"Scott is a person of rare integrity and character. He's the personification of the professional soldier who embodies those noble ideals of duty, honor and country. Whenever I think of Scott, commitment and devotion to duty come quickly to my mind.

"I propose a toast to two of God's most beautiful people. May their future be filled with happiness, joy and children. I'm proud to call both of them my friends." The clinking of glasses and jovial sounds of agreement reverberated through the small room. Later, towards the end of the celebration, Bright Cloud danced with Scott while Mark promised Marie that he would give it a try.

"Dancing was never one of my strong points, Marie, but I wouldn't think it right not to have tried a slow waltz with a beautiful bride we've come to love like a daughter."

"Colonel Leroux," said Marie, gliding into his arms. "Thank you for helping to make this such a special day for us."

"Bright Cloud and I will also remember this day. We're happy for the two of you. I want you to know that if either of you are ever in need of anything, you have but to ask."

"You're going to make me cry, Colonel…"

"I don't mean to. I've been married for almost thirty years to the most wonderful person in the world, so I know what I'm talking about when I tell you that a marriage blessed in heaven is a rare gift. I think you and Scott will feel the same way in thirty years. You're a vision of loveliness. I pray that the two of you can enjoy each other as much as Bright Cloud and I have been lucky enough to share."

"Thank you… I'll always remember this dance with you."

"Your husband can't keep his eyes off you, so I'm going to let him cut in to finish the dance with his new bride," said Mark, passing Marie over to Scott while he picked up Bright Cloud's waiting arms.

"You know, Bright Cloud," whispered Mark in his wife's ear, "Scott reminds me of DJ so much it's almost as if a part of him has come back to us…"

"I've had the same kind of feelings, too. What a lovely couple they are. I hope they can build the same kind of life we've been able to share," remarked Bright Cloud, laying her head on Mark's shoulder. Mark didn't answer her. He didn't have to, for she understood what was in his heart!

After the reception, Steve and Bright Star drove them to Bangor where they booked air passage to Hawaii. Marie fell asleep on the long ride over the Pacific Ocean. Scott was content to watch her and hold her close. They planned to spend three weeks at the tropical paradise before flying to Japan. Scott had already rented a house on the Army base where his battalion was stationed. They lived an idyllic existence enjoying the flowering softness of lazy days and nights in a tropical world filled with exotic aromas and sounds that excite and stimulate the senses.

Scott and Marie spent a memorable honeymoon in a dream-like existence on the sandy beaches of Oahu, where they became as one. It was like living in a fantasy world of make-believe that would never end. They had been married two weeks when an announcement came over the hotel loudspeaker system that shattered the paradise dream they were sharing.

"Attention, all armed service personnel! North Korea has just invaded South Korea with massive penetration southward of armored forces. You are urged to contact your individual units for instructions. Repeat..."

Chapter Seventeen

The happiness of the past two weeks was quickly forgotten. Suddenly, their world was shattered by events Scott and Marie knew would affect their lives.

"What are we going to do, Scott?" asked Marie, frightened about what the announcement could mean to them.

"This is a time to be calm, sweetheart. We can't be sure about anything. A lot of things have been happening in Korea. First, we've got to confirm what's going on. I'll call the Far East Command in Tokyo right now."

Scott and Marie returned to their hotel room where he called Tokyo. He had a premonition that this was the real thing, but he did not want to worry Marie needlessly until it was confirmed. The operations officer was a classmate, so Scott was able to determine the tactical situation better than the press was reporting in the papers.

"We've got a full scale invasion on our hands, Scott. The North Koreans broke through the defenses of the South Korean forces with ease. General MacArthur immediately put all units in Japan on alert notice." The operations officer urged Scott to return to Japan as soon as possible. His battalion was one of the best trained units in the area, and he could be certain that it would be used in any resistance force assembled by the Far East Command.

Scott hung up the phone and sat down beside Marie. "The situation is probably more serious than the press is reporting. We must get to Japan as soon as possible."

Marie sat motionless for several seconds before responding to the news. "I always wondered what I'd think and do if a situation like this came up. I was sure that at sometime or another, my soldier husband would be asked to do what he had been trained for. Now that it has interrupted our honeymoon, my first reaction is anger that a civil war in Korea couldn't be postponed for at least a little while longer."

"I'm sorry this had to come now, too."

"Don't be sorry, Scott," answered Marie bravely. "We'll face this thing together. Where you go, I'll follow if I'm able."

"I love you for the support, sweetheart. I should call to see if we can get a flight out of the islands to Japan. The airways will be busy, so we had better get on the list as soon as possible."

"You know what you have to do," said Marie, responding to his embrace.

Space on a military plane was available first thing in the morning. Twelve hours later, they were in Hokkaido checking out their new quarters on the Army base. It was a small cottage-style house with two bedrooms, kitchen and large living room. Scott's fellow officers had decorated it for their return and provisioned the refrigerator with an assorted supply of drinks and food. A gala homecoming celebration was planned, but the circumstances in Korea changed everything.

Scott proudly carried Marie over the threshold of their permanent home, and spent some time showing her the layout of the rooms, and directing her to the kitchen appliances and the adjoining bathroom.

"I'm going to be fine, Scott," said Marie as soon as she oriented and familiarized herself with each room. "Now, you've got things to do. Don't worry about me. I'll know this place inside out in no time!"

"I feel terrible leaving you so quickly in this strange house. I'll be back as soon as I check in at the regiment headquarters and my battalion command post. Thanks for making all of this so easy, Marie."

"Go and do whatever has to be done, Scott. I would feel terrible if I thought my presence here was going to interfere with your responsibilities to your men. Don't forget, I'm a soldier's wife, so be the soldier I'm so proud to call my husband."

"Yes, ma'am," responded Scott playfully kissing her on the lips. "Remind me to tell you I love you."

"I will, every day of our lives."

The briefing at regiment was a grim affair. The situation was more serious than Scott expected. The United Nations had just voted for the authorization of force to oppose the invading North Korean forces. General MacArthur was made Supreme Commander of all UN forces, but it was a hollow force. The only American forces available were a few occupation troops in Japan and a small contingent of advisors and specialists in South Korea, that had already been heavily battered by the invading enemy.

US troops in Japan were woefully unprepared for the rigors of combat. Equipment of all type was desperately needed to bring the units up to their normal table of organization standards. To send such troops into combat would have been irresponsible, and Scott was relieved to learn that his regiment was first on the priority list for replenishment of supplies and manpower before they would be considered for combat roles. Colonel Friedricks congratulated Scott on his marriage and informed him that it could be one or two months before they left Sapporo for action in Korea.

Marie received the news with mixed feelings. She was thankful for the few weeks they had together before he had to leave, but the prospect that his battalion would be one of the first to mount out for combat sent chills through her body. There wasn't anything she could do about the fact that he was soon going to be in mortal danger. So she made a vow that the time they shared together would produce meaningful memories for both of them when they were separated.

"The battalion is going to be on an accelerated training schedule from now on," said Scott over breakfast the next morning. "I wanted our first meal in the house to be something special. Now, those plans are thrown out the window, too."

"This breakfast has been special," countered Marie, placing a finger to his lips in admonition. "I'm not going to let Korea rob us of these special times together. We'll do the best we can with the time allotted to us. I want you to know that I'm with you every minute of the day supporting whatever is asked of you and your battalion. I don't wear the uniform, but I'm marching beside you wherever you may be."

"That fact is truer than you think," answered Scott, scooping her into his arms and swinging her around the room. "I'll be back as soon as I can."

Troops from United Nation members were promised to General MacArthur, but it could be a costly delay before they arrived in enough force to halt the North Koreans. The US Army troops present in Korea when the invasion started fought heroically with obsolete equipment and inadequate supplies at their disposal. They were readily expended against overwhelming hordes of tough well-trained North Korean soldiers equipped with Russian weapons and tanks. If the existing forces in Korea were not augmented with fresh troops, there was a danger that the Korean peninsula war would be lost before it really got going, creating a disaster of major proportions.

MacArthur was still under the command of the US Joint Chiefs of Staff, and he showered them with demands for additional troops, or the failure to stop aggression in Asia would be their responsibility! His forceful demand for a full marine division, with a brigade to be sent immediately, got their attention. The brigade was desperately needed at the southern tip of the country, where remaining US and South Korean forces had dug in for a determined last-ditch-stand.

Arlo and Michelle had recently closed up an apartment in Washington, DC, previous to attending Scott and Marie's wedding. They visited with Mark and Bright Cloud for several days before leaving the east coast for Camp Pendleton Marine Corps base in southern California, where Arlo took command of a division. Like all other military formations of the time, it was a division in name only. Building up the division to its full complement of men and material was a daunting task. Arlo predicted and understood the urgency of assembling a full brigade around his best regimental combat team, and he started collecting small detachments scattered all over the hemisphere for that purpose. By the time MacArthur requested the brigade, it was ready for shipment to Korea and the Navy was still scrambling to find ships to transport them.

In the meantime, Scott worked long hours conditioning his battalion. His hard-nosed methods previous to the current crisis made believers and supporters out of his subordinates, and they enthusiastically responded to his demands. They knew that combat was imminent. The battalion was fortunate to have a number of combat veterans and Scott wisely scattered them throughout the ranks so that their experience could be shared with as many younger soldiers as possible.

On his own initiative, Scott scoured the Army supply depots for additional support and firepower for the battalion. He was able to collect fifteen infantry support vehicles that the men reconditioned. Ten of them were White armored half-track vehicles equipped with four-fifty caliber machine guns mounted on a turret in the rear. The other five vehicles were twin forty millimeter cannons mounted on a tank chassis. Both weapons provided the battalion with anti-aircraft protection and lethal infantry support. The twin 40's were a potent weapon for longer distances, while the quad 50's were a fearsome close-in weapon that was looked upon with a sense of security by the doughty infantrymen.

Colonel Friedricks looked upon Scott's scrounging methods with silence. Scott's battalion was the best in the regiment. "Your battalion is going to have a chance to find out just how good it really is. You've got the best trained and best equipped battalion in Japan, Scott. Consequently, you'll be given more missions to perform than others that are less prepared, but I have a feeling we're all going to pay dearly for not maintaining a better fighting ability among the troops. You may be unfairly used, but it should be taken as a compliment that you're more capable of completing a mission than others."

In mid-August Colonel Friedricks called his battalion commanders to his headquarters for a conference at which he was able to bring them up to date on the tactical situation in Korea. UN troops were arriving steadily in small numbers. The troops holding the Pusan perimeter were holding on by a thread, having been bolstered by the brigade of marines. They helped to stabilize the small stronghold, but a much larger force was needed before an offense could even be contemplated. Colonel Friedricks advised his officers to continue the training programs and to stockpile their equipment and supplies so that they could move out on a very short notice.

Scott was included on the list of officers who were to accompany Colonel Friedricks to a secret meeting the next day at the Far East Command in Tokyo. Scott knew from experience that such a high level conference was usually the first stages of a troop movement. He decided to alert Marie to that possibility without telling her the specific details.

Marie was still getting settled into Army base life. With the war raging in Korea, the base was alive with activity. Before long she developed a friendship with several of the officers' wives. She was amazed to learn how accurately they could predict events in advance of their happening. They frequently knew about them before their husbands. They all agreed that a movement of the regiment was forthcoming, within hours possibly. When Scott told her that he might not be home for the next few days, Marie confided to herself that the "information grapevine" was probably right as usual. Every time Scott left the house, she would send him off with love, good cheer, and support.

The meeting in Tokyo finally gave everyone a chance to learn the truth of what was ahead of them. As soon as they entered the situation room, Scott recognized a familiar face walking toward the podium to address the group.

"Good morning, gentlemen. I'm Major General Arlo Korsman. We're gathered here today to set plans in motion for an amphibious assault landing in Korea that should shorten the war and ease the pressure on the Pusan perimeter at the same time.

"Before we get into details, let me say that a lot of work remains to be done before the invasion takes place, but I can tell you that the marine division I command is charged with planning and executing the landings at the port of Inchon on the west coast of Korea a few miles from the capital city of Seoul. It's our intention to pull the brigade from the Pusan perimeter to participate in the landing. One of my regimental combat teams is enroute from San Diego as we speak while my third RCT is still in the Mediterranean and will not be available to assist in the landing as expected.

"Therefore, the Corps command has made an Army RCT, commanded by Colonel Friedricks, available to us as a substitution. Would you please stand, Colonel Friedricks, so that we can all see who you are."

Colonel Friedricks stood up and bowed to the other members in the room. "My regiment is at your disposal, General Korsman," shouted Colonel Friedricks proudly.

"Thank you, Colonel," answered Arlo. "It's good to see you again. The last time we worked together was on Peleliu and Okinawa. Tentatively we plan to use your RCT as a floating reserve during the assault phase, and when we position our forces for the capture of Seoul, you're scheduled to be part of the attacking force under my jurisdiction. Corps has already delineated our areas of operation. We can and will go over that in more detail at a later date. If you'll be patient with me, I've got just three more items for you this morning:

"One, be prepared to load your units on Navy transports within a twenty-four hour notice. That means loading of everything you need in the field to conduct an offensive for thirty days before additional supplies are needed.

"Two, I've already assigned a tactical air controller to each of your battalions. The crew chief and three assistants should be waiting for you at your headquarters when you return. This will give you the capabilities of calling in fighter planes for ground support. During the assault phase, planes from aircraft carriers will answer the calls for support. Later, when we capture Kimpo airfield on the road toward Seoul, we'll be able to use Air Force and other UN squadrons for the same function.

"Three, I know I don't have to tell you, but I'll say it anyway. Keep what has been said here to yourself.

"There will be more planning and coordinating conferences as soon as I leave the podium, so sit tight a little longer. Welcome aboard, gentlemen. May our endeavors help to bring this war to an early and successful conclusion." Arlo left the podium and walked directly to Scott and Colonel Friedricks, who came to attention and saluted him as he approached.

"This is a hell of a thing to happen to a newly married man, Scott, but I'm glad you're here with us," remarked Arlo good naturedly. "How's your lovely bride?"

"She's settling in just fine, Sir. The wedding was only two months ago, yet, it seems longer than that. We heard about Korea in Hawaii and came directly to Japan. She's been a real trooper."

"Colonel Friedricks is an old friend," announced Arlo, shaking hands with him. Both officers seemed to be glad to see one another. "We went to staff school at the same time, and we probably sweated it out more than you did, Scott."

"Those stars look good on you, General. There isn't a man I'd rather serve under than you. I just hope we're ready for the big leagues again," answered Colonel Friedricks solemnly.

"This is a hectic time for all of us, but listen, why don't we get together over lunch?" suggested Arlo, looking at his watch.

"You set the place, General."

"The Officer's Club located just across the street from this building will be fine for me. I can make it for noon sharp."

At the close of the last conference of the morning, Scott and Colonel Friedricks hurried to the Officer's Club across the street where they met Arlo and enjoyed a leisurely meal. There was much speculation about what would happen after Inchon and Seoul were taken. If it went as expected, the United Nations forces would have a unique opportunity to destroy the North Korean forces in the southern half of the country.

The capture of Seoul and Inchon would essentially sever the supply line of the enemy troops fighting at the Pusan perimeter. MacArthur planned to increase the UN forces in Pusan to drive them northward. Arlo's Division would be the anvil while attacking UN forces from the south would be the hammer driving the enemy against their blocking position. The plan was to block their line of retreat and end the war by Christmas.

Arlo mentioned that Steve and Bright Star had been ordered to active status and was not sure if they had left Fort Lewis or not. The lack of manpower in the armed forces was sending shock waves throughout the world. There was a pervasive fear that Korea was just a feint to a much more dangerous threat from Russia in Europe. It was a late hour to find that American forces had been allowed to deteriorate in quality and quantity to such an alarming state of readiness.

"I didn't think they'd call up the reserves on such a short notice," said Scott, thinking aloud. "What's going to happen to the school at Fort Lewis?"

"I don't know, Scott. I'm sure something will be done to keep it going. The last time Michelle spoke to Star she said that her mother, Bright Cloud, may go to work at the infirmary while Star's away. I don't know about the school. If I have anymore news from home, I'll pass it along to you. Right now, we've got a big job ahead of us right here. If Lady Luck is on our side, we should be able to pull this off with minimum losses."

Arlo and Colonel Friedricks reminisced about staff school days. Scott was not surprised to learn that they had remained close friends over the years and frequently kept in touch with each other. Scott knew that Arlo was a very private person and very selective about his friends. The fact that Colonel Friedricks was one of them was significant, and it reinforced the opinion that Scott had already made about his regimental Commander. He was in good company.

When Scott returned home he told Marie about Steve and Bright Star. "I can't believe that Fort Lewis is going to lose both of them at the same time," exclaimed Marie. "What a stroke of bad luck for them. Scott, why don't we call Colonel Leroux and Bright Cloud? They'll know what's going on."

"If it will make you feel better, Marie, we can call," answered Scott. "Honey, are you thinking what I think you're thinking?"

"Yes. It would be terrible if the school had to be closed down. On such a short notice they'll have difficulty locating substitutes. The other wives calculate that the regiment will be in action by mid-September. I'm not asking you to deny or corroborate their estimate, because I understand the need for security, but if that is the case, then you'll probably be away from here for most of the winter even if the campaign is successful."

"The grapevine point of view is not unrealistic, honey. If you feel that strongly about it, we'll call right now. Then, we'll know for sure."

"I do, Scott. I love being with you and you know how happy we've been these past two months. The thought of being alone here without you is something I would do to support what you're doing, but if I'm really needed at Fort Lewis and I chose to stay here when you're gone, then I'd feel as if I'd abandoned the children."

Scott saw the concerned look on her face and understood the dilemma that confused her. A part of him agreed that she would be able to handle his absence better in familiar surroundings than biding her time at the house on an empty Army base. He checked a notebook next to the phone and called the Leroux's home in Maine.

"Hello," answered Mark.

"Hello, Colonel Leroux. This is Scott Taylor."

"What a pleasant surprise, Scott. We were just talking about you and Marie. Steve and Star have been called up for active duty. Steve's squadron of Mustangs has been activated and is scheduled for duty in Korea. Star is not sure where her duty station will be. Steve has already left Fort Lewis and Star reports to Norfolk, Virginia by the end of the week. I have a feeling that she's going to be assigned to a hospital ship, but my hunches are sometimes wrong."

"I can't tell you much about things here, Sir."

"I understand your position."

"I'm going to put Marie on the phone. She can talk for herself. It's been nice talking to you Colonel Leroux. Give my regards to Bright Cloud."

"I will. You take care of yourself, young man. Our prayers will be with you."

"Thank you, Sir. Here's Marie."

"How are you, Colonel Leroux?" asked Marie hesitantly. "We're calling to find out about Steve and Star, and what will happen to the school when he leaves."

"Well, Marie, it appears that our little Eagle Nest is about to be drastically reduced in size. Steve has left, and the teacher that was replacing you is also leaving. He's an American, and has been drafted. There's no way he can avoid the call to duty."

"Oh, my...parts of the school will have to close down then. Would you hold on for a moment, Colonel Leroux? I want to ask Scott something." Marie placed her hand over the receiver of the phone and turned towards Scott with a troubled look on her face. "Scott, the school is going to need me this coming year. Do I have your blessings if I go back?"

"Yes, my darling. It will probably be better for you to keep yourself busy while I'm gone. Of course you have my blessings."

"Colonel Leroux, what would you say if I came back to teach for this year until a replacement can be located?"

"That would be like a dream come true, Marie. Bright Cloud is going to spend the fall and winter at Fort Lewis to replace Star at the infirmary. I've been giving serious thought to volunteering as a substitute at the school. If you come, Marie, we could keep the school going. You can help me. I don't know how well I'd do, but I'm willing to give it a try. Are you sure this is what you want?" asked Mark, having second thoughts about her offer. "After all, you're still on your honeymoon."

"We've considered that," answered Marie haltingly. "Under the circumstances, we think it's something that should be done."

"God Bless you and Scott. I think your decision to help us at Fort Lewis is most unselfish of both of you. Bright Cloud will be pleased to hear the news."

"I'll call you again when our plans are settled."

"Thanks for calling and thanks for the offer. We pray that the situation in Korea is going to be quickly resolved, but I have a bad feeling it's going to be a long pull."

That night Scott and Marie clung to each other with more intensity than ever. They were facing their first separation and they worried about the future. Everything seemed to be turning out differently than they had planned. The horrible war in Korea was pulling them in different directions, threatening their life together, and there was nothing they could do to change the course of events.

"Are you afraid of what's ahead of us, Marie?" asked Scott, holding her close to him.

"Yes, I admit it. I'm afraid, but my faith keeps my thoughts positive instead of negative. What about you, Scott? Are you afraid, too?"

"I'm afraid in a lot of different ways. I'm afraid that something will happen to me so that we won't be able to share the dreams we've shared for tomorrow. I'm afraid I won't measure up to the demands of a battalion commander when hard decisions are needed, and I'm concerned about leaving you alone when I'm gone. It's easier to be doing things than to just wait for time to pass. So I'm relieved that you're going to Fort Lewis."

"My darling husband, if I could steal you away somewhere so that you would not have to go into combat again, I'd do it. I love you. My life really began when you became a part of it. This period we're going through will pass, hopefully soon; when it's over we'll be stronger than ever and more thankful for what we have together. Tonight, I have some news that should make you happy."

"What news is that?"

"Here, give me your hands." Marie took his hands and placed them on her stomach. "While you were in Tokyo, Mrs. Friedricks took me to the base doctor. Colonel Scott Taylor, you are going to be a father in another seven months. I'm pregnant!"

Chapter Eighteen

"Oh my God, Marie," exclaimed Scott, quickly sitting up in bed. "Imagine me a father. But, how can you think of going into the North Country so far from a hospital at such a time?"

"I haven't thought much about it, but I can teach right up until the due date provided things go well."

"That's just it, Honey. What if things don't go well? Who'll take care of you?"

"Scott, I'm only pregnant, I'm not coming down with an incurable disease. I couldn't ask for anyone more capable than Bright Cloud to watch out for me and the baby. I was thinking of the baby too, but when I heard Colonel Leroux mention that she was returning to the infirmary, my doubts disappeared. After all, she's delivered more babies than most doctors."

"I don't deny that."

"Listen my darling soldier husband," she said, wrapping his arms around her. "The last thing I want is for you to worry about me whether I stay here in Japan or if I return to Fort Lewis. You have an important job ahead of you and I want you to be free of worry and distractions about my welfare. I promise you, I'll leave Fort Lewis if the baby or myself should ever need specialized care. I could go to my parent's place or to your mother's if that becomes a necessity."

"Anytime I'm away from you, Marie, is the time when I'll worry and be concerned about your welfare. Now, we have another person to think about," whispered Scott in her ear.

"Isn't that wonderful?" Marie smiled and turned out the light.

* * *

Most of the units in Colonel Friedricks' regiment were rapidly being brought up to full strength. There was a new raw energy present at the Army Base as they prepared themselves for duty in Korea.

Scott returned home one night and told Marie that the battalion had just received a tactical air control group of four marines just as Arlo had promised in Tokyo. The leader of the group was a short muscular, plain-speaking Captain Les Jones. He was a former pilot that had been grounded because of an eye injury. The group came with a radio and generator truck and a command jeep. Their powerful radio made it possible to talk directly with the pilots even when they were several miles from the front lines, making it possible for Scott to call in aircraft for close air support of ground troops. He was a believer in the concept, even if a short drop did almost kill him once.

Steve's squadron of Mustangs had made a specialty of close ground support. The air branches were rapidly changing over to jet-powered aircraft, but they were not as effective in the ground support role as the older piston-powered planes like the Air Force's Mustang and the Navy and Marine Corps' gull-winged Corsair.

In mid-August the regiment received a warning order to prepare for embarkation of vessels at Sasebo Naval Base. Movement from Sapporo was imminent! The timing corresponded perfectly with Marie's departure from Japan. They each experienced a wide range of emotions when it came time to say good-bye. Anticipation and excitement of what tomorrow held for them was mixed with dread and heartache of separation. Scott walked Marie onto the airplane that would take her to San Francisco, the first leg of a long flight to Canada's wilderness.

Marie bravely bit her lip to contain the tears. She and Scott held each other for a long time without saying a word. Marie kissed Scott one last time.

"Whatever happens tomorrow, my darling, I'll always cherish these past few weeks. I'll pray for you and no matter how many miles separate us, you'll be in my heart. Good-bye, my love." Marie tenderly ran her hands all over Scott's face. It allowed her to complete the mental picture she had of him. He took both of her hands and kissed them softly before he left.

"Until next time, Marie," he whispered with a lump in his throat. The stewardess requested that he leave the aircraft. They were cleared for takeoff.

Scott watched the plane disappear over the horizon. He had never felt so alone. He walked back to the waiting Army command car which took him to dockside, where his battalion was being loaded on the Army transports.

Scott boarded the transport and watched the port of Sasebo fade into the distance. An announcement for a conference of staff and battalion commanders in one of the wardrooms came over the loudspeakers. Now that they were under way with the promise of combat ahead of them, a more serious group of men listened with rapt attention. Colonel Friedricks pushed his chair away from the table and carefully took stock of the men in the room before he spoke.

"Men, now that we're at sea I can bring you up to date on what's ahead of us. Inchon is our destination. Two Marine Corps Regimental Combat Teams (RCT) are going in on the first assault wave. A RCT composed of our regiment and other attached units, will act as a floating reserve for the landing operation as a substitute for a Marine RCT which won't be able to make it in time. The scheme of maneuver is to land and secure the port of Inchon as rapidly as possible. Equipment and supplies are scheduled to come in right after the landing teams have cleared the waterfront area. We'll remain aboard and at sea for one day in case we are needed at any particular point.

"Once Inchon is secured, we'll land and take our place in the line of attack eastward against the capital city of Seoul. We'll be attached to the Marine division until our own division staff establishes a command post ashore. In general, we're going to be a part of the blocking and holding force to the right of the Marine's right flank south of Seoul while the main elements of the division make a wide left hook to envelope the city from the west and north.

"Part of our job as a blocking force will be to contain enemy units trying to escape from the city proper. United Nation forces will be driving the North Korean troops concentrated in the Pusan perimeter area northward against the blocking line the Marine division will establish across their line of retreat. We'll be a part of the anvil against which they're being driven. It's a big job and we could drastically shorten the war if we're successful at closing the line of retreat of the enemy. Take this period to double check your equipment and rest as much as possible while the ship's crew carry us to our destination. There will not be any orders issued until we receive them from the Marine division. At that time you'll be notified immediately. Good luck, gentlemen."

* * *

Far from the scene of anticipated battle, Marie lay on her bed at the Eagle Nest and listened to the cry of the loons across Lac Diamante. It sent spasms of loneliness and longing through her tired body. Three weeks had now passed since she left Scott in Japan. She wrote to him daily even if the courier plane did not pick up the mail pouch. She received two letters that he wrote on the transport to Korea. Bright Cloud volunteered to be the reader for Marie while she typed the contents onto her Braille typewriter. Bright Cloud finished reading the letters and said: "Waiting and wondering is always the hardest part, Marie. I don't have any magic formula that makes it easier. It almost drove me mad. I understand what it is to be alone and not know if your loved one is alive or dead."

"Sometimes I'm all tied in knots inside. I can't eat, I can't sleep, Bright Cloud," confessed Marie.

"Of course, it's only natural. One thing did work for me, Marie. Faith in the Almighty helped soothe my soul when it was most needed. I think you have that same kind of faith."

"Sometimes I feel abandoned by my faith," admitted Marie.

"There aren't any easy solutions except the need to continue with the matters of everyday living."

"Yes, I think my coming here to teach has made it easier to handle. Scott thought so, too. You and your husband have been so kind and helpful to me."

"The children have settled for the evening. I plan to be at the infirmary for a while longer. Goodnight, Marie. You and Scott are in our prayers." Bright Cloud gave Marie a warm hug before leaving.

Marie listened carefully to the news on her short-wave radio every morning and evening. During the second week of September she was mesmerized by the words that flowed from the radio speaker: "UN forces under General Douglas MacArthur have landed at Inchon and were pressing towards Kimpo airfield and the city of Seoul east of Inchon. The Marine division was supplemented with a RCT from an Army division and they are now fighting in the outskirts of the city." This could mean that Scott's battalion would be involved if for no other reason than it was the best equipped and the most ready unit in the Far East.

The busy skies over Seoul were filled with black smoke and flames from burning buildings. Destruction from artillery shells, bombs, and naval gunfire rained down on the metropolis. The few clouds that hovered above the city glowed with an eerie orange hue filtered by wisps of black smoke. The ferocious battle raged for days, ending when most of the buildings were destroyed and the enemy strongholds eliminated.

Scott's battalion held onto a prominent piece of real estate called South Mountain, at the southern edge of the city. It was fiercely defended by a large contingent of North Korean troops. Scott ordered Captain Les Jones to call in air support to soften the mountainside as a prelude to their attack up its slopes. Scott watched carefully as the black corsairs systematically hammered the hillsides.

Scott commanded his battalion from one of the half-track trucks. It gave his command post mobility and the heavy duty radio on board gave him communication links with all three companies in the regiment without having to leave the vehicle. He preferred being where the fighting was the heaviest so that he could direct operations based on information he could verify with his own eyes. It was the reason he kept Jones' team close by and assigned two of his half-tracks, with four fifty-caliber machine guns mounted in the body, to give them protection from all sides so that the tac air team could do their job with a minimum of interference.

The firepower of the quad fifties was awesome. They were capable of destroying anything in their path out to a half mile. The half-tracks were frequently used to pinpoint enemy strongholds by firing tracers in the area for the circling planes above to register their targets. Captain Jones knew some of the Navy and Marine pilots on a first name basis, and after the team directed their first strike Scott was satisfied and gave them the added ground protection so that they could concentrate on their jobs. Jones called in another strike when the attacking platoon called the mobile command post to announce that they were still getting heavy resistance from the same location.

Scott was standing on the hood of the half-track scouring the hillside with his binoculars when Jones called out to him: "Colonel, this is something you can tell your grandchildren about. We've had Marine, Navy and Air Force pilots supporting us, but this group overhead is unusual. We've got a squadron of South African Mustangs for this run. I'll turn my speakers up so that you can listen in." Jones pulled his headphones back on and began directing the pilots to the targets.

"Cheetah One, this is Ground Hog. Your target is the western face of South Mountain. Make a single run on the aerial tramway structure midway of the slope, out."

"Ground Hog, this is Cheetah One making an initial run on target, out."

They watched a single Mustang peel off from the circling formation and position itself so that its run on the target would be perpendicular to the ground troops, dropping one napalm canister squarely on the tramway building from a very low altitude. The fiery explosion momentarily engulfed the climbing Mustang.

"Ground Hog, this is Cheetah One. Is that where you wanted it? out."

"This is Ground Hog. Cheetah One, you are on target. Using the initial strike as a reference point, continue on the same axis of contour 200 yards to the north and carry your coverage up to the summit with your remaining ordnance. Good luck. Ground Hog out."

"Ground Hog, this is Cheetah One. We read you loud and clear, out."

Scott watched the South African pilots cut the mountainside into grids. The skill and nerve of the pilots was reassuring to the infantrymen watching. "Jones, tell those South African pilots we are most pleased with their skill and professionalism. Well done."

"Cheetah One, this is Ground Hog. Ground Hog One sends congratulations for a job well done. We'll be glad to call on your services again. Ground Hog out."

Before the smoke settled, Scott ordered the three infantry companies to take the mountain. He wanted to get his observers to the top as soon as possible so he warned the company commanders to not spend a lot of time eliminating strongholds. They should be contained and bypassed so that they can be taken out at a later time.

"I want an artillery spotter and a phone link to Marine Operations on that hilltop before darkness," Scott shouted into his mouthpiece. "If the half-tracks can't negotiate the slopes, continue without them and call for air support if needed. Good luck."

The driver of Scott's half-track located an abandoned trail leading to the top and Scott directed him to take it as far as he could go. His command vehicle was equipped with a single fifty-caliber machine gun mount on the left rear corner of the truck body. The armor-plated body was filled with boxes of ammunition for the machine guns on the other half-tracks, which were busy spraying the areas on both sides of the trail. They carried as much extra ammunition as they could, creating a heavy load for the trucks. They needed the additional ammunition because they expended large quantities of bullets when they were attacking and supporting infantry. Scott had allowed for that contingency by using five of his precious half-tracks as ammo carriers. They also did sterling duty as supply workhorses and as casualty evacuation vehicles.

Part way up the hill the attacking squads met heavy opposition from machine gun and mortar fire from the concrete structures at the mountain top. Scott's command vehicle was hit with small arms fire and a mortar round showered them with debris. He ordered a concentration of fire from the climbing half-tracks and asked Jones to bring in anything he had available.

Within seconds of requesting assistance, two South African Mustangs dropped their load of napalm bombs on the top of the concrete bunkers eliminating the enemy gun crews. The planes banked sharply and returned on the same axis spraying the flaming bunkers with machine gun fire. Scott ordered an immediate follow up and led the battalion to the base of the cement structures, where he jumped from the half-track and started climbing over the walls and debris. Within a short time the top was occupied even though it was not completely secured. Scott told his radioman to notify regiment that South Mountain was occupied. Regiment failed to answer so he told them to inform Marine Operations of the situation.

When the message had been sent, the radioman removed his headset and shouted to Scott: "Colonel Taylor, Division sends a well done and requested that we reinforce our position and be prepared for heavy counterattacks. The enemy is being pushed out of the city and we're on one of the major avenues of escape. Our artillery spotter will have high priority for artillery shooting missions."

"Thanks, Sergeant. Try to contact regiment again and pass the info to them. Tell them we'll hold this position, but we'll have to be resupplied with ammunition."

Scott jumped down from the concrete wall to continue his reconnoiter of the hilltop, when a bullet struck him in the leg throwing him to the ground. A platoon leader saw him fall and caught the movement of the enemy sniper out of the corner of his eye and snapped several shots from his M-1 carbine at the enemy soldier. "You got him, Lieutenant," shouted a soldier on the other side of the wall. "How bad is the Colonel hit?"

The platoon leader ran to Scott's side expecting the worst, and was relieved to see Scott holding onto his right leg. "How is it Colonel?"

"It's my leg. I don't know if it's broken or not. It just burns," Scott hollered to make himself heard over the battle still going on at the summit.

The Lieutenant could see blood seeping from Scott's leg above the knee. He picked remnants of cloth from the wounded area and reached for the dressing bandage fastened on his web belt. "I think it's a flesh wound, Sir. I'll cover it with my field bandage. You're losing quite a lot of blood."

Scott felt a little light-headed, and as soon as the Lieutenant told him it looked like a flesh wound he was relieved. With a tight wrap around his leg he could continue checking out the area for defense before nightfall settled in. Standing up was awkward at first, but the Lieutenant helped steady him. He moved his leg and agreed that nothing seemed to be broken. As soon as he had the summit secured and properly defended, he would have the medics clean up the wound and dress it properly.

* * *

While Scott and his battalion were fighting in the outskirts of Seoul, Marie continued her teaching chores at Fort Lewis. She passionately listened to the radio for news or listened to reports from the older students in the school that read the papers brought to the settlement by the courier plane.

There was a penetrating cold blowing from the north which forewarned the forest dwellers that winter was knocking at their door. Within a short time after Marie returned to Eagle Nest, it was almost as if she had never left. Steve's guiding hand and helpful disposition was missed, but Marie was amazed at how smoothly things went with Mark taking over Steve's duties. Mark was like a father to her and his gentle encouragement endeared him to her more than ever. He was always checking to see that she was eating and resting properly and never failed to be available when she needed a helping hand.

At first the children tested Mark to find out how much they could get away with. They soon discovered that even though he was soft spoken and easy going, and had their best interests at heart, he was nevertheless, more strict and demanding than Steve. They learned to live with the limitations he established without complaint. He had a way of getting their attention with his quiet authority.

At the end of the day, Mark usually went to the Mounted Police station to see if there was any news about the war situation in Korea. Whenever a courier plane dropped off mail, they left a supply of newspapers which were hungrily devoured by the Fort Lewis inhabitants. Mark would then return to Eagle Nest and bring Marie up to date on pertinent events in Korea.

One day early in October Mark dropped off a letter from Scott to Marie. The headlines in the newspapers gave Mark a feeling of uneasiness. "MacArthur sends UN troops across the 38th Parallel to North Korea." He relayed the information to Marie but kept his anxieties to himself.

"Arlo seems to be doing well with the division in Korea. It's the most prestigious command job in the Marine Corps. He's been preparing all his life for this time in his career. He'll make us proud, wait and see." said Mark, dropping off the letter.

"It's nice to have friendships like you two have," answered Marie caressing the letter in her hands.

"We go back a long ways. He's been a part of my life ever since I started college before World War I. Arlo and the irreplaceable Inspector Clough have been two of my best friends. I'm a lucky man."

"Perhaps, Colonel Leroux, they're fortunate to have a friend like you," responded Marie with a smile. "Friendship is a mutual thing, you know."

"You're getting technical on me, young lady," laughed Mark. There was much about this blind school teacher that impressed him. She was a delight to work with and he enjoyed her subtle sense of humor. He understood why Scott loved her the way he did.

225

"I'm going up to the infirmary. I'll send Bright Cloud along. If you need me send one of the children after me."

"Thanks, I'll be fine."

Bright Cloud left the infirmary as soon as Mark showed up. She heard the courier plane and assumed that a letter from Scott would be on it. She hurried down the well-traveled path, for she knew how precious letters could be.

"Why don't we go into your room where we'll be quiet. Your Braille typewriter is already in there," suggested Bright Cloud. "I'll make sure the kids be quiet." Marie walked into her private sanctuary without touching any wall or door jamb on the way. Her ability to orient herself to her surroundings was a gift she was proud of.

"Let's see what your husband has to say," exclaimed Bright Cloud enthusiastically. Marie handed her the letter.

Korea
October 1, 1950

My Darling Wife;

I hope that you and the baby are doing well. I think of you all the time and would give anything to be there with you. I still have a hard time believing that I'm going to be a father. I hope I'll be a good one.

The weeks we had together were wonderful. I think of those days and a warm glow fills my heart. I'm fortunate to have a wife like you.

I'm sure you're following the news as much as possible. By the time you receive this letter, a lot of things will have happened. My battalion was part of the force that captured the city of Seoul. General Korsman did a fine job at Inchon and Seoul. We were attached to his division for a while, but we're back with our Army division now.

MacArthur may know what he's doing but I have a bad feeling about attacking north of the 38th parallel with winter not far away. Our division left Seoul and is gathering at a staging area for advances to the north, with the Yalu River as our ultimate objective. That seems to be optimistic with the forces we have available, but in reality, the resistance these past few days has been light. There's a lot of talk about being home by Christmas, and the euphoria is good to a point, but it has a tendency to give the troops a false sense of security that can dull their alertness to the dangers out there.

I'm not sure if the censors will pass this or not, but we are in Wonsan on the East coast. The men have been great. The training schedules I forced on them have been paying dividends. In many ways, combat is not any more difficult than realistic training exercises except for the casualties.

Speaking of wounds, I got hit in Seoul. It was just a flesh wound on my right leg. The bullet went through the muscle missing the bone. I was lucky again! Don't worry, Honey, I had it dressed and it's healing now. Colonel Friedricks checked it out to make sure I could still do my job. We lost four men dead and eighteen wounded in Seoul. It was our baptism to combat for most of the men. Our losses were light, but then we didn't have a very active front.

You and the rest of the gang will be pleased to know that I ran into Steve the other day. His squadron is based at Wonsan airfield where we were doing perimeter security for a few days. It was great to see him. He's in good spirits (I've never known him when he wasn't that way) and sends regards to everybody.

I've got to run, Sweetheart. Until next time, I love you. Take good care of yourself and our baby.

Love You xxxxooooo,
Scott

Marie was in her own world with Scott at her side. Bright Cloud understood the feeling and sat quiet when she finished the letter.

"Thank you, Bright Cloud," said Marie calmly.

"You're more than welcome, my dear. Scott reminds me of my son in so many ways. As difficult as it is to sit here and wait, we can never know the horrors the men are subjected to in combat. The biggest miracle is that most of them survive it."

"In my heart I know that's true, too," reflected Marie. "Bright Cloud, could I impose on your generosity again?"

"Why yes."

"Would you stay here with the children for a few minutes? I'd like to be alone for a while and get a breath of fresh air. I...I won't be very long."

"I understand. I'll watch out for them."

Marie buttoned up her heavy parka, pulled the fur hood over her head and walked towards the dock at the lakeside. The cool air blowing across her face was refreshing. She did not hear the water splashing against the shore or the dock pilings so she assumed that the water was coated with ice.

Her head was filled with so many things, she was confused and frightened. The words "I've been hit" pierced her heart like a bullet. The reality that thousands of enemy soldiers were intent on killing men like her husband, had never before registered in her consciousness like it did now. It was frightening. She was too scared to cry. The fear that her husband could be one of the "Killed In Action" statistics fired a rage inside her that was difficult to control. Without thinking where she was, Marie stepped off the edge of the dock and fell against the rocks near the shore. She tensed her body and cried out when she felt herself falling. After, she lay motionless in the icy water with her head against a rock. Blood started to trickle into the water.

Constable Snow was outside the Mounted Police station getting an armful of wood when he heard Marie scream. He looked towards the sound and saw her falling. Some of the children playing in the school yard also heard the scream and saw the policeman running to her. They excitedly called Bright Cloud who ran as fast as she could toward the wharf. Constable Snow quickly checked Marie for broken limbs and gently lifted her out of the water aware of the possibility of back injury.

"I'll take her to the infirmary," stated Constable Snow briskly. He ran faster with Marie in his arms than Bright Cloud could keep up. One of the children opened the infirmary door and held it for the policeman to pass through. He took her into the examination room and gently laid her on the table.

"What in the world is going on?" asked Mark, recognizing Marie's unconscious body on the table. "No…"

"She fell off the dock and hit her head on the rocks," interrupted Bright Cloud.

One of the nurse's aides came into the room and gently herded Mark and Constable Snow outside so that they could care for Marie. Bright Cloud quickly removed her soaked clothing. The wound above Marie's temple was still bleeding, but Bright Cloud was less concerned about the bruise than she was about possible injury to the baby she was carrying.

She found no physical evidence of injury. After completely removing her clothing, they wrapped Marie in several layers of soft blankets to ward off the danger of shock. Bright Cloud checked her eyes and was thankful that her pupils were normal. Concussion was still a possibility, but her condition was encouraging.

Marie remained unconscious for an hour or more. They moved her into a regular bed in case the examination room was needed for an emergency. The room was lit with a single lamp on the table beside Marie's bed. Bright Cloud was sitting with her eyes closed and her head against the chair, resting. Suddenly she heard movement and saw Marie with her hands covering her eyes.

"What's wrong, Marie?" she asked, standing over the bed.

Marie cried hysterically. Bright Cloud cradled Marie in her arms until she calmed down. "Bright Cloud, look at me!"

"What is it, my dear?"

Marie wiped the tears from her eyes with the bed sheet and looked deeply into Bright Cloud's eyes. "I can see you, Bright Cloud. I can see you," Marie stammered. "Everyone told me how lovely you are. Now I can see that it's true."

"This is a miracle," cried Bright Cloud, taking Marie into her arms again.

"I thank God for answering my prayers. I prayed every day since my accident for this moment." Marie touched the bandage on the side of her face and focused on objects around the room. She looked out the window and saw the tall cone-shaped spruce trees that lined the shore of Lac Diamante. Her heart pounded at the thrill of seeing the world around her. Tears of joy cleansed her bright eyes.

"I'll be right back, Marie. I want to get something in our cabin." Bright Cloud returned with a picture frame in her hands.

"You've never seen what your husband actually looks like," said Bright Cloud, approaching the bed. "Here's a picture we took of him on our trip to France." Bright Cloud handed the photograph to Marie who held it out in front of her.

"He's handsome, isn't he?" she questioned proudly.

"He's as wonderful a person as he is handsome, Marie."

She caressed the picture. Tears of joy flushed away the darkness. "What wonderful news I have to share with you, my darling Scott."

Chapter Nineteen

Fighter-bomber aircraft were taking off and landing at the Wonsan airfield on a continuous basis. Ground crews scrambled to refuel and rearm the planes as quickly as possible. Steve and his squadron of Mustangs had been carrying out close ground support missions ever since they arrived in Korea. Lately, however, they were flying a few long range strategic bombing missions that took them to the Yalu River and the Manchurian border.

Steve led one of the first long range strikes at enemy supply dumps and transportation systems. They were trying to isolate the battlefield by bombing bridges and railheads to stop or slow down supplies reaching the North Korean troops still fighting in central Korea. Navy and Marine Corsairs were also flying similar strategic missions north of the front lines.

In order to reach some of the distant targets, the Mustangs carried auxiliary fuel tanks that could be jettisoned when they were empty. It took less fuel to return to Wonsan from any given targets, so many of the pilots dropped their partial filled tanks on targets of opportunity along with their normal load of bombs and rockets. The six fifty-caliber machine guns in the wings of the planes were used as little as possible in case they were intercepted by enemy fighters. At the same time, they were frequently given ground support missions when they flew back over the front lines. Machine gun fire from the planes was enough to suppress most enemy strong points the ground troops wanted eliminated.

One day in mid-November, Steve and five planes from his squadron flew a mission against bridges close to the Manchurian border. A Marine squadron preceded Steve to the target by half an hour. They met the returning Corsairs fifty miles from the proposed target. Two of the Corsairs were flying in a circular pattern over a downed marine plane in a rice field.

"Red Dog, this is Bluebird One. We are loaded with napalm and have been ordered to the same target. Have you called for a helicopter? Bluebird out."

"Bluebird, this is Red Dog. Affirmative. Estimated time of arrival is one hour and a half. I have barely enough fuel to make base. Red Dog out."

"Red Dog, this is Bluebird. Stick around as long as you can. We'll run our mission and retain auxiliary fuel tanks so that we can fly cover for the downed pilot until the helicopter arrives. Is pilot injured? Out."

"Bluebird, this is Red Dog. Pilot okay and will stay with the plane. His radio is functioning but his batteries are weak. Our fuel supply is marginal. We are heading for base. Get back as soon as you can Bluebird. Red Dog out."

"Can do, Red Dog. Bluebird out."

The silver Mustangs located their targets and made their runs straight in so as to not waste time checking for potential anti-aircraft fire. When they approached the railroad warehouse area heavy plumes of black smoke filled the sky around them, yet, the Mustangs never deviated from their selected angle of approach and continued to make their bombing runs. As soon as Steve released the bomb load he hit hard on the right rudder and climbed rapidly to check the site for damage. Satisfied that the mission was accomplished, he set a course for the downed plane at full throttle.

"Bluebird One to squadron. We'll fly cover for the downed pilot until the helicopter arrives. Do not, repeat, do not, drop your tanks unless they are empty. I'll fly closest to the pilot in a circular pattern. Expand upon my pattern several miles out and report what you see on the ground. We don't want any of the North Koreans to get near our man. Bluebird One out."

"Bluebird One to Red Dog, do you read me, out?"

"Red Dog to Bluebird One. Batteries are low so will use sparingly. I hear noises in the brush to the west, out."

"Red Dog we'll stay with you until helicopter arrives. We'll sweep the area around your plane, out."

Steve flew around the Corsair and was aghast at the number of soldiers making their way towards the downed plane. He made a tight circle close to the plane bringing in machine gun fire right up to the tip of the aircraft's wing, pulled up sharply, and repeated the same maneuver on the other side of the plane.

There was reason for concern, so Steve called base rescue to get an update on estimate of arrival. He was told that the initial flight had to be aborted because of mechanical problems, and another could not be dispatched for twenty minutes. He knew it would not be possible for him and his men to stay in the air until the second helicopter came on scene. If they vacated the area it would place the helicopter and the marine pilot at extreme risk from the heavy concentration of North Korean soldiers.

A low sweep close enough for Steve to see the apprehension and fear on the face of the marine pilot, who had been listening to the conversation, was enough for him to explore another option. The crashed plane was in a rice field that was built up around its edges. One side was wide enough for a roadway or cart track between the two fields. Steve looked it over closely and decided to effect a retrieval of the pilot by landing on the cart path.

"Red Dog, this is Bluebird One. Can you run to the northern edge of the rice field if I drop in to pick you up. Remove any excess gear on you. Keep the pistol in your hand until you climb aboard. You'll sit in my lap and handle the stick, I'll run the pedals. Do you read me? Bluebird out."

"This is Red Dog. I read you loud and clear, Bluebird. I'm picking up rifle fire from all directions now. I'll make it to the cart track. Red Dog out."

"Bluebird One to squadron. Give us all the suppression fire you can muster. I'm going in on the east-west path between the two fields. If something goes wrong, hang around as long as you can. I'm starting my landing approach. Bluebird One out."

Steve aligned his plane on the east-west axis, dropped his landing gear and feathered the engine back to an idle. He wanted to land in as short a distance as possible so that he could continue on a straight course after he picked the pilot up. He sprayed the area directly in front of him with a long burst of machine gun fire. The marine was running feverishly towards the Mustang.

As soon as the pilot evacuated the wrecked Corsair, Steve's team mates circled lower and concentrated on the enemy soldiers closest to the downed plane. It was impossible to get all of the enemy but they could buy a little time for Steve and the marine to get out of the area. Steve came to a stop in a flurry of blowing snow which blurred his view of the cartway. One miscalculation could pull the wheels off the snow-covered bank. The marine leaped on the wing and climbed aboard.

"You got a helluva lot of grit, Bluebird, and I'm grateful."

"Welcome aboard, Red Dog. I'm glad you're not a heavyweight, our space is limited, but we'll make it." As soon as Steve felt the marine in his lap he closed the cockpit cover and rammed the throttle full speed. "Lift us off when it's up to speed, we'll pull a hard right and climb as fast as we can."

The plane slipped sideways several times, but quick foot work on Steve's part averted a mishap. The powerful Merlin engine lifted the aircraft off the ground with ease. The two pilots were not in perfect coordination maneuvering the plane, and it banked sideways as if it was standing on its right wing while they were climbing. Rifle fire from the ground increased as the plane became airborne. Two bullets smashed through the Plexiglas canopy, destroying the altimeter and the compass. Fragments from the glass and instrument panel showered the bubble canopy and the interior of the cockpit.

"Are you all right?" Steve hollered in the marine's ear.

"Yes. I'm Joe Lance. Thanks for the lift."

"I'm Steve Taylor, Joe. Glad we were in the area. Any of us may find ourselves in that same predicament someday. As long as we've got an escort to follow back to base we're going to be fine."

Shortly after climbing to cruising altitude and speed, an emergency request from an air controller in the Chosin Reservoir area came over the radio for support of ground troops from any planes in the vicinity. A battalion of marines was under heavy mortar attack from surrounding hills on the main supply road between Hagaru-ri and Yudam-ni.

"Bluebird One to Bluebird Two. Take charge of situation and answer the call for help. I'm without compass but will fly low and use land marks back to Wonsan base. Good hunting. Bluebird One out."

"This is Bluebird Two to Bluebird One. Good luck, Colonel. Welcome to the squadron, Leatherneck. Bluebird Two out."

Scott took inventory of his situation. It would soon be dark and the landmark peaks and valleys below were getting hard to distinguish already. They continued in a southern direction and ran into snow squalls eliminating any chance of picking up landmarks. They were still flying level, but the swirling winds could be pushing them in any direction. Steve said nothing to Joe who was aware of their predicament. The small wooden cross in Steve's pocket was a source of comfort to him and as soon as Steve reached for it a strange feeling of security settled over him.

"What do you think, Steve? We've got plenty of gas to get to Wonsan if we knew where it was," cried Joe, who had just finished stuffing the holes in the Plexiglas bubble with an old pair of gloves from his pockets.

"I have a feeling we're heading south, Joe. Within a half hour we should reach the coast where we turn southwest to Wonsan."

"It's worth a try, Steve. Maybe the snow shower will lift as we get closer to the salt water."

For three quarters of an hour the two pilots anxiously strained their eyes to pick up anything on the ground. They were still flying blind. Visibility was less than one hundred feet. Both men knew they were in trouble.

"If we have to ditch, what's your preference, Joe? Ride the plane down or bail out?"

"I threw away my chute so I guess I'll vote to riding it out," answered Joe.

"I've still got mine on. We could jump and hang on to each other. We might have a rough landing, but…" Before Steve could finish the sentence, a strong light source blinded them in the cockpit, then streamed out of the canopy in a direction about seventy degrees to their right, forming into a thin white glowing line pointing miles ahead.

"What in hell is that?" screamed Joe.

"I'm not sure," answered Steve. "But I have a strong feeling we should turn and follow that light line to where ever it takes us." Joe didn't answer but quickly moved the stick so that the plane was in alignment with the axis of the light.

Scott fondled the wooden cross in his hand and thought back to the time when he and Bright Star said good-bye at the dockside in Fort Lewis. She fought to keep from crying in front of him. The Mounted Police pilot was waiting in the plane to take off. At the last minute Bright Star grabbed him and thrust the crucifix into his hand. He knew the significance of the cross.

It was a gift from Flying Eagle to Bright Cloud, who gave it to Bright Star when she was a young girl. Steve had heard the story of the cross being found at the Tomb of the Unknown Soldier when it was left behind at the hotel by Bright Star. Mark claims that it was responsible for his miraculous recovery when he was near death from wounds in World War II. The tiny icon was a sacred possession and Bright Star entrusted it to Steve with the words: "My darling Steve. I pray that this will keep you safe. I love you."

Could it be possible that the hand of Providence was, once again, reaching out to protect Bright Star and those she loved through the intercession of Flying Eagle? Steve couldn't answer the question he proposed, but he was inclined to think it was possible.

"Trust me, Joe," Steve told Joe, grasping his shoulder with a reassuring touch.

"I don't have much of an alternative…"

For fifteen electrifying minutes they followed the ribbon of light in a straight line and continued following its beam when it tilted downward. Steve and Joe nervously adjusted their elevation to ride it down. Suddenly the engine skipped several times, smoothed out for a second or two and stopped completely.

"There goes the rest of the gas," said Joe, reconciled to riding out another crash landing.

"When we hit I'll try to hold you, Joe."

The plane glided through the winter sky without a sound except the flow of air over the fuselage. They looked to see if they could make out anything on the ground suitable for a crash landing, when powerful lights lit up the runway of their base at Wonsan.

"Quick, Joe. Crank down the landing gear. The handle is to your right below the canopy. Joe cranked furiously to get the wheels down before they touched the runway, then he took the stick and guided them to a perfect landing while Scott applied the brakes.

"Steve, I'll ride with you anytime anyplace. I thought we were goners. What was that light? We were heading straight out to sea before it showed us the right way."

"We've just witnessed a miracle, Joe," said Steve, holding up the wooden cross. "This is the item responsible for directing us home."

"Whatever it was, I'm grateful. I'll never bad mouth the Air Force as long as I live."

"Let's get a cup of coffee," suggested Steve, putting his arm around Joe's shoulders. "It's been quite a day. I'll tell you the story behind the crucifix." The two men jumped in the jeep sent to get them, thankful to be alive.

In the meantime, north of Wonsan airfield, the United Nations forces were fighting the piercing cold winter that blows straight out of the Manchurian highlands. Temperatures in and around the Chosin Reservoir plummeted to twenty degrees below zero with a steady wind that penetrated any amount of protective clothing. Vehicles had to be kept running or the oil would congeal to such a hard consistency the engines could not be restarted.

From the coastal port of Hungnam to the central regions of the Chosin Mountains the UN forces relied on a single military supply road that twisted and turned through the mountains and valleys. Arlo's division of marines was strung out along the road following their orders to attack northward. The grand strategy involved the Eighth Army on the western coastal plain of Korea, with Arlo's marines holding the center. The wide gap between them worried Arlo a great deal. An Army division was being formed on Arlo's right flank which would coordinate attacks to the north where all three UN columns would converge near the Manchurian border.

Colonel Friedricks was ordered to assemble a Regimental Combat Team at a staging area on the eastern side of the Chosin Reservoir as part of the right flank of the grand strategy. By late November Scott's battalion and a scattering of smaller units had arrived at the staging area prepared for advances to the north. He went into a defensive position at the most northern point of the Reservoir where he sent out light patrols to reconnoiter the terrain around them. The general feeling was that they'd all be home by Christmas, but Scott felt uneasy about their situation. They were heavily committed in a brutal winter campaign in the mountains a long ways from their base of supply without proper supporting arms. The single track road was covered with ice and was treacherous for vehicle travel. The situation did not cultivate optimism.

The possibilities for disaster were present. The realization of Scott's fears were played out on the second night after their arrival at the staging area. The cold night started with a light fall of snow accompanied by a massive attack simultaneously mounted from the north, the east and the south from hardy well-disciplined Chinese Communist Forces. The attack was announced by screaming front line troops and blasting bugles all along the line of attack.

Several of Scott's listening outposts were overrun. He pulled his mobile command post and one company into a tighter circle that could be defended easier. His other two companies were strung out along the trail back to the staging area where Colonel Friedricks maintained the Regimental

Command Post. He was still waiting for additional troops which were on their way somewhere along the supply road. The small cart track between Scott and Colonel Friedricks had been cut in several places by the Chinese. They were two isolated pockets in danger of being demolished one at a time.

The CCF also hit Arlo's two forward regiments which were a short distance northwest of the Chosin Reservoir. Their forward movement was stopped by superior enemy forces that threatened to fragment the two Marine regiments. Arlo was aware of the danger and warned the commands to maintain supporting proximity to each other. That rule of basic infantry tactics saved the regiments. Now they could halt the attack and retreat down the supply road to Hagaru-ri, a small town at the tip of the Chosin Reservoir. The movement to Hagaru-ri would be a tenuous operation and air support was a necessity during every daylight hour to help shepherd the long columns of men and equipment.

The road was chopped into several sections where the enemy roadblocks had to be blasted out of the way one mile at a time. Time was against them. If they could make it to Hagaru-ri they would have all three Marine regiments in a continuous body that could withstand anything the CCF threw at them. For now, they needed time to concentrate their forces before the enemy could organize and enlarge their breaks in the supply road. It would be possible for the enemy to cut the moving column into small pieces with superior forces concentrated at those segments and destroy them. Similar tactics had been used by the Finns against the Russian soldiers that had invaded their country in 1939.

The CCF attacking from the east side of the Chosin Reservoir was intent on destroying elements of Arlo's division at the southern end of the Reservoir in conjunction with the CCF attacking further to the north. Their intelligence had failed to note the presence of Army units east of the Reservoir, so the attacking CCF bumped into Scott's battalion and Colonel Friedricks' Command post without realizing they were in the area. The timetable of the enemy was altered by the stubborn resistance of the poorly equipped and incomplete Army Regimental Combat Team.

Scott and Colonel Friedricks knew they were faced with a nearly impossible task. Friedricks had his headquarters company, an infantry company and three 105 mm howitzers mounted on tracks, plus miscellaneous specialty units at his CP. He had a total of thirty five hundred men under his command, and that included Scott's battalion of twelve hundred. Scott lost ten men killed and thirty wounded in the initial engagement. His single company was returning fire at a rate he knew could not be maintained without running out of ammunition.

Colonel Friedricks called Scott on the wireless. "Do you think you can counter attack back towards me and pick up your other two companies along the way?"

"I can try, Sir. We're vulnerable if we stay here. I'll organize an attacking column and have it ready to roll at the crack of dawn, when air can be called in."

"Do the best you can and don't leave anything behind that they can use."

"Yes, Sir."

"Good luck, Scott."

It was a long night. Pressure was maintained at all points by the enemy. They would pull back to rally their troops, then they'd attack Scott's pitifully thin defensive line with increased fury. The three quad fifties spaced out as part of the perimeter defense took a horrendous toll of the attacking enemy infantrymen. The operators fired the weapons until their barrels glowed white in the darkness. Some barrels failed completely and had to be replaced by anxious troopers wearing protective gloves. The precious supply of ammo and barrels were dangerously low.

Scott ordered Captain Jones to get whatever he could locate for support of his breakout to the south. Demands for air power assistance came from all over central Korea. Scott drew two Navy Corsairs which showed up on station just as the sun was beginning to rise. Scott warned his two isolated companies to mark their outer perimeters with smoke grenades or mortar shells so that the pilots could ease the pressure at their flanks.

The two planes executed their runs to drop napalm bombs close to Scott's Command Post. He ordered the trucks and half-tracks into motion as soon as the planes started their runs. The planes continued to plaster both sides of the track until they ran out of ammunition. They notified Jones that the areas around them were filled with large concentrations of CCF.

Four miles separated Scott from the rest of the regiment. The first mile was traveled without incident except for sporadic sniper fire. Two miles down the road, the enemy had established a roadblock at a bridge over a small brook that fed into the Reservoir. It took two hours for the battalion to smash through the road block and it cost the column dearly. Two trucks loaded with wounded were hit by mortar shells. Scott placed his half-tracks with the quad fifties at the outer edge of his skirmish line while he tried to salvage what he could from the burning trucks. Over fifty casualties were on the vehicles. It was difficult to tell the wounded from the dead. The quad fifties hammered constantly at the endless number of enemy soldiers stopping long enough to replace empty canisters before starting up again.

Scott knew he would be overrun if the ammunition ran out or the half-tracks broke down or ran out of fuel. The medics worked feverishly on the wounded men. The snow cover on the ground around the trucks was red from the blood of his soldiers. He was proud of the way they responded to the seemingly hopeless situation. The carnage that his battalion inflicted on the enemy at the first roadblock was substantial. He estimated that at least ten mortars had been positioned by the enemy to register on the convoy. Twenty minutes after the convoy stopped, the mortars were silent.

Luckily, the bridge was still usable. The wounded and dead bodies were loaded on the remaining vehicles and the column moved cautiously forward. Several of the walking wounded took up positions in Scott's mobile CP. He gave warning to the column that the trucks and half-tracks had to be protected at all cost by the walking infantry. By now he was certain that the CCF did not have any artillery with them, so he ordered both sides of the road for a distance of two to three hundred feet, to be swept free of enemy soldiers. He didn't have enough men to clear any further out, so they would have to take their chances with the enemy mortars.

The flanking squads sustained as rapid a pace as possible. When a stronghold was located, the infantry shot a steady barrage of all weapons against it until the column had a chance to drive past it, then the infantry bypassed the point and continued with their flank protection. Ten hours later, they pulled into the regimental compound. The trucks were running on gas fumes.

The situation at the compound was not encouraging. Scott's battered battalion added to the firepower of the existing units, but both he and Colonel Friedricks knew that a heavy push by the enemy would succeed, they lacked the firepower and ammunition to resist a determined siege for more than a few hours.

Colonel Friedricks went over their predicament with Scott in a small warming tent. The welcome heat renewed his determination to continue resist. "X Corps really put us out on a limb this time, Scott. There's no help available right now, so we've got to defend this encampment. Officially, we're attached to the Marines again. They're struggling to consolidate their scattered forces. Several different CCF divisions have already been identified by X Corps and the Marine Operations Center. General Korsman wired us through the artillery battery radio, we still do not have direct radio contact because our radios are working on different frequencies. Anyway, he told me they cannot mount any relief effort to help us because it's not certain they can hold Hagaru-ri. When his two Regiments come together, they'll be able to do something. We're on our own, Scott."

"It could be worse, Colonel," answered Scott, trying to be optimistic. "We need to assess what we're up against, so I suggest we call in air to scout for us. They can sweep our perimeter and give us an estimate of where the most likely threat will come from. I'm reluctant to place the half-tracks directly on the perimeter. I'd like to use them as a mobile force to reinforce those points being hit the hardest.

"We need air drops of food, ammo, medical supplies, blood plasma, and fuel. We can mount a strong defense but we've got to have more supplies to do the job."

"I agree, Scott," said Colonel Friedricks. "Have Captain Jones get cracking while I check the perimeter positions again. I've placed the 105 MM howitzers in the center of the compound where we can defend them easier in case of a breakthrough. I suppose the balance of our Regimental Combat Team components are stalled on the supply road. They probably are better off out there instead of being stranded the way we are at the compound," reflected Colonel Friedricks. "If anything happens to me, Scott, get as many of the men out as possible."

"I'll try, Sir," answered Scott, avoiding Colonel Friedricks' penetrating glance.

Scott left the warming tent so that others could take their turn at the life-saving heat source. He helped arrange some tenting material over the trucks with the wounded. The wind was severe. Scott watched the pitiful faces of the injured in silence. They knew what the score was. It fueled an intense rage in Scott's head and heart against the higher command who so miserably failed these brave men. As bad as it was, though, Scott was determined to fight until General Korsman's situation improved. He knew that the doughty Marine General would make some effort to relieve his Army brothers across the Reservoir.

The drone of aircraft in the distance picked up everyone's spirits, for the fiery birds packed a punch against the enemy that temporarily helped to equalize their situation. Scott watched a flight of three silver winged Mustangs approach their air space. They were loaded with bombs and rockets and a feeling of pride and thanksgiving came over him as he saw the sleek aircraft begin circling the perimeter.

Captain Jones gave them directions to reconnoiter the area out a few miles for enemy concentrations. The planes scoured the area north and east of the compound with their rockets and bombs. Then they peppered the area within fifty feet of the outposts until their guns were empty. Jones motioned Scott to the radio truck. "Colonel Taylor, Bluebird is on the line. He asked for you."

Scott leaped up on the truck eagerly reaching for the earphones. "Bluebird One, this is Ground Hog One. You look mighty good to us down here, Steve."

"Ground Hog One, this is Bluebird One. Great to hear your voice, Scott. Rest assured we'll do everything in our power to cover you. It doesn't look good out there, Scott. Don't relax your guard. I've never seen so many enemy soldiers in one area as there are east of the Reservoir, out."

"Thanks for the update, Steve. I expected as much. We're in a bit of a jam but we're not licked yet. It's great to hear a friend's voice, out."

"I understand, Scott. Running low on fuel, but we'll be back. I'll make sure that air dispatch pays particular attention to your calls. God be with you, friend, out."

"He was best man at my wedding," said Scott, passing the earphones to Captain Jones.

"I'll try to bring in another strike before nightfall, Colonel."

"Thanks Captain." Scott slapped Jones on the shoulder and started to jump off the truck, but changed his mind. "I haven't told you before, Captain Jones, but the men and I really appreciate the great job you and your team are doing for us. We would've perished without your help. It's important to me that you know how much I admire your professionalism and perseverance, and I'm sure I speak for all the command."

"Thank you, Sir. It's been a privilege to serve with you."

Loud explosions and gunfire erupted from the area where Colonel Friedricks went to check on the outpost positions. Scott ran towards the noise and realized it was getting closer to the compound. He saw enemy soldiers firing at one of the trucks. One of the Quad Fifties was prepared to open fire when Scott told him to stop. "We don't know how many of our men are in the line of fire."

Collecting a dozen riflemen, Scott led a counterattack to repel the invaders. They pushed the Chinese soldiers beyond the last outpost eliminating as many as possible. The listening outpost had been overrun. Four men were dead and six men wounded. One of the dead was Colonel Friedricks. Scott assigned new men to the outpost and helped carry the wounded and dead to the center of the compound. He was now in command. There was little time to mourn his friend and commanding officer.

Before the wounded could be placed in the warming tents, firing erupted all around the perimeter, even on the Reservoir side, which meant the enemy was out on the ice. Scott checked with his surviving officers to evolve a scheme of maneuver and counter attack. He suggested that a short aggressive counter attack should be used to parry any enemy intrusion of the compound. He told them that they would lose very quickly any battle of attrition with the large numbers of enemy surrounding them. When the enemy knew that any breakthrough would be met with a determined counter thrust, they may hold off for a while, which would buy some time and give the air controller time to direct air support to the rupture.

For the next four days and nights the small force continued to hold their ground. The command, now known as Task Force Taylor, was close to the end of its ability to fight. They were almost out of ammunition, half of the trucks had already run out of gas and no one had eaten anything for the past day and a half. The hundreds of wounded in the command suffered from lack of medical supplies. What blood plasma they had was frozen solid, and there was no fuel to thaw it out. The brutal cold was as much an enemy as the Chinese soldiers. The end was in sight for them. Every member of the command walked and talked as if they were in a trance. No one had slept for days.

The last message they received from the marine division was devastating. They were told that help was not available. The situation was serious at Hagaru-ri, the two regiments were still fighting their way back. General Korsman suggested that the remainder of the command should try to fight their way to the marine encampment. They would be given first priority for air cover. Seven miles separated them, it looked like seven hundred to Scott's exhausted soldiers.

On the last night, Scott sat behind the wheel of his Command Post truck with a poncho over his head and started to write a letter to Marie by flashlight. Periodically he had to hold his hands under his arm pits to warm his fingers enough to use the stubby pencil he usually carried in his pocket. He was chilled to the bone and there was no relief from the stinging cold that blew across the windswept reservoir.

Chosin Reservoir, Korea
November 30, 1950

My Dearest Marie,

So much has happened in such a short period of time it seems like years since I last saw you at the airport in Japan. I'm not sure you will ever get this letter. Our situation is volatile at best. I'm writing this letter to myself as much as to you, sweetheart. I'm so tired it's difficult to think straight anymore. I'm fearful of making stupid mistakes that could cost lives.

This is a time when reality and honesty must motivate our actions. The truth is we may never get out of this Godforsaken country alive, and the world will never know how difficult these past few days have been and how proud I am of the men in my command. They've withstood all that mortal man is capable of enduring, and they have done it with honor and courage in the face of certain death. We may not survive our ordeal, but the world can be assured that the enemy which surrounds our compound will pay a high price if they hope to overrun us.

Like most of the men, I haven't slept for four days. We are almost out of fuel for the trucks, and it's been a long time since we had basic medical supplies for the wounded, who have suffered terribly. I'd give anything right now for a steaming cup of coffee. We ate our last rations two days ago. I'm writing this with a pencil, as you can tell, because the temperature is twenty-five degrees below zero and the ink in my pen is frozen.

We are forming a convoy of our remaining vehicles for a breakout to General Korsman's marine compound across the Chosin Reservoir from us. It will be our last effort. Whatever happens is in the hands of Providence. His division has had a difficult time, too, and he has handled it extremely well like the professional he is. I hope that our sacrifice has bought him enough time to concentrate his forces. They can't send any help to us. We're out on a limb. We've become expendable. That word is not as harsh as you may think. Every professional soldier realizes that at one time or another he may be in that situation.

I can't close this letter without telling you again how proud I am of the men. They've fought like tigers even when relief was not in sight. We haven't been very well served by the Far East Command. General Korsman has done all he could to assist us. The available air support has been our greatest hope for survival. Steve and his squadron have flown some of the sorties for us. We've lost our ability to vector the planes now. Our gallant air-controller was killed by a mortar round that also destroyed his radio. It was our last link to the outside world. I have lost ninety percent of the command.

If I don't survive this last effort, my love, you will be in my heart and in my last thoughts on this earth. Thank you for being a part of my life. Until I met you I never knew what real love was all about. Tell the baby that daddy will always love him like he does their mother.

Until next time, Marie. God, I love you so much. I pray that we may be together again. If that's not possible, then I'll wait for you to come to me, and I'll be as close to you and the baby as our Creator allows.

I hear the sounds of guns at our point. Good-bye my darling.

Scott

Chapter Twenty

It was still dark when Scott and the few surviving officers of his command organized the remaining twenty vehicles, including three half-tracks, into a convoy. The most seriously wounded were placed in truck bodies separated with odd scraps of lumber and metal so that four layers of stretchers could be stacked one upon another. Any wounded men who could walk were assisted by the able bodied, but they still had to walk. There simply were not enough vehicles to transport all of the wounded men. Scott estimated that the column contained over fifteen hundred wounded. Three to four hundred non-wounded were all that was left of the Regimental Combat Team. Fifteen hundred soldiers had been killed in the four day siege. They were buried in a mass grave beside the Chosin Reservoir. When Scott was lucid enough to comprehend the magnitude of the losses, it made him physically ill.

Considering the extreme exhaustion of the men, it was a great achievement to get the convoy loaded and ready to move before daylight. As soon as it was light enough to see the roadway without lights, Scott ordered them into motion. They planned to run along the track beside the reservoir to the Marine encampment at Hagaru-ri. The three half-tracks were placed at the front, rear and midway of the column. Nervous soldiers, showing the strain of the ordeal they had endured, kept their eyes open for any sign of enemy activity.

Aircraft engines could be heard shortly after they started down the track. It was four Navy Corsairs. There wasn't any means of communicating to the pilots, but they waved their hands to show the pilots they were going to try for a breakout, and assistance from the air was certainly welcome. The lead

Corsair buzzed the convoy and wagged his wings to acknowledge he understood their intentions. The planes started to make runs parallel to the track. One plane, nobody could remember which one it was, misjudged the distance and dropped two napalm bombs dead center of the column wiping out two trucks loaded with wounded and the center half-track.

The strike completely demoralized the exhausted survivors. Scott, sickened with anger and disbelief by the mistake, was quick to react to the potential of even greater losses if they did not get the column moving again. The napalm incinerated everything in the trucks and surrounding area. There was no hope of survival for the men in the truck or half-track; he had to think of the living. He jumped to the side of the roadway where he directed the vehicles behind the burning trucks to pull around them and catch up with the rest of the column that had already started toward Hagaru-ri.

Halfway to the Marine compound the column approached a destroyed bridge. Bypassing the bridge looked out of the question for the wheeled trucks. The banks on either side were steep and slippery. As soon as the column ground to a halt, hundreds of Chinese communist soldiers closed in on the vehicles, hurling grenades into the cabs and truck bodies. There was little chance for the members of the column to defend themselves. The carnage in the trucks filled with wounded men was unspeakable. Screams could be heard for miles around in the cold damp air. Scott recognized that the breakout would have to be made on foot. It was every man for himself. At that point his command became a mob and he encouraged everyone to walk or crawl across the ice of the reservoir to the Marine compound.

The lead half-track was able to negotiate the embankment and reach the edge of the ice where Scott ordered it to stop and collect as many wounded as they could pack in it. He also had them collect ropes and chains to drag behind the half-track so that some of the wounded could be dragged along the smooth ice. The rear half-track fired its quad fifties until all of the canisters were empty, then it tried to go down the steep bank. It slipped sideways and ended up breaking through the ice in a marshy area where it worked itself in deeper every time the driver turned the tracks. It was hopelessly stuck. Chinese soldiers quickly surrounded the vehicle killing the driver and its gun crew.

The planes overhead were powerless to assist the outnumbered soldiers. Within a short time the enemy completely overran the column. Only those capable of running away from the scene were able to escape capture or death. The planes did warn the Marine compound that a line of stragglers and survivors were heading towards their perimeter across the ice. When Arlo heard of the tragedy taking place, he ordered his outposts to be alert for the soldiers and ordered extra warming tents to be established close by the most likely locations the soldiers would enter their perimeter. He also warned the kitchens to be prepared with plenty of coffee and hot soup.

Scott limped with a look of horror on his face two hundred yards behind the half-track helping a young medic drag a discarded Jeep hood along the ice with two wounded men on it. He had been shot in his left arm and left leg at the bridge. The wounds hurt at first, but the closer he got to the safety of the Marine lines, the less he thought about them. Both wounds bled freely staining his jacket and fatigue pants which quickly froze into a solid mass. They were challenged by a nervous sentry as they crossed the perimeter into the relative safety of a well supplied defense force of marines. Several jeeps and light trucks soon left the compound in search of additional stray soldiers. They contained medics and corpsmen supplied with life savings drugs the soldiers had been denied for days.

Scott refused to enter a warming tent or to leave the area until every possible survivor had come into the compound and been cared for. He leaned against a sand bagged machine gun post with his eyes riveted against the wide stretch of ice in front of him. He was cold and weak and he felt like laying down on the dry sand bags. He was close to collapse, but the magnitude of his losses filled his head with feelings of inadequacies and hatred for himself. He felt guilty surviving the ordeal. Out there across the Chosin Reservoir, in four days, he had lost the equivalent of fourteen senior graduating classes the size of his hometown in Pennsylvania. What could he say to the families that would justify their tragic loss?

A young marine captain in a heavy parka approached Scott and saluted him respectfully. "Colonel Taylor?"

"Yes, I'm Taylor," answered Scott slowly. It was difficult for him to talk.

"I'm Captain Martin Seton, aide for General Korsman. He asked me to locate you and urge you to come back to our Command Post where you can be cared for. May I offer you a cup of coffee, Sir? It's not the best in the world but it's warm and sweet."

"I'd like that, Captain. Its been a long time..." answered Scott deliberately.

Captain Seton poured a canteen cup full of steaming coffee from a thermos bottle in his parka pocket. Scott's hands shock so much he had to grasp the cup with both hands. "Thanks, Captain."

A wounded soldier being carried on a stretcher past the outpost recognized Scott. The wounded man saw the painful expression on his commander's face and saluted him from the stretcher and shouted: "You did the best you could, Colonel."

"The whole command was lost," said Scott in a low voice, straining to look for more survivors. "Three thousand men killed and wounded in four days and five nights. How can I ever face all those mothers and fathers who entrusted their sons to my care?" He silently wept for the dead souls out there on the frozen reservoir who were never coming home.

"We'll place groups of corpsman here and at other likely points of entry to assist any survivors, Colonel," stated Captain Seton. "Why don't you let me escort you to Operations? General Korsman is anxious to see you and you can get warm and have some hot chow? I guarantee we'll take good care of your men."

Scott slowly took a long drink from the cup of coffee, savoring the magic liquid as it warmed his cold body. His stomach was still tied in knots. "Okay, Captain, I'll go with you."

Captain Seton pulled the jeep close to an abandoned school building and helped Scott through the door. The warmth of the room was like a tonic to his exhausted body. Scott tried to adjust his eyes to the glare of the overhead light bulbs and felt disoriented. He reached out for something to support himself and suddenly collapsed.

General Arlo Korsman saw the two men enter the main classroom. He was alarmed at the sight of Scott Taylor who was obviously in an advanced state of exhaustion.

"Seton, get a doctor in here now!" Arlo ordered firmly, rushing to Scott's side. "This man is dying and we've got to save him."

"Yes, Sir"

"I'll notify the nearest station," volunteered a clerk at the operations table.

They picked up Scott's limp body and stretched him out on the General's folding cot. They tried to loosen his outer clothing but had trouble removing it. His body was covered with frozen blood. The leg wound continued to bleed all the way across the reservoir, freezing as soon as it exited the wound.

"General, this man has been wounded at least twice," remarked a marine working over Scott. "He's lost an awful lot of blood."

Before Arlo answered, the door flew open admitting a doctor and a naval corpsman. They instantly set up a blood transfusion apparatus and a bottle of glucose in Scott's arms. The doctor cut away the outer clothing so that he could assess the severity of his condition, applying large bandages to the two open wounds.

"General, this man is dying. He's hanging on by a thread," announced the Doctor calmly.

"What can we do to help, Doc?"

"Bring me more blankets and clean clothing. He severed an artery and shattered part of the bone in his leg, I don't see how he made it on his own."

"He's a determined young man," Arlo replied. "I've known him for a while. I attended his wedding a few months ago."

The doctor gave Scott a large shot of morphine to relax his muscles and give him some relief from the pain the doctor knew he must be feeling. Scott was out for twenty-four hours. In that period of time he was transferred to an aid station in preparation for evacuation by aircraft from the Chosin Reservoir battlefield area.

Arlo showed up at the dressing station shortly after Scott woke up. "It's good to see you again, Colonel Taylor. You had us worried for a while. I wanted to see you before you were evacuated, to tell you personally how proud I am of you and the performance of your regimental combat team."

"I lost most of them, Sir," answered Scott sadly.

"I know that, Scott, but your efforts made it possible for us to link up to all three of our regiments. While you were sleeping, our two regiments from the north marched into the perimeter. Now I can assure you and the world that we'll be able to fight our way out of these mountains to Hungnam where the Navy is waiting to evacuate us. The precious time your command bought us with their courage and perseverance has most likely averted a much greater disaster then that which it was your bad luck to endure."

"I'd like to make a statement to the families that are wondering about the fate of their loved ones."

"A couple of correspondents are waiting just outside your tent to interview you. Shall I send them in?"

"Please do, General."

Scott was still very weak and the two correspondents agreed to not press him too hard. "If you'd like, Colonel Taylor, we can take your statement. After we transcribe it, we'll show it to you for your approval."

Without looking at the reporters, he stared across the tent and carefully stated: "Approximately three hundred men accompanied me across the ice to the relative safety of the Marine compound. Most of us walked the last few miles and I'm thankful to the Marine division for the way we've been treated. For four days and five nights our Army task force fought against a numerically superior Chinese Communist

Force. I never realized that a piece of real estate could cost so much.

"Those who may study the battle after we're gone, should know that we fought and died as professionals with courage and determination. And let it be stressed that we didn't retreat or surrender, and we gave better than we got until we fired our last bullet.

"Let it also be known that we ran out of food, medicine, fuel and ammunition, but we never ran out of the will to resist. What grieves me the most are the tragic losses we sustained and the lack of support from those in higher command, whom we had a right to expect support from, but never received. Thank you gentlemen."

"Thank you, Colonel Taylor. Best of luck. May your recovery be complete."

Arlo made his rounds of the compound on foot. He was more than satisfied with the defense situation now that all of his components were together. The Army survivors from Scott's regiment formed a composite battalion and took their place in the defense perimeter with full stomachs. Arlo said nothing about the lighter aspects of interservice rivalry, but he was concerned at the widespread misinformation that some members of his command possessed regarding the decimated Army Regimental Combat Team that showed up at their door in such a bedraggled and exhausted condition.

He was determined to squelch the rumors so he called for an officer and staff meeting in the operations building. Arlo made his way through the crowded classroom and climbed on top of a desk to address the men.

"The soldiers that some of the men, and I hope it doesn't include any officers, have been referring to as 'doggies,' cry-babies, etc., implying that marines could have done better is pure unadulterated bullshit. You had better start sending the message up and down the ranks that the survivors of the Army RCT that have joined our ranks are to be treated with respect. We most likely would have been overrun piecemeal by the Chinese, if they had not conducted themselves the way they did.

"The Chinese divisions were stopped when they ran into your Army brothers on the eastern side of the Chosin Reservoir. Those soldiers held off the enemy for four days and five nights even though they were surrounded, outgunned and heavily outnumbered. They were put out on a limb at the most vulnerable spot imaginable when the Chinese struck towards the marine division from the north and east. They ran into the Army RCT which had no supporting arms and was still lacking a full infantry battalion and a company of tanks which are still on the supply road unable to meet their parent unit.

"The ad hoc Army units that were on the eastern side of the reservoir were bled to death. It should never be forgotten that these brave soldiers ran out of food, ran out of fuel, ran out of ammunition and they ran out of medical supplies to care for their wounded. They also lost all communication with the outside world. They ran out of everything, including luck, but they never ran out of guts and courage. Step back, marines, and thank your God that such men were on your right flank where they traded time and space with their lives.

"The cold snow of the Chosin is awash with the blood of American soldiers that gave us time to concentrate our forces. Their losses are not known at this time, but it is in the vicinity of ninety percent casualties, which speaks adequately of the magnitude of the tragedy they had to endure. Could you have done any better? You'll never know. Pray that you'll never be put in the position where you have to confront the test your Army brothers have already passed."

The day after Scott spoke to the correspondents he was placed on a Greek Air Force transport for shipment directly to Japan. General Korsman specifically ordered that plane full of wounded to go to Japan.

The newspapers and radio were filled with reports of the successful withdrawal from the Chosin Reservoir. It was one bright spot in an otherwise dark period for UN forces in Korea. The euphoria of a few weeks earlier vanished when the CCF dealt a crushing defeat on the forces that threatened the integrity of the Chinese-Korean border.

Scott was placed in a naval hospital near the port of Sasebo, Japan. They treated his arm wounds and placed his leg in a cast. The wounds were badly infected but a routine of antibiotics and frequent dressing changes arrested the infections. The doctors and staff were less concerned with his physical wounds than they were about the man himself. He was despondent and spoke very little. He had lost twenty pounds during the battle. It showed in his gaunt face. It was his eyes that touched everyone who treated him. Dark circles beneath his eyes gave him an emaciated tormented look. He seemed to be in a different world, a forlorn purgatory that he could not escape from. His staring eyes frequently filled with tears that ran down his angular cheekbones.

When spoken to, Scott responded slowly and somberly. He continued to worry the staff. The horrors that he kept to himself were reflected on his face, and in his heart he held himself responsible for the loss of his command. The guilt was tearing him apart.

Arlo had his hands full bringing the division out of the reservoir, but as soon as they resettled in the Pusan area, he asked his aide, Captain Seton, to locate the whereabouts of Bright Star. She was serving on a hospital ship off the coast of Pusan. Arlo made a request that she be transferred to the hospital in Sasebo where Scott was being treated. Maybe a familiar face would help the young soldier.

Bright Star arrived in Sasebo by helicopter. She was briefed on Scott's condition and soon appeared in his room where she found him watching the ships in the harbor. At first she didn't believe it was Scott. He looked old and tired. Her heart went out to him as she hastened to his bedside.

"Hello, Scott," her soft melodious voice was instantly recognizable.

His eyes lit up and a cry of relief pierced his dry lips. "Bright Star, am I glad to see you! I can't believe this…"

"I'm going to be stationed at the hospital for a while," she exclaimed, reaching for him.

"I must look terrible, Star."

"On the contrary, you look great considering the circumstances, and we're going to get you on your feet in no time."

"I can't get a lot of things out of my mind," he cried helplessly.

"I know, Scott. The whole world is proud of what you did."

"All of our records were lost or destroyed. How can I notify the families of my men and what can I say to them? They trusted me to look out for them and I lost them..." Scott quietly sobbed. It was a cry for release of the pain that went to the depths of his soul and had tormented him day and night.

As painful as it was, the intense emotional moment was a cleansing ordeal. It left him weak and exhausted, and Bright Star eased him back on the bed and covered him with extra blankets. He was drenched with sweat, but she was relieved. She was certain that Scott Taylor had just taken the first step of his recovery.

Arlo Korsman intervened once again on Scott's behalf. He personally called the hospital and asked for Bright Star. She had read the papers describing his performance at Chosin with pride, but she was not surprised. It was what she expected of him. They talked about Steve, who was stationed at Pusan, and things at Fort Lewis. Arlo asked what she thought about bringing Marie to Japan.

"That would work another miracle for Scott, Uncle Arlo. It's a long trip for her."

"She's a strong young lady. I'll see what I can do. What about Eagle Nest if she leaves?" asked Arlo directly.

"They'll survive, Uncle. Right now, Scott needs her more than Fort Lewis does. It would be wonderful if she could come here while he's recovering. I know first hand how important a friendly face can be," answered Bright Star recalling Steve's long convalescence at Pearl Harbor after his plane crash during World War II.

"I'll check into the situation, Star. Take care of yourself and don't say anything to Scott just yet."

"I won't, Uncle. I love you."

"I love you too, Star."

Bright Star had a warm feeling in her heart as she hung up the phone. Her Uncle Arlo never used his rank or position to obtain extra favors or considerations for himself, but when anyone in his circle of friends or family was in need, he was capable of pulling any strings available to help them. Right now, Arlo was making arrangements for the transport of Marie to Japan. Bright Star had no doubts that it would be accomplished.

Within ten days Marie stepped off the Military Air Transport plane near the Sasebo hospital. Bright Star met her at the airport. Marie was six and a half months pregnant, so she walked a little slower than usual, but she was radiant with happiness. This was the first time Star met Marie since the recovery of her sight. Star was standing near the ramp when Marie came down the steps. Their eyes met and instantly Marie knew who she was.

"Bright Star," exclaimed Marie with arms open. "Let me look at you. You're more beautiful than everyone said you are."

"Flattery will get you anything," laughed Star, relieved to see Marie again. "You look wonderful, Marie. Motherhood is becoming to you."

"How is he, Star?" asked Marie nervously.

"He's doing better, but your presence here is going to do the trick and put him on the path to full recovery. He's been injured and those physical wounds are healing well. He's been through a terrible ordeal which would have broken many men, but your Scott is made of tough stuff."

On the way to the hospital in a Navy sedan Marie told Bright Star how her Uncle Arlo had arranged for military transport for her even out of Canada. The hospital staff placed Scott in a private room. Marie held Star's hand walking up to the door of the room.

"Good luck, Marie," Bright Star whispered in her ear.

Scott didn't pay any attention to the opening of the door at first. It gave Marie a chance to observe her husband for the first time. He looked thin and tired. When his eyes met hers, his mouth dropped in disbelief and shock.

"Marie, is that really you?" She raced into his waiting arms. They held each other for a long time without saying a word. Marie was the first to speak.

"I have news for you, my husband. This is the first time I've been able to see you with my eyes."

"I knew there was something different about the way you came to me from the door. Thank God." His eyes moistened and he held her again.

"We have much to be thankful for, Scott. You're finally safe from harm and we're going to have a baby," declared Marie.

"You look wonderful, Marie."

"I've got another piece of news for you, my love. Arlo has recommended you for the Medal of Honor. He told me that it should go through without a problem. There was no question about the worthiness of your performance."

Chapter Twenty-One

Steve banked the sturdy Norseman circling Lac Diamante, flying close to the ledge outcrops near Lookout Point west of the village. The sparkling blue waters of the lake were a welcome sight to Steve and Bright Star, and for Scott and Marie, sharing the back seat with their four and a half month old son, Scott, Jr. The baby was sound asleep in his father's protective arms.

"It's like coming home," said Scott, squeezing Marie's hand. "I have a lot to be thankful for."

Marie looked at him with her beautiful hazel-green eyes and smiled. She was happy, and she, too, had much to be thankful for, placing her head against her husband's broad shoulders.

They had just returned from Washington, DC, where President Harry S. Truman awarded the Medal of Honor to Scott in a simple ceremony in the Oval Office of the White House. Steve and Bright Star accompanied them. The President was his normal energetic self. He was moved by the meaning and solemnity of the nation's highest award for gallantry and intrepidity at the risk of life, above and beyond the call of duty.

The President graciously received each of them. He was a common man who maintained the dignity of the office he held. He said, "I'm glad you could come today. I'm humbled by the sacrifices of our men and women who defend our country. I believe that the American soldier is the embodiment of the highest ideals of mankind. Colonel Scott Taylor, you have given new meaning to the sacred oath you took on the plains of West Point. Duty, Honor, Country, have been a code which has guided your life. Awarding the Medal of Honor is one of the privileges I enjoy as President. Your commitment to duty and to the men in your command have elevated courage and valor to a new level. When your son is old enough to understand what his father accomplished, he'll join the rest of the nation in proudly saying 'thank you'."

Scott wore the Medal of Honor on a sash around his neck. He joined the distinguished fraternity of men who had been thoroughly tested and rose to the challenge. The President shook hands with Scott and Steve and embraced Bright Star and Marie. Then he gently kissed little Scott, Jr. on the head. "God bless you all. We sleep better at night knowing that young men and women like you are watching over us."

Steve gently set the plane on the lake and idled to the dock where several people were waiting to greet them. Bright Cloud and Mark were especially anxious to congratulate Scott and Marie and to see the new baby. They were joined by Arlo, Michelle, and Maria. It was a gathering of friends who found it important to reach out to each other and celebrate life in the peaceful surroundings of Fort Lewis.

As they were all walking towards Eagle Nest, Bright Cloud handed Scott and Marie a letter. Marie had a puzzled look on her face as she read the letter with Scott.

June 30, 1951

To Scott and his wife, Marie:

I'm not sure if you'll ever receive this letter, but I feel it's one I have to write. I've read about you at the Chosin Reservoir, and was touched by the performance, but I was not particularly surprised. The qualities that sustained you in Korea were evident to anyone who chose to look close enough.

I've been reflecting a lot upon my own life these days. I've certainly made a lot of bad choices that I would do differently if I had a chance to go back. One choice I regret was to not follow my instincts about you, Scott, but, alas, it's over now.

Your wife, Marie, must be a very special person. The two of you have my sincere congratulations and best wishes for a happy life together. You deserve that.

I'm trying to get on with my life. The trial in Japan has helped me to evaluate those things that are really important. I won't take the wrong turn again.

I want both of you to know your steadfastness and decency at my trial was an inspiration to me, Scott. I'll always regret what might have been, but I now have a chance to build a new life and I want to thank you for giving me the courage to press forward. May your tomorrows be filled with joy and peace.

Leslie Kerr

"I feel sorry for the woman," admitted Marie. "It took courage to write such a letter. I wish her well."

"So do I," said Scott.

Just before the sun set, another float plane landed on the lake and taxied to the wharf where a young Marine captain stepped out onto the dock and looked around. Steve was on his way to the Eagle Nest when he heard the plane in the distance. He had an idea that it might be his friend, Joe Lance. Steve invited him to the village if he had a chance to come. Ever since their great adventure, they had become close friends.

"Welcome, Joe, you're just in time," greeted Steve warmly.

"You're right, this is a beautiful spot," remarked Joe, impressed by the raw beauty of the Canadian wilderness.

They walked to the Eagle Nest where a banquet was prepared for the gathering of friends and loved ones. Steve introduced Joe to those present. They sat at a long table filled with fine wines, fruit, breads of all types and several serving pans of fish, meats, and vegetables prepared by the villagers in appreciation for all the work the people at the table generously gave to the people of the North Country. Mark, wearing his Medal of Honor, sat at the head of the table and acted as the host. He was, as always, a standard of grace and civility.

"It's my pleasure to welcome all of you to the small outpost of Fort Lewis. My wife and I are proud to be a part of this gathering of friends and loved ones. We welcome you with open hearts, Joe. We've come together on the shores of Lac Diamante to renew our fellowship with one another and to give thanks for the safety of those who have just returned from the battlefield. One in particular, our dear friend, Scott Taylor, has just returned from Washington where he was awarded the Medal of Honor. I'm proud to share that honor with him."

Scott exchanged looks with Mark and stood up holding a glass in his hand. "I'd like to propose a toast to those brave souls who never came home. They fell in defense of a way of life they can no longer share. I remember a few months ago in Korea when it looked as if the end was in sight for me and my command. We were cold, hungry, and scared. My half-track driver, Sergeant Mike Castle, God rest his weary soul, asked me on the last night before our attempted breakout, what I'd ask for if I had just one wish. I selfishly and jokingly answered him that I'd take a big steak smothered in onions and mashed potatoes. He simply said in that unique Texas drawl of his, 'they could give me tomorrow'. The next morning he was killed by a Chinese mortar.

"To Mike and all the others lest we forget, lest we forget." 'Lest we forget' was repeated around the table. Scott raised his glass, blinded by tears, and drank the toast.

Arlo, a gentle warrior with the soul of a poet stood up and raised his glass. "I also want to propose a toast to the fraternity of brothers who join us here. I'm reminded of the passage from Shakespeare's Henry V, Act IV, Scene iii:

But we... shall be remembered;
We few, we happy few, we band of brothers;
For he to-day that sheds his blood with me
Shall be my brother; be he ne'er so vile,
This day shall gentle his condition.

"I am honored to be a part of this band of brothers. To that fraternity of brotherhood."

They drank to the brotherhood and sat around the table enjoying an evening of fellowship and sharing. They gave tribute to the past and reached out to embrace the future with a celebration of life, the most precious gift of all.

The End

Other Historical Romance Novels
BY
Clifton LaBree

A Song for Lisa   A Historical Romance

This is the story of a young American woman captured by the Japanese in the Philippines, 1941. Like most prisoners, she was brutalized and sadistically treated with a cruel disregard for human life. Three years later, Lisa and her companions had reached the low point of starvation and abuse .....

Lake of Three Sorrows   A Historical Romance

A warm spiritually uplifting story of courage, commitment, and sacrifice. This is the story of Dale Cooper, a battle-weary American soldier who served in two world wars.

Flickering Flame (Colonial Series Book One)

A historical novel, about the Cullen family who settled in Portsmouth, New Hampshire, and their participation in events prior to the French and Indian War. Freedom and opportunity were on the march, but it extracted a heavy price. Frontier settlers were ruthlessly killed and butchered by rampaging Indians lead by French officers and Jesuit priests who frequently incited them to greater levels of inhumanity...

Raising the Torch (Colonial Series Book Two)

A continuation of the saga from Flickering Flame, Colonial Series book one, of the Cullen family in Colonial Portsmouth. This is a moving story of love and sacrifice when a small colony had the audacity to fight for independence from their motherland...

Non-Fiction Books

By

Clifton LaBree

New Hampshire's General John Stark, Live Free or Die: Death Is Not the Greatest of Evils

Publisher - Fading Shadows Imprint

A fresh look at one of America's staunchest defenders of liberty and freedom. John Stark was a courageous New Hampshire citizen-soldier who fought in both, the French and Indian War, and the Revolutionary War. His pursuit of leadership excellence on the battlefield distinguished him as one of the most successful combat commanders of the war, and one of the least appreciated.

His selflessness, modest life style, and devotion to the cause of freedom are an inspiration that time has not diminished. He remains today the embodiment of the frugal, independent, and cantankerous New Hampshire Yankee.

Gentle Warrior, General Oliver Prince Smith, USMC

Published by - Kent State University Press. Kent, Ohio, 2001

The Story of one of the United States Marine Corps best General Officer. His flawless performance in Korea is a story that needed to be told.

www.ingramcontent.com/pod-product-compliance
Lightning Source LLC
Chambersburg PA
CBHW072207170626
46813CB00003B/832